Marcella Bell is an avid reader, a burgeoning beader, and a corvid and honeybee enthusiast with more interests than hours in the day. As a late bloomer and a yogini, Marcella is drawn to stories that showcase love's incredible power to inspire transformation—whether they take place in the vast landscapes of the west or imagined palaces and exotic locales. When not writing or wrangling her multigenerational household and three dogs, she loves to hear from readers! To reach out, keep up, or check-in, visit marcellabell.com.

Growing up near the beach, **Annie West** spent lots of time observing tall, burnished lifeguards—early research! Now she spends her days fantasising about gorgeous men and their love-lives. Annie has been a reader all her life. She also loves travel, long walks, good company and great food. You can contact her at annie@annie-west.com or via PO Box 1041, Warners Bay, NSW 2282, Australia.

D0522870

HIS BRIDE WITH TWO ROYAL SECRETS

MARCELLA BELL

ONE NIGHT WITH HER FORGOTTEN HUSBAND

ANNIE WEST

MILLS & BOON

First Published in Great Britain 2022
by Mills & Boon, an imprint of HarperCollins*Publishers* Ltd,
1 London Bridge Street, London, SE1 9GF

www.harpercollins.co.uk

HarperCollins*Publishers*
1st Floor, Watermarque Building,
Ringsend Road, Dublin 4, Ireland

His Bride with Two Royal Secrets © 2022 Marcella Bell

One Night with Her Forgotten Husband © 2022 Annie West

ISBN: 978-0-263-30080-2

04/22

MIX
Paper from
responsible sources
FSC C007454

HIS BRIDE
WITH TWO
ROYAL SECRETS

MARCELLA BELL

MILLS & BOON

To Innovation and Hope

CHAPTER ONE

JAG STRODE INTO the bright, vast garage in time to witness a dark-haired woman wearing an obnoxious lime-green jumpsuit reach out to delicately caress his priceless vintage Ferrari GTO.

The Ferrari, which gleamed in glacier-blue perfection, rested atop a round white platform beneath a bright spotlight.

The woman's hand upon it was gentle and lingering, like that of a lover's cupping of the curved hip of their beloved.

Something unfamiliar and powerful jolted through Jag's body at the sight of it, though he remained where he stood.

Hard or soft, the pressure of her touch didn't matter.

She did not have permission to touch his car.

"Mmm…" she purred, unaware of Jag's presence, her voice lingering on the sound with the same sensuality with which she handled his vehicle. "Practically perfect," she continued in a low, throaty voice. "In every way. It's an outrage that I don't get to keep you all to myself. Only I know how to take care of something as precious and rare as you."

Her words were slightly breathless, each syllable heavy and erotic, as if she and the car existed in a private world of their own.

Jag swallowed, his hand clenching at his side so that he didn't involuntarily lift it to accept an invitation that he logically knew she was not offering to him.

But maybe by proxy?

Shaking the outrageous thought out of his head, he blinked slowly, intentionally unclenching his hand at his side.

That he was here at all, at the very western edge of the United States—as opposed to attending to any number of the many interests he had as Crown Prince of the independent emirate of Hayat—was absolutely ridiculous.

To have arrived in time to discover a strange woman pawing his precious jewel was utterly unconscionable.

Equally offensive was the fact that the car was the one thing left in Jag's world that could be used to manipulate him. And while NECTAR did not directly control that, he'd certainly revealed to the world that it was true.

Which was, naturally, the point that offended Jag the most.

Manipulation by means of the heart was the thing he hated most in all of creation.

Through restricting the output of his love, doling it out rarely and only to those in command of their own security forces with at least a modicum of demonstrated martial acuity, he had thought himself to have been thoroughly cured of that particular weakness, and for a very long time now.

But he had been utterly immovable on the decision to travel all this way—against his better judgment and adviser's wishes—for the humble pleasure of having his own property back.

Adding insult to injury, he had done so at the demand of a man whom literally no one had ever met, no one could physically describe, and now, only Jag knew the location of. Well, now Jag and his security team. Obviously, he had not walked into an American blind spot without a contingency and retrieval plan. He was too important for that. That would have been irresponsible.

But at least the beauty that shone before him was worth it—beauty of the four-wheeled variety, he mentally insisted.

Though her back remained to him, he could sense that the woman, too, was beautiful, as well as appreciate the tantalizing view of her generously rounded rear end and shapely thighs and calves.

But he didn't have time for the woman. He was here for the car.

While Jag was happy to play light and carefree in the company of the few individuals he loved in this world, and to become a master seducer when he needed to let off a little steam, since stepping into his role as Crown Prince and officially instituting his plan to bring his father to ruin, his playboy prince persona had been put firmly behind him.

His people wanted their prince to be a wholesome family role model and, to the best of his ability, he would give his people what they wanted—both because a good leader put the needs of his people above his own, and because he needed to be popular if he was going to overthrow his father without bloodshed.

For not the first time, Jag deliberately pulled his attention away from the curvy creature of flesh before him and returned it to his angel on four wheels, drawing in a long breath as he did it, and exhaling only once he got there.

The car was pristine. Possibly in the top tier of most stunning objects he had ever laid his eyes on.

And there would be plenty of time to admire it, and women, when he returned to Hayat.

But between planning the largest international event that Hayat had ever seen and launching the final phase of his plan to oust his father from the throne, there was not a lot of room in his schedule for leisurely exchanges with reclusive automotive geniuses.

There was simply too much at stake.

Even if it was true that NECTAR had never spoken directly with a single client—Jag included—until demanding to meet with Jag face-to-face.

But the success of Jag's exhibition depended upon that car, and the success of his coup depended on the success of the exhibition, so here he was, waiting for NECTAR while a strange woman pawed his prize.

And on that matter, the clock was ticking. In truth, both he and his car had bigger concerns than smudges and fingerprints, and it was past time they get on with them.

Clearing his throat, surprised at the thickness that had accumulated there while he'd watched the mechanic, Jag managed to get out a low, more or less smooth and ominous, "Careful, there," though his voice still caught as it exited his throat. Strengthening and carrying more of the original remonstrative disdain than he had intended, he added, "I'm sure your employer wouldn't appreciate you smudging the finish."

But rather than startling and pulling her hand back like a thief caught in the act, the woman instead went absolutely still, her hand remaining firmly affixed to the side of his vehicle.

And as she turned to face him, he was forced to admit that she was a risk to him of the oldest and most potent variety.

She was gorgeous.

Her hair was dark, and glossy, and thick.

Her skin was bright and clear, an umber tone that glowed, silky, smooth and warmth.

Her dusky-rose-colored lips matched the rest of her full and expressive beauty, while her nose was well shaped and adorable and her eyes large and brown.

If she weren't dressed up in mechanic's gear, she would have looked like a princess from a fairy tale.

Their eyes locked.

Her straight eyebrows drew together, the deep color of her lush lips pressing into a line.

And from the light burning in her dark brown eyes, it was clear that she had the audacity to be offended by *him*. *She* had been the one fondling *his* car.

"Prince Jahangir, I presume," she said, as if *his* property were not the subject of their conversation and his title were simply a superfluous adjective.

Nothing in what she said neared an apology, nor an explanation, nor anything remotely remonstrative. In fact, there was not an ounce of regret in her voice.

If anything, she sounded as if she were disappointed at his behavior, and not just that. Her voice also made it clear that she was additionally disappointed with herself—for expecting better of him.

It had been so long since anyone had used a tone like that on him that it took the Prince a moment to place it.

Only his mother had ever spoken to him like that. *And where had a thought like that come from?* Shaking his head, he pushed the memory away, rather than let it linger.

"Indeed," he responded, instead. "I am here to retrieve my vehicle at NECTAR's…*request.*"

The woman laughed, and it broke through the irritation on her face. Lifting her lips, her glorious eyes crinkling at the corners, she appeared to emanate her own light, though Jag knew that couldn't be true. It had to be because she stood beneath the car's spotlight.

Jag stared, unable to quite adjust to the wattage of her smile as well as a bit taken aback by the whole situation itself.

If he wasn't mistaken, she was laughing at him.

As her laughter died down, though she remained smiling, she said, "I'm NECTAR. In person, though, people usually call me Rita."

As though he had not been thrown for a loop, Jag verified, "*You* are NECTAR?"

Meeting his eye, which was a feat he had long ago given up on expecting of most people, the woman said, "I sure hope so. Otherwise you just paid the wrong person a lot of money for this car. Not to mention entrusted a car worth its weight in gold to the wrong person."

Jag blinked once, then nodded as if the information were to be expected when it entirely was not.

NECTAR was a woman.

NECTAR was a beautiful woman. Possibly the most beautiful woman he had ever met.

And her tone was chastising.

The facts that she had been the only individual he'd seen on the premises, apart from the driver she'd sent to pick him up from the airport, and had had her hands all over a car that most kings and queens would be afraid to touch, should have made it all obvious, he realized now.

As had the fact that she had not been intimidated by him in the least.

And why would she be? He might be a crown prince, but so were most of her clients. And hadn't she just successfully demanded that he jump at her command?

Jag said, "I assume that's my car?"

Rita moistened her lips, leaving them plump and glistening, and said, a bit breathlessly, "It's the only 1962 Ferrari GTO that's ever come through my garage."

There were those who said it was the rarest car in the world.

And the purists of the world would decry that he had ruined it by ordering the conversion.

The two of them, however, knew that her work had made a unicorn into a legend.

"It's lovely that you appreciate its rarity," Jag said, unable to stop the bit of humor threading into his voice. Clearing his throat before he spoke again, and straightening his already upright posture, he added, "However, I imagine that there was a greater purpose to your summoning me here than a discussion of that. Otherwise, I'm afraid I need to take it home now."

To his utter shock, she held her palms up, with a firm, "No."

"Excuse me?" Jag asked, apparently still capable of being surprised despite the fact that she had already proved exceptionally bold.

"Wait—"

"I can't," he said, and there was some real shame in that. But kingdoms came before beguiling women. They had to when people's daily lives depended upon the behavior of a handful of individuals. "It is an honor to own one of the world's most precious automobiles, and an even greater one yet, that it is also the work of such a renowned engineer as yourself. However, I cannot linger nor offer any more than my appreciation, compliments and the substantial amount of money I've paid you for the privilege."

She disabused him of the notion that she was looking for more money, however, with the next thing she said.

"Take me with you," she blurted out, the words running together in her rush to get them out. "I heard about the exhibition, I know what you're planning to do, and you need me around to make sure it happens. If you're going to succeed, the car has to be perfect at all times. No one can keep it that way other than me."

Jag froze. She had no idea what he was planning to do with his exhibition. She had likely read the official marketing materials about the exhibition and thought it was all about the cars.

"And what's in it for you?" he asked, voice low.

"I have to be there. It's the best place I can showcase my work, my talent. The place to make the connections that I need to in order to achieve my long-term goals. The most important names in electric vehicles will be there, so I have to be there, too. The connections I could make…

you wouldn't even need to acknowledge me. I just need to be in the room where it happens," she pleaded earnestly.

It made sense.

Of course she would want to be a part of it—she was the world's leading engineer when it came to electric vehicles.

But electric futures were not the only thing his exhibition was about, and she had no idea the kind of danger and intrigue that boiled beneath the surface.

Only his close friends, the total of whom he could count on one hand, knew just what his plans were. There was no conceivable reason to add babysitting a strange and alluring woman into that mix.

Except for the fact that she was right about the car.

And that she was alluring and strange and beautiful.

But most importantly, the car.

It did have to be perfect, for every moment of the exhibition. And not just for the race, but for the countless showcases and press events and demonstrations as well. Old cars, as well as converted cars, were high-maintenance under the best of conditions. A weeklong showcase of the power, range and capacity of electric vehicles, starring a vehicle that had been born in the same year as his mother, rest her soul, was not exactly the best of conditions.

NECTAR guaranteed lifelong service for all of his—or rather, her—vehicles, but that service required to and fro international transport and resulted in intolerable waiting times.

Her offer made absolute sense.

But still, Jag refused. "Absolutely not."

He owed it to her to protect her—even if it was just against her own recklessness.

Honestly, what was she thinking?

She didn't know the first thing about Hayat, she didn't speak the language and, most importantly, she had no idea what she was asking. Did she have no sense of self-preservation?

Probably not. Like most Americans, she probably believed that the world was wild and free and full of desperate dreamers.

In Hayat, she would merely be another soul he was responsible for keeping safe and happy while simultaneously staging a coup.

But damn, she was right about the car.

His eyes found hers desperate, and he paused.

For an instant her expression shuttered, and she took a deep breath. Then a layer of resolution settled over her.

On an exhale, she said, "I'll let you pick out a car from my personal fleet if you let me come."

Jag blinked.

She was beautiful and ingenuous and enigmatic, and he simply didn't have the time to take care of her while he dealt with his father.

But that was before she'd offered him a vehicle from her personal fleet, a sly voice inside reminded.

And there was the point she'd made about maintenance. And, as she was one of the world's foremost experts on electric cars, he could build her into the program, even this late in the game.

An idea was beginning to form in his mind.

His advisers had told him multiple times since his permanent return to Hayat that marriage would greatly boost his popularity. It was a step he had resisted, however, despite being willing to refrain from having public romantic associations, because he had not been willing to take the risk of making a woman his bride.

A marriage of convenience with a logical peer—a woman of high status, wealth and connections—was simply too big a risk, given his plans.

The kind of woman who would go into a partnership like that with open eyes would undoubtedly bring a level of honed cynicism that just wasn't a good idea to have around when one was planning a coup.

That left him with the alternative of pursuing and wooing, which he had neither the time nor the duplicity for.

He would not present himself as a genuine lover to a woman when he knew that was something he would never be.

He had learned long ago that love, affection and closeness were liabilities when one had a father like his. It would not be right to capture a heart that he had no intention of caring for and keeping.

And, of course, there was the matter of the vow that he and the three men he considered friends had made while still young foreign men doing a long stint in English boarding school.

Jag and his friends had done their damnedest to fight back at every step, and even making plans into the future, such as in their promise to one another that when the time came, they would each find the most unsuitable brides they could.

Vin, Rafael and even Zeus may have pushed the boundaries of their vow by falling into real love with their unsuitable brides, but each had met the terms without causing harm to their people.

Jag could do no less, particularly when a brilliant and beautiful opportunity knocked.

Bringing a thumb and forefinger to stroke his beard, Jag reconsidered Rita, otherwise known as NECTAR. She was equal parts famous and mysterious.

She had an eye for design and detail, a mind for engineering and complex systems, and in making demands of a powerful man she barely knew, had shown herself to be both dangerously bold and categorically reckless.

She was wealthy—if the fees she charged and her property were any indication—and charismatic. She was passionate about cars, as he was famous for being, and a leader in electric transportation at a time when he was leading Hayat into becoming a world leader in clean energy.

She made sense as much as the absurd plan forming in his mind did not.

And she has a body that begs to be driven along with the face of a heavenly maiden, his own internal reckless-ness pointed out—though that point he ruthlessly pushed aside.

Her body and face were irrelevant insofar as the future of their relationship was to go.

He was not considering this outrageous idea because he wanted her.

He was considering it because as she was neither a steely-eyed socialite nor a woman he had to fool into love, she was safe to bring into his circle.

He didn't need her to be attractive.

He needed her to be a woman who wouldn't bring shame to his nation or people while simultaneously pos-ing no threat to his plans, nor any risk of emotional en-tanglement.

She was a lovely stranger with her own prerogatives, and as he'd encountered thus far, as transparent as a glass window, and, as genius as she was, when you boiled it down, she was a mechanic.

She was perfect.

She would get whatever it was that she wanted to get out of attending his exhibition, and he would gain in pop-ularity without trouble, risk or wasted time.

If she were willing to agree to his terms, she would get what she wanted, he would get his car back, and, as the Lord had apparently coordinated it, get an added boost in public support while at the same time fulfilling the terms of an agreement he'd made with his closest friends when they'd been only hints of the men they were today.

A wicked and decided grin lifted one side of his mouth and then the other.

Opening it to speak, Jag countered her offer. "A car, even one from the world-famous NECTAR's personal fleet, is nowhere near enough for the kind of inconvenience you're asking of me. However, there is a condition upon which I would be willing to bring you along."

She swallowed, but she didn't look away, and her voice was resolute and earnest when she promised him the world without knowing what it was. "Anything."

"Marry me."

CHAPTER TWO

"WH-WHAT?" RITA STAMMERED, the wind knocked out of her as if she had taken a hit to the chest. "Why?"

She had offered him a car, and he had asked for her hand in marriage instead. But this was no open-air market, and they were not a buyer and seller haggling over the price of goods.

This was real life.

The Prince's wicked smile somehow grew, even as his tone remained even-keeled, as if they discussed the weather rather than marriage. "I need a particular kind of wife, of which you fit the bill, and you want to come with me to Hayat. It will be a business arrangement."

A business arrangement?

The words rattled around Rita's mind. Did she want a business arrangement for a marriage?

As if summoned in answer, her mother's long-ago words rose in Rita's mind.

Marriage is always an arrangement. It is an arrangement in which two people have to wake up every day and work with each other to make a good life. No matter how it starts, the arrangement is the same, and it's hard enough that, love or no love, it falls apart almost as much as it doesn't.

Rita hadn't thought about that conversation in years, hadn't even realized she remembered it until now. Once again, she was looking at the prospect of marriage—but this time it was a business arrangement.

And her dad had been wrong after all.

Someone *had* asked to marry her.

And not just any someone, but an honest-to-goodness, real-life prince.

If he had not also been a client whom she'd only just met and had spent less than an hour with in her entire life, the situation could have been plucked straight out of a fairy tale.

"What kind of arrangement are we talking about here?" Rita asked, caution tingling in her limbs.

Pressing his lips together, moistening them almost effectively and seductively as if he'd licked his lips, the Prince said, "Strictly business. Nothing physical beyond presenting the image of a happy couple to the public."

The man who had just asked her to marry him was, without contest, the most compelling man she had ever seen in her life.

His nose was straight and true down the center of his face. His eyebrows were thick and coal black, an exact match to the gorgeous mane on his head and neatly trimmed facial hair that framed his defined face and square jaw.

At the moment, his eyes glowed a glorious amber, his expression captivating her, willing her to hold contact.

Just the eyes alone had enough voltage to power her whole system.

And that wasn't even considering the way that his incredibly tall and broad body filled out the impeccable lines of his suit.

Had she ever used the word *impeccable* in the context of men's clothing before? She didn't think so.

While she struggled to return her inner world to any semblance of order, his gaze remained fixed upon hers like that of a hunter who moved silently and struck in the night.

His astounding irises were rich amber encircled in a deep brown ring and striped throughout with small streaks of equally dark brown.

The intensity of the glow that shone from within them was a reminder that although he had been gifted with a body that was more than enough to house all of that power, being caged only made it all the more desperate to escape.

And, for all intents and purposes, he'd just asked her to marry him.

But why had he asked her to marry him? If he was looking for a business arrangement, what singled her out as the woman to make it with?

And did the answer matter?

"What's the catch?" Rita asked.

He swallowed, and she realized that he was just as caught in their stare as she was.

"Some women might consider marrying a stranger all the catch they needed."

"Some women wouldn't think twice about marrying a handsome and mysterious prince."

Laughter flared in his eyes, though he only released a chuckle. "Don't forget rich beyond limit."

Rita swallowed this time, and it wasn't just because there was something magnetic about his awareness of his own power.

As NECTAR she had done well for herself, her years of struggle behind her now, but she was far from living a life beyond limit—wasn't even sure, really, if she knew what that meant.

"There has to be a catch," she insisted.

He inclined his head with respect. "In addition to marrying a stranger, you will be inheriting a ruthless tyrant for a father-in-law. Being my wife will keep you safe from him, but he, unfortunately, exists nonetheless."

Rita knew a thing or two about complicated and tyrannical fathers.

"And you're not after anything physical?" she queried.

Nodding, the Prince said, "I am, in fact, unequivocally rejecting anything physical. A physical relationship would undermine what makes this such a good arrangement."

"I'm not sure I'm clear on what makes this such a good arrangement."

"My people would like to see me married, but I am interested in neither a life partner nor a confidant. You can see how being up-front about that might turn prospects away. On the other hand, it would be disingenuous to pretend to be interested in a wife when, in reality, I am merely in want of one. An acquaintance with some common ground and her own life, however, stands out to me as a solution. One that only works if we remember between the two of us that it is all an act. Sex can complicate keeping that in mind. To that end, I reiterate that there is not and never will be anything romantic about our arrangement. This arrangement could work well for the two of us for many reasons, but romance is not one of them," he said.

"I can see how marrying a stranger could make it easier to maintain distance," she mused on the thought. Taking it further, she asked, "So you're proposing that we remain as close as we can to strangers in matrimony for the rest of our, mostly separate from the sounds of it, lives?"

The Prince's eyes once again danced with humor. "Hardly," he said, as easy being interrogated as he was tossing out proposals. "A few years is all I expect, and then we can divorce like normal modern royalty."

Something shuddered through Rita at the word *divorce*, but she told herself she could handle that stigma as well as she could handle the stigma of having been disowned.

But she wouldn't be taken advantage of in the process.

"What about a prenup?" she asked.

The Prince's eyes narrowed and cooled ever so slightly, but he replied smoothly, "My assets will be protected, I assure you. I had not taken you to be the kind of individual I needed to protect them from, however. Should I revise that opinion?"

Rita let out a short laugh, shaking her head.

All she cared about was her cars.

According to her family, cars were all she had ever cared about.

But if she and the Prince were planning a marriage with an expiration date, she was getting it down in writing that her babies stayed with her when that date arrived.

"My private fleet is a collection of priceless one-of-a-kind vehicles. How do I know this isn't just some elaborate scheme to take them from me?"

Just because he was wealthy beyond limit and royal did not mean that he was above trickery.

For years now, Rita had worked among the rich and famous, and in those years and from those people, she had seen some of the most outrageous attempts to get more than their fair share out of her for free. Worse yet, were those who had outright tried to steal from her.

Reluctant as she was to think cynically about the people she met, as a young brown female innovator operating in mostly male-dominated realms, Rita had learned that a vast majority of the powerful men that she encountered were, at the very least, going to try to intimidate her, and that the only way to combat it was to look past their facades, speak clearly and firmly, and stand up for herself.

The suspicious edge leaving him, the Prince's eyes heated once again. "If you want one, I'll have one drawn up immediately, ensuring that every single one of your vehicles, sans the Ferrari, which is mine, and the one I select, as you so generously offered, remains your own."

Rita frowned, unsurprised that he would hold her to the offer of his choice from her selection, even after he had raised her offer to this more audacious deal himself.

"I must continue my work," she said, the outcome of the entire agreement hinging on this one point.

She had not let her future husband and in-laws, nor her own father, bar her from pursuing her calling, and she would not let the Prince do so, either.

He nodded without hesitation. "Of course. Your work is the thing that makes any of this make sense. You will have your own garage in Hayat, preferably equipped to your most extravagant and expensive whim and delight."

He didn't have to know her well to know that he offered her the kind of thing that only a very few men in the world could—and that she would have a hard time resisting.

Her kind of garage didn't come cheap.

But he doesn't know you, a cautionary internal voice reiterated.

But for the first sixteen years of her life, she had known that there was a great possibility that her husband would not know her until their wedding day, as had been the case for her own parents.

The Prince might be a stranger, but unlike the marriage she had thought she was going to have back then, beyond residence and legal status, he was not asking her to make any significant changes to her life or person.

And while romance might not be on the table, what *was*, was a marriage that did not expect her to sacrifice herself to anything but a tepid dynamic.

That was certainly more appealing than familiarity or love.

In Rita's experience, love demanded too much—was conditional and controlling. Love clipped the wings and drained the batteries, using the heart to trap and coerce. Love left no room for creativity or innovation or freedom.

Instead of intimacy with an overbearing known, she could marry a stranger and continue her life of celibacy and fulfilling work alongside.

She could marry a man who was content to let her remain entirely as she was right now.

"In sum," the Prince concluded his offer, his voice as

convincing as any shaitan's, "if you agree to be my bride, you remain free to continue your work, your body remains your own, and you retain all but the agreed-upon vehicles in your fleet. And, following a few lavish years abroad, your life will once again be your own. Only you will have gained invaluable contacts and an incredible story to tell."

When she had been given the choice as a young woman between the cold comfort of trying to change the world and the warmth and love and devotion of starting her own family, Rita had chosen the former.

Now she was faced with a similar choice: a cold marriage that came with a real shot at changing the world, or staying right where she was as NECTAR, chipping away at her dream alone, one commission at a time.

Licking her lips, Rita drew in a deep breath and said, "I'll do it."

Like a pair of Venuses in the night sky, triumph lit the prince's already-glowing eyes further still. His lips carried his mouth into a genuine, uncontrolled, smile—one that revealed bright, straight teeth.

And then he laughed.

The sound was round and full and echoed in her garage, swirling around Rita like a fairy godmother's magic, changing her irrevocably as if this were the beginning of an adventure and not a marriage of strangers.

When his mini solar flare began to settle, his eyes still glowing, his smile still wide, he said, "To Rita, the motorhead princess." Raising an invisible glass to her, he added, "I am certain that this is the beginning of a beautiful arrangement."

Rita's stomach flipped at his words, her heart fluttering at the same time.

It was the beginning of something, she knew. She just wasn't sure she'd use the word *beautiful*.

Maybe impeccable... a sly voice teased in her mind, but she tamped it down.

The Prince had been clear, and she had agreed: theirs wasn't that kind of arrangement.

For her, it was about the dream that she had formed at her father's knee, a dream she was going to make come true, whether he was around to witness it or not.

Across from her, the Prince stood, his form simultaneously still and thrumming, activating every area of her being—her imagination, her appreciation for beauty, her determination, her humor, her acknowledgment of fantastic design, her curiosity and even her body.

Though that isn't what this is about, she reminded herself.

Had she ever met a man who made machines seem primitive and weak in comparison to before?

She didn't think so. Humans were lopsided and prone to imperfection, but he was symmetrical, beautiful and strong.

Even her father had seemed small beside their family's fleet of big rigs.

She couldn't think of anything here the man who was going to be her husband would seem small beside.

With his car and his exhibition, and access to the world stage as a gorgeous prince's pretend wife, the Prince had just handed Rita a very real opportunity to change the way the world drove—far more of one than she had ever even had as NECTAR, boutique auto engineer for the globe's rich and famous.

Reaching into the pocket of her jumpsuit, she dug out her phone and dialed a number.

When she looked back up, the Prince had a slight furrow to his brow, as if he had not liked the fact that she had escaped his gaze.

He would have to just learn to deal with that kind of frustration, though, because, as per their agreement, there were a lot of things she would be keeping to herself.

Her thoughts, for example.

He might be her fiancé, but they were still strangers, after all.

Infusing her voice with the cheerful distance she used for client phone calls, Rita offered, "I don't know what your transport plan was for the Ferrari, but I'm happy to arrange to include her in my barge."

She could hire services to transport the irreplaceable items she would need from her garages, as well as to prepare the rest of her small compound—built with the money she'd earned as NECTAR—for a long absence.

Retaining the groundskeepers on their regular maintenance schedules would ensure that the landscaping retained its private oasis-like charm while she was gone, as well.

Her cars, however, she would coordinate the care and transport of herself.

"Barge?" the Prince questioned, breaking into her preparations with a faint trace of distaste darkening his remarkable face. "You need to bring so much that you have to coordinate a barge? There is nothing you have here that I cannot replace to your liking in Hayat."

Looking at him as if he'd made the most ludicrous statement in the world, *because he had*, Rita lifted an eyebrow and said, "Except for my cars."

As if he had temporarily forgotten about her private fleet and only now remembered, the Prince's face lit with delight.

If he were truly a boy, rather than a man whose dominating presence had just had a devastating effect on her five-year plan, he might have clapped and jumped for joy at the reminder of her fleet.

The man she was now engaged to might be stranger, but he had a passion for cars, and that was something.

Great love stories had been kindled out of less.

Not that theirs was a love story.

CHAPTER THREE

JAG HAD COME to get his car, and along the way he had picked up a wife.

What an unexpected development that had been.

He had already anticipated reaching his desired level of popular support within Hayat following his successful world exhibition, but with the added bonus of announcing his marriage, there would be no doubt.

And he had thought the trip to the United States was going to be a waste of precious time when he was so close to achieving his ends.

He was serious about his takeover being nonhostile. His people deserved peace, and he would do nothing to shatter that for them.

And he would secure that peace by first securing their love.

After all, there was no stronger force to compel human behavior, he knew, than love. In fact, he knew it better than most.

It was another reason why his little jaunt had proved so fruitful. In Rita, he had found a woman with whom he would never worry about manipulating with emotions.

Rita was a virtual stranger, and by not allowing them the space to become close there would be no emotional coercion and no accidental heirs—as his three friends had stumbled into in the fulfillment of their vows.

If love itself was powerfully coercive, then children were its most effective tool.

People were willing to do anything for their children—even die.

Jag was fond of free will.

Which did not mean he looked down on his friends.

On the contrary, he was happy for them. In their cases, love had crept past their defenses and enriched their lives, the lovers they'd found trustworthy in their commitment to not manipulate.

The children they had produced were blessings.

In fact, reflecting on it now, Jag oddly preferred to see his friends happy and settled with strong women and joyful families than where he sat, unexpectedly tied to a brilliant and beautiful but unwitting accomplice, that many steps closer to achieving his ruthless goal.

But if his goal was ruthless and methods resolute, it was at least to the benefit of the people he ruled and the woman he had joined himself to.

Following his proposal, his legal team had coordinated expedited US licenses, documents and a local judge, who had arrived at the NECTAR compound with the required paperwork and witnesses within the hour.

The ceremony had taken place in Rita's garage, surrounded by the cars she had engineered, and perhaps because of it, it was an experience that Jag found more personal and unique than any wedding he'd ever attended. Of course, the feeling could have come from the fact that it was his own.

Like everything else about their meeting, it was completely unlike any context within which he had ever imagined getting married—and as a prince there had been many of those—and yet it had been sentimental at the same time.

And funny.

In all of the rush of preparing for their hasty marriage and immediate departure, Rita had not changed from her jumpsuit.

She had been married in NECTAR lime green, his new wife, the world-famous genius mechanic.

And when she first laid eyes on the private plane that now belonged to her as well, and which was just one of many, he heard her gasp even on the gusty tarmac.

It was rather adorable.

"Nice plane," she said breathlessly, gazing around the interior with adoration in her eyes as they boarded.

An unexpected surge of pride and pleasure at having decided to take the Cessna coursed through him as if it had always been his intention to impress her when, in truth, he had simply wanted something that was both comfortable and fast.

He could have flown in his G6 but had chosen speed over power for his unplanned excursion, and it made all the difference.

Seeing her enthusiasm, now he was glad he had for other reasons.

There was something cozy about the sweet little jet with its designer interior.

Of all his jets, this was the most intimate and comfortable and close, and sliding into the supple comfort of the branded leather reclining seat across from her, he appreciated that the small jet created an atmosphere of intimacy around their fake arrangement that he could not.

Was it fair that he had corralled this beautiful and brilliant woman into a such a cold and transactional marriage?

If she had not been so desperate to enter into their deal for her own reasons, the answer would likely have been no. But for whatever reasons—and he knew it was more than the need to ensure her work showcased well—she was.

"Why do you want to attend the exhibition so badly?" he asked, interested in the backstory now that they were on their way back to Hayat.

To his surprise, his question brought a real blush to his wife's cheeks.

"I told you. No one else can take care of the Ferrari but me. She's perfection on wheels, but with a race and the eyes of world leaders all around, she'll need maintenance. This isn't your everyday showcase."

She laid it all out very matter-of-factly, as if it were a completely reasonable justification for agreeing to marry a stranger and hare off into unknown waters.

Yet again, he could only admire her bald audacity.

The woman was completely undaunted.

She was also lying.

"What's the real reason, though?" he asked in a voice that brooked no denial.

Perhaps unsurprisingly, she denied it anyway. "That *is* the real reason. My name is on the line."

"It's bigger than that," he insisted. "It has to be."

If he had not been surprised by her continued denial, he *was* taken aback when her resistance crumbled.

"It's dumb," she muttered in a low voice.

"It's obviously not 'dumb' to you," he pointed out. "In fact, I would hazard a guess that it has to do with something you care about very much."

"I want to change the way the world drives," she whispered, almost under her breath, as if she were afraid to say it out loud to another person.

A number of feelings set off within him in reaction to her reluctant confession.

An unwarranted surge of protectiveness, the urge to fight and crush any force that threatened her fragile confidence and dream.

As idealistic as the words sounded, her decision made more sense now. Like every American he'd ever met, she wanted to save the world, and she was serious about it.

And, unexpectedly, he admired that dream and her dedication to it.

She had agreed to his terms not simply because she wanted to further her career as NECTAR, as he had assumed, but because she was truly committed to a better future, no matter how large a sacrifice it asked of her.

It was noble.

Because of that, he wasn't cynical when he responded. "If there is anywhere you can make an impact, it will be at this exhibition. You will have the attention of the world for however long it holds. There will be no better time to make a statement that will align it to your way of thinking."

Blush growing, her eyes glistened beneath the plane's lights, and he found himself caught in their wells.

Had she sparkled like she did now in the garage? he wondered. *Or was it simply a trick of their current lighting?*

Clearing her throat, she broke their stare and looked around, swallowing as she did so. Speaking only after another beat of settling herself. "The CJ has it all," she said finally, continuing, "She can go far, she's comfy and cute, and she has a pair of wings that were made to fly. If I ever get the chance to try my hand at a plane, I'd start with a CJ."

Unable to help himself—and why should he even try when he was wealthy and powerful and could not give much beyond trinkets and platform to a woman who wanted to save the world?—Jag indulged her.

"You can start with this one," he said, smiling at the delight that swept across her beautiful face.

"Don't tease," she said cautiously. "If you don't mean it, don't say it."

He appreciated the casual way she ordered him around. No one else had ever done that with him, not even his friends.

"Why would I joke?" he said with a shrug. "If you mess it up, it's my oldest and smallest plane. I'll just get a new one."

Snorting, her smile still wide, she mocked him. *"'I'll just get a new one.'"*

Grinning, he sighed, "Airplanes. They just don't seem to make them like they used to anymore."

"I can guarantee that no one will make one like the one I make," she said, full of herself, and seeing the confidence on her made his grin stretch wider.

She had earned every ounce of cockiness she possessed.

Like her, the vehicle that she had built for him surpassed every one of his impossible standards.

Her work, her mind and her body were all exceptional.

All of that aside, however, they still needed to get their stories straight before they touched down in Hayat.

A frown coming to his brow along with the thought, Jag leaned forward in his seat.

"You've reminded me that even for an engineering genius there are still matters we should discuss before arriving in Hayat."

Teasing at his new seriousness, Rita leaned forward, bringing her elbows to her knees, her eyes direct on Jag's, and said, "Lay it on me, Prince Jahangir."

Across the aisle from her, Jag grimaced. "Save me from Americans…" he muttered to himself, before he said, "Well, for starters, you will not be calling me Jahangir."

The name left a bad taste in his throat every time he said it, each syllable a reminder that his father saw him not as a human being, but as a prized possession. His name had been a reward to a favored lackey, evidence from before he was even born that to his father, Jag's entire life was nothing more than an accessory to his power.

Rita frowned. "What should I call you then?" she asked.

"My friends call me Jag," he said gruffly.

A slow smile spread across her face, mischief lighting her eyes as she asked, "Does that mean we're friends now?"

Snorting, he said, "Absolutely not. We're married. Friends is the last thing we are."

Smile not budging an inch, she slyly retorted, "Whatever you say... *Jag*..." emphasizing and lengthening his short moniker.

Or at least that's what it sounded like to him, though in reality, it was probably only her teasing and forward nature unable to resist an opportunity to needle.

He may not know his wife well yet, but he had become quite familiar with those elements of her personality in the time they'd known each other.

Regardless of intent, however, he liked the sound of it more than he probably should have.

He would need to be careful around the woman he had just married.

She was forbidden territory, and recalling that he really did have serious things he wanted to go over with her, he attempted to steer the conversation back to them and far from the threat her open and easy nature presented. "Now that we've settled that, we can move on to more important things."

Clearly starting to enjoy herself, Rita leaned in even closer. "Is there really anything more important than what I should call you? Maybe your birthday?" She tapped her finger to her chin in thought.

"October twenty-ninth," he snapped, continuing, "I will have a dossier drawn up for you with pertinent biological and preferential details later."

"Ooh, a dossier," she said, mocking his stiffness and formality in a way that he refused to smile at.

There were serious matters to discuss. Holding back his grin with effort, he said, "While we will have some time before the public finds out about you, and while I have been assured that my people will adore any bride I bring to them, we still must have a story to tell them. Obviously, we will limit and minimize your public role as

Crown Princess for the tenure of our agreement. You're quite occupied with your work, I'm sure, and there is no need to get the people attached to a temporary figurehead. While our ruse serves many purposes, I am committed to ensuring that it does not negatively impact the people of Hayat. In fact, beyond providing them with something fun to write about in the tabloids, this arrangement should not affect them."

"Admirable," Rita said sarcastically.

"What?" he asked, giving her a look. He only raised normal considerations for a monarch.

"Nothing. Go on." She gave him a "carry on" gesture with her hand that he had the most infantile urge to ignore simply on principle, *and he would have,* had the continuation of their conversation not been necessary.

It was too bad she would not be serving in the capacity of a real princess, however, because her little wave had been filled with enough royal condescension to make a queen proud.

"As I was saying," he went on, nonetheless dogged by the strange sense that she had somehow outmaneuvered him, "we'll need an entertaining and believable story to explain how an American mechanic, albeit a world-famous one, snagged the Crown Prince of Hayat."

"That's funny, I remember it the other way around, with the Crown Prince of Hayat snagging the American mechanic," she said flatly.

"Regardless of how it happened, we need a unified story to tell."

"Forgive me for suggesting that it might be best to stick as close to the truth as possible," she said, the sarcasm in her voice slipping a notch closer to irritation.

"You think people are going to believe that?" he asked, lifting a brow as his urge to settle the matter shifted more into one to egg her on further.

His new wife had a sparky temper, as he'd seen in the

garage and throughout their acquaintance, and he found he liked the jolt of touching it.

And unlike most of the people he knew, Rita never seemed reticent about sharing that part of herself with him.

It was refreshing to be in the company of someone unafraid to put him in his place the way only his friends seemed to.

Not that his new wife was his friend.

Rita was merely his business partner, which he would just have to keep on reminding himself since it was dangerously easy to forget while in conversation with her.

Wisely, she said, "I think people will believe whatever they want to believe, regardless of what the official story is."

"So cynical, Rita," he said, tsking at her with a disapproving shake of his head before continuing, "And now you're confusing me. One minute you want us to tell the truth that our alliance is really just a strange political move, and the next you want us to make up a story that's worth believing?" Though it might have been rusty, his comedic tone achieved what he had been going for, and the stiffness in her posture and expression broke with an exasperated smile.

"No, no," she grumbled, hands up in surrender as she deflated. "The people want good tabloids, so we will give them good tabloids," she added.

He didn't expect the strange surge of approval that coursed through him at her words, a misplaced sense of pride rising in him to have found a woman who, like him, was willing to put the needs of the people of Hayat before her own.

That, he believed, was the single most important trait of a good ruler.

Ruling together, however, was not a part of their deal.

And keeping that in mind was already showing itself

to be slightly more complicated than he had initially anticipated.

Once they landed in Hayat, he would endeavor to restrict the amount of time he spent in her presence.

It was perhaps unsurprising, but her combination of brilliant mind and royal irreverence made it far too easy to relax his guard around her. He excused his lack of foresight with the fact that it was an experience he hadn't often had.

"So, *Jag*, what kind of story do you propose?" she asked, doing that thing where she made his name sound like honey on her tongue again.

Once the wave of caress-like tingling stopped coursing across his skin, Jag reflected that it had perhaps not been his brightest idea to give her his casual name.

"Like-minded tech-loving young lovers' paths cross over one-of-kind commission and sparks fly?" he suggested flirtatiously, as if he'd momentarily lost his mind.

The deep wells of her eyes locked on his, and she licked her lips before replying, "Better, Prince falls for mysterious engineer known the world over only as NECTAR."

A slow grin lifting the corners of his mouth in a way he knew that women loved, Jag's eyes lit with dare. "My version is closer to the truth."

Rita's breath quickened. "Mine is a better story."

"Says who?" he asked, his eyes never leaving hers.

"It's got mystery and romance, enough of both to keep people occupied filling in the details themselves."

"And just how did you become such an expert at subterfuge, I wonder, Rita," he murmured, eyes never leaving hers.

Rita waited a beat, swallowing and clearing her throat before replying, "Just the past six years of becoming one of the most famous conversion specialists in the world all while no one knew my name, face or gender."

"Strong points, dear wife. So why did we marry, then?

Why not simply become famous lovers? Princes do it all the time," he teased, pushing her because the effect when he did—the way she got all strong and firm before his eyes, refusing to back down or be intimidated—set off thrills in his blood.

And she did not disappoint him now.

Tossing her head, throwing that thick, glossy hair of hers over her shoulder in the process, she angled her chin up. "That was never on the table, prince or not. The mysterious mechanic might work on the cutting edge of technology, but she is still an old-fashioned Muslim girl from an old-fashioned Muslim and South Asian family."

Jag could not stop his eyes from flaring with the triumph at yet another welcome, if utterly unexpected, development. "Is that true, Rita? About you, I mean? Are you a Muslim?" he asked.

Guardedness creeping into her eyes, Rita nodded, her answer a tentative, "Yes."

"Unbelievable," he uttered on an exhale, and she frowned.

"What?" she asked warily.

"I just couldn't have planned it better myself. Unsuitable, and yet infinitely suitable."

"What do you mean?" she asked, eyes narrowing with suspicion.

"You being a Muslim woman, I did not expect it, but am beyond pleased."

"Why?" she asked.

"As a Muslim woman, you have removed my father's greatest potential argument against our marriage. I was prepared and, according to national polls, Hayat was prepared for its first non-Muslim princess, but now that is irrelevant. When I debut you to the world as my bride, my father will have no excuse with which to invalidate our marriage."

"Your father would do that?" Rita asked, less aghast than he might have anticipated coming from an American.

"I warned you that he was a ruthless tyrant. He believes it is a king's right to dictate the lives of all of those he encounters. As you might surmise, I have been less than amenable to those beliefs. A great deal of your appeal as my wife lies in your being the antithesis of what he would want in a daughter-in-law, but while I am happy to take every shot I can at my father, I never like to do so at the expense of my people. The fact that you are Muslim, however, will make it easier for them. He will not be able to use religion to stir up the wrong kind of controversy, and they will find you more relatable."

"And here I'd always thought faith was a personal thing," she said dryly.

Jag laughed. "Nothing is personal when you are royal."

"Yippee," she responded darkly, and Jag could not hold back his laughter.

"Relax," he said, still quietly laughing. "You are exactly the woman for the job. Our marriage is expressly for the purpose of securing the approval of my people, and I would never bring them a bride who I did not think would serve them. The wrong woman in the position could be disastrous, no matter how temporary the arrangement might be. But you, you just keep proving yourself more and more suited to the role. You're nothing my father would want for my wife, and yet everything my country is clamoring for. Announcing to the world that I have made NECTAR, the world's greatest electric conversion engineer, my bride as the grand finale of my international electric energies exhibition will not only be the coup d'état of my exhibition, but has the potential to be the kind of story that captures the attention of the world."

It was all so close, he could almost taste it.

CHAPTER FOUR

As USUAL WITH her conversations with Jag, Rita's mind zeroed in on the minutiae of what he said while sailing over the probably more important parts.

"Debuting NECTAR?" she asked, fingers and thumbs suddenly and inexplicably numb.

Jag smiled, the visions of the future in his eyes much clearer than what was before him. "Of course," he said. "The future Queen of Hayat being the world's foremost expert on electric engines and systems will catapult my vision into reality far more efficiently than even the world's rarest car."

"No one in the world knows who NECTAR is," Rita said, as if stating the well-known fact was evidence enough of the point she was trying to make.

"And because of that, the reveal will be that much more a sensation."

"I've kept my identity a secret for a reason." Many reasons, in fact, not the least of which included not having to wade through the nonsense of men who didn't respect women and being able to get away with charging what she did for her work. She was the best there was at what she did, but there was just no way her clients would pay a woman that much money for a job. Especially when she had first started.

And then there was the fact that she hadn't wanted

to cause her family to lose any more face. There was no need to flaunt her disobedience—to either of the families involved.

Jag shrugged insouciantly and waved the concern away. "I'm sure it was a good one," he said. "Circumstances now call for a change."

"It is easier to do my job when people think they are dealing with a man," Rita tried again.

Leaning forward, he took her hand, his amber gaze trapping hers. With deepest conviction he said, "Imagine how easy it will be once they know you are a princess."

Rita blinked, for a moment stunned by imagining it. Jag was right.

Princess.

She could probably charge even more.

But at the expense of the world knowing who she was.

It was part of the deal—he had mentioned it multiple times, in fact; she had just somehow not put two and two together.

"We can't be more...*discreet* about that?" she asked, already knowing the answer.

Seriousness coming to his stare, Jag gave the lightest of head shakes. "Absolutely not, Rita. Not for what I'm about to do, and certainly not for what you want to do. You just said you wanted to change the world. That's not the kind of thing you do discreetly. This is your chance to jostle your place to the center of the world stage and sing as loud and strong as you can. People must know and love you if you have any hope of getting them to do what you say."

"You don't think it's a little overrated? People? I mean, look at all I've accomplished so far with just the help of a few people along the way," she said, gesturing around the cabin.

"You said you wanted to change the way the world drove, Rita. You don't achieve that by taking the driver seat in every car."

Again, he was right, though she only ceded the point with a nod.

She didn't think she liked it when he was right, the idea triggering a memory of her mother saying the same thing about her father.

She had thought of her parents more in her short time with her new husband than she had in years.

But it made sense that they would be on her mind on the day she got married. Her getting married had been what set everything off, after all.

Just like everything Jag was saying to her made sense. She had been willing to sign up for a facade of a marriage for the sake of this goal. She would not let it be for nothing simply because she didn't want to stand in the spotlight and speak.

And why, in all that was good and beautiful, did her mind keep coming back around to sex?

She knew it had to be because they had expressly established that they would not be having sex, but even in defiance it was out of character.

She never thought about sex. Her mother had drilled it into her that sex was a part of marriage and when marriage had been taken off the table for her, so too had sex.

And while others might have taken being shunned as freedom and permission to abandon the edicts and values that had been imposed upon them for the first eighteen years of life, Rita had not. Instead, she had clung to them as the only proof that she had ever had a family at all.

The fact that her family had been right—that she'd only ever been interested in cars—made it easier. It was easy to walk what was left of the line when she only noticed steel frames attached to wheels.

Rita wasn't sure now if it was because she'd already started down the slippery slope of forgoing her morals and ethics by marrying him, or if it was just that she found herself sitting in the sky under the spell of some kind of stunning and wicked djinni, but for some reason, that wasn't the case with Jag.

She was honestly having a hard time *not* noticing Jag.

They had made the right choice in committing to a marriage without physical intimacy. She was sure of it, even as areas of her mind and body were apparently in the process of waking from their twenty-seven-year slumber.

She did not care about sex, even with Jag—*especially* with Jag.

In fact, she hardly thought about either the opposite or same sex throughout the whole of her existence.

It had been one of the greater divides between herself and her peers all the way through school.

While early childhood friendships had flourished in the playground context of racing and chasing, as she had aged alongside other girls, her attention had remained fixed upon the interests that had driven her childhood explorations, while her peers became more and more interested in, well, each other.

Like all of her idiosyncrasies, Rita had assumed the difference was just part of how she was uniquely engineered. Her disinterest, in addition to the headscarf she had worn during that era of her life, had not exactly prevented her from making close friends, but certainly didn't help her find common ground with anyone her age. Being the only *hijabi* at her school often meant that curiosity got in the way of friendliness, and none of her classmates liked cars the way she did.

But it hadn't mattered to her.

Her parents' opinions had been the only ones that mattered to her back then.

And after that, she had been matched and in school and occasionally meeting her intended for chaperoned outings, and then after that, all she'd had left were cars.

No marriage, no sex, and there hadn't been time for it

anyway—not when she had been on her way to becoming NECTAR.

Spending time in the presence of the stunningly and unconsciously sensual Crown Prince of Hayat, however, was doing things to her system that she had never before experienced—uncomfortably activating processes that she had been certain she lacked and sparking questions and curiosities she had never felt.

And here on the plane with Jag made for neither a good time and place, nor partner, to be setting anything like this ablaze.

CHAPTER FIVE

As THE JET descended into Hayat, having stopped once midway through the journey to refuel, Jag took in his homeland. It took him a beat longer, though, to recognize the unfamiliar apprehension he felt as caring about what another person thought. Did the woman who was his wife see an expanse of large flat inkblot-black seas broken by stretches of abysmal beige—as he'd once overheard a Westerner describe it—or did she see the turquoise-azure sea meeting the ivory-cream ocean of sand, pulsing and mixing at the point of contact like freshwater meeting salt, as he did?

As they neared the ground and Hayat City proper, did she note the incredible and whimsical shapes of the great sand works that seemed to float like lotuses at the top of the churning sea? Did she see the incredible architecture, how the traditional and ancient met the bold and new, the oldest of humanity's histories jumping right into the scientific and technological future of their collective imagination?

Did it matter?

Appreciating the beauty of the country she was the pretend Princess of wasn't why he'd married her. She was here to serve a different purpose.

It was absolutely irrelevant what she thought of Hayat or its capital.

But that did not stop him from feeling a sense of pride when she gasped as they touched ground and she got a good look at the city around her.

"I never realized… Would you look at the size… Is that a mosque?" Each statement was more like exclamations, most left incomplete, abandoned in favor of the next.

The flow of her words didn't stop, all the way through the airport and into the car that awaited them.

If he had wondered what she thought of Hayat, her enthusiasm gave him a strong suggestion as to the answer.

"And you're telling me that three of the world's ten tallest buildings are located here in Hayat?"

At his nod, she made yet another note in her phone. "We'll have to see all three."

She had begun taking notes as soon as their driver entered traffic and they passed two parked police vehicles.

"That was an Aston Martin One-77 and a Lykan Hypersport!" she had squealed joyously. "For the police!"

Since then, she'd hardly stopped jotting things down.

Observing her, he sent a text to the head of his team to coordinate a new encrypted device for her use. Her US-based carrier and model would be too easy to break into here in Hayat.

And, while his mind was on the topic of preparing her for Hayat, he needed to do something about her clothing.

As was the case in Dubai, Hayat City's citizens prided themselves on living on the front lines of fashion, with straight-from-the-runway couture a common sight on the streets.

Her wide-legged American blue jeans, baggy sweatshirt and canvas sneakers would not do.

Beyond that, the getup was inappropriate because it was far too warm to wear in Hayat City—even for the purpose of strolling from a climate-controlled car into a climate-controlled building interior.

Retrieving his phone from his pocket, he called his

secretary, catching Rita's attention in the process. "Alert my tailor that we are on the way and will be using the private entrance."

Rita had paused her back-seat tourism and was looking at him quizzically.

"We need to outfit you like a princess," he explained.

She looked down at her clothes, then back up at him. "I thought we were waiting to announce until the race. I was really hoping to see the stadium first."

And to push the debut from your thoughts. He noted her lingering reticence on that point, but said only, "There will inevitably be photos of us taken before then. The moment we leave this vehicle, our game is on. There is no room for misstep. You must look the part even while playing the mysterious stranger at my side."

She narrowed her eyes at his words, pressing her lips into a line, but ultimately shrugged and returned to taking in the city as they traveled through it, and he found himself curious as to what she was thinking.

The driver made the turn into the belowground entrance of the secured building, and Jag smiled.

Their wardrobe problem would soon be a thing of the past.

Rather than a standard elevator, the driver guided their car into a vehicle elevator.

Visitors to residents of the tower drove right into the elevator with an access code and were lifted, in situ, to the private floors of the individual they were calling on. The majority of residents had selected the floor plan that included the facade of indoor/outdoor living, which allowed their visitors to exit the elevator into the facade of a residential street front.

Jag's chauffeur parked faux-street side and came around to open the doors for both Jag and Rita.

Stepping out, Rita was agog. "We're inside a building

still, right?" she asked, looking around at the shockingly realistic outdoor residential street scene.

The "sky" above them was intelligent, programmable according to the owner's weather and daylight preferences. Currently, a balmy blue sky shone above while an artificial warm breeze swirled a floral scent around them.

Jag nodded, smiling at the note of awe in her voice. "We are."

Rita's eyes sparkled as she took it all in, the glowing wonder in them stopping here and there to peruse the hidden joints that held up the mirage.

She examined the one-way windows, which let light stream in for the "outdoor" plants without interfering with the artificial climate.

"How extraordinary," she breathed, sounding more like a scientist at the moment of eureka than a garage denizen.

As NECTAR, perhaps the mad scientist label was more accurate.

She should not have looked the part in the least, this woman dressed like an American teenager, but she did.

She had the kind of wild genius that had a hard time hiding itself.

Despite clothing being the reason they had entered the luxury building, Jag could not help but note that, more so for her than anyone else he'd ever met, clothes did not make Rita.

Nothing she wore, it seemed, had the capacity to hide her bright intelligence, nor her beauty, nor the way her eyes constantly darted around and analyzed—not a lime-green jumpsuit, and not a sweatshirt and old trainers.

In every setting and costume, the woman was stunning.

But just because form could not hide her function, it did not mean that her form could not be enhanced.

And as if the conclusion conjured him, Jag's tailor chose that moment to open his front door.

"Prince Jahangir, your visit is as welcome as it is unexpected." The man's voice was loud and warm and, as always, modulated to convey friendship.

Jag was willing to tolerate a certain level of theatrics in the pursuit of a perfect suit.

"Jameel, you are a paragon of style, as ever," Jag said, smiling.

Jameel waved off the compliment. "I wear the same thing every day."

"There is no need to change when you are leagues ahead of the rest."

"Flattery, Prince? You must have a dire need."

Jag laughed before indicating Rita's presence with a nod of his head. "Not I. I bring you a challenge from America."

Jameel's gaze traveled from the Prince to Rita, who had returned to Jag's side from examining the mirage walls that were in truth one-way windows.

"Oh, dear," Jameel said, shoulders slumping as he took in the whole of Rita's person. "How much time do I have?" he asked, a slight wobble in the shield of confidence he typically exuded.

"For a complete wardrobe? A week. For something more appropriate for daywear in Hayat City? None. She cannot leave the premises like this."

Taking in a shuddering breath that concluded with an expression of resolution, Jameel nodded. "I don't have much here right now, but your timing is impeccable, as always, Prince. Your father's youngest wife recently commissioned a new set. I've a few pieces completed that I can make adjustments to." Eyeing Rita, Jameel began taking mental notes. "Let out the bust, bring in the waist, lengthen the pant, and we'll be set."

Bemused, Rita laughed. "Just all that?" Her voice was charming and melodic, bolstered by her curiosity and engaged mind, and even the jaded tailor looked momentarily mesmerized.

Jag could not have found a better partner in this endeavor.

However, he had brought her to Jameel not to assess her capacity to make everyone she met fall in love with her. He'd brought her for some clothes.

Answering his wife in order to remind the tailor of their purpose in being here, Jag said, "Like in all design, impeccable attire comes down to the details, my dear."

Directing his attention more fully on Rita, Jameel said, "You're rather beautiful, you know," as if he were surprised to only now realize it.

Brushing aside the strange spurt of possessive aggression that rose within him upon noting the other man's gaze, Jag agreed. "Indeed, she is a diamond in the rough."

An odd expression flashed across Rita's face at Jag's words, but she smiled at Jameel and said, "Thank you."

"Who are you?" Jameel's question seemed to slip free without his realizing that it was a monumental breach of the discretion he was famous for.

For his part, Jag understood.

There was something powerfully magnetic about his new bride. Something about her approachable appeal frayed the seams of even the strongest sense of propriety.

Because of that, and because there was no time like the present to practice the winding navigation of their story, rather than ignoring Jameel's question, Jag answered with a careful truth. "She is NECTAR."

Jameel's mouth dropped open, and again Jag was impressed by the uniqueness of the situation.

Jameel regularly outfitted the kings and queens of the world—that he was moved to shock upon meeting this particular woman spoke volumes.

"B-but… I had no idea NECTAR was a woman…" Jameel stammered.

"I trust you'll have no problem outfitting a woman."

"Certainly not," Jameel said absently, tossing a "help

yourself to the refreshments" over his shoulder as he led Rita off.

Two hours later, Jag's diamond had been polished to a shine.

"Prince Jahangir, may I present the newest NECTAR conversion to hit the world, the mad genius herself?" Jameel's voice held the humor of an inside joke, and Jag opened his eyes to another surge of possessive feeling.

He had not brought her to Jameel to develop a rapport; he had brought her here for a casual outfit for a princess.

But upon laying his eyes on her, thoughts of jealousy fled Jag's mind.

A change of clothing should not have transformed the woman the way it had.

And to be fair it wasn't that she looked different, per se.

The same bright glowing brown face smiled at him, with the same big glossy eyes and the same lushly full lips.

Her heart-shaped face was the same, with the same charming pointed chin, with its faint hint of cleft, and the same perfect white teeth and the same straight brown brows and thick curling lashes, each feature emanating the same sheen of health and vibrancy that they had had before she'd gone away with the tailor.

It was only her clothing that had changed, but the difference was night and day.

Jameel had outfitted her in slim-cut ankle-skimming black pants whose thick black satin material retained a gentle structured form while at the same time flowing smoothly with the movements of her legs.

For her top, Jameel had chosen black as well, dressing her in a three-quarter-length-sleeve tunic with a mandarin collar and decorative clasps.

It was the astounding embroidered long coat, though, that truly made the look.

Technically a long sleeveless vest, the black garment was made to be worn open, falling to about knee-length and embroidered with what Jag knew would be real gold thread that had been woven into intricate and detailed geometric and star patterns along the front and lower edges of it.

The effect was natural and effervescent, bold and future-minded, while remaining respectful of tradition. She looked exactly like the conversions she created.

Once again, the clothier had proved himself to be of the highest order.

Jameel did not merely drape fashionable clothes on bodies. He used fashion to express the souls that the bodies contained.

Rita's accessories were gold and glittering—her hands and wrists and ears and neck draped with copious amounts of diamonds and black pearl–accented rings, bracelets, necklaces and earrings. Each piece caught the light in much the same way as her skin tone did, catching and refracting it back out into the world more joyously.

Jag swallowed, unsuccessfully attempting to recalibrate himself in the material world.

"Fortunately," Jameel said, midway through explaining Rita's attire, which Jag only now realized, "your stepmother had not yet seen my concepts or pieces so she will never know what she missed out on."

"It was meant for Rita," Jag said.

"Without a doubt," Jameel added, his eyes aglow with his creation.

Jag looked to Rita, catching her gaze, unable to pass up an opportunity to feel the strange bolt of connection that came every time their eyes met.

Her pupils dilated, distracting him from her clothing as they pulled him deeper, lulling him into following her lead.

The smile that blossomed on her face was wide and unguarded and sweet as anything that Jag had ever seen, and he was transfixed. Until he shook himself free with a frown.

As much as it might appear from the outset that they were here spoiling his new bride, that was not the case and he, above all apparently, needed to remember that.

"I'm never taking it off!" Rita exclaimed, proud of how she looked despite the war going on within him.

Her delight was fresh and nourishing like a dip in the nectar she'd so aptly named herself for, making him realize how starved for simple, honest sweetness he had been all this time.

But not from her. He could find that sweetness from any other source but her.

To remind them both of the distance they'd agreed to, Jag nodded to break their connection and cleared his throat, offering a stiff smile and a clipped, "Excellent."

Glancing between the two of them, Jameel laughed. "It was an honor to dress you, Rita. You have my number. Don't hesitate to call if you ever need anything."

Not liking the sound of that, Jag lifted his arm to his wife. She crossed to him to take it without thought, brushing off Jameel's very serious offer as if he just gave his direct number out to all of his clients.

Leading her back to the artificial street and their driver, Jag was glad to return to the vehicle elevator and once again capture her attention. She had the confounding habit of finding anything and everyone outside of him infinitely more fascinating than she seemed to find him, and he didn't like it.

"What did you think of Jameel?" he asked as soon as they were comfortably situated within the car.

"He cares about clothing the way I care about cars and was full of advice about Hayat."

"Well said. And what advice did he give?"

"There is always someone watching."

"Again, he's correct. Fortunately, now you are dressed for the audience."

She snorted, and he smiled, glad she had heard the joke in what he had said and proud of her.

As far as dry runs went, their stop by the tailor's had been perfect.

Rita had charmed Jameel exactly as Jag predicted she would charm all of Hayat.

Now Jag just had to figure out how he felt about it.

"Where are we going now?" she asked.

"The stadium," he replied, and was rewarded by another megawatt smile. She was like a living Edison bulb—almost too bright to look at directly.

At the stadium, the driver had barely opened the door before Rita launched herself out of the car, virtually running toward the construction site. Only waving an American flag as she ran could have better displayed to the world where she came from.

But her enthusiasm was rather pleasing. And he was proud of the stadium.

Very near completion, it was the largest structure in the world of its kind.

Catching up to Rita where she stood in the shade of scaffolding, her palm placed flat against its surface, Jag asked, as if in all seriousness, "What do you sense?"

Laughing, she pitched her voice into the realm of science fiction and horror, and crowed, "It's alive!"

Surprisingly, he caught himself smiling alongside her though he was not typically one for such silly jokes. His sense of humor and play was best showcased in situations that he and Rita would not be finding themselves in.

Had agreed not to.

Attempting to pull his mind back from the edges of what it was thinking, Jag defaulted to the dry and factual. "In truth, it *is* alive. When completed, this building will be the largest biophilic structure in the world."

At his side, Rita nodded in appreciation. "Outstanding. I took a course on biophilic design over a summer semester once. It inspired a lot of the renovations I did in my home and garages. It's really the way of the future…" She trailed off as she explored the wall in closer detail, noting especially where the living elements joined with the artificial.

Jag watched her, oddly rapt, as she gently probed and felt the structure.

Her hands were quite small, he realized only now.

He had not noticed the fact while in her garage, nor during their plane journey, but now, as if every moment with her promised a new revelation.

How unexpected it was, that such small hands were solely responsible for creating some of the most advanced electric engine systems on the planet.

"You do renovations as well, now?" Jag asked, a single eyebrow lifted. "I didn't know I had conscripted a woman of all trades."

Rita turned to him with a smile and a laugh that knocked him back a bit, though she didn't seem to notice. "You do everything when you're just starting out and growing a business at the same time."

"And here I thought it was all about the cars for you."

Still easy and smiling, she returned to her exploration of the building as she answered, "It is, but as hard as it might be for a man like you to imagine, there are a lot of roadblocks along the way to progress, and they're usually financial. Whenever I ran out of funds to pay for garage or home improvements, which happened pretty much between every commission at first, I was left with the choice of either scrounging up materials and figuring out how to do it myself or twiddling my thumbs and waiting."

Jag smiled, familiar enough with her by now to know she was not a woman who waited for things. "Impressive." He commended her with a nod.

Turning, she caught his eye and once again they shared a heartbeat of simply staring, before she remembered to smile and gave him a shrug. "It's just the way my family always operated."

"Well, it's made you well-versed. You should make something for my father," Jag said, trusting she had gleaned enough of the picture now to realize what an absurd idea that was.

She didn't let him down.

Chuckling, she said, "From what you've told me, I'm sure he'll love that. 'Here you go, Father-in-Law, even more evidence that your new princess is…dun-dun-dun… handy.'"

Laughter danced in Jag's eyes, even as mention of his father reminded him that until the announcement was made, it was still better to limit the amount of time Rita spent out and about. "Imagine his horror," he agreed, before adding, "As excited as you are, my dear, it is best I show you your new home."

He hadn't meant to call her *my dear*, just as he had not meant to allow his mind and body to drift off into familiar and flirtatious behavior the countless other times they had since he and his bride had agreed to keep things professional between them, but it happened nonetheless.

After a good night's rest, and some time away from his blushing bride, however, he would have no problem maintaining the warm and unemotional facade of a royal husband.

And in the meantime, he would take her to his mother's old palace. With its custom design and elaborate gardens it was the only one of his palaces or residences that seemed remotely right for the vibrant woman at his side, despite the fact that he hadn't set foot inside it in years.

CHAPTER SIX

A WEEK LATER, Rita met Jag in the palace's central open-air courtyard beside its gorgeous centerpiece, a massive mosaicked fountain.

She hadn't intended to be there when he arrived.

She had simply finished the project she was working on too late to start a new one before dinner so had gone early to clean up in the palace baths and just happened to be crossing back at the same time that Jag entered from the hallway that led to the old garage.

She had only been in residence for a full week, and her new garages were nearly complete.

Smiling, her wet hair wrapped up in a towel and her body draped in the lovely linen pants and fitted cotton T-shirt that Jameel had made for her, Rita said, "Hi."

His answering smile was warm and sexy and a little surprised, and Rita had to tamp down the series of events that it set off in her body.

We might be husband and wife, she had to remind herself, *but we both agreed that real intimacy, emotional or otherwise, would only complicate things.*

She had not had to remind herself of the fact in a while—not since the Prince had settled her in before leaving the palace for wherever he resided the first night they arrived.

In fact, she had not seen him in person since then.

They had spoken on the phone and exchanged multiple messages in the preceding week—about her needs, and the construction of the new garages and discussions of how she might be incorporated into the exhibition at this late stage—but she had not seen him.

And it only took a few minutes for the wild thoughts to begin, her inner critic noted tartly. *You need to get more serious about keeping things professional.*

"Hello to you," he said, a faint trace of breathlessness to his words. "You've been enjoying the baths, I see."

Appreciating the opportunity the small talk provided to settle her system, Rita nodded. "They're wonderful. I can't believe I never thought to do something like that back home."

"They were my mother's pride and joy. She designed them herself. It's been years since I've used them, though. I should."

"You absolutely should! It's a shame to think they'd gone unused. It's the first thing I'm going to add when I return home. I bought my property because there was enough room for my garages and it was close to the city, but the house wasn't much when I got it. Nobody else wanted it because it's a heritage building and couldn't be torn down, only renovated. It took me a while to get to it since the garage had to come first, but as soon as I could, I refurbished it back to its mid-century brilliance. I haven't touched the old pool yet, though. It doesn't even have any water in it—" She stopped herself when she realized she was rambling on and gracelessly shifted subjects. "Your mother was a designer?" Rita asked, the question slipping out before she could think to stop it. Asking personal questions wasn't any more of a good idea when they were trying to keep things collegial between them than thinking inappropriate thoughts.

But rather than withdraw further, her question seemed to relax his guard.

"She was," he said with a faint smile. "Interior, as well as an architect. She was rather brilliant, not unlike yourself," he added with a nod to Rita. "This palace was her doing, in fact."

Heat came to her cheeks at his words, the experience of being praised by someone whose opinion mattered unfamiliar after so many years.

In fact, she couldn't recall it since the day her father had announced the acceptance of her match when she was seventeen. Had it really been ten years?

"It's stunning," Rita said honestly. It really was. In the week she had been here, Rita had truly come to feel as if Jag's mother's palace was a home away from home, with its somehow warm and comfortable elegance and class.

"I shared many happy memories with her here," he added, unprovoked.

As if the volunteered information were permission to prod more, another question popped out. "What happened to her?" Rita asked, once again unable to keep her curiosity to herself, but this time it was not rewarded.

Rather, when he next spoke there was a thread of distance in his voice that hadn't been there before, as if her question had brought him to his senses and he'd closed entirely up, which was probably for the best. At least one of them didn't seem to be having trouble recalling the terms of their arrangement. "That's a sad story for another time," he said. "But I appreciate the reminder about the baths. A long soak in the large hot pool would no doubt do wonders for my shoulders."

Rita's mind's eye snagged on the image of Jag's long, muscular body stretched out in the largest of the otherworldly baths. Chest strangely tight and breathless, she nodded, focusing on bringing her system back under control rather than pushing further.

She wasn't supposed to push. She was supposed to smile and retain professional distance.

Making another attempt at it, she said, "You're here in time for dinner. Will you be joining?" She kept her voice light and airy for all that she looked him in the eye, trying, if not entirely succeeding, at keeping things bland.

But it was a challenge, because in the week that she had been living in the palace, this was the first time she had seen Jag since he had dropped her off.

The corners of his mouth lifted ever so slightly and he swallowed before nodding. "I canceled my call with Sheik Ahmed. He will attend the exhibition or he will not. I found I didn't care enough either way to miss Rafida's cooking in order to convince him."

"Is that so?" Rita asked, her breath oddly shallow and chesty.

It couldn't be just Rafida's cooking that had lured him back to the palace, though.

Rafida had confided to Rita that before Rita arrived in Hayat, the Prince had rarely set foot in the home of his childhood.

"I had a craving I could not resist," he said, and Rita would have sworn he was not talking about food, had he not been the one between them most firmly committed to the terms of their agreement. "I assume we're dining in the blue room?" Jag asked, shaking her from her thoughts as he took a step back from her as if he only just now realized he stood too close, though she supposed that she, too, only now realized how near they had come to each other.

He had taken his suit jacket off as he spoke, having opted for Western attire for whatever business the day's agenda had included for him, and this time it was Rita's turn to swallow, nodding her response to save herself from having to clear her throat.

The blue room was one of her favorites in the palace.

A small formal dining room, it wasn't simply blue; that was merely the shorthand for it. In actuality, it was a gorgeously decorated room, graced with teal-trimmed wainscoting that was delicately overlaid with a faint gold leaf lattice pattern that seemed to shimmer and glow in both natural and artificial light, and floor-to-ceiling panel windows. Above the wainscoting, a stunning lagoon scene was painted across the walls, with cranes and weepy foliage all in lovely muted water tones.

Against the backdrop of the high-tech city, the room— the entire palace really—was a tranquil retreat, despite the fact that she hadn't explored Hayat City enough yet to need a retreat from it.

On the car ride from the racetrack to the palace, Rita and Jag had agreed that it was best for her to keep a low profile, remaining for the most part in the palace, until after the exhibition.

That would keep the public's attention focused on the event while Rita's wardrobe was completed. It also allowed her to push the whole idea of debuting to the world to the back burner of her mind.

Thus far, nothing this wild arrangement had asked of her had caused any permanent changes to the way she did business, but revealing to the world that NECTAR was a woman undoubtedly would.

If Jag was right, being a princess would offset the loss of respect she would undoubtedly experience in the public eye once everyone knew she was woman, but if he was wrong, it would take a long time to recover.

And it wasn't like princesses exactly commanded respect in the auto industry—not to mention in engineering and computer science. They were fields that, unfortunately, still just didn't really take women seriously.

But she *would* be able to weather the storm because she *would* be a princess.

At least temporarily.

And when she was no longer a princess, she would have been openly operating as NECTAR, the woman, for long enough that her work would once again speak for itself.

She hoped.

"What's going on in that mad genius mind of yours?" Jag asked, breaking into her thoughts.

Starting, she had to pause in her steps for a moment.

Readjusting to the reality of company was a strange novelty. She had spent so much time alone that she wasn't used to someone pulling her back from her thoughts.

In fact, dinner tonight, with company, unexpected as it was, was something that had not happened in her life since she'd graduated from college.

After being disowned by her family nearly a decade ago, she had not been invited to any family gatherings, following the Friendsgivings of college. When her few friends had returned to their families of origin or begun starting families of their own, she'd felt like too much of an imposition to sit in.

In fact, far more than the physical intimacy they were committed to avoiding, sharing a meal together felt dangerously close and personal.

But that was probably just because she was used to the life of a hermit.

She was sure the Prince knew what he was doing.

Arriving in the dining room, they found that Rafida had set the table, but not yet laid it with food.

Jag sat at the north end of the table and Rita took the seat to his left, it being the spot that made the most sense, conversation-wise.

She didn't want to have to yell at him across the table.

As they settled, Jag asked, "How did your work go today?"

Smiling, Rita said, "Good. The tools that have arrived so far are already making me realize how out-of-date my garage had become. I can't wait for the whole work space to be completed. It's so much more fun to work with top-of-the-line equipment," she said, pleasure rippling through her. "What about you? I mean besides the phone call you skipped."

Chuckling at her sass, Jag said, "Oh, I got a few things accomplished, one of which was approving the final schedule for the finale and NECTAR's, and my wife's, debut. It will take place at the race after-party. Where a highly selective guest list and a great deal of media will be in attendance. I anticipate announcing not just the triumph of the remarkable NECTAR Ferrari, but also the triumph of having won the infamous engineer's heart."

Once again there was a skip in the smooth flow of their conversation as Rita stilled upon hearing his words.

Of all the sacrifices she had been asked to make for her chance to change the world, the loss of her anonymity and the protective shell of the world thinking she were a man was the most difficult.

It had not been easy to protect who she was, and a part of her still wasn't convinced that giving it up was the best call.

When Rita waited too long to nod her enthusiasm or say something in response, Jag frowned at her. "You're still nervous."

Seeing no point in denying it, Rita didn't. "I am. Anonymity has been a security blanket for me," she admitted. "It's hard to let it go."

"You're not a little girl, Rita, and you don't have little-girl ambitions. I say that it's well past time you let go of the blanket."

"Well, if you're going to put it like that," she said, teasing to keep things light, but he wouldn't let her.

"I am, because it is true. As I said on the plane, you might have had your reasons and convictions for keeping yourself a relative secret from the world for this long, but you're going to have to be brave enough to set them down if you want to do the thing you said you want to do, that I believe you want to do. You wouldn't be here if you didn't. Don't let self-doubt sabotage you now that you're here. Unless you are ashamed of being a woman," he added the last to his little speech as if the idea had only just now occurred to him.

"Of course I'm not," Rita sputtered. "I'm extremely proud to be a woman, especially in my field."

"Your field? So it's being a mechanic, then?"

Rita snorted. "There's nothing else I've ever wanted to be. Absolutely nothing. But the field doesn't feel the same way about women in the ranks."

He waved her words away. "You've so far surpassed the skill and reach of all of the good old boys that that reality, unjust as it may be, is no longer an excuse. If you're not afraid and ashamed, then I can see no reason why you would hesitate to own who you are on the world stage. Evolution is the constant process of releasing that which no longer serves you. Anonymity was merely a tool to make your way to a place of real power. Now that you've arrived at the threshold, you can't let fear and old habits keep you from walking through the door."

Unable to think of anything to say to him, Rita smiled, knowing the expression was flat because she didn't particularly feel like smiling, and Jag frowned in response, but Rafida chose that moment to enter with their dinner service, saving her from having to say more on the subject.

The table was soon filled with platters of succulent seasoned and grilled meats and vegetables served over flavorful steaming rice, bowls of delicious slow-cooked porridges seasoned with freshly ground herbs and spices, and a large tray of fresh-baked flatbreads, as well as dishes overflowing with dates, homemade yogurt topped with honey and sesame seeds, fresh sliced fruit, deep-fried dough balls liberally sweetened with date syrup, and a large, condensation-dripping pitcher of water infused with mint and honey.

How Rafida and her family managed to find the time to

care for and run Jag's large palace as well as do the cooking for three meals a day—as she had been since Rita's arrival—was beyond Rita's comprehension.

Of course, much to the dismay of her mother, the greater bulk of domesticity was beyond Rita's comprehension. It had been one of the things that had made negotiating a marriage arrangement for her initially difficult.

Sure, she was smart, but mothers wanted to know their sons and grandchildren weren't going to starve. It was just another one of the reasons the offer from Rashad's family had been so warmly received by Rita's.

They hadn't needed a girl who could cook, just one who could become a doctor.

But Rita had just never been able to find the same kind of passion for putting together a meal or healing a wound as she had for building an engine, and it showed—even if she hadn't known about the doctor part back then.

"It's love that makes the work fulfilling, dulali," her mother had assured her. *"I was just like you as a young woman, never interested in the housework or cooking. But then you and your sister came, and it all changed. When you have children, you will see. You will want to feed them."*

But children had not featured prominently in her future visions then. And now they did so even less.

Though her current business-arrangement marriage was something different, normal arranged matches were still common in her community, even among American Bengalis.

Like Rita and Jag, her parents had only met for the first time on the day they were married, but practices had changed since then.

When it was clear that Rita would be on a successful and advanced track educationally, her parents were approached with match offers. Realizing the time had come whether they were ready or not, they officially began the process with the caveat that no marriage could take place before she had graduated from college.

The process was eventually settled with Rita engaged to a fellow Bengali-American young man from a family of doctors.

Because Rita had been so young, still just seventeen at the time, she and Rashad had been granted six years to finish their undergraduate educations and date and get to know each other before they were to be married. And Rita would go so far as to say she had become comfortable with Rashad. He was smart and nonthreatening and made easy small talk.

But then she had gone and unwittingly violated the terms of their arrangement, causing her family to lose face and her to be disowned. So here she was, instead, eating a delicious meal that she had not prepared in a business-arrangement marriage with a handsome prince and no prospect of change.

Which was exactly what she wanted.

In fact, her only regret was not realizing for so long that her parents' love and approval had hinged so strongly on that of her future in-laws.

That would have been nice to know way back in the beginning.

Fortunately, things with Jag had been spelled out from the start.

"You've gone quiet again," Jag noted, bringing her back into the present moment once more.

"Just enjoying the delicious meal," she lied, smiling and hoping he didn't look past her explanation.

Of course, taking in the fascinating lines and planes of the Prince, noting the curves of his lips and the barely restrained electric power in his gaze, it wasn't long before there were no more morose thoughts to hide.

"Rafida does not disappoint," he said.

Rita agreed. "She does not. She made the most delicious *balaleet* this morning," she said, grasping at the straw of chatting about food.

Jag made a noise of disappointment at the news, and Rita was struck by the normalcy of the moment.

It would be so easy to believe they were a normal husband and wife, when in truth, they were merely business partners.

"Rafida's *balaleet* is the best in the world. It was my mother's favorite," he said, a soft, unguarded smile on his face.

For the second time that night, he had brought up his mother. This time, she knew better than to push too hard.

"Really?" Rita said, forcing her voice to remain casual. "I hadn't realized Rafida had been in your service for so long."

"Rafida was my mother's housekeeper," he said.

"Really?" Rita exclaimed, genuinely taken aback. While Rafida was no spring chicken, neither did she seem old enough to have been with a family through multiple generations.

Laughing, Jag said, "She was very young when my mother hired her. Just fourteen."

"That is legitimately child labor," Rita noted.

Looking askance at her, Jag waved her words away. "Some rules are better broken until someone in a position of power can come along later and change them. Rafida was assaulted, and her family shunned her as a result. At the time, that was more common. Since I have stepped into my role as Crown Prince, things have changed."

"That's so awful for Rafida, though," Rita said, heart heavy.

Jag nodded. "My mother defied everyone, including my father, and gave her a good job. She offered her education as well, but Rafida refused, knowing she would not be as welcomed at school as she was in my mother's home."

In a single anecdote, he had revealed the kind of woman

his mother had been, far more than the details he had mentioned earlier. And he had revealed how strong and resilient the woman Rita had been sharing a home with was, as well.

Solemnly, Rita said, "Your mother sounds like a generous and brave woman. And Rafida stronger than I even realized." Sensing without his indicating that he had once again gone as far as he was willing, Rita then deliberately joked, "With two powerful women as role models, it's too bad you turned out the way you did."

What her gibe lacked in sophistication—which was a lot—it made up for in efficacy.

Instead of the flare-up of flame in his copper eyes, of his walls going up again, the Prince moved.

As quick as a mongoose, his finger darted out to bop her nose.

Her eyes widened and her breath caught, her skin instantly sparking to life where he'd touched her, but he was unaware of the affect his contact was having on her.

Instead, his eyes triumphant but still somehow light and teasing, he said, "And what about you, Rita?"

"What about me?" she hedged.

"What about your family? Parents, siblings, all of it. Tell me about my in-laws." His questions were not requests but commands, given as if he'd only now just realized she might have a family history herself.

Likely, he only had.

Even without the need to defy him out of principle, family was a subject about which she didn't have much to share.

"My family," she repeated, buying herself time.

What should she start with? What could she tell him that would satisfy a mind that she knew would be looking for hints and details into her background without also revealing dark secrets and wounds that she did not know him well enough yet to discuss?

As curious as she was herself, she knew it was a delicate balance to satisfy someone while retaining your privacy, which was why as NECTAR she didn't even bother.

She lived in the mystery.

"My family owns a long-distance trucking company,"
she said. "My grandfather started it when he came to the
United States with my grandmother as a young man and
currently my father and US-based uncles run things. I
grew up going on long-haul runs with my father every
summer." Rita paused, thinking of what to say next. What
she came up with would have to be personal enough to
reveal a truth about herself without giving any hints as
to how it all ended. Even years after it had all happened,
she could not shake the stings of guilt and shame, nor the
fear that—in the end and in the eyes of anyone outside
of the situation—her actions had not been principled and
righteous, but selfish.

"My parents had an arranged marriage," she said. "My
father flew to Bangladesh where he met my mother on the
day of their wedding. They stayed there for one week and
then flew back to the United States to start their life together. My mother had never been to the US before then."
Rita focused on the parts of the story that had always fascinated her, dangling them like shiny distractions in hopes
they might stave off more probing inquiries from Jag.
"Two years later, I was born, and three years after that my
sister, Nadia, arrived. That's the lot of us, Mom, Dad, sister, uncles, cousins and me." She ended on a chipper note,
her voice light and easy, even as her stomach turned over.

"Long-distance trucking? That's—once again, I
couldn't have come up with something better," he said.

"And why is that?" she asked, knowing she shouldn't.

"Not only are you a mechanic, but you come from a line
of blue-collar immigrants. While I know that immigrants
grow and strengthen the economy, it's not generally the
population one chooses a princess from. Among his many

flaws, my father is also a bigot. He despises Hayat's immigrant population, who happen to be primarily of South
Asian origin, like yourself, and will hate it even more that
you come from immigrant American stock, in addition to
your plethora of perfectly imperfect traits. The common
people of Hayat, however, are going to love you, even as
my father seethes!

"I assume," he said, moving on as if positioning one's
wife in opposition to one's father was done every day,
"that trucking is where your interest in mechanics and
engineering came from?"

Nodding, Rita said, "Yeah. Cars, and trucks, and things
that go. I was all about them from an early age. Honestly, it
was all I was ever interested in. My dad took me on drives
with him every summer as soon as I was old enough to
not need a car seat. Those were my favorite."

Examining her, he said, "It is easy to imagine you as
a little child in a big truck."

Rita laughed. "When I was really small, before the
drives, I had to sit on a stack of telephone books just to
see through the window."

"Telephone books?" he asked.

Holding back her laugh, she said, "Telephone books
were these old things that used to hold the phone numbers
of area people and businesses."

"They just gave that information away for free?" Jag
asked, shocked. "That seems like a breach of privacy,"
he added.

Laughing now, Rita said, "Things were different back
in the Wild West days of America, especially when you
were not royal," she said. "You had to ford rivers and use
wired telephones."

Smiling, he indulged her joke, saying gravely, "The
hardships you've endured," before shaking his head as
he said again, more to himself, "Long-distance trucking."

Rita rolled her eyes, relieved more than irritated to

be in the safe territory of discussing her family's trucking history.

In truth, her family was never far from her mind, but as her life as NECTAR had blossomed, she had arrived at a place of balance in which thoughts of them operated in the background rather than as a constant grievance at the forefront.

Dinner tonight with the Prince, however, had pushed them back to the surface, if only because it had reminded her once again of what it was like to be a part of a unit.

Their unit might only be just the two of them, but even with all of the restrictions and stipulations they were operating under, they had still managed to form a team of sorts.

For better or worse, their bond was growing stronger, drifting, if not toward a true marriage, then precariously far from simply being a pair of colleagues involved in a business deal.

But perhaps most dangerous of all, thorny conversations included, tonight's dinner had forced Rita to recognize what she'd been unwilling to admit over the past week: she wanted more, and she wanted it with Jag.

CHAPTER SEVEN

Ten days later

"THIS IS QUITE the event you have going on here," Vincenzo Moretti, the current ruler of the European nation of Arista, said as Jag entered the room where the three men that meant more to him than any other living beings stood.

Pushing aside the image of Rita that filled his mind in contradiction of the idea, Jag opened his arms to Vincenzo, a true smile coming to his face for the first time that day.

"Brutal and monstrous my father may be," Jag said, "but he has an unfortunate affinity for making money. It is my only joy, then, to spend it lavishly."

Vin's father, the former King of Arista, had not been so gifted.

Like Jag's father, the man had lived as if his pleasure was the only important truth. And, like Jag's father, cruelty to their wives had been a pleasure that both Jag's and Vin's fathers shared.

"You couldn't have found a little more useful pet project, Jag? A hospital, for instance, seems perhaps more practical than the 'world's largest biophilic structure'?" Rafael asked without hope, knowing Jag well enough to know the question to be pointless.

"I've completed six state-of-the-art hospitals within

the past three years. No one in Hayat City lives more than twenty minutes from a brand-new, fully equipped hospital. I wanted to treat myself, as they say in America."

With a scoff, Zeus said, "Since when did you begin dabbling in American aphorisms?"

It would be Zeus, Jag thought with a mental sigh, to pinpoint the unconscious revelation in a statement.

When a matter needed to be cut through with a heavy, relentless tool—something powerful enough to shatter and destroy any attempt at obfuscation and illusion—it was always Zeus.

The Aegean Prince was a living broadsword.

With these men who knew him so well, there was no point in or need for deflection or hedging.

"Since I made an American woman my bride," Jag answered openly.

It was as if the very room in the secure downtown office sucked in its breath then, freezing the three men within it in a moment of silence before all of them began speaking at once.

"You married?" from Rafael, a grimace ready in place across his swarthy visage.

"Who is she?" Vin asked.

"When do we meet this bride of yours? I assume she is as desperately unsuitable as planned?" Zeus drawled. Eyes lighting, he added, "Tell me she is hideous."

Jag said stiffly, "She is not."

With far greater restraint, Rafael suggested without sarcasm, "Her being an American is enough."

"Excuse you," Vin said testily, his own American bride likely on his mind.

"Then what is it that makes this bride of yours so unsuitable? Or is she not? Did you go and fall into the same love trap as the rest of us?" Zeus asked.

Waving Zeus's words away, Jag said, "Oh, no. My bride

is most perfectly unsuitable. And we are most certainly not in love. She's a mechanic from Oakland."

The three men in the room burst into laughter.

"It seems you're the only one of us who made it, chap," Zeus said, laughter lingering in his eyes.

Even Rafael chimed in, a thread of rare amusement lightening his voice. "While there is nothing wrong with being a mechanic," he said, "it certainly isn't a background that would prepare one for ruling a nation."

Vin's voice and smile were rueful when he said, "I would have liked to welcome you to our side of this game, friend, but I must admit it sounds like, of all of us, you may be the only one to have fulfilled the terms of our agreement so thoroughly."

With a smile devoid of humor, Jag said, "It would appear so…"

"But? I sense a but there." Zeus asked.

"Is she proving to be too unsuitable?" Rafael asked, ever astute.

Shaking his head, Jag said, "No. She is truly ideally unsuitable, a study in contrasts really. She's reckless, and brash, and daring and foolhardy, but she's also shy and reserved. There is not a subtle thing about her body, and yet she excels at maintaining mystery and her own counsel. She's certifiably brilliant. Rarely have I encountered a mind as quick and discerning as hers. And, for the record, she is as far from hideous as it's possible to be. She represents everything my father hates while offering everything the people of Hayat could want in a princess. I could not have discovered a more perfectly imperfect woman if I had been trying. And I wasn't. I was just picking up my car."

"I'm beginning to see your problem," Zeus said dryly.

"As do I," said Rafael.

"Clear as day," Vin added.

"And just what is that?" Jag said testily, lifting an eyebrow, ready to deny whatever wild theories they put forth.

Until Zeus said, simply, "You want her."

"That's absolutely absurd. Were you listening to what I said? She's utterly unsuitable."

"We heard the important part," Vin said with a grin.

"*Perfect* was the word I believe you used," Rafael added.

"Couldn't have discovered better if you'd been trying," Zeus served his words back to him.

Jag closed his eyes and forcibly set down the violent urge to deny it again.

His friends would never believe it, and neither could he.

He *did* want Rita.

His want of her was an ever-increasing presence in the back of his mind, constantly growing in size like a monstrous tumor, threatening the life of the arrangement he had made with her as well, not to mention his own. He could not afford to want anything, not like this. Not the kind of want that led to feelings and attachment. It was too much of a risk.

No relationship could ever again become a tool with which he could be manipulated.

But he could no longer deny it. Not to these men and not to himself.

"I want her," he said, lowering his head in defeat.

While his plans were by no means completely devastated by his desire for Rita, he would be a fool to deny that it put everything in jeopardy. It was already too much that he had eaten dinner with her each night since the first, and that he'd come to crave her company enough every day that he made excuses to ensure that it happened.

"So have her. So long as she wants you, too," Zeus egged on, ever the voice of the devil on his shoulder. "Isn't that one of the few known benefits to come with the baggage of matrimony?" he asked, as if he were not more than happy being burdened by the baggage of matrimony and family himself.

"Did she reject you?" Rafael asked, his characteristically bored tone lifting with the ring of real incredulity.

Jag wished there were space inside him to take pride in the thread of disbelief and doubt interwoven in his friend's question, but it didn't truly matter if there had never been a woman interested in denying him before if he could not have the woman that he shared a life with now.

Shaking his head, he said, "No. But I must keep my distance."

"Must." Zeus shivered with distaste. "Such an ugly word."

Jag agreed. "The only way this works is if Rita and I remain professional. Otherwise, she becomes a liability. This close to seeing things through with my father, there is no room for trust and opening up. Not in Hayat. It was different with the three of you. My father is on his home turf. If he were to sense even the slightest hint of emotion he would use that, and her, against me."

A new seriousness coming into his voice, Rafael said, "If you think that is even a possibility, you must keep her as far from you as possible."

But Jag waved his warning away. "It's not. Not with Rita. The woman doesn't have a grasping bone in her body. All she wants to do is save the world, one car at a time," he said, and if he sounded exasperated by his own devil's advocacy it was only because it was true.

He could not seem to stop going back and forth when it came to Rita.

"If you're that certain, then once again I do not see your problem," Zeus said. "You trust her, so have her."

Incensed, Jag whipped toward his friend. "I can't risk a kingdom on a hunch, Zeus!"

"I don't envy you your position," Vin said.

"It is rather sticky," Zeus added, unperturbed by his friend's outburst.

"No, it's not," Rafael said. "It's clear what you need to do. There is no challenge to it whatsoever. As you said, you can't risk a kingdom. Not on a hunch, and not on pent-up desire, either. Under no circumstances allow yourself to be alone with her. All you need to do is remember how long you've been implementing this plan, how much you have sacrificed along the way, the peace of your people, and what remains on the line while your father is still in power. And if that is not a strong enough deterrent, think about your mother."

A bastard, as well as having served as regent of his nation for his child half brother, family ties—as well as mothers—were simultaneously fraught and rigid subjects in Rafael's world view.

Vin let out a laugh that sounded like a cough. "May we all be blessed with such self-control, Rafael. I know the three of us have not shown ourselves to be so endowed."

"Self-control is overrated," Zeus chimed in. "All one truly needs is power."

"Well, power—" Jag grabbed on to the idea like it was a lifesaver "—is something that I have in spades. Therefore, worry not, my friends. Today is not a day for ominous warnings. Today, I have the rare triple pleasures of visiting friends, enraging my father to the glory of my nation, and announcing my marriage to a brilliant and beautiful woman. What more could a man want?"

"Well, I for one can't wait to meet the more that you want," Zeus said, at which Vin smiled and Rafael's eyes lit with humor.

Only briefly, Jag wondered if he needed friends as much as he'd thought.

After weeks now dedicated to putting together a showcase for her work at the exhibition, she could not believe it was all ready for the grand finale.

Her babies had done exceptionally on the world stage, her private fleet of vehicles making its world debut as if it had been born for the moment. Her inbox was overflowing with commission requests and she'd made some connections that she was excited might mean her dream was that much closer to becoming real.

And her baby, the astonishing car that she had been dreaming of her whole life until the day the Prince had sent it to her garage, the very catalyst for all of it, had eviscerated the competition in the all-electric race.

All of it had been better than she'd even imagined.

But now it was time to get ready for her debut.

Rita squeezed into the long black throat-to-ankle, shoulder-to-wrist bodysuit that Jameel had sent with mild trepidation.

Made of shimmering stretchy formfitting material that had the appearance of leather and the breathability of a mesh, the suit hugged every nook and cranny of her form, leaving little to the imagination.

The legs of the garment were accented with diagonal motorcycle stripes across the thighs, and the overall impression it gave was one of a woman who had been born to ride and ready to kick ass.

"I—I can't wear this," she stuttered. She looked sexier than she ever had in her life.

This was not what one wore to debut to the world.

And then she saw the accessories.

A belt made of pearls the size of baby's fists—bigger than Rita had even known possible—glowed in the living, breathing way that only pearls seemed able to do.

A chandelier necklace was obviously intended to wrap around the turtleneck neckline of the catsuit and drape decadently across her collar and chest.

Stunning earrings matched the belt, with diamond posts and three pearls dangling below each.

To the left in the case, a set of three intricately filigreed diamond-encrusted tennis bracelets glittered contentedly, and on the right was a lovely diamond anklet with tiny tinkling platinum bells swinging from it.

None of it, however, compared to the enormous ring that lay in the center of it all.

Rita brought a hand up to cover her mouth, equal parts horrified and amazed.

It was a ring fit for a princess—a ring fit to let the world know she was a taken woman, and, if by outrageous ostentatiousness alone, by whom.

Closing her eyes as she began to put it on, the rest of her senses attuned to the gentle pressure of the jewelry as she lay it across her catsuit-clad skin.

She could not see them yet, but she could sense that the jewels would be breathtaking—if only from the glare shining up from her chest.

She was beginning to wonder, however, when and how her outfit would transition from that of a bedazzled femme fatale into that of a proper international daughter-in-law making her debut.

And then she saw the overlayer.

An expanse of sheer fabric that shimmered in the light, it was thick, yet transparent.

Most astoundingly, it was in a shade of blue that was an exact match to the iridescent paint she had used on the Ferrari.

It was a long fitted jacket that buttoned up the back, with enormous billowing bell sleeves that gathered at the wrist just below where her bracelets rested.

When worn over the catsuit and jewels, what had begun as a revealing outfit on the cutting edge of fashion transformed into something modest and chic.

And although the jacket obscured the view of what lay beneath, because it was transparent and eye-catching, and because the jewels beneath shone through so clearly, it also begged the eye to look closer.

She somehow looked as ready for a spin around the racetrack as she did an elegant twirl around a ballroom.

Which was good, because it was time to go.

The car was waiting to shuttle her away to her grand debut.

Rita was to meet the Prince at a private entrance of the capital city's world-famous botanical gardens where the closing gala was taking place and the announcement would be made.

In no time at all, the driver was parking and walking around to open her door.

Taking his hand, she stepped out, finding the shoes surprisingly stable, easier to walk in than any heels she'd ever worn before.

She turned to thank the driver when a movement in the corner of her eye caught her attention.

It was Jag.

He had changed clothing as well.

No longer did he wear the full traditional Hayat-style clothing that he'd been wearing in the various photographs she'd seen of him from throughout the day, though he still wore his white ghutra and agal.

Paired with his bespoke suit, he was a sight to see.

The deep black of his suit set off the constantly burning fire in his eyes.

As always, he was captivating, commanding her attention and focus like a machine made for just that function.

His eyes shone as he took her in, gaze falling on her hand and, impossibly, flaring even more before returning to her face.

"Ravishing," he said.

The wonder in his voice worked its way around her heart and squeezed.

"Not so bad yourself," she said, awkwardly, wishing she had a greater lexicon for this moment than the one she'd picked up from romantic comedies.

Unfortunately, there was not another genre that could lend her vocabulary for the situation she found herself in.

What compliments did you give to a man who was your husband but not your lover?

What level of physical appreciation was appropriate with someone you were not allowed to be attracted to, but were?

How could she not be, when he looked like that? How could she resist when he was a force for his people who accepted nothing less than excellence from everyone around him, and gave back tenfold in response? Jag was dedicated, and shrewd, and hardworking, committed to providing the very best for those he was responsible for, and loyal to his core.

He was everything her mother would have told her to hope for in a husband. The kind of person it was possible to fall in love with.

Rita didn't know how long they stood like that, staring at one another, but it was long enough that it was a jolt to be reminded of what they had come here to do.

"Are you ready?" he asked, offering his arm.

Was she ready? She wasn't sure it was possible to be ready.

They were going in there to tell the world that she was his wife, and not only that, but that she was NECTAR.

And only half of it was true.

They might be married, but she was not his wife.

Hands trembling faintly at her side, Rita shook her head. This was a terrible idea.

"What's wrong?" he asked, concern deepening the timbre of his voice as he drew her to him, interlacing her chilled fingertips with his warm ones.

"This isn't a good idea. We can't pull this off. No one will ever believe the two of us are really married."

Tilting her chin up, Jag faced her, expression serious. "You are so brilliant and beautiful that they will believe anything you tell them just for a chance to be in the same room with you. You don't go in there to be shamed, but to shine in front of an adoring crowd. *Your* fleet was the surprise hit of the exhibition, *your* car irrefutably attested to the world the power and speed potential of electric, and your reveal tonight is the first step in getting the world to reconsider how it gets around. You're the star of this exhibition, whether the world knows you are or not. We don't have to do this this way, Rita. The results of the exhibition were better than even expected. I can close the exhibition myself and we can create a more formal debut for our marriage with an altered origin story. But you will never again have another opportunity like tonight with which to step on stage and transfix the globe. The choice is yours, Rita."

Rita stared at him, unable to even settle on an expression, let alone a course of action. He was willing to let her keep her secret identity but unwilling to let her off the hook.

Like her dad had been, before the whole matching thing.

He would let her hide, but he wouldn't do it without letting her know the consequences.

She knew Jag was right, not because he said it, but because she herself had seen her reach expand over the course of the exhibition. Her work had caught the attention of the international community.

What she did now would determine whether they forgot about her as soon as her moment had passed or stuck around to listen to what she had to say.

She had hidden behind NECTAR because people had not listened to what she had to say when they thought she was a woman. She had done it because women weren't supposed to do and like and study what she did.

And now her strategy was threatening to become a different kind of silencer.

She had to trust that she was ready to hold her own in front of the world. She had to trust Jag.

But what if they rejected her? Could she handle the wider public saying all the things her parents had said about her hopes and dreams?

Squeezing her hand, Jag said in a low tone, "You've gone quiet."

Rita cleared her throat. Then clear and loud and strong—as far a cry from the similar declaration she had made sobbing to her parents so long ago—she said, "I choose to change the world."

Jag's smile in response was beyond blinding and it occurred to Rita that, though he had been willing to let her lead, it had been his dreams and plans that had been on the line as well.

"You will blow them all away, Rita. None of them will know what hit them, even as they will be desperate for more—not the press, the people of Hayat, nor the heads of the industries you will transform." He held her hand as he spoke, squeezing again before he asked her quietly, "Are you ready to become a national pride and joy?"

Chuckling to herself, the sound bubbling up to burst through some of the anxiety, she squeezed his hand in response and nodded. "I am," she said.

Not everyone was going to love her, she knew.

Her father-in-law was somewhere in the crowd tonight.

But that was also her part in their arrangement, and she was prepared.

Tonight would mark the first time she met the man in person, but having gone nearly four weeks in residence in Hayat, she had now seen his image enough times to know what he looked like.

Jag had warned her to expect that her father-in-law would be nasty, reminding her that the man was a ruthless tyrant even as recently as the last dinner they'd shared.

Having her own history of nasty encounters with fathers, Rita could handle herself.

She would be everything Jag needed her to be, when it came to his father and the public. It was the least she could give in return for the man who not only supported who and what she was but also believed in her capacity to push both toward achieving her dreams.

Stepping through this door represented entering into a new future, for all that Jag hadn't asked her to change herself.

It was a dangerous future in which the world knew who she was.

It was a future as the wife of the man at her side.

There was no going back once everyone knew.

Looking up at Jag, she was once again caught by the fiery amber of his gaze.

Something tormented and pained struggled in his look, his lips taking on an unfamiliar grimace as he opened them to force out the words, "Last chance to turn back."

Shaking her head, Rita said, "No. That moment passed. We're in it together. Let's do this."

Relief returned Jag's face back to the confident mask she was coming to know so well, and he nodded. Then he opened the door.

Rita gasped.

Massive walls of green glass arched overhead and around.

Stepping into the room, she walked into a wall of humidity, the perfumed air thick and moist in the room despite the ventilation provided by the many open windows.

Being inside it was as if she had stepped into a prehistoric jungle.

The room housed three long shallow rectangular pools each graced with lily pads, lotuses and other gorgeous water plants that Rita had not come across in any of her gardening classes.

Partygoers dotted walkways, standing on small arched bridges, swirling glasses of effervescent liquid while tuxedo-clad servers replenished drinks and handed out hors d'oeuvres.

As she gained her bearings, Jag scanned the crowd, his eyes coming to rest on a group of white-clad men in a far corner.

Though they were far away, Rita could just make out the features of the man who was her father-in-law.

She swallowed, and once again Jag squeezed her hand.

"I will keep you safe," he promised, reading her accurately.

And because he had already done the most important thing of making it safe to be the woman she was—with the interests she had and the goals she wanted to achieve— she believed he would.

But he was mistaken if he thought it was his father that she feared most tonight.

Resolute or not, she was most afraid of coming out to the world.

But there was no more time to worry.

With a signal to a server, Jag indicated it was time.

The man lifted a glass and clinked a fork against its side with enough force to cast its tinkling sound out and over the crowd.

That such a small sound, in a sea of noise and chatter, had the power to catch the attention of so many people was just one of the many mysteries of life.

As Rita watched, a wave of calm focus descended upon the attendees, each of them turning their faces toward the sound of the glass only to land upon the Prince of Hayat and Rita at his side.

"Good evening, ladies and gentlemen," Jag began. "After two weeks of astonishing sights and sounds, and the out-of-this-world race of tonight, it hardly seems fathomable that more excitement could emerge from this exhibition."

A light cheer rose in response to his words, with more than a few lifting glasses, before he continued, "But I would not be the Prince of Hayat—" he paused, allowing time for another small round of applause, before continuing "—if I let such a grand event close without an even grander finale."

More applause met his words, and Rita's stomach did a flip.

With each word, they drew closer to the point of no return.

"And I assure you, what I share with you now has been worth the wait."

The silence of rapt attention greeted him.

"You have all been dying to know, how did that rascally Prince get his hands on so many of NECTAR's custom specials? Well, here is your answer." Raising Rita's left arm, ensuring that the massive ring she wore caught and refracted the light, Jag said, "I present to you, revealed for the first time to the world, the ingenious and incomparable NECTAR. She is the woman who has blessed me by becoming my wife, Princess Rita of Hayat."

Deafening cheers and a blitz of flashing lights greeted his announcement, and it was all Rita could do to maintain her grip on his hand and smile for the cameras.

Hours that felt like lifetimes later, Jag was hot and ready to have Rita back as his private treasure.

In the past weeks he had gotten used to enjoying her company alone.

And while both the debut and exhibition had gone exactly as he had intended them to—better even—he realized he was ready for things to get back to the normal they were establishing.

Introducing her as his wife as the finale of the exhibition after revealing her to be the infamous NECTAR, drawing in the flare of romance and intrigue while his attendees were already rolling high on the exciting cocktail of enthusiasm for electric energy and innovation and fast cars, made for exactly the instant sensation he had desired.

He would have final data back only following tonight's grand finale, but the preliminary information his team was sending him even now showed that the exhibition and announcement of his marriage had had exactly the impact he wanted.

Rita had handled it all like she had been born for it, including the media.

"How did the two of you meet?" one reporter had asked, while others shouted out their own queries. "Tell us about yourself, Princess Rita. Who are you? Where are you from?"

"How long have you known each other?" still another asked, and so it went for the rest of the evening.

Rita navigated it with grace equal to that of her stunning beauty.

Jag was used to being the center of attention in a room, to being constantly in demand and fielding personal questions, to graciously smiling when asked for selfie after selfie.

Rita, however, was new to all of it. And yet she handled it with open warmth that only added to her charm.

"I'm from California," she answered one, before adding, "in the US."

And when she was asked the follow-up question of, "But where's your family *really* from?" Jag was impressed by the diplomacy with which she answered.

"If you mean ancestrally," she said, "my grandparents immigrated to the United States from Bangladesh. My father was born in the US, as was I, but my mother is Bengali."

Enraptured, the reporter said, "Now that you are Princess, do you feel that you're going to bring greater visibility to the large South Asian population living here in Hayat?" and belatedly Jag realized that he and Rita had spent very little time discussing the history, politics and realities of Hayat.

But Rita did not need his help.

"Of course," she said. "It is an honor to be a woman of South Asian descent and to bring representation of South Asians to a higher level here in Hayat. As an American, I have a lot to learn about the complex history and people of Hayat, but for now, I'm just glad that my presence brings greater visibility to such an important national demographic."

The woman took his breath away. How was it that he had only known her for a matter of weeks, when she stood by his side as if she had been training for the role? She was so much more than the perfectly imperfect sensation of a bride that he had thought he found in a Northern California garage. Over and over she had proved to him that she was not a ruse, with each new facet he encountered more evidence that she was, in fact, actually perfect.

Had their announcement been authentic, had she been the love that swept him away in every sense of the world, at this moment, Jag would have been the proudest man on earth.

Even still, he knew there was no better choice in all of the world.

And that was a real shame, because for all of her perfection, his union with Rita was temporary.

She was not his wife. She was not his queen.

Their paths would separate in the near future—must separate—and when they did, there would be no one who could ever stand a chance of replacing her.

Stepping closer in a show of their affection and unity, as well as to savor the nearness that was as close as he could get, Jag cultivated a mischievous twinkle in his eye and said, "You must all forgive me. My darling wife swept me away in such a whirlwind that it has been all I could do to keep her to myself up to now. Our unexpected romance coinciding with this exhibition has given me little time to introduce my bride to the complexities of Hayati history. But with a mind like hers, I am sure it will only be a matter of time before she becomes a better national representative than even I."

They chuckled in response to his words, and he led Rita away, directing them toward the small group of men that made up the full list of people he trusted in the world.

If she was not his forever, she was at least his for now, and if it had been real, this would have been a moment he eagerly anticipated.

He watched his friends as their gazes landed on Rita, more eager and proud to introduce them to his bride than he should have been.

In a way, it had been them who had brought the two of them together—and their long-ago pact.

Zeus smiled first, eyes alighting with masculine delight on Rita. "You must be the bride we've heard so much about," he said. "I begin to see what has blown our friend in such a wildly new direction."

Smiling, Rita offered her hand. "The blowing is mutual, I assure you. I certainly never expected to end up here."

At Zeus's side, Vin choked, quickly taking a sip from the champagne flute he held.

Catching his eye over Rita's head briefly, Zeus replied to her, "Probably not as mutual as Jag would like."

And Vin quickly came in with, "What Zeus means is that no man is truly prepared for the moment that a transformative woman enters his life and changes everything he ever imagined for himself."

At this, Rita narrowed her eyes, though Jag was grateful for his friend's smooth cover.

Tilting her head to the side, still eyeing them closely,

she asked, "You must be the 'few men I call friends' that I keep hearing about?" pitching her voice as she mimicked Jag.

All of the air fled from Jag, not for fear their conversation would be overheard—her words were easy enough to explain away—but at her directness. Of course, Rita wouldn't beat around the bush with the men he had told her she did not need to.

With a small chuckle, Rafael spoke up finally. "We are, indeed."

Looking from man to man before settling her gaze on Zeus, one of her eyebrows lifted, she said saucily, "Well then, isn't it just so nice to be in company where we can speak freely."

A bolt of pride jolted through Jag at her, as she showed no signs of being intimidated by these men who controlled nations. Not many dared to meet them head-on.

Laughing openly, Zeus agreed. "It is, indeed, Princess. And, speaking freely, I can say that it is truly a delight to make your acquaintance. I have no doubt, you will drive our friend Jag here to absolute distraction."

"Let us just hope that distraction is not synonymous with ruin," Jag said, pitching his voice jovially as another group of reporters neared them, mics at the ready.

Taking Jag's cue for the warning it was, his friends shifted their bodies into their royal public personas as the media arrived.

Jag noted a murmur running through the crowd of reporters and knew the time for light inquiries had come to an end. His father had finally made his move.

Jag brought an arm around Rita's shoulders protectively before gently turning her to face his father, himself offering the man a nod of the head that was just shy of respectful.

"Father," he said, watching him closely.

The helpless rage that boiled in his father's eyes was of

an intensity unparalleled in Jag's experience, and a part of him thrilled.

Learning that his son had married without his consent or input this way, in a public forum after the fact, and that his daughter-in-law and the future Queen of his country was all of the things he despised in modern women, was nowhere near the shock and pain that Jag himself had felt when he'd learned what had happened to his mother, but it was enough that it felt good.

It was a start.

Staring at his father, seeing his rage all the while knowing that his plan to take the only thing that had ever mattered to him—just as his father had done to him, so long ago—had begun in earnest, was the closest thing to justice that Jag had ever felt.

And this was only the beginning of a grand scheme that had started with an electric exhibition and an unexpected daughter-in-law and would end in prison.

Jag's blood sang, his eyes lighting with the satisfaction of things going exactly according to plan.

His father refused to look at Rita, averting his eyes upward for all the impression he gave of gazing at her with fatherly love and affection.

Rita was everything that his father detested in a woman: smart, ambitious, hardworking and bold.

And though he had learned of his son's matrimonial status for the first time tonight, like everyone else in attendance, the King would have to pretend that he had not only known but approved, when in fact he had not even given his blessing—that was an immense disrespect.

But the worst of the situation would have been the arrangements and concessions his father would have to give to whomever he had already promised Jag's hand in marriage to. Jag had no doubt that his father had always intended to select a bride for him, and a bride who would be a benefit to himself—not Jag nor the people of Hayat.

By making his announcement so painfully public, his father was forced to play along or lose face. It was no less than he deserved.

And his father knew that Jag meant every bit of it.

"My son!" His father's voice was booming and jovial, the size of it intended to dominate for all that he sounded harmless.

The room quieted.

"You have outdone yourself as ever with your astounding exhibition, global leadership and committing Hayat to a one hundred percent electric society within the next fifty years. As in everything, you have proved once again that the innovation and style and groundbreaking leadership of Hayat is boundless."

Muted applause followed his father's remarks and his eyes—the same burning brown orbs that stared at Jag in his own mirror—sharpened, glued to Jag's face as he spoke, conveying threat and fury even as his face presented geniality.

Jag angled further toward Rita, placing his body between hers and his father's.

Turning, his father finally addressed her. "My daughter," he said, a hint of poison in the word. "Your unbelievable achievements are living proof that even the lowliest can climb to great heights when given the example and trappings of quality. Through your toil you have earned the attention and affection of my son. Your accomplishments are a testament to our house."

While those gathered applauded, Jag did not.

He had anticipated an encounter like this, had looked forward to it even, but he had not accounted for his own reaction to his father's taking aim at Rita.

He had not anticipated that he would be filled with the urge to tear his father apart.

Beside him, Rita gave Jag's hand the faintest of

squeezes—enough to remind him that he needed to get himself under control.

Unable to let the insult slide completely unaddressed, however, Jag said, "Come now, Father. You and I both know that it is Rita who redirects our jaded and capitalist eyes toward the things which truly matter. It is her heart that is beating new life into the house of Hayat."

Again, Jag was rewarded by his father's glare that meant the barb had hit its mark.

Cheeks reddening, his father opened his mouth, no doubt to issue another disparaging remark, when Rita startled them both, her bright smile and fearless American accent tromping right into the fray like a lost tourist. "We must give the credit where it is truly due. It is family that teaches us—" and here she looked up at Jag, her eyes sparkling as she put on an outstanding performance of a blushing new bride "—that it is only through learning together that we ever truly discover anything."

The room burst into boisterous applause.

She was incredible.

Jag swallowed, and in the action regained his center, or perhaps more accurately, recentered with her.

In the lighting and humidity, she was big-eyed and dewy and hopeful—a princess the world could love—and she had completely stolen the spotlight from both himself and his father.

He couldn't think of another woman in the world who could have done it better.

He was ready to have her to himself.

Fortunately, one of the perks of being a prince was leaving when you wanted to.

Lifting Rita's arm while the applause died down, Jag announced, "We are sorry to say farewell, my friends, but after two weeks of electric mania, an exhilarating race and this wonderful party, I am afraid I must whisk my bride away."

The room let out a collective sigh of disappointment, and Jag had to stop himself from smiling. His father did not have a chance against Rita.

It was slow going, making their way out in an endless parade of additional waves and farewells, but he and his newly revealed princess made their way through the red-carpeted main entrance of the botanical gardens to the driveway where the valet waited for them, holding open the door of the Ferrari.

Rita sucked in an audible breath, a bright smile coming to her face. "You had a fresh set of rubber put on," she said, cheeks darkening.

He laughed. Only Rita would comment on tires. But beneath the words, there was a trill of real excitement, and he knew he'd made the right choice.

"After you, Princess." He had not intended to draw the word out, to make it into a sensual caress, bold and telling when uttered while staring into her eyes.

Her lips parted and then closed again as she swallowed, rapt and otherwise frozen.

And then she blinked, as if snapping out of a spell, and licked her lips with a fleeting frown that disappeared as soon as her eyes returned to the car. Her gaze cleared and she took a deep breath, smiling before she slid into the passenger seat.

Taking the keys from the valet as he walked around the front, he got into the driver's seat beside her.

"You're driving?" she asked, surprised.

He sighed, drawing out the sound though he felt no real irritation. She could question the obvious as much as she wanted, so long as she never stopped being her open and honest self with him. "Did you think I was going to ride in the back?"

"I've just never seen you drive before," she pushed, and he laughed.

"Well, then, you're in for a treat. I hope you like to go fast."

Lighting up like a star in the sky, she answered, though she didn't have to. "Do I ever."

Laughter extending, Jag shook his head as he turned the system on.

He loved it when she spoke like a character from a film.

And then they were off, her squealing in delight the whole way.

CHAPTER EIGHT

SOME WOMEN LOVED expensive gifts. Some women loved cuddly things. Rita loved cars.

Jag raced through the streets of Hayat City at unconscionable speeds, dashing past unbothered police officers and through lights that were somehow always miraculously green. Rita's heart thundered and her body felt skin-tinglingly alive.

The man could drive.

He drove fearlessly and with purpose, and it was everything she could do not to stare at his profile at the wheel.

The car, the man—it was nearly too much.

And then they were abruptly outside the city, racing down a long stretch of night-dark freeway hugged on either side by smooth dunes of sand and tucked beneath a blazing quilt of stars.

And that was when he really got going.

Like a bolt of lightning, they struck out into the desert at blazing speed.

In what felt like the blink of an eye, they were alone on the road, just the two of them cradled in the car of her dreams.

Rita couldn't hold back the sigh of contentment that escaped her lips.

Jag looked over at her then, just for an instant before he

turned back to the road, but there had been enough heat in his gaze to burn her to ash.

Ever so gradually beginning to slow, his fingers flexed around the steering wheel.

Licking her lips to moisten them, Rita asked, "Where are we going?"

Taking her offer of small talk, he answered, "I'm merely taking us home, the long way. There is something I thought you might like to see out here, but mostly, I thought you'd like taking the baby."

Heat coming to her cheeks, she gave a self-deprecating laugh. "I do. More than I probably should. Thank you."

Having slowed to a normal cruising speed, Jag had time to scan her before he said, "There is nothing wrong with loving cars, Rita. I do. I don't know if you know this about me, but I have been known to spend exorbitant—dare I say extortionate—rates for vehicles."

Rita snorted, comforted even if she didn't want to be, but outside, she retorted, "Some things are priceless," as she stroked the dashboard that she'd spent hours of her life lovingly restoring.

Jag noted the motion of her hand, watching it for a moment with an intensity at odds with the cockiness of his voice as he said, "I've heard that said, though I've never found it to be so."

She rolled her eyes. "It must be good to be a prince."

"If you don't mind the King," he said, a mixture of bitterness and heat in his voice.

Shuddering, Rita made a face of distaste thinking about the man who was her father-in-law. "I have to admit, he was worse than you described," she said.

"Unfortunately, it is hard to encapsulate his brand of ill will," he said flatly.

Waiting a beat, she asked, "Why do you hate him so much—I mean, beyond his being so obviously hateful?"

For a long time, he didn't say anything, simply stared at the road ahead.

When he finally spoke, his voice was dry and cracked, sounding older than he was.

"My mother was born in Egypt, but her family is from rural Hayat," he began. "She was beautiful, and kind, and smart. She loved horses and handbags."

"And you?" Rita guessed, now more certain than ever that it had been his mother who had given Jag his heart.

Closing his eyes, Jag agreed, "And me." After drawing in a choppy breath, he picked up again. "And at one time, she loved my father. But the feeling died long before he took me away from her."

Knowing the pain of separation, Rita ached for him. "I'm so sorry, Jag."

Shaking his head as if he could shake off her concern, he said, "He played us against each other. He sent me to boarding school and would use access to her to manipulate me into being the son he wanted. Any transgression could mean the loss of a visit or phone call, so I became perfect. Soon, even perfect was not enough, however. For years, he would set impossible standards, knowing I would never be able to achieve them. I had nearly completed school, the model son, when I learned that the reason for the change had been that she had died. He hadn't wanted to lose his bargaining chip so he simply didn't tell me. She died by herself, and for that alone I would never have been able to forgive him, but he'd gone further than that. For years, he paid someone to forge letters from her so that he could use our correspondence to spy on me. He let me write letters to a ghost in order to mine my most private thoughts and feelings."

Rita brought a hand to her mouth in horror. "Oh, Jag."

With a bitter face, he added, "And when I finally stepped into the role of Crown Prince, three years ago, I learned that the same cruel tactics he used on me, he had been using on the people of Hayat. He loves nothing more than illegal surveillance and emotional deception. Except perhaps skimming from the top."

Rita's stomach roiled, her entire being sickened by what Jag's father had done.

That a father could be so monstrously cruel was nearly beyond belief. She might not have believed it, in fact, had she not met the man herself—had she not come to trust in the prince at her side.

And in trusting, she gained greater understanding of why he had been so reticent to build emotional connections.

How could he take the risk of caring when he knew his father would stop at nothing to manipulate and control him?

As it had in her own life, love and closeness had been coercive and overbearing forces in his—chains with which to dominate, rather than to hitch onto toward joy and fulfillment.

It might have been bloodthirsty and merciless of her, but she wished her father-in-law everlasting torment for the cruelty he had bestowed upon his wife and child and people.

Rita shuddered again. The world would not suffer when his reign ended—even if, from what she could glean, these days it was close to a thing in name only.

Jag, as she understood, had taken the bulk of the functions of his government under his lead already, as if for him, too, that day could not come soon enough.

"No inspiring words of forgiveness and hope?" Jag asked, attempting lightness while the lingering harsh rasp of his voice belied his efforts.

Shaking her head, Rita said, "None. If this were a movie, it would be the kind of situation that would warrant grandiose vengeance."

With a strained laugh, he said, "Is that so?" before side-eyeing and nudging her with a sly smile and alluding to her words from earlier in the evening, "Family is so important, after all."

He was joking, merely making fun reference to her earlier words, but the reminder was akin to being wrapped up tight in a wet blanket.

Like Jag, she was estranged from her family because the demands of their love had been too much to bear, but after hearing his story, how could she ever share?

She had thought her family's demands were unfair, but compared to Jag, they'd simply asked for the same kind of commitment from her that they had given.

They had made big sacrifices for the happiness of the whole. Demanding the same of her was a far cry from the deception and manipulation Jag's father had employed.

What would he think if he knew that she had walked away from her family in favor of chasing dreams?

Knowing that he had been so cruelly ripped from his mother, would he think her spoiled and wasteful for throwing away something as good and precious and priceless as she had?

Her parents might have been unrelenting in their desire to mold her, and they may have not fully understood the beat of her heart, but they had always loved her.

That fact of that stood out in sharp contrast to Jag's experience.

From what she knew now, it seemed like the only one who had ever loved Jag was his mother, and unlike Rita's family, with whom reconciliation might still someday be possible, she was long gone.

"Rita." A serious note had come into Jag's voice, one at odds enough with the tone of the moment that it shook her out of her wallowing and had her glancing at him with a frown, her eyebrows drawn together.

"What is it?" she asked. "What's wrong?"

"In a moment, I'm going to pull the car over. I want you

to take off your overcoat and wrap it around your head, then I want you to curl up in the footwell. Do you understand?" His voice was forcibly calm, steady and even, and all the more unsettling for it.

"What's wrong? What's going on?" she asked, struggling to shrug out of her jacket in the narrow confines of the car as she spoke.

Still staring straight ahead, he said, "We are directly in the path of an oncoming sandstorm."

He spoke as if he delivered the most mundane news... even as he carefully untucked the folds of his ghutra and removed his agal.

Following his lead, she wrapped the sheer jacket around her head, doubtful the flimsy thing would provide much coverage through one of nature's disasters but unwilling to freak out.

Jag was remaining calm. She could remain calm.

"Curl up as tightly as you can." His muffled voice came through his own layers of wrapping, and she did as he said.

And moments later, they were swallowed by a wall of sand.

The sound was incredible and horrible. A crescendo of scratching and scraping wind, punctuated here and there by the screeching of metal being bent against its will.

Sand pummeled them, somehow able to make its way inside the car and beneath her wrapped jacket, grains of it forcefully aggressive in their push to get into her mouth and ears and tightly shut eyes.

The roar continued, seemingly endless.

And then, blessedly, it was over.

Coughing, Rita struggled out of her curled position, crawling up to sit on the sand-covered seat that she had abandoned.

At her side, she could hear the sand shifting as Jag moved as well.

With a cough of his own, Jag asked, "Are you all right?"

"I think so," Rita said, unwrapping the layers of her jacket from around her head and sending a cascade of sand falling down all around her.

There was sand everywhere.

And not just sand, but dirt and bits of rock—even nestled among the crooks and crevices of her gargantuan jewelry.

Abruptly overwhelmed by the sensation of drowning in sand, Rita reached for the door handle and pulled it open, stumbling out of the car amidst a river of sand and more coughing.

On the other side of the car, Jag did the same.

Upright, Rita began the process of shaking the invasive grains out of all the places they had bombarded.

Removing her hair tie, she bent forward, flipping her hair over in the process to rake and comb her fingers through it, shaking free as much sand as she possibly could.

Like glitter, the rain of it seemed never-ending.

Finally, after reaching the limit on the amount of rattling her brain could handle, Rita came upright, letting her now-loose, dusty black hair fall. It tumbled freely over her shoulders and down her mid-back.

Further examination and dusting of her person, however, revealed that aside from the now-sand-encrusted over-jacket and collection of slightly sandy priceless accessories, her outfit had come through the harrowing experience not much worse for wear.

Whereas she wasn't sure she would ever get all the sand out of her ears, the catsuit had somehow prevented any and all sand from penetrating its barrier.

Saved from the well-known horror of copious amounts of grit in unmentionable places, Rita was more than glad to see that Jameel's fashion efforts had proved to be so practical.

The same could not be said for Jag.

"What are you doing?" she asked, though it was very clear that he was in the process of removing his shirt, dexterously unbuttoning it from the top down. Strangled panic gripped Rita's throat, squeezing as her eyes locked on the motion of his deft fingers quickly working their way down the fastened column.

"What does it look like?" he said, not looking at her from his task. "I'm getting out of this sand-sodden clothing."

"And into what?" she croaked.

Rolling his eyes, he said dryly, "Why, into the change of clothes you can see that I packed."

He was being sarcastic. She knew it. There were no clothes in the Ferrari.

"You're just going to go naked?" she said, panic rising. He couldn't go naked. Outside of images, Rita had never seen a naked man.

"Men have been known to go without clothing," he noted, amusement at her obvious embarrassment overwhelming his earlier irritation.

She knew that, rationally.

He had to disrobe to shower, and she didn't imagine he had been born wearing clothing.

But that didn't mean that she was prepared to be around him in all of his naked glory.

Heat coming to her cheeks, she whirled around, turning her back to him as she belatedly gave him the privacy she should never have breached.

"I'm so sorry," she said.

"For what?" He chuckled. "The fact that my ensemble doesn't appear to be as sealed as your own?"

"N-no," she stammered.

"Then what is it, Rita?" he asked, a wicked smile in his tone. "Or have you never seen a naked man before?"

"No," she lied. "I just shouldn't have looked. Our agreement…" She trailed off.

"That's right," he said, irritation once more bringing stiffness to his voice. "Our agreement. I haven't forgotten our agreement, Rita. You need not worry that my lack of clothing represents anything beyond an effort to prevent chafing. It will get chilly soon, though. The place I wanted to show you is nearby. We can stay warm there while we await assistance."

"Assistance?" Rita questioned, turning to face him in her surprise. "We aren't going to just drive?"

But by the time the words had left her mouth she was no longer interested in the answer.

Her mouth went dry.

She wanted to blame the dust and sand, but that storm had already passed—and had nothing to do with a storm whipping up inside her now.

Jag stood glistening in the moonlight, shirtless, the fastens of his pants undone, the front folds hanging open. His chest and arms were all muscled and gleaming strength, as perfectly formed as any automotive frame she had ever laid eyes on.

Curling hair dotted his pectorals before disappearing among the lines of rigid definition that made up his abdominals, only to reappear below his belly button, this time marching in a straight line that led downward and disappeared beneath the top fabric line of his boxers.

Rita swallowed hard, her entire focus attuned to that line of fabric, her breath coming shallow in her breast.

She had been aware of the fact that Jag was handsome, had noticed how well he filled out his clothing, his hard body a rigid form so perfect it seemed to have been made for the task.

But she'd had no idea that beneath the perfect tailoring and exquisite materials lay a body that was enough to put the works of the great Renaissance masters to shame.

His skin was the exact shade of a perfect white mocha,

creamy with a hint of tan, and in the bright moonlight, it glowed as much as the pearl belt she wore.

When she tore her eyes away from his body, yanking them back up to his face, what she saw there stole her breath all over again.

She was used to the eternal burning flame of his eyes, but the fires she saw now raged out of control, hotter than she had ever seen them.

And yet she had the sense that touching those flames would not bring her harm, but the opposite, in fact—the promise of immense pleasure.

Where such an idea came from, she had no idea.

No experience thus far in her life had prepared her for this moment with Jag.

With his gaze glued to her face, his hands came to the top of his pants.

Gasping, Rita ripped her gaze away from him once more, desperate for anything to take her mind off the growing heat in her body.

Casting out for anything to save herself, her eyes landed on the sand-buried form of the Ferrari, and for the millionth time that evening, her mood swung from one extreme to another.

Freed from the entrancement of seeing Jag's near-naked body, Rita now understood exactly why he said they would be waiting for assistance.

The Ferrari had been sheared by the sand, its light blue paint stripped in a flash by nature's cruel buffering.

Chipped-out spots, divots left by bits of rock and sand, dotted its surface until the hood resembled a cheese grater.

A massive spiderweb crack crossed the windshield diagonally from corner to corner.

Instead of a grille, there was now a solid brick of sand.

Fist coming to her mouth with a gasp she could not hold back, Rita's stomach knotted even as her mind continued to catalog the damage.

Dropping into a crouch, she examined the dust and sand-packed undercarriage. She had never seen sand as thick and solid as a brick wall before.

The excessive particulate must also be why her own eyes could not seem to stop welling over.

It wasn't because the car that she had dreamed up alongside her father so long ago and waited so long to bring to life was already gone, its life even shorter than the amount of time that she had spent as her father's pride and joy, all of its beauty and flair stripped and gone with just a shell left behind.

She did not look over when Jag crouched beside her, could not look away from the wreckage even as she sensed the heat and nearness of his presence and could catch the sandalwood scent of his skin on the wind.

He was fully naked now, she knew it without looking, but being unsettled by his nudity seemed suddenly childish and unimportant when faced with the wreck of the car.

Her tears fell just as Jag's arm came around her shoulders.

The feeling of warm pressure of his bare skin through the thin material of her suit unleashed the floodgates.

Great racking sobs coursed through Rita's body as she leaned into him. And he just let her cry—for the pain of having to choose between family and future, for the loss of the magnificent car, and for the complications that kept them from being everything to each other that they could.

When finally her tears had subsided, Jag's voice was low and gentle when he said, "We should go. We're not far from the place I wanted to show you. We can walk there and call for assistance where it's warmer."

Gently, he drew her to her feet, and the movement, coupled with the reminder of his nudity, inevitably drew her eyes downward toward the apex of his thighs, where a great mystery of the world lay revealed to her.

As if powerless to the thrall of her hormones and force

of her curiosity, Rita could not look away as he stood before her riveted gaze.

Fiery heat flamed her cheeks, but she couldn't tear her eyes away.

Free from the cover of his clothing, the trail of hair that began beneath his belly button could be seen leading in a straight line to the dark hair at the base of his shaft.

She took note of the details of him as if she had never before seen a human body.

And perhaps she never had.

She certainly had never seen a body like Jag's.

Swallowing once more, her arm reached toward him without her say-so or permission, as if driven by a need all of its own. And, as if the small, unintended motion were enough to break the heavy spell that had entrapped them, Jag cleared his throat loudly and stepped back, severing the connection that held their gazes.

"We should get to the ruins," Jag said thickly, adding, "The desert cold catches one quicker than you'd imagine. Just give me a second to shake these out." The last was said as he rummaged through the pile of clothes that she had been certain only moments before that he was going to leave beside the wreck to retrieve the small black cloth of his boxers.

Looking away as he pulled them on, not cold in the least, Rita said, her voice viscous and heavy, knotting and tangling in her throat in the jumble of all of the erotic details her eyes had taken in, "Absolutely. Certainly. Take your time, it's fine. Being comfortable is the most important." She had to force herself to stop talking, realizing the stream of repetitive assertions would only continue if she let it.

Stepping away as if even a little more space would magically render her unaware of the powerfully attractive man she was with, she asked with determined casualness, "Which direction?"

Eyeing her for a moment before answering, Jag lifted an arm, pointed in a direction that looked the same as every other direction in Rita's eyes, and said, "That way."

Nodding decidedly, uncomfortably aware of every private feminine place that the sight of her naked husband had activated, her new sensual alertness only further exacerbated by the intimate hug of her catsuit, Rita took a determined step in the direction Jag had pointed, angling her body and face so that his was just outside her line of vision. Even now, clad in boxers, he was too much stimulation. "Great. Let's go."

Behind her, Jag laughed. "Don't forget your jacket. We're going to need it."

Stopping in her tracks, Rita returned to the car to retrieve the jacket.

The walk was short, thankfully for Rita, who soon followed behind Jag trying to look at the stars, and the miles of dunes all around them, and her shoeless feet sinking in the sand, and anything but the rear end of the man who led the way.

Dragging her eyes back up to the round and full moon overhead once more, Rita asked, "Where are we going again?"

"You'll see soon," Jag answered enigmatically.

"I had no idea there was a destination out this way," she noted.

"It's something not many people know about. I wanted to show you," he said.

Shortly thereafter, Rita wondered no more.

Appearing almost out of nowhere was a small ruin mound, its ancient stone walls crumbling into the dune that had built up around it, filling and burying parts of it, furthering the erosive process of the structure and the sand becoming one and the same.

In the bright moonlight, the ruin's arched doorways and

crumbling pillars cast long dark shadows, only enhancing the sense that magic and mystery lurked all around.

A copse of date palms grew nestled into its shaded side, hidden from view by the direction from which they had approached the ruin, lending a sense of life to what otherwise might have seemed a lonely home for ghosts.

The shadowed beige of the stone blended seamlessly into the color of the sand around it, giving everything the impression not of an ancient structure, but of one built to match the existing landscape.

Impossibly drawn, Rita stepped toward the nearest doorway, fearless, led by her curiosity to see what lay inside.

Jag's hand on her shoulder stopped her.

"Another time," he said, "and in daylight."

Startled, as she always was by the experience of having another person weigh in on one of her decisions, Rita's face made a moue of disappointment, but she nodded.

What he said made sense.

She didn't know anything about what the desert held or what might be waiting inside the dark for her.

Leading her by the arm, Jag took her toward a crumbling staircase that led up to the flat square rooftop of a sand-filled rectangular structure.

Her bare feet touched the warm stones with relief, some of their chill dissipating instantly.

As usual, Jag's next two words indicated his preternatural ability to read her mind. "The stones heat up during the day and hold on to the heat long into the night."

Rita nodded. It made sense, and for a much more comfortable experience in the nighttime desert.

On the rooftop, Jag laid Rita's jacket on the ground. Then, beckoning her to come to his side, he lay down on his back, his arms under his head.

Rita sat down and joined him in lying back to look at the stars overhead.

They lay there, alone in the world and quietly together for a time before Rita reluctantly reminded him, "Weren't you going to call someone?"

He nodded but made no move for the phone that he had carried through the desert and which now lay at his side. "Soon enough. I'm finding, however, right now, amidst the oddity and discomfort of our situation, an unexpected feeling of peace. I want to enjoy it a little longer."

There was a quiet vulnerability in his voice, and Rita didn't know why, but something about the words warmed her.

While she couldn't take credit for the sandstorm, and wouldn't want to, she had had a part in creating this moment beneath the stars with him, and even facing the devastation of the Ferrari, she sensed that that was an accomplishment.

"What are you thinking about, my princess?" he asked, ever alert to her energetic and mental shifts.

With a sad chuckle, Rita sighed. "The car is ruined."

Jag shrugged, saying, "I'll get you a new one."

This time Rita's laugh was incredulous. "You can't just get me a new one," she said. "There are only so many of them in the world. And that one was one-of-a-kind."

"It will be one-of-a-kind again when you rebuild it, as I know you will," he said, unconcerned. "And I will still get you another one."

Smiling, Rita said, "You know, there is such a thing as having too much money." She was wearing the pearl belt, and chandelier necklace, huge earrings, and megawatt ring to prove it.

"Impossible," he said, looking as if she had said the most ludicrous thing in the world. "In the case of the royal family of Hayat, truly. It is not possible to spend through the riches my family possesses in one lifetime. It is why I am so extravagant with our wealth. Well, that and because it enrages my father to see his money enjoyed by anyone other than him. But what other municipality can boast of having world-class hospitals and entertainment venues without having to spend any of their tax revenues? None that I know of. I mean it when I say I will get you a new one."

The revelation of his wealth was slightly breathtaking, even as she knew this pain was about more than simply access to another car. "It was horrible to see it like that."

But rather than indulge her, this time he shrugged and said, "It is just a car."

With a noise of outrage, Rita sat up to look down into his laughing eyes indignantly, saying, "It is not just a car."

Unrepentant, Jag merely rolled his eyes. "Forgive me. It is a one-of-a-kind NECTAR conversion."

Smacking his shoulder, she said, "That's not what I meant."

Sitting up himself, bringing a layer of seriousness to the question, he asked, "What did you mean, then? What is so special about that car that it brought you to tears for the first time in our acquaintance? You left your home and country without a backward glance, and yet a car that is only yours through marriage makes you weep?"

Unprepared for the turn the conversation had taken, Rita paused.

Here was the opportunity to confess, if she were brave enough to do so.

If a night that had included her world debut as NECTAR and as a princess, as well as surviving a sandstorm, had reminded her of anything, it was that she was brave enough to do anything she set her mind to.

She didn't know what Jag would make of her decisions, didn't know if learning just what she had given up in pursuit of her ruined dream would make him look at her in disgust.

But he had shared his secrets with her; it was only fair that she take the same risk with him.

CHAPTER NINE

"WHEN I WAS seven years old," Rita said, "my father got a commission from a collector to transport his 1962 Ferrari GTO from the Bay Area to Los Angeles. It was already my dream car. It had been ever since I saw one in an episode of *Scooby-Doo* when I was five. When my dad got the order he promised to take me along and he did. We had an amazing time, eating out of gas stations and chatting about cars and the future and electric vehicles. It was so much fun that I promised—to my dad and to myself—that one day I would change the way the world drove, and I would convert a 1962 Ferrari GTO of my very own. My dad laughed at that, pointing out the slim chances of that ever happening."

"Not so slim after all," Jag observed.

Smiling, Rita said softly, "About as slim marrying a prince, I'd say."

"So it is not just a car but a shared dream with your father?" Jag asked.

The innocent assumption chased away Rita's smile.

Shoulders dropping, she shook her head. "No, not a shared dream," she said. "Just mine, it turned out. And one I wanted a little too much in the end."

"How's that?" he asked.

"You mean beyond marrying a stranger to get it?"

she asked dryly, proud of how well she echoed his own honed aridity.

Laughing at her, he said, "Yes, beyond that."

Not knowing where to start, Rita drew in a long, slow breath to buy herself a little more time.

Then she opened her mouth and said, "I got into college when I was sixteen years old. My parents were elated. For a moment, I was the pride of my family. But they didn't realize that I had worked so hard and been determined because I wanted to achieve a specific dream, as opposed to being driven to succeed. I wasn't striving to do well because I wanted my family to be proud—honestly, I wasn't even striving for anything at all. I was excelling because I was following a passion that had burned within me from before the time I could talk. I strove because I wanted to impact the world working with the objects that I loved most within it, not because I wanted to impress anyone. Out of that well of passion and conviction, the force and determination behind it, I surprised everyone, not only by graduating early, but by being accepted to a top university."

"You, forceful and determined?" Jag asked, gently teasing.

Closing her eyes, Rita laughed, shaking her head. "I know. It's not shocking. What was shocking, or at least what shocked my father when he found out two years later, was that unbeknownst to him I had not enrolled in the pre-med track that would put me on the path toward becoming an obstetrics and gynecology doctor, but had instead registered as a dual major in mechanical engineering and computer science. He was also rather shocked by the fact that by the time he found out, I was halfway toward completion as well as one of the top students in both programs."

Jag let out an uncharacteristic whistle and Rita couldn't help but smile, even if there was little joy in the expression. Even she was impressed by how bold the story was when she said it out loud.

"I knew I was dealing with a mad genius, but I had no idea she was so titled. I take it that Papa wasn't very pleased when he found out, though?"

Shaking her head, Rita said on an exhale, "Not by a long shot. In fact, he disowned me."

"Excuse me?" Jag asked, utterly serious. "How old were you?"

"Eighteen," Rita said. "A full-fledged adult, in his defense."

"Hardly. And a man who can disown his daughter because she dared to excel in a way he did not approve of needs no defense," Jag said.

Though she hadn't known she needed it, his being defensive on her behalf soothed an old hurt.

Tired, she said, "I deliberately deceived him, and in doing so, stole not just trust and tuition from my family, but also their reputation and my future."

"Explain to me how pursuing your passion stole from your future," he demanded.

Grimacing because they'd come to the shameful and guilt-laden part of the story, Rita said, "When news broke out in our community that I had been accepted to Berkeley at such a young age, it kick-started everything. Families began approaching mine in interest of making matches with their sons, so my family began making arrangements to ensure that I did not miss out on a prosperous future."

"When you were sixteen?" he growled, voice low.

She lifted her palms. "With the caveat that no marriage would take place until I had turned twenty-two. The idea was quite progressive and exciting for the families involved, mine and the one I matched with. My and Rashad's futures would be secure, despite our young ages, while also giving us an opportunity none of our parents had received. We would have the chance to get to know each other, to perhaps fall in love the American way along the process as well."

"And you were fine with all of this?" Jag pressed.

Rita shrugged. "Outside of cars, my family was the most important thing in my world. It didn't seem like a big sacrifice to play the role I was expected to, especially because I didn't understand at first what I was being asked to give up. Rashad was kind and funny and easy to get along with, if a bit distant and aloof. At seventeen, a difference in age of even two years can be a long time, especially with how sheltered and tunnel-visioned I was. But he came from a medical family, which I knew, and the reason they accepted me despite my working-class family, which I did not know, was because of my intelligence, particularly in science and math. With the promise that I would join the medical track, which my father never told me, simply enrolled me and expected me to obey, Rashad's family had offered and my family accepted. In hindsight, it makes sense now why my father took me to register in person. I thought he was proud, but it was really so that he could make sure I was signed up for the right courses. He underestimated my willfulness, though. He didn't understand that I wasn't inherently brilliant, but because I loved cars. And I didn't understand that by going behind his back to change majors and continuing on with him none the wiser, I had unwittingly broken my marriage contract, as well as made my family look foolish and grasping. My father didn't disown me because of what I had done, though. He disowned me because when he found out and gave me the choice to stop chasing cars and behave in a way that put my family first, or to continue to pursue my dream alone, without the love, support and warmth of a family and future, I chose to walk out the door."

She didn't look at him as she finished her story, afraid of the judgment she might see in his expression, but even fearing that, she felt there was a weight lifted off her chest in the telling.

Whether or not he thought her selfish, it felt good to have no dark secrets from him.

"That's no choice," Jag said, his voice heavy with condemnation, but not of her. Of her father.

"Come again?" Rita asked, startled, having expected any number of reactions but not protectiveness on her behalf, and in the surprise, another part of her stitched itself back together.

"What kind of father asks his child to choose between her dreams and her family? The worst thing you did wrong was lie in order to do what you were born to do. Even in deception, you remained a testament to your family. As far as youthful transgressions go," he said with disgust, "I'd say your father got off easy."

"I don't think you understand how poorly my behavior reflected on my family as a whole. If I could be so willful, what did that reflect about my family's values and lessons, about my parents and uncles and sister?"

"I don't think you understand that a real parent's love is dependent not on how their child behaves, but on the miracle that they exist at all. Real love is not conditional, like your family's or my father's, but boundless and unfettered."

"Like your mother's," Rita finished for him softly.

A shadow banked the fires of his eyes, but he did not pull away or deny it. "Like my mother's."

With a soft sigh and smile, Rita said, "What it must have been like to have felt such unconditional love like that."

With no trace of hyperbole, Jag said, "Terrifying," confirming with a single word what Rita had suspected.

"Until the day my father found out," she said, voice still low, "that's what I thought my family felt for me. I never realized that their years of tolerating and indulging my fantasies and dreams had actually been payment in advance for doing my part when the time came."

Taking her hand, he caught her eye to say earnestly, "You made the right choice, Rita. In my experience, conditional love is never truly satisfied, even when its demands are met. It will simply demand more and more until failure is guaranteed because conditional love is not about love at all, but power. If you had sacrificed the things that made you *you*, they would have only asked for more. Instead, here you are, better to yourself and the world than you ever would have been had you allowed them to clip your wings."

It took a moment for his words to penetrate, as if they had to travel through thick layers of calluses left by years of hard feelings between her and her father.

But as they did, something broke open inside her, a box filled with grief, and guilt, and shame—all of the feelings that she had carried and shoved deep down inside in order to survive the pain of separation and loneliness of being cast out from her family.

All of the self-doubt and second-guessing that she had taken on as her responsibility and used to create a hard protective shell started to crack and crumble and fall apart like the ruin she and the Prince sat atop.

For the third time that night, Rita's eyes welled up with tears, this set years overdue.

Unlike those she'd cried for the car, these were silent tears, racking her body with force that felt like it could tear her apart.

Like before, Jag's arm came around her, drawing her into the warm circle of his embrace, this time all the more comforting for the heat that radiated upward from the stone they sat upon.

Rocking her, he made soothing sounds, like a mother.

The experience was so unexpected that it took Rita a moment to realize, between heaving gasps and big wet tears, that the shooshing noises were not coming from the wind, but from him.

"Shh. Shh. Shhh. There, there," he murmured, voice a low rumble against her form.

She didn't know when she had crawled into his lap, but at some point in the process of enveloping herself in the arms he'd offered, she had.

Giving in fully, she nestled her head in the crook of his neck and closed her eyes, letting the warmth and comfort he provided seep through her suit and ease the ache of being alone all these years.

He held her there, quietly rocking her back and forth, for a long time.

Long enough that her body stilled, calming in its silent hyperventilating, and her tears ebbed and dried.

Long enough that other inputs began processing—his bare skin, the smell of him on her and all around her, the feeling of being wrapped in the safety of his strength.

She slowed her breathing so that she could savor every warm strong inhale of him.

He stilled further at her movement, his own breath going shallow as hers went deeper.

Wrung out, not even a lifetime of lessons and inhibitions were enough to overcome the powerful tide rising in her now. She had shown him her full self, and he had affirmed her right to be and think and feel just the way she was.

Like love, he made demands of her, but unlike love, when he pushed her, it was into bravery, into being more fully and authentically herself. He wasn't trying to mold her; instead he affirmed time and time again that he wanted her because of exactly who she was.

And if he'd affirmed that what they'd told her about love might be wrong, could he not do the same for sex?

If love did not always have to coerce and demand, then perhaps sex didn't either. Perhaps it was possible to be two people committed to caring for each other, enjoying each other's bodies. Perhaps it was okay to simply feel good.

Wrapping her arms around his waist, pressing her face deeper into his neck, she squeezed.

Above her, he groaned, the sound like something in him giving up, and his arms closed fully around her, trapping her now whereas before he had merely held the space for her—as if he held something precious.

Twisting in his arms, she rearranged her body, maneuvering into a new position in order to assuage the urge that demanded she get closer still. Straddling him, lifting her arms up to wrap around his neck where her fingers could dive into his thick, silky hair.

He did not squander the opportunity that their new position offered, either, tightening his hold on her so that her breasts pressed against his chest and her core against the rigid hardness at the apex of his thighs, ushering in a rush of liquid heat at her center.

He brought one arm up the middle of her back to cup her skull and slowly tilt her face toward the sky, gently exposing the column of her neck.

When his lips pressed against the tender, delicate skin there, a fireworks explosion of sensations went off inside her.

Never before had another person's lips touched her in such a way, and she marveled at the pliable pressure that masked the insistent demand of his mouth against her.

Here and there, his tongue darted out, taking tiny tastes of her, leaving her tingling and breathless.

He kissed her shoulders and collarbone through her suit, drawing her attention to those and countless other sensitive places she'd never been aware of.

Working his way up her neck, he left a trail of stirring kisses, soft warm breaths, and teasing bursts of cool air pushed out through pursed lips.

When he reached her jawline, his hands joined in the

action, trailing up the sides of her body to cup her face, cradling it as he placed long, soft kisses at the outside corners of each of her eyes, her temples and earlobes before coming back to kiss the spot between her eyebrows with the same deliberate tenderness.

Pulling back only slightly, he caught Rita in the mesmerizing fire that was his gaze once more. "Do you want me, Rita?" he asked, tension in every word.

"Like I have never wanted another," Rita breathed.

His pupils dilated at her words, understanding what she said beneath them—it was what she had meant when she'd told him that she was from an old-fashioned family before, that she had never been intimate with anyone else—and then he was kissing her, their lips meeting in a dance older than the ruins they sat upon.

She hadn't known what she expected him to taste like, but it hadn't been honey and cardamom, a sweet thickness she could gladly lose herself in.

Nipping his bottom lip, there was no timidity in her exploration of her prince.

When she ran her fingers down his neck, scratching the bare skin of his shoulders and trailing down his back, he groaned, pulling her closer and pressing her hips to grind against the hard shaft of his erection.

The tender, sensitive buds of her nipples hardened further, raking against his bare chest, the only thing separating them the thin high-tech material of her clothing, which was barely a separation at all.

And at the same time, it was unbearable.

Her body cried for the freedom to feel, skin to skin, the hands that caressed her up and down, that gripped her bottom and spread her thighs to press her molten core closer against the hard plane of his abs.

Suddenly, she was bitter for the excellent quality of her clothing.

If it had not been sealed so well she would already be

as bare as her husband, already have achieved the further closeness her body knew was possible and strained for.

With a dry laugh, Jag whispered in her ear, voice strained, "Slow down, my sweet, sweet wife, this is no race. I've imagined savoring you like this, like the NEC-TAR you so aptly named yourself, so many times, I would be shameful to rush."

His words, their deep rumble yet another form of sensual simulation, traveled the lines of her body like rivers of lava heating and stirring in their carnal promise.

Rita had waited long enough, though.

She had waited twenty-seven years to be accepted and adored as she was now, with reverence rather than the intent to mold.

Hands growing bolder, Rita explored Jag's body freely, trailing over the sculpted shoulders and arms, squeezing, scratching, lingering and digging in as she pleased to the intoxicating chorus of the sounds of his pleasure.

His tongue probed deeper, hands to her breasts, his thumbs caressing her hardened nipples once more. The dual attack split her focus, splintering and captivating the forces that had only moments before been intent on conquest.

Her breasts, high and tight and fully alert, trembled beneath the onslaught of his attention, and the sensation threatened to carry her away, though into what she had no idea.

Crying out, she gripped him tight as he tortured her through the thin barrier of her clothing. She could not have stopped the moans of pleasure coming from her if she had wanted to and as it was, she didn't want to. In this moment, the only thing that existed was her and him in the vast expanse of empty night desert around them. She could be as loud as she wanted to.

"It's time to get you out of these clothes," he said, an

implacable chord of certainty woven throughout his voice like rebar.

And she agreed.

With more patience than she would have been able to manage, he reached up behind her neck to release the clasp that held the heavy chandelier necklace in place.

Setting it to the side gently, he went for the belt next, his hands lingering on the outer edges of her thighs and trailing up to cup her bottom and squeeze, before rounding the curve to remove the belt of astounding pearls.

Next, placing his palms on her shoulders, he trailed his hands down her arms, gently slipping her bracelets off when coming to them in his unhurried caress.

He then took her left hand, turning her palm upright, gently spinning the ring into the center of her hand and folding her fingers over it so the mighty rock lay safely tucked in the palm of her hand. Then his hands came back to her neck, finding the hidden zipper that blended near seamlessly into the line of her catsuit.

Staring deep into her eyes, he began to pull down the zipper, gently peeling the fitted material down, exposing the bare skin of her shoulders, then her sternum, pausing only after releasing the large soft globes of her breasts.

Eyes smoldering, he told her everything she needed to know about his reaction to what he saw with the heat in his gaze.

But as if sensing how far an affirmation would go, he said, "Even more beautiful than I imagined."

Heat flushed Rita's skin, a dusky blush deepening the brown tone everywhere that it was visible.

Licking his lips, Jag returned to her true unveiling.

Though this was the first time any adult had ever seen her naked body, Rita felt entirely comfortable.

More than comfortable. Powerful.

The man before her might be a world leader capable of

commanding the respect of the international community, but in this he was helpless to his desire for her.

She held the key—was the answer—to the only thing he wanted.

Only she could give it to him. Only he could give it to her.

And then she was as naked as he was, but for the enormous ring on her left hand that sparkled in the moonlight.

Bared to her husband for the first time, no barriers between them, she was filled with a sense of virtue. They might not have entered marriage this way, but here, finally, they came together for the right reasons.

His eyes consumed her, raking over her form, leaving invisible marks of their possession in their fiery trail.

He swallowed, the sound audible to them both in the hyper-focused bubble that had grown up to encircle them.

Clearing his throat, he said, his words thick and rough, "You are perfection."

And seeing it in his eyes, she believed him.

CHAPTER TEN

RITA IN THE moonlight was beauty incarnate. Blessed with a shockingly hourglass figure—shocking because perfect symmetry was rare in nature and yet abundant in her— Rita's breasts were buoyant and full, exactly the size and density necessary to neatly counterbalance the glorious round peach of her hips and bottom.

Her legs were proportionally long and shapely, her feet adorable, with red-painted toenails.

The cinch of her waist emphasized the balance of top and bottom, while her stomach was an expression of smooth slopes rather than cut definition—just the way he liked it.

By everything that was good and holy, she was sex on wheels.

Jag's palms itched, ready to be all over her once more, this time unimpeded by the barrier of her clothing.

He wanted to trail hot kisses down her stomach and beyond.

He wanted her from the front, from behind, and on top of him—riding him, holding him in the vise grip of her strong thighs—all at once.

Guiding her to lie, he rose above her, taking in her satiny expanse of brown skin and the way her dark hair feathered around her. Her eyes were huge black pits in the moonlight fixed upon him. She would follow where he led, and he did not take it for granted. Not with this woman, whose ferocious independence had given her the courage to strike out on her own in a world not made for her. And she had made it, had proved to herself and the world that she needed no man to lead her.

But here she was willing to follow, trusting he would take them through the labyrinthine halls of pleasure to both of their benefits. Suddenly grateful for his lifetime of dissolute practice.

Lowering himself over her, he brought his lips to hers in yet another long, lingering kiss. Despite the driving urge to possess her, he'd meant what he said to her earlier. As much as he knew this woman loved speed, what happened tonight between them would be no race.

Trailing kisses from her lips down her throat and over between the valley of her breasts, he began his southward journey, reveling in the out-of-this-world softness of her skin with every press of his lips.

Underneath the blanket of his attention, she writhed and moaned, her hands taking on a mind of their own as her control dissipated in wave after wave of sensation.

Could he thank her without words? Could he send her body into the throes of ecstasy in repayment for the dark and twisted game she had agreed to play with him? Could he repay her for her perfection, her capacity to meet each of his demands and still have more to give?

He could.

Rita was a revelation. Her skin as smooth as satin, its scent reminiscent of the heavy sweetness of night blooms, she beckoned him to touch, caress and taste.

And so he did.

Savoring her textures, he kissed his way down her body. But he did not make a beeline for the heated center of her. There was so much to explore before.

He licked and kissed and nibbled a path, leaving a trail of his marks.

He rubbed his beard along the sensitive skin of her inner thighs and she shivered, as responsive to his touch as the vehicles she created.

Had he ever had a lover who was so attuned to everything he did?

She was a woman of eagle-eyed focus, and now all of it was tuned in to the things he did to her. Had he ever had this power?

He had been born a prince. In the desert moonlight, she made him a god.

Trailing his fingertips from the arch of her foot up her inner thigh, he pressed a hot palm against the silky expanse of her skin, gently opening her thighs and exposing her further. She sucked a breath in when the night air touched her most intimate seam, and he had to take a slow breath himself in order not to plunder what lay before him.

He had promised them slow, even if her hips moved in a way that was nothing if not an invitation to dive in. She didn't know what she stood to miss in a race to the finish line—he owed it to her to show her.

While continuing his oral adoration of her thighs, her brought one palm up to cup her mound, holding her there, his steady grip firm, hot and gentle, and her sensitized sex opened further, its liquid heat evidence of her growing readiness.

He began to undulate his fingers in slow waves with gentle pressure against the sensitive bud at her center, confident the steady, slow motion would take her exactly where he wanted her.

She arched her lower back on a long moan before falling back again with a shiver.

He could not have dreamed up a more responsive lover. Would never dream of another.

Where he cupped her, her deepest layers pulled at him, their slick invitation an irresistible siren call. Deviating from his intention, if only slightly, he pressed the heel of his hand against her core.

Bucking in response, she shuddered out a hiss of a breath, and he smiled again.

She was ready for him now, her body eager to welcome him in its slick, wet embrace—but they still had so much to explore.

When her moans rang out across the desert to the beat of his heart, he kept up the motion with an even speed and pace until she was left panting and whimpering, her fingers reaching for him desperately, seeking his skin to grip and hold.

It took all he had not to be greedy with his gift, to gobble her all up in an instant.

He had at least taken his time enough to have earned a taste. The reasoning drew him toward her center, had him kissing the core of her.

If her flavor had hinted at sweet blooms before, she was a full bouquet now, thick and syrupy and celestial. It was not enough to taste, he had to feast—and so he did.

She cried out his name, her hand finding a hold in his hair, and the sound drove him on, urging him to take more ground, and faster, like the most relentless charioteer.

To draw it out for her, he resisted, held back the will whose every whim was the status quo. A prince got what he wanted. A man could bow to her needs.

He tasted her steadily, lapping at her core until she was trembling and moaning and teetering on the edge of collapse.

Bringing his fingers to join his mouth, he traced the edges of her while devouring her, and she screamed, body going rigid for an instant before she curved around him, her thighs tightening around his head in an intimate clinch.

She remained locked around him like that for the sweetest eternity before collapsing back against the still-warm stones, temporarily gone to the world, undone by her orgasm.

A moment later, because she had been blessed to be born in the form of a glorious woman, her eyes opened, luminescent, and she smiled, the expression brighter than the moon.

Reaching toward him, she pulled him up to wrap her arms around his neck and bury her face against him, nuzzling and squeezing, her legs simultaneously curling around to hold him as if it were not enough to hold him in the embrace of just her arms. It was intoxicatingly sweet.

Without guile, she angled her body into the exact position necessary for his access, her body a beacon that his was instinctively driven to seek out, and his muscles strained while he continued to hold himself back.

There was no going back from this point; the knowledge was a truth in him as certain as his need to venture forth anyway. The last of his will faltering in the face of the heat that radiated from her, he knew he was lost.

The tip of his erection pressed along the hot core of her, and he paused.

Her focus, too, was zeroed in on the place where their bodies touched.

"I—" The word came out rough and unwelcome in the face of the perfection of this moment. "I don't have a condom," he finished. He hated the words for being true, himself for being unprepared on the most important night of his life. As attuned to her emotion as he was now, however, he wouldn't take what was not clearly given.

Irritation—primal and fast and the most merciful sight he had ever seen—flashed across her eyes. But he did not move until she spoke.

"I don't care. Don't stop. You can't stop now," she demanded.

Immense relief washed through his system to mingle with everything else she stirred up. She was strategic and thoughtful. She would not be cavalier if pregnancy was a possibility.

Most important to him in this moment, however, was that she did not want him to stop.

Mindful of her inexperience, he eased in gently, he entered her, slowly and steadily relying on the controlled application of his weight for pressure, giving her body time to open and adjust to his intrusion, even as the vise-like grip of her undulated and pulsed around him, dragging him close to climax faster than any self-respecting lover would admit to.

Not even during his first time had the simple act of sliding inside a woman brought him so close to the precipice.

Ever the rebel, Rita blew away what he'd thought sex was, redefining the act into something more intimate and dangerous than he had ever experienced.

His muscles strained, torn by the barrage of his conflicting needs. He needed to please her, he needed to fully sheathe himself within her, he needed to break away from her, to run before the tendrils of emotions that floated between them hooked into him and never let go.

Beneath him, she moaned, and the sound curled around him, as much of a trap as the way their bodies joined, fitting together like two pieces of the most complicated human puzzle.

And when their bodies clenched and his shaft was fully encased within her, he lost his breath, his sight momentarily replaced by flashes of light, like the twinkle of stars in the night sky, and the only thing that held him back from shaming himself was his commitment to make her come again.

After two long, slow strokes, he knew they could not continue this way, not with her breasts grazing his chest, her inner thighs caressing his flanks, and the dark wells of her eyes, incandescent and mesmerizing in the moonlight, staring up at him. She wanted him to release his ultimate

core of control and give it all to her, to let himself crack
open in her presence. She didn't ask for it in words, but
with her body. Her energy seducing it from him, promising that it wouldn't hurt to be vulnerable with her, that it
would feel sinfully good.

Unable to take it, he drew her up, maintaining his
steady, impossibly sweet stroke as he repositioned her,
bearing the bulk of the weight of her pleasure-limp form
until he finally had to reluctantly withdraw in order to
guide her onto her hands and knees.

He would not embarrass himself if he could no longer
see her pleasure in her eyes, if her breasts did not brush
against him each time their hips met. He told himself the
lie even as the new vision she presented him threatened
him as well.

But if he didn't let it wash over him, the primal urge
from seeing her perfectly round behind in the air, her hips
waiting for his grip, he would be fine.

In his calculations, however, he didn't account for the
intimate physics of human joining, hadn't recalled that
when he slid into her from behind, he would not find
space but even more profound joining. He had forgotten in his drive for distance that the position would only
carry him deeper.

But still he held back, biding his time, patient without
grace, as he stoked up the growing tension in her body
again, building her to a crescendo once more, edging her
closer and closer to another collapse.

Nearing the point where he could either continue to
see to his woman and lose himself or direct all of his
focus to holding back, he released one hip with a caress
of farewell before reaching his hand around her to once
again cup her mound. The move drew her closer, tucked
her body tighter in the protective arch of his own as his
thumb found the sensitive bud at the apex of her opening,
bringing a tendril of tenderness to their tireless dance that

sweetened and thickened the joining, even as he sought to bring them both the escape of climax.

They could not get closer, he reasoned, if they both fell apart.

But the increased sweetness between them only deepened the pleasure of the experience. Rita reveled in it, arching her back and crying out, unconsciously deepening his access as she shattered around him again. Her inner muscles spasmed in powerful waves, the pull and tug of them drawing him further still. A surge of final need thickened his shaft within her, locking him in place as he spiraled toward the inevitable and impending death of everything that he had been before her.

His climax destroyed him, as if his sole purpose in life—the very reason he had been put on this planet—had been to give her this moment. To love her.

And because his body, still pulsing with tremors of pleasure, still beating and throbbing inside hers, wanted only to ease further into her, he did not pull her close to hold and cushion her comedown.

He couldn't, not when his own protective barriers were down, his system rocked as it never had been before. He was exposed to her in this moment, as vulnerable as the sanded Ferrari because he could not separate the one-of-a-kind experience he'd just had with her from the her herself.

Neither did he allow himself the reprieve of falling back against the warm stone to breath deep and look at the stars overhead while she snuggled in beside him, as his instincts urged him to do.

Instead, he painstakingly withdrew from her, gentle even as he was thorough in his distancing. Their bodies resisted separation, held on to each other like lovers lingering at a train station.

Her small sound of protest at his leaving pierced his chest, but as the transcendent bliss of having her cooled, it was replaced with resolved contrition.

He had had her once, and he could never risk it again. Not when just a single taste tempted him to stop fighting, to let down the barriers, reveal everything he held within inside and give her the power to compel him—to twist him to her will.

And if not her, then anyone who wanted to get to him through her.

In having her, he had created that doorway. There was no way things would go back to being as simple and smooth as they had been up to now.

He should never have brought her here in the first place.

He should have heeded Rafael's advice and taken greater strides to avoid being alone with her.

Obviously, it was too late for that wisdom now; and *shoulds* and *oughts* were a weak man's nostalgia. The breach had already occurred, but the damage could yet be controlled. He simply need not do it again. Now that he had tasted the ambrosia of NECTAR, now that he knew that she held within her a wellspring of the sweetest elixir, however, the task would be easier said than done.

It was saying something when losing a priceless Ferrari to a sandstorm was the least of an action's consequences.

Constructing an invisible wall between them, he reached for her hand and kissed the back of it, smiling a smile that did not reach his eyes, and said, "I'm afraid that our stone heater here is running out of fuel, so it's time to bring our lovely little party to a close."

Eyes wide, filled with confusion that battled hurt, she stammered, "O-okay."

He felt her baffled sting as if it were his own, but could not allow the situation to go any further. It was better for both of them that this fire be doused now—and thoroughly.

The success of their partnership depended upon them not developing feelings for each other. They could never get close enough that they introduced the opportunity for betrayal. Acquaintances could not hurt each other. Could not be used against each other.

Looking away from her, freeing himself from the shame and sting of her bewilderment, he reached for the phone that lay cold on the warm stone. He dialed quickly, calling their pickup and a change of clothes with efficiency that only highlighted how foolish and unnecessary a risk this little excursion had been. He should never have broken the seal, neither of her innocence nor on his ignorance of what it would be like to be inside her.

He had made love to his wife when it had been entirely avoidable, and now, inevitably, given the nature of their situation, nothing would ever be the same.

CHAPTER ELEVEN

DESPITE BEING POSSESSED of a mind powerful enough to send her to Berkeley at sixteen and to create some of the world's most innovative vehicles, postcoital etiquette was an area in which she had no basis of knowledge.

For example, she had no idea if it was normal to feel not pain or awkwardness or shock in her body, but a relaxed liquid joy, as if the muscle of her happiness had flexed to its utmost tension before letting go with a sigh.

She wanted to curl into Jag, not to go another round—though a giggly part of her insisted that wasn't a bad idea—but because she wanted to bathe in his scent and fall asleep in his arms.

He, on the other hand, seemed more interested in getting them home.

Maybe he was tired? Maybe he was just depleted now and eager to get to his bed.

She wouldn't mind a glass of water herself, and while they weren't helpless, they were currently stranded in the desert.

But a part of her protested the idea.

If it was considered rude to use one's phone at the dinner table, it seemed like the rule would apply the moments following an experience like the one she had just shared with Jag.

Never in her wildest dreams had she ever imagined

that sex would be anything like what had just happened between them.

No wonder the world was obsessed.

No wonder Jag had been so certain it would change things between them.

Rita didn't think it was possible to open oneself to another human being the way that they each had just done and have things remain static between them—but after her night with him she no longer agreed that it couldn't be done.

Remaining strangers couldn't be done, but that wasn't because they'd had sex. It was because over the course of the past weeks, they'd become friends.

They could see their arrangement through simply because they cared about supporting each other.

If anything, she was more sure of that now than she had been before.

In fact, watching Jag, the only thing she could even think of to change was the comedown, and even on that front was willing to accept that there were drawbacks to outside in the moonlight.

Wrapping up his conversation, Jag hung up the phone before saying to Rita, "Our ride will arrive shortly. We should make our way back to the car and the road—the time it will take us to get there should mean our path and the driver's will converge upon arrival."

His tone was all business and clipped, nothing like the way he'd been talking to her since they'd left the exhibition, nor even over the past weeks. Resisting the urge to frown, she told herself it was a sign he had realized the same thing.

However, after his next words she began to wonder that they had not come to exactly the same place.

The administrative clip in his voice confirmed her suspicions when he said, "Don't forget your bracelets. I set them just there," he said, pointing to the small pile of precious jewels beside her jacket, before adding, "and about tonight…" He paused, as if he searched for the words and they did not come easily. But then he confused her even more, with his next words. "In the interest of keeping things simple, I suggest we put this little incident behind us and return to business as usual, moving forward."

While she had been thinking in a similar vein, her train of thought had contained some very critical differences, including the character and nature of what they had shared.

Was he serious? Business as usual? It seemed pretty clear to Rita that that wasn't one of the options on their table.

But it was clear he thought it was, and not knowing what else to do, she simply nodded.

There was no route by which she could return to the way things had been before, but if he thought that meant they must be even more vigilant that it should never happen again, then she couldn't coerce him.

Instead, she said, "Sure," lightly, matching his energy.

He said nothing to her anemic reply, and she took his silence as a reprieve from the effort of pretending to be less affected than she was.

With wobbly hands, she tugged the zipper of her suit, snagging it when she came to the collar seam at the base of her neck.

"Let me help," he said, his warm fingers replacing her rapidly chilling ones to clasp the tiny metal tag. His hands lingered on her neck, warm and tender, before leaving with a light caress, its faint touch so soft it could have been accidental.

Then he stepped away from her once more, and the coldness rushed back in to surround them again.

Though she had been coming to feel like she was learning to read him, she could not understand him now.

Rather than his usual firm and efficient, his actions

now appeared brittle and edgy, and yet outwardly he merely ensured they would make it home before daylight.

When she was dressed once more, they made their way back down the crumbling staircase to the desert floor, and from there they walked quietly back to the wrecked vehicle they had abandoned earlier.

As he had predicted, their driver awaited their arrival in a sleek black town car.

Once he saw them, the driver stepped out holding in his hands a bundle of folded clothing.

Taking the clothes from the man, Jag walked around the other side of the car and clothed himself while Rita entered the back seat through the door the driver had opened for her.

Moments later, Jag joined her, sliding into the seat, his attention focused on the phone in his hand.

They spent the rest of the drive that way, Jag engrossed in his device, Rita staring at the night outside, her mind wrapped up in wondering how long they were going to pretend their arrangement could go on as it had before.

CHAPTER TWELVE

EIGHT WEEKS LATER, Rita was no closer to an answer, and had, in fact, only driven herself sick in dwelling on it. The most obvious reason—that she'd become pregnant from her night with Jag—had already been ruled out by the particularly emotional period that had followed it, just days later.

She was utterly exhausted and could not remember the last time she had made it through an entire night without her bladder waking her at least once to use the restroom.

Her skin, too, seemed affected, becoming sensitive and tender as if now that she had had sex once, she should experience actual pain from the lack of it.

Maintaining the line Jag had reestablished for them even as the ashes of it still burned from how thoroughly they had set it aflame, they had not had sex again.

In fact, she hadn't really seen Jag since.

It appeared that their intimacy had had opposite effects on each of them, even if it came to the same conclusion: deeper commitment to maintaining their agreement.

And now she had lost her appetite and could no longer reliably keep down even the scant food she felt like eating.

Losing weight as a result, she could suddenly understand what people meant when they said they were wasting away.

She found herself spending long stretches of time,

sometimes entire days, replaying the night of the debut and what had happened afterward in her mind, trying to figure out how a man could go from making her the center of his attention to behaving as if she were an acquaintance in the blink of an eye.

True to his word, Jag had indeed endeavored to keep things professional between them, no longer coming home for dinner most nights, and scheduling a three-week trip abroad, leaving Rita in Hayat.

Now that she was publicly his wife, and gaining her own popularity with car-loving citizens, he had told her before departing, with her security detail, she would be safe enough from his father that Jag believed they could reasonably afford the risk of the trip.

Or so he said.

With all of that time to herself to think, Rita had come up with other theories, as well as more questions.

Mulling over it all once again, however, she meandered into the blue dining room to have yet another meal alone.

Walking into the room, she was welcomed by a bouquet of aromas.

Rafida had set the table already, including the cinnamon porridge she knew Rita loved, fresh fruit, dates, and yogurt with honey. There were fragrant flowers, as always, and freshly squeezed orange juice. It all looked beautiful—and Rita got one whiff of it and dropped to her hands and knees, gagging, as dry heaves overtook her.

Rafida walked in carrying a tray of bread and, seeing Rita, dropped it with a clatter and ran over. She placed her hands on Rita's cheeks and forehead before bringing them to rest on Rita's shoulders as she guided Rita back out of the room and into the cooler, less aromatic hallway.

Moments later, Rita was more settled, her wave of nausea having passed. After propping Rita against the wall, Rafida hurried off to retrieve something for her to drink.

Rita had expected a glass of ice water, but Rafida came back with a mug filled with what looked like hot water.

"Here, have a sip of this," she said.

Trusting, Rita took a drink and nearly spit it out. Inside was not just warm water, but vinegar and, if she wasn't mistaken, sugar.

The combination of strong yet nonspecific flavors was an attack on her senses—until it wasn't.

As the sip settled, so too did her stomach—her whole system, really.

The strange concoction had done the job, and Rita was grateful.

Gingerly, she rose to her feet, Rafida hovering nearby to offer a hand of support if she needed.

Smiling and mildly embarrassed, Rita said, "Thank you, Rafida. I'm glad you were there. I don't know what came over me, but your vinegar drink has cured me."

She turned back toward the dining room as she spoke, prepared to return to the beautiful breakfast that Rafida had laid out for her, when the older woman reached out to take her hand and stop her.

"I don't think you want to go back in there, Princess."

Frowning at the title—she'd tried to get Rafida to stop calling her that—Rita said, "Of course I do. Whatever is going on with me is my problem, not breakfast's. Your food looks delicious as ever."

A smile growing on her face, Rafida shook her head. "Not a problem, a pregnancy. I'm no doctor, but I'm certain when I say that you're going to have a baby."

For a moment nothing processed. Rita didn't breathe. No thoughts crossed her mind. No maternal warnings, voices or images rushed in to guide or provide understanding.

Just a moment of utter blankness.

But like the disappearance of the shoreline before a tsunami, the silence was no reprieve but a dire warning of the wave to come.

There came a rumbling and roaring in her veins and ears, the sound of the abrupt transforming of the very landscape of her life.

Thoughts whipped around in her mind like whirlwinds, further churning the already-roiling incoming tide.

Her husband had gotten her pregnant.

At her side, Rafida beamed, her reaction the standard and congratulatory joy for an expecting newly married couple.

Like nails on a chalkboard, it raked against Rita's nerves.

She and Jag were not a joyfully married young couple.

Rafida has to be aware of that, Rita thought crossly. She saw them interact—or *not*, rather.

There was no way she could be as deeply embedded into their household as she was and not know that it was purely business beneath their romantic facade.

Her husband's absolute lack of meaningful feeling toward her had to be obvious for anyone who had eyes to see.

And this was the same man she was going to have a child with.

That she was married to.

She had given up her anonymity and her country for the chance to change the world but instead she wound up pregnant, abroad and alone.

And she didn't even know where her husband was.

She was thousands of miles away from her home base and now she had become responsible for another being's life—a being whose father had already made it clear that he didn't want things getting awkward between them.

With the emerging development of her pregnancy, there was no way to prevent things from getting extremely awkward.

They were going to have a baby.

CHAPTER THIRTEEN

IT WAS 2:00 A.M. when Jag returned to the palace, walking the halls quietly on his way to the room that was his to sleep in had he ever decided to.

In the two months that had passed since he'd made love to Rita, he had become such an expert at keeping busy that he had finally hit a wall in which he had nothing more to do. Pregnancy was not his concern—she would have surely cared about a condom had that been a possibility—but the experience nonetheless harried his every spare minute as if he were a young man worried about getting a girl in a bad situation. He'd used that energy to drive his recent efficiency until that well ran dry, too.

Considering all of the follow-up necessary for an event as large as the exhibition, and everything that was needed to take down a corrupt king, he should have felt triumphant.

Instead, it had only further complicated matters.

He had nothing left to distract himself with. And with nothing left to distract him, his mind invariably returned to Rita.

And tonight, he returned in person. But only to sleep beneath the same roof. He would not sleep with her again. He had tasted her forbidden fruit once and was already struggling with withdrawals. Twice and he would surely go past the point of no return.

But he could be near her. He had nothing left strong enough to keep him away.

His popularity had skyrocketed. International interest and tourism spiking, with Rita's name at the center. And Jag was the most popular living monarch Hayat had ever seen—and he wasn't even reigning.

And because of it, the press conference in which he would reveal and condemn his father had been scheduled.

He had had a personal hand in planning every element of the event. It would be perfect. But now all there was to do was sit back and wait for the big day.

And though he expected more to come in, he had finally made his way through the backlog of international trade offers and shiny new contracts that had been on his desk after the exhibition.

Now there was nothing else to keep him away from Rita.

So he had come home.

Was it home because it was the only place he had spent happy years, or was it because she was here?

He hated himself for asking the question.

Since Rita had arrived, even when he dined with her, he had been so good about leaving for whatever residence was nearest with traffic at the time. It didn't matter; he was only going to toss and turn dreaming about Rita anyway.

And that had been before he was inside her.

But tonight, as weak as his will had become—or more likely because of it—there was nothing that would stop him from at least sleeping in the same building as her.

This was how he broke.

This was how he drove himself to the only place he'd ever called home, uninterested in a driver or witness for the trip, staring out at the long stretch of desert beyond the city and seeing Rita.

Slipping into the room that was his. Or would be if he ever spent the night here.

Closing his eyes as he passed through the doorway, he could almost smell her, his mind supplying the details. Her scent reached out of his memory to wrap around him like the climbing and clinging vines of the sweet night-blooming jasmine that she always brought to his mind.

Then he realized that though the room was darkened, he wasn't alone.

His memory had not supplied her scent in such vivid detail that his nose could not tell the difference between imagination and reality, but rather her living and breathing self had in his bed.

He had set her up in a different wing when he'd installed her in the palace. It appeared things had changed in his absence.

He wished the observation did not make the corners of his mouth want to lift.

"I know you're here, Jag," she said by way of greeting, her body still and back to him as she lay on her side.

"How did you know it was me?" he asked quietly.

"I could smell you," she said.

Frowning, he said, "My apologies. I didn't mean to come into your room. I thought you were in the guest wing."

Rolling around to face him, her expression still shadowed in the dark room, she said, "Rafida moved my things here as soon as she heard the news."

Jag bowed his head to the absurd logic of it. Of course; he had not anticipated it, but it made sense nonetheless.

And because of it, not only did he find himself beneath the same roof as the woman he desperately needed to get off his mind, but in the same bedroom.

He needed to get out.

Clearing his throat, he said, "In that case, I'm sorry for disturbing your rest. I'll let you get back to it." He began to step out, pulling the door closed as he spoke, knowing he shouldn't even be in here.

"Jag, stop." Her voice was a command, and he stopped.

He pushed the door back open with a creak, though never in his life had he ever recalled a palace door creaking.

He stood silhouetted in the door because as low and gentle as the hall lighting was, it was still brighter than the dark of the bedroom.

The dark from which Rita's disembodied voice emerged to say, "I'm pregnant."

He had been worried about the wrong threat all this time. He had been worried that the tendrils of warmth and homecoming he felt when he was around her, the threads of connection that had only grown, exponentially, since he'd made love to her, were the thing to watch out for.

But no. It was the one that should have been the most obvious from the beginning.

He was no different from Vin, nor Rafael, nor Zeus.

Undone by the oldest side effect in the known universe.

Rita was pregnant.

She had obviously become so the night they made love in the desert. The timing and the circumstances made sense, after all.

She had never been with anyone else. They had not used a condom, could not have, as in his undress he'd been in the rare state of not having one. There you had it.

As a healthy modern male, he maintained excellent sexual health, getting the appropriate tests and checkups regularly enough to ensure that he posed no risk to the partners he took, and still, he was typically very careful to ensure that he was protected in return.

Making love to Rita had been the most transcendent experience of his life, and one that he had been patently reckless regarding the possible consequences of.

But for this to happen.

He was undone. And what about his plans? Should he change them now, the risk of unrest not just a matter of the comfort of his people but the safety of his child?

This was almost to a T the exact situation he had taken such great pains to avoid.

To have things unravel at the end like this, because of this, was just so, so primitive. For it to have come down to a condom was so damn *old-fashioned*.

"You're not on the pill? You said you didn't care about a condom. What does that mean, if not that contraception is taken care of?" he asked, his tone sharper than he had a right to, unthinking to the fact that those would be the first words he would say in response to the first time he found out about his impending fatherhood for eternity.

He could think about that later.

Right now he wanted to know why the woman who created the world's leading electric vehicles and was passionate about the future and technology and machines was not on the pill.

She was all that was modern and liberated from natural cycles. Shouldn't she be on the pill?

"Excuse me?" Rita asked, outrage lifting the volume of her voice.

Belatedly, Jag realized that she had likely played out a number of scenarios in preparing to deliver the news to him. She had likely feared his reaction and worried that he would be angry with her, and the edge in his voice and immediate interrogation were not likely to be dissuading her from those notions.

But he couldn't seem to find the control he was famous for to do anything about it.

He was angry.

But not at her.

He was angry at himself. How could he have let this happen? Because far more fairly than his words implied, he knew it had been his fault. He should have had greater self-control. He should have resisted.

None of that, however, stopped him from digging his hole deeper. "The pill," he repeated. "Aren't you on it?

Aren't all women on the pill these days?" he grumbled, recognizing that the answer was obvious.

Lifting to her elbow, she cocked her head to the side and lifted an eyebrow. "Are you done?"

Sighing, he closed his eyes and answered his own question. "Obviously the answer is no. If you'd been on the pill, you would not be pregnant." He was being an ass. He was being an ass because if there was any fault to be had, it was primarily his own. He had let desire drive away logic, assuming far more than she'd ever implied. A man in his position knew far, far better than that. Opening them again, he said, "I'm sorry, Rita."

Only now did he realize she wore an ice-blue silk nightgown beneath the sheet that draped over her hips, hugged her curves, while the gown framed her cleavage.

Only now, his eyes adjusted to the dark and his life no longer his own, was he able to take note of her breasts, and how their increased size already hinted at her pregnancy.

Stepping back into the room, his nostrils flaring to catch the scent of her, he remained in control of his voice at least, when he said, "I should have never assumed."

How could he have been so reckless?

Rita was pregnant.

The world's most remarkable, beautiful and ingenious woman was going to have his baby.

He went to the bed, kneeling to take her hand, which remained stiff between his palms until he repeated, "I'm sorry, Rita. None of that is what I meant to say. I was a fool. What I meant to ask was how are you feeling?"

And then she melted into him, her lush body pliable and lovely in his arms. "Sick, but Rafida assures me that it's a sign the baby is healthy."

Breathing into her hair, he closed his eyes as the wave of realization swept over him.

He had a child to protect.

"Rafida would know."

For the third time since he had met her, Rita split him in half. There was a Jag that had existed before this moment, and a Jag that existed now.

The first time had been when she became his wife.

The second, when he made love to her in the moonlight.

And now, the third, as she made him a father.

Their agreement was shot.

There would no longer be an end date on their contract—they would share a child for the rest of their lives.

As rich and powerful as he was, there was nothing he could do to stop this train now that it was in motion. All he could do was recovery and damage control.

They would need to renegotiate. He would need to increase her security, and he was going to have to move up the date of the press conference.

With a little more time to sit with the information, it was obvious to him that he had been wrong to even consider postponement at the news.

With Rita's announcement, his worst nightmare was coming to life, and in a world like that, there was no room for men like his father to have power.

And in the meantime, he would keep watch over Rita himself, here in the palace, with the support of additional security.

Soon he would have the kind of obligation in the world that he would be willing to die for. He would not allow any harm to come to it.

But she didn't have to worry about any of that now. No, he would make sure she was happy, healthy and well—the most supported pregnant woman on earth. He owed her that much for his part in things, and for the fact that she was the future mother of his child.

Lifting from his kneel, he rose, loosening his shirt and sliding into bed beside her.

Her body was stiff, resentments and tension still lingering in her muscles. He had done this to her. Fortunately, since everything else had crumbled around them, he knew a way to make it right.

As if she could sense the shifts in him, she gazed at him, her brown eyes like two deep wells. Her lips were parted, plump and the prettiest pink, and he'd held back and punished them both for so long.

He caught her lips with a growl, and she melted into him, and he set about easing her stress one of the best ways he knew how.

She would have questions tomorrow, and he would not only have answers, he would have come up with entirely new ways to keep her out of his heart.

For both of their sakes.

CHAPTER FOURTEEN

As much as she had wanted this, as many times as she had imagined it, only to just once again curse him for being stubborn and foolish, Rita could taste the edge of panic in Jag's kiss and knew that this was not the way.

He had been so infuriating, and yet it had also all been so obviously fear.

She understood it. She felt it, too.

This wasn't what they had planned.

If making love in the moonlight had not made it clear to him that things had changed past the point of insisting they remain the same, then this certainly had.

She imagined it was hard for a man as powerful as he was to accept things not going according to plan.

But the unexpected could be good. It could have a silver lining.

They were not and would not be in love—Rita could accept that with only a mild tightness in her chest—but they cared about each other, and now they were going to have a baby. They could still be a family. They had to be, because there was no other family she had to offer to their child.

But she knew better than to present it that way to Jag.

She didn't know how she knew it, but she had sensed it the moment Jag was hers again. Just as she realized that in this moment, the lead was hers to take.

Fortunately, she was no longer new to all of it—not

the palace, not the man and not the passion that flared between them—and she knew exactly what she wanted.

Bringing her hands up to cup his jaw, rather than explore the broad planes of his chest that virtually begged her to grab hold and climb on up, she gently took the reins of their kiss and told him in a different way.

And only when his own hands reached for her body, their gentle and smooth exploration tempting her to hand things back over and let him ravish her, did she take their kiss deeper.

For the second time in her life she kissed the same man, and just like the first, the experience of it threatened to carry her away.

But she wasn't going to just let them go where the wind took them.

He had given up on something tonight. His plans had collapsed, and their futures had changed.

But if the future was not what they had thought it would be, Rita could at least show him the silver lining.

They were the silver lining. This was.

They didn't have to profess love in order to build a good life together. They'd both learned the hard way the meaning of unconditional love. They could both give that to their child without having it for each other.

And they could give each other companionship and conversation and, after long last, family.

She could be happy with that if he could. Happier even than she might have been two years from now, had the terms of their original deal come to fruition.

Trailing her hands down along his jawline and neck, over his shoulders, she followed the lines of his arms all the way down to interlace her fingers with his before softly breaking the kiss.

"Come with me," she whispered, her voice only slightly uncertain until he nodded.

He hadn't wanted a family, but as she'd lived in his

childhood home, she had realized that in many ways, he no longer recalled what family was.

And so tonight, she took him to the baths.

Rafida had told her he'd spent so much time in them as a boy that they'd joked he was half merman.

Since she'd been in Hayat, he had not even visited them once. The memories of his mother, she realized now, were too strong there. And how could she not be? The baths were as much her art as cars were Rita's.

Upon realizing their destination, a rapid-fire series of emotions crossed Jag's face. Joy, pain and something more complicated came and went almost as soon as Rita had identified them.

Feeling as if their roles from the night of the debut had reversed, she squeezed his hand in the doorway, telling him without words that she believed he could do this—not just go into the baths, but be a father and not lose himself to the process.

Though his spine remained as upright as ever and the embers of his eyes burned as strong, she had never seen him so unmoored. A voice inside told her that she had the capacity to be his anchor if she dared.

An anchor did not need to be in love, so she dared.

Releasing his hand, she looked him in the eye as she reached up to slide the nightgown she wore off her shoulders.

Beneath it, she had on only a pair of panties, simple and plain, but it didn't matter. Clothes were armor for the outside world. Tonight their challenge was intimacy.

The baths provided the perfect environment.

Filled with low amber lighting that set off the glow in his eyes, the baths consisted of multiple pools of water in various sizes and at various temperatures.

Like the rest of the palace, the design of the room showed its age with grace. In this room, that meant that traces of the seventies lingered in the amorphous shapes and overall lagoon impression of the pools, as well as in the large tropical plants that had had plenty of time to grow and mature over the years beneath their glass ceiling and accent walls.

Water permeated even the air in this room, a far cry from the setting in which they had first made love.

Rita slid her simple underwear over her hips and then stood naked before her fully clothed husband. This, too, was different from their night on the ruins.

Then he had been bare before her. Tonight she bared herself for him.

He stared without words, the fires in his eyes dancing and flickering in the gentle lighting of the room.

In this space, mirrors had been strategically placed to make both the room and foliage seem somehow bigger and deeper, but they had also been positioned so as not to reflect the bodies of anyone who might be enjoying the pools. Her display was for his eyes alone.

As always, they burned, but the fire within them now was of an intensity that put even his normal inferno to shame.

She didn't know how long they stood like that, him fully clothed, lighting her ablaze with only the caress of his gaze, while she stood completely naked before him, but her instinct to be patient paid off when he drew her to him with a growl.

He took her mouth with need but care, his kiss nothing like the tender, reverent things he'd bestowed upon her atop the ruins.

Whereas before he had been delicate, now he was fire and force, but controlled.

Fearless, she met him head-on, exploring his mouth with her tongue as he explored hers, running her hands along his clothed body even as he ran his along her bare one.

And when she finally grew impatient with his progress in removing his attire, she simply took over the job herself, deftly releasing buttons as their tongues danced.

Only when he was naked did she break their kiss, and only then to see him in full, illuminated by the glow of the bath lights.

When she began to lead him to a warm pool, however, he shook his head, apparently tired of following. Now he was in charge, and the pool he led them to was hotter and larger than the one she had selected.

He was in a mood, and who could blame him? Years of planning had gone down the drain. But without knowing where the knowledge came from, Rita knew she had what it took to shake him out of it.

The recipe wasn't secret or complicated. He just needed her.

Or her body, at least.

How she knew when she was an utter novice on the subject wasn't important. What mattered was giving him what he needed—whether that was to lead or follow.

The heat of the pool provided a fascinating contrast as they stepped in.

The water lapping around their thighs added another layer of sensation to the exploration of their hands and mouths, and Rita moaned as the combination thrilled her senses.

Capturing her mouth again, his kisses grew in intensity, building as his frustrations funneled themselves into the kind of handling reserved for off-roading.

No matter the terrain, it seemed, the man could drive.

Cupping her breasts in his hands, he nibbled and sucked his way toward her nipples, licking and kissing the sensitive flesh along the way, and by the time he'd reached the hard buds, her breath was fast and shallow and she was arching her spine, curving to give him greater access.

"Do you like it when I touch you like this, Rita?" he asked, voice low and harsh, and she could only offer a moan in response, bringing her hands to his shoulders, trying to steady herself against a storm that came from inside.

"You're going to love the rest even more," he promised.

In the moonlight, he had been the epitome of the tender lover. Here in the baths he made her want to bite and scratch.

She was surprised to realize how much she liked it both ways.

In the relatively short time that they'd known each other, he'd already shown her so much that had been a mystery to her.

It was almost unbelievable to her that there was anything she could give in return. But at the same time, as he gripped and held, kissing her neck and doing things to her sensitive breasts that threatened to push her over the edge, she sensed that she remained the steady one.

She was the calm at the center of his storm, and she could take whatever he threw at her.

He pleasured her as if it were a competitive sport, driving her mercilessly to and over the edge multiple times with his fingers and mouth before finally lifting her up to wrap her legs around his hips in a shameless straddle.

Holding her weight with one muscled arm, he positioned himself at her entrance with his other hand, teasing and caressing her before finally sliding in.

Her moans echoed around the humid room, their sound warped and changed by the water in the air, mingling with the rhythmic sound of their bodies contacting each other's and their panting breaths.

The combination of it all, the sensual overload intertwined with their locking bodies, was enough to thrust her to climax yet again, ripping through her with enough force to carry him along for the journey, and their final primal groans happened in sync, before they both collapsed, sinking into the warm relief of the pool.

For a long time, neither of them spoke, both seeming

to understand that with what had changed between them, words were just not quite enough.

Planned or not, they were well and truly partners now, committed to each other in a way neither of them had anticipated or agreed to.

And if it wasn't exactly what either of them had wanted when they set out, if their baths session had just reaffirmed anything, it was the fact that they could certainly make it work, and even feel good doing it.

CHAPTER FIFTEEN

MARRIAGE, AS RITA'S mother had explained to her, was a long twisting road, filled with unseen curves as well as massive hills and valleys—and that turned out to be true even for a fake turned not-so-fake one.

Jag took real residence in the palace alongside Rita, accompanied by an inordinate number of new security professionals. He insisted that it was simply that she was unused to the size and scope of his full retinue, but she could not recall ever seeing that many guards around him.

Along a similar vein, his arrival had also apparently necessitated an upgrade to the palace alarm system, which had been completed within the first week.

Sharing the palace, they had each fallen into individual daytime routines until their paths converged at the dinner table—which, due to Rita's new sensibilities, had become much simpler affairs.

And then, more nights than not, they shared a bed, making love and falling asleep.

And they didn't talk about any of it, not their arrangement, not their expectations, not their future.

But as much as she didn't know what to make of it, she wasn't exactly unhappy.

Jag was an attentive expecting partner, doting and involved, if not romantic, and if he was getting a little haggard and going a little overboard in terms of security, she had read that some expecting parents got that way.

He would settle down once the baby arrived. It was certainly making its presence known in every conceivable way.

Hovering on the cusp of fourteen weeks now, not only had her breasts increased in size—as most resources predicted—but her abdomen as well, the famous bump appearing rather shockingly around the twelve-week mark and having only grown since.

The same resources suggested that that was unexpected.

But she felt wonderful. Her current project—the plane Jag had promised—was flourishing, and she was alive, and steadily cared for in the company of other people in a way she had not been for a long time. As unlikely as it had all seemed in the beginning, she was going to have a family.

That was what was important. Not love, but a happy family in which no one expected anyone to be anyone that they weren't.

Overall, though she still was plagued by occasional nausea, she generally felt like a flower in bloom.

A hothouse flower hidden away from the harsh light of day and the prying eyes of people, but a flower nonetheless.

In fact, the only drawback over the past few weeks had been the intensity with which Jag was treating the effort to hide her pregnancy.

He was leaving the palace less and less and had stopped taking outside meetings.

In fact, though she was fourteen weeks pregnant and showing, she had only seen a doctor once, in part due to Jag's paranoia.

The only doctor that Jag trusted had been dealing with family matters abroad. Jag would allow no one else to know of Rita's condition. The doctor, who had made the initial house call to confirm the pregnancy and pronounce Rita exceptionally healthy before going abroad, vowed to return as soon as possible.

"As soon as possible" had still not arrived, though.

The ultrasound machine that they had tersely reminded Jag that he would need to purchase if he was going to insist that Rita never go to the clinic or hospital for care, had, however, arrived.

And the doctor was due next week.

Soon, she would see her baby for the first time.

And in the meantime, she had days filled with adjusting her work to her pregnancy and Jag.

The thought filled her with a sense of well-being. Even if things remained the way they had ended with her family of origin, Rita had found herself a family after all.

A week later, however, Rita was forced to reevaluate her sentiments as she looked at the brand-spanking-new three-dimensional ultrasound image that showed she was carrying not just one baby, but two.

"Well, that answers why you're so huge!" the doc said with a chuckle. "I didn't want to alarm anyone, but I was already considering the conditions that could have resulted in that…" The sentence trailed off as the hand moving the wand around in the mess of jelly on Rita's abdomen stopped. "Oh, and there's the smaller one again. Such healthy babies. Of course, healthy or no, this being a twin pregnancy means the risk is higher. That is just a fact. Therefore, you must be even more vigilant about eating right and getting proper exercise and sunlight. Not too much stress either, and no harsh chemicals. You may need to take a hiatus from your garage, Princess, and—"

Jag cut them off impatiently with the words, "What do you mean, healthy or not? How can she be healthy and high-risk at the same time? That makes no sense."

Shrugging with a knowing smile aimed at the Prince,

the doctor replied, "Twice the baby, twice the potential for complications, twice the development that could go wrong, twice the baby to safely deliver. A singleton pregnancy requires a woman to operate at the height of human endurance for months at a time. A woman carrying two babies is doing double that. But do not worry, my prince, our princess here is healthy and strong and so clever that I bet she'll think of a brand-new way to deliver entirely."

The doctor gave parting advice and left. Rita placed a cool palm on Jag's thigh. "I can handle this."

For a moment, he did not reply. She wondered if he was so lost in his worries that he had not even heard her speak. But then he smiled, kissed her forehead and said, "I have no doubt."

CHAPTER SIXTEEN

THE PRESS CONFERENCE had been moved up and his palace made as secure as it was possible to be with a fully functioning home office and the comings and goings of his staff, but Jag felt helpless.

How was he supposed to keep Rita and his children safe from his father, conduct his work, and keep her stress levels healthy for the next four months? And after that?

He couldn't do it here.

Rita didn't know it, but his father had been becoming increasingly aggressive in his attempts to breach the protective ring of security that Jag had established around her since the announcement of their marriage.

He had already attempted to get to her multiple times, and that was without even knowing she was carrying the future of the family line. Both of them.

Twice the baby, twice the risk.

He had to get Rita and their children out of his father's reach entirely—had to make sure they were literally and physically outside of the range of a man who had already shown Jag that he wasn't above using any means necessary, and then he needed to get rid of the threat altogether.

Even here, with his near-constant presence at her side and within the palace that had been built to ensure privacy and security, they were not protected enough.

Nothing could happen to them; he would not be able to function.

He trusted Rafida and his security team with his life.

He trusted no one but Rita with the life of his children.

And that meant there was only one option.

She wouldn't like it, but there was only one place on earth that he could trust to be completely out of the reach of his father, one place where he could be certain that Rita and their babies would be safe.

"Pack your things," he told her when he found her in her garage, his voice implacable and firm, before adding, "We leave in an hour," and no further explanation.

There would be plenty of time to explain everything on their journey there, and she would have the rest of her pregnancy to come around to understanding exactly why they had to go.

This was their only option.

Rita claimed to understand the risk she was in, but she didn't truly. She thought Jag was overreacting, because she had never truly had to deal with a man as ruthless and distanced from healthy bonds of love as his father was.

That was what made everything that his father had done to him so particularly twisted. His father had undertaken everything that he'd done to Jag and his mother in the name of love.

From the day of his birth, Jag had been his father's pride and joy. Unfortunately, his father had long ago confused love with control.

He loved his perfect son; he just happened to see no problem in using psychological warfare to ensure that perfection.

He never beat his son—he'd simply played a lifetime of mind games, surveilling him and monitoring all of his relationships in order to influence his behavior.

When bribery didn't work, he resorted to more menacing and long-term solutions, such as separating him from his mother and sending him to boarding school.

Nothing like that would ever happen to either of his children.

He would get his family to safety and then he would return and deal with his father once and for all.

Now that he knew he was becoming the father of not one but two souls, that he would be beholden to two beings who could run in opposite directions while he struggled to keep them safe, one thing was absolutely clear to him: the time for subtlety had ended.

Hayat had a room for only one ruler, and his name was Jahangir Hassan Umar Al Hayat.

The moment of his ascendancy had arrived—Rita's life and his children's lives depended on it.

All hail King Jag.

He'd given her less than an hour, which was hardly enough time to carefully pack the drapey new wardrobe pieces that Jameel had created for her under the guise of making her loungewear.

Without time for even a lingering goodbye to her fleet, she rushed through the palace garage that was now home to her fleet on the way to the Mercedes touring van that would take them to their mystery destination.

The vehicle suggested it might be a long drive.

Under normal circumstances, Rita would be looking forward to it. But newly aware that she carried twins and was saddled with a paranoid husband, the whole thing lacked adventurous appeal.

It seemed there was a limit even to her patented brand of recklessness.

And yet here she was, following the lead of her husband.

The father of her children.

Not *child*, as she'd spent the past weeks cooing, but *children*. *Had one of them been feeling left out this whole time?*

Suddenly, she felt as paranoid as her husband, but for fear that she had already begun failing as a mother and had not yet even met her children.

But beyond protective, how did *he* feel about the news? Was he happy?

She didn't know. She knew only that he was resolute and certain of a next move that he still hadn't let her in on.

It was, indeed, a long trip—long enough that she was grateful that the tour van had a bathroom. She hadn't known it was possible for a human to need to use the restroom so many times in one day.

Jag had been silent and broody as he drove through the first still-dark hours of their journey, and while she had had every intention of forcing him to talk, the combination of the late hour and the smooth motion of the van and her pregnant state made her fall asleep.

When she woke, the sun was close to setting and they were driving on an otherwise empty road in a stretch of bleached-out desert without a thing in sight.

Her husband's aura appeared no less inclined to talk, but now she had daylight and alertness on her side.

"Where are we going?" she asked, for not the first time.

Miraculously, this time he answered. "My mother's oasis."

The image of date palms clustered around a small pond in the sand filled her mind, but it didn't fit with her sense of Jag's tastes. "Your mother's oasis?"

The nearing twilight brought another miracle with it— he smiled.

And as much as she wished she could be immune and unmoved, seeing him crack—even if it was just one corner of his mouth lifting—made her heart beat faster.

"It's not what you're picturing," he said, reading her mind, as always.

"Then what is it?" she asked.

"My mother's family had land at the far western point of Hayat. By appearances, it is a wasteland of sand, far off the beaten path of traditional nomadic routes," he said.

Catching his drift, she said, "But appearances can be deceiving?"

Nodding, the other corner of his mouth joining the first to bring a real, full smile to his lips, he said, "They can, indeed. The land has been in my mother's family for generations, its true worth kept as a cherished secret in order to preserve and protect it. It was a wise move. Because she kept the secret even from her husband, she was able to leave it to me when she died and my father, thinking it useless and valueless, had no incentive to steal it. And when I came of age, I made sure it was no longer possible."

"But really there's an oasis there?" she asked.

"Not naturally. But naturally, there is groundwater. Lots and lots of it. Formed by a large underground porous stone system, in the desert, it is more priceless than gold. My family found the water by chance. They built, maintained and kept secret the oasis, by choice."

"And you couldn't tell me when we were at home because of the secret."

He nodded.

"I thought you trusted Rafida," she said softly, a hand coming to her abdomen.

Jag's face went hard. "I do. You, however, are the only person I've ever trusted with this. Our family has managed the water for hundreds of years, going so far as to engage in a state-of-the-art catchment to refresh from what little rain we get. This is not mere wealth, but survival."

"Is it abandoned, then?" she asked.

Shoulders loosening, he gave his head a brief shake. "No. There is an entire village responsible for managing, monitoring and protecting it."

"Protecting it?" she prodded, picturing armed soldiers in fatigues.

"It's water in the desert, Rita."

So her picture might not be that far off.

"And it's very remote?"

He nodded. "As remote as you can get and still be in Hayat."

"And why are we going?"

"It's the only place I can be sure the twins and you will be safe from my father."

Flatly, she said, "Well, thanks for telling me."

"Everything's changed now," he countered. "It's one thing to take responsibility for the safety of an adult woman who can consent to a certain level of risk. It's another to protect a woman pregnant with twins from a man who would not think twice about threatening his unborn grandchildren if it meant controlling me."

Again, her hand came to shield their growing babies. "I see."

"Do you?" he pressed, temper fraying. "Do you see what has to be done?"

Rita's eyebrows came together. She understood that the threat they were facing was graver than she had initially imagined, but she did not see how that led them to driving to a secret oasis in the remote desert.

"I'm taking you to Jana to stay there for the remainder of your pregnancy. It is the only place I can be assured of your safety. My father cannot get to you in a place he does not know exists."

"What?" Rita shrieked, her hand coming down to grip the armrest at her side.

Jag remained calm, despite her outburst. "I am taking you to the oasis for your pregnancy," he repeated calmly.

"No," Rita said.

Jag kept his eyes on the road. "We're already halfway there."

"I don't care. Turn the car around."

"No," Jag said.

She crossed her arms in front of her chest. "Then you're kidnapping me."

He shrugged, the move incredibly American. "So be it."

Dropping her arms, she smashed her fist against the armrest. "Not so be it. You can't kidnap me."

"It seems I already have. And I seem to recall you packing your own bags and getting into the car willingly."

Narrowing her eyes, a new suspicion forming in her mind, she asked, "And what are you going to be doing?"

Brushing her question off, he said, "Everything I normally do, in Hayat City. I would stay with you, but I cannot. Not if I hope to keep it a secret. People are already remarking that they have seen very little of me of late. Your retreat from the public is one thing, but a prince cannot disappear for six months. My responsibilities require my presence in the capital."

She hissed in response, and he took a sudden left, veering the vehicle onto a steep, hidden road to a hidden rocky valley, nestled in the folds of which was a cozy oasis lagoon and town.

Under any other circumstances, Rita would have been thrilled at the sight of the lush, beautiful surprise, lit up by a colorful sunset, but at the current moment, she would have been happy to burn it all down with a glare.

Glorious water that went from blue-green at its shallows to deep turquoise at its depths pooled in the large, long lagoon that was surrounded by rocky outcrops on one side and a tidy stone village built into the surrounding hillsides on the other.

While most of the structures in the village looked ancient, there were modern buildings mixed in among the old.

Few cars dotted its roads, and most of them were parked.

Figures moved about on the streets, but from this distance it wasn't possible to tell if they were men or women, adults or children.

"The hospital in the village is brand-new and staffed with excellent practitioners whom I personally selected to service the people that live here. For all of its isolation, you will not lack quick medical care."

Rita could not help but be blown away, not by the advancement of this remote village—which was impressive—but by her husband's ability to simply charge forward as if they were not in the middle of an active argument, and he was not in the midst of depositing her like so much trash in the desert.

"I'm sure there's a library, too," she said sarcastically.

"As a matter of fact," he said tersely, "there is."

"How convenient for me."

He said nothing to that.

Curving their way out of the village around a long bend, the landscape opened up to reveal a gorgeous massive stone fortress. From size alone she would have guessed that this was the familial home of the rulers of this isolated microcommunity.

Outside of it, gorgeous foliage softened the stone facade, naturally blending into the surrounding landscape, and if she wasn't mistaken, there were frankincense trees mixed in with the date palms and shrubs.

To the right of the grand stone palace was another open lagoon, deep and still and clear, its mirror finish so crystalline and reflective that Rita would not have been surprised to look into its depths and see all the way to the center of the Earth.

Stopping the Mercedes in front of the timeless structure, Jag said, "We're here."

"I'm not getting out of the car, Jag."

"Then I'll carry you."

"Then do it," she challenged, not exactly understanding the energy that washed over her but willing to let it take the lead. Perhaps it was pregnancy.

Or perhaps it was that she was tired of being dictated to by tyrannical men.

Whatever it was, Rita had reached her limit as far as being pushed around went.

He could listen to her dictate things for a change. "You can drag me kicking and screaming and leave me here and no one will be the wiser. But you and I will know, and neither of us will forget the wrong you were willing to commit against me because of your own fear and pride. This single action will fester between us until our relationship deteriorates because you know it's wrong."

"Fear and pride? You think this is about fear and pride? You think it was fear and pride that led me to drive you all the way out here? To share one of my family's oldest secrets with you? To do everything in my power to keep you happy and safe and satisfied? Look around you, Rita. I'm doing all of this because I love you." He hadn't raised his voice, not truly, but shouted the last, nonetheless.

Rita's eyes widened, her head shaking back and forth in denial.

"It's true, Rita. I love you. It all ended for me the night in the ruins. Before that. When you stood up to my father at the finale and I realized that you weren't merely the ideal woman for my aims, but the ideal woman for me. You shine as my partner, my queen and already as the mother of my children. You're everything I will ever want. I must know that you and the babies are safe from my father. It's not forever, Rita. Just until I've taken care of my father. I just need this peace of mind. If you can't do it for the babies, if you can't believe me about my father, do it for me. I love you, Rita."

He said it a second time, his voice lighter, as if he felt better in the telling, while Rita stared at him in horror, mouthing the word *no*.

"No," she finally voiced, when sound came through her throat. "No," she repeated. "No, Jag. No. No. No. Don't do this. Don't ask this of me. Don't make my family contingent on bending to your will. Don't tell me you love me while you're demanding I sacrifice myself to your needs. Don't you do this to me, too, Jag. I thought you were different."

Color draining from his face, Jag raised his palms as if to stop her from going on, from taking the train of thought any further, but it was too late.

"Don't be my father, Jag," she begged, adding, "Don't be yours."

Fire flashed through his eyes, but Rita didn't look away. She'd meant every word she said. If he left her here, right now, she would never forgive him.

"Rita, that's not what I meant..." he began, but she shook her head. There was only one thing she wanted to hear from him, and it wasn't excuses.

It was that they were going back to Hayat City.

She had a right to stand up for herself; facing off with her husband in the desert, she realized the truth of that.

She had always had a right to stand up for herself. With Jag, and with her father, so long ago.

She wasn't the one who had been in the wrong all those years ago—her father had been. She had been young and willful, but Jag had been right. She had also been a loyal testament to her family. The transgression of staying true to the passion that had taken her so far was not one that was worthy of losing her family.

Just as the transgression of being pregnant with twins was not worthy of twiddling her thumbs in the far reaches of the desert. She was healthy and strong and would stay that way only if she had the space and freedom to keep both mind and body occupied. She needed her workdays in her garage and her dinners and nights with Jag.

She didn't need to be hidden away in a desert tower—no matter how beautiful an oasis it was.

Like Jag was now, her father had overreacted and over-reached. Back then, she had been too young to do any-thing about it.

Today, she was a grown woman carrying twins.

Jag blinked and looked away.

Staring around him at the astounding architecture of the Jana palace, he cleared his throat. Then he got back into the van.

Rita didn't crow in triumph, because there was no tri-umph in learning that her husband was not above using the same techniques as her father, but she took comfort in the fact that at the very least, this time she hadn't stood for it.

CHAPTER SEVENTEEN

JAG DROVE BACK to Hayat City with Rita in tow because she was right.

He could have easily left her there, confident in her safety and security, and in doing so, would have become just like her father, demanding she bend in the name of his love.

He could not believe he had confessed to her as he had done. The frantic moments between acknowledging it himself and throwing it at her the way he had was matched only by the poor quality of his delivery.

And yet avoiding that slippery slope brought Jag no closer to a solution regarding what to do to keep Rita safe from the man.

It had only left him outside her good graces.

It was ironic that the things he had so feared—falling for Rita, having children with her—in the end had paled in comparison to the damage he had done simply by speaking.

And yet as bumbling as he had been in his communications with Rita, he knew he was right to not shake his concern regarding his father.

He would sort things out with her later, in the lifetime they had ahead them, even if it meant he had to spend the whole of it making her fall in love with him.

His father he would deal with now.

In T minus ten minutes.

In moments, he would go on national television and bring shame to his family name. He hoped he would also restore honor to it, taking his father down in the process.

The space between the conclusion of his broadcast and his father's arrest would likely be the most dangerous for Rita and the children, and he had doubled palace perimeter security to coincide with the timing.

He had told Rita—she refused to go anywhere safer, of course, but Rafida was to send him updates regarding his wife's status.

No updates had arrived, but he had sent in the extra guard after waiting a generous amount of time anyway.

He wanted her and their children safe.

Twenty-seven minutes later, the same number as Rita's age, Jag noted, he stepped out of the bright television lighting and offstage.

Like his exhibition, the broadcast had gone off with a hitch.

The grand finale of his plan had been set in motion.

There was no telling how far his desperate and enraged father might be willing to go until the special services caught up with him, but his reign of manipulation and control was over.

Unfortunately, the answer arrived a few moments later, with the message that came through from the head of security.

Rita had stepped out for a moment of air in the courtyard and disappeared.

They were searching for her, the team leader assured Jag, but he could have told them not to bother.

He knew where she would be, and what he would have to do to get her back.

CHAPTER EIGHTEEN

For the second time in her life, Rita was face-to-face with her father-in-law.

As far as evil villains went, her father-in-law appeared frail and weak.

But as he had just successfully kidnapped her from her own home despite a crack security team, she recognized that it was probably time to revise her opinion.

Long past, really.

She also recognized that she had perhaps taken the threat he presented for granted.

She had not truly believed the man could be cruel enough to harm his own grandchildren. She could admit that to herself now, as she was uncomfortably tied to a chair in the center of his private balcony.

Admitting that also meant admitting that perhaps Jag had meant what he said when he tried to leave her at Jana, and that it might actually have been the only place he could think of that would be safe for her and their children.

Of course, while these were important truths to discover, they paled in comparison to the necessity of escape.

Her babies were depending on her.

"So this is why he disappeared with his whore," her father-in-law said, stroking the thin beard that graced his chin, eyeing her growing bump.

But hiding her pregnancy was no longer her top priority. Keeping her babies alive and getting away from her father-in-law was.

And though she didn't have an escape plan yet, she did have the wherewithal to engage in one of the oldest strategies in the book: stalling.

If she could get him talking and keep him talking, she might buy herself enough time to figure out a way out.

"I am not a whore," she retorted.

Making a face at her oversharing, the old king scoffed, saying, "Everyone knows American girls are easy. You may have fooled my son, but you will never fool me. And you have brought as much shame on my house as I will allow. My son has done me a favor in hiding your pregnancy. No one need know more than the fact that you died in a tragic accident. As a widower, my son can make a more appropriate selection for his next wife."

The idea of Jag with another woman was a knife in her chest, but she would not let this cruel man see it.

"You know what?" Rita said. "I'm getting real tired of everyone talking about what's wrong with me."

Taken aback, her father-in-law looked mildly surprised and confused, as if perhaps he thought she might not have heard the words he'd said.

Taking advantage of the pause, she jumped back in with, "It's always how my interests are not the right ones, nor my choices, nor passions. First it was my father, and now you, each one telling me that I am somehow inappropriate, that I need to change to better fit your image of the world. Well, you know what," she said. "I'm tired of it. And it was your son who made me see it. Never once has he asked me to change who I am to better fit his requirements. He delights in who I am, without alteration or revision, and I have been a fool to not realize what a precious gift that kind of love is. Unconditional. It is something you will never understand, so I won't waste my breath trying to explain, but I will not allow you to call me a whore. I am no man's whore, but I am your son's wife. I will be the mother of his children and your grandchildren, and what is more than that, I love him and them with every fiber of my being. I will not tolerate you disrespecting what we have built. I was accepted to the University of California at Berkeley at the age of sixteen. At the age of eighteen my father cut me off in one of the most expensive cities in the world and not only did I manage to pay for my life with my work, I also paid for the remainder of my tuition. By the age of twenty, I had a dual master's degree in computer science and mechanical engineering, as well as a start-up valued at two million dollars. And while I don't expect you to be impressed with that kind of money, I do expect you to be impressed by the fact that seven years later I had invented multiple technologies with the capacity to change the world. Interest in Hayat has skyrocketed since the world found out about its new American Bengali Muslim working-class princess, and your son is the most popular royal your line has seen in generations. By my calculations, I'd say that means your reign is coming to a close, and, in addition to being absolutely suitable to be a princess exactly as I am, I am exceptional at math."

She was under no impression that her little speech would inspire her father-in-law to release her; it was merely a way to eat some time and release a bit of righteous indignation and fear she felt.

So she was surprised when, as soon as she finished speaking, a massive commotion erupted at the entrance to the room, and like an ancient warrior, Jag flew in.

Seeing him, knowing he knew where she was and trusting him entirely to get her and their babies safely out of there, she surprised herself by bursting into tears.

She and her babies had narrowly escaped disaster.

And she wouldn't have to do the rest on her own.

She was ready to tell him now how desperately in love she had fallen with him. Having been brave enough to say it out loud once, she was ready to do it again for real with him.

She had finally learned to speak up for herself and to fight for what she loved—people, places and things.

She was brave enough to own her emotions, her hopes, her dreams and her actions.

And because of that, she could demand the same of others, including her parents.

Jag had been her safe space and testing ground for the theory, and once he'd taken care of things here and they were in a bit safer a spot and she'd had a chance to shower him with her declarations of love, she vowed to take everything that she'd learned and make her family listen, too.

CHAPTER NINETEEN

JAG HAD DRIVEN from his palace directly to his father's, where he knew Rita would be.

Arriving there, he took the stairs two at a time before sprinting toward his father's private chambers, in time to hear Rita, strident and proud, declare to his father that she loved him and their babies and she would tolerate no disrespect on the matter.

As if he had sprouted wings at her words, he tore through the distance to find what was truly his nightmare come to life, all of this familiar as much as it was new.

Falling in love with Rita and getting her pregnant had not been the nightmare. His father was.

Seeing his father standing before his wife, who was tied up in a chair and crying, was a real nightmare.

His father intended to throw her off the balcony.

Jag was as certain of it as he was of his own name.

The man who had consigned Jag's mother to die alone would not hesitate to throw the woman he loved and their unborn children off a balcony.

His father loved his power positions, and his private balcony had always been his favorite.

Jag did not think, plan or strategize. Impossibly, he simply sped up—running at his father and Rita far faster than the pace of his father's deranged retreat.

With a roar, he leaped, reaching out to clasp Rita's

wrist with an iron grip before swinging his body to kick his father away from her, catching the man in the chest.

His father flew backward, but as soon as Rita was free from his grasp, Jag had no more attention for the man. Law enforcement had been quick on Jag's heels; they would deal with his father.

Instead, all of his focus landed on his wife.

"Are you hurt?" Jag asked her, frantically checking her arms and legs where the ropes chafed against her skin.

Rita shook her head. "No. Not even scared now that you're here."

"I'm not sure your confidence isn't misplaced, but I'm grateful for it," he said.

"Spare me the romantic reunion," his father croaked from the floor behind them, where he had pushed himself to his feet. "Your bride and I were just discussing the happy news."

"You have nothing to discuss with my bride," Jag said coldly, "now or ever."

His father clucked his tongue at him. "Now, is that any way to speak with the father who loves you?"

Rather than engage his father in his games, though, once again, Jag turned his back on the old man, giving his attention instead to his wife. "Let's get these ropes off you, shall we?" he said to her.

"You will look at me when I speak to you. I am your father and you will love and respect me," his father warned ominously. "Dammit, Jahangir, look at me. Your king addresses you!"

But Jag did not turn.

Instead, he worked on the ropes that held Rita in place.

Only when she was free did he address his father, finally turning to look at him with nothing but pity in his eyes.

"I neither love nor respect you, Father, and your days as King have come to an end."

Scoffing, his father said, "Youthful defiance and arrogance."

But Jag shook his head. "I'm afraid not, Father. I have just finished debriefing the people of Hayat on the collection of information and evidence I have put together to depose you a thousand times over. You are not my king, nor the people's king, and you ceased to be my father a long time ago. You will be tried and punished through the legal system according to your crimes, and it will take the people some time to rebuild their faith and trust in the royal family, which they will because of my and my wife's efforts, but you, you will never rule again."

Choking on his own rage spittle, the old King sputtered, "You will never sleep again, knowing I am out there, plotting."

Rita sucked in a quiet gasp, but Jag held firm. "I know you will try. I just won't be losing any sleep over it. It's finished. I should have ended this a long time ago. You're going to prison, Dad."

As if the drama were being staged rather than lived in real life, the authorities chose that moment to finally make their entrance, converging on the former King to arrest him.

But Jag had no time or attention for his father any longer.

Pulling Rita into his arms, he held her to him as closely as her enormous belly would allow, pressing desperate kisses on the top of her head, grateful to press her into the safety of his arms.

Only when he heard her muffled "Jag, I can't breathe" did he release her from the lock of his hold, and even then, only wide enough to allow her to pull back a fraction.

"How did he get to you?" he demanded when she did.

Smiling, her eyes filled with tears again. "It was just like you warned me. It was like getting jumped by a bunch of ninjas, rappelling in from the roof."

Shaking his head, he said, "I'm sorry, Rita. I broke my promise. I didn't keep you safe."

Wrapping her arms around his neck, her embrace delicate yet strong, she said, "Oh, Jag. You tried. I just didn't listen. You were right about Jana. I'm sorry I was too headstrong to see that."

Pulling back to look at her, he shook his head. "No, Rita. You were right. It wasn't right to ask you to hem yourself in because I could not handle how much being in love with you, loving our children, terrifies me. I am so sorry you had to experience this, but there is one thing I am grateful for—a silver lining, if you will."

"What is it?" she asked.

"Who knows how long it would have taken you to calm down enough to admit you were in love with me if we'd just stayed home?" he teased.

But this time, she did not match his energy.

Instead, the tears left in her eyes spilled over and she swiped at them quickly, never losing her smile. "I know I wasn't supposed to, but I love you, Jag. More than even planes, trains and automobiles."

He closed his eyes and drew in a long, deep breath, pressing his forehead to hers, letting the warmth and completion of her words roll over and dig into him. "Thank you for loving me, Rita. I am sorry for running from you and trying to control you. Love had been absent in my life so long that I feared both its return and then the risk of its loss again. I love you, Rita. More than life itself."

Beaming like sun, her tears flowing freely, Jag had the strangest thought that she might sprout a rainbow.

It would be only fitting. A storm had passed, after all.

"You're going to be an amazing king," she said.

A half smile on his face, he said to her, "And you will be my queen."

EPILOGUE

APPROXIMATELY TWO MONTHS LATER, hovering around twenty-six weeks pregnant with twins, Rita stepped onto the long red aisle, but the phenomenal dress that Jameel had created for her did a remarkable job of flattering her bump.

Fitted at the neck and chest, with a high lace collar above a sheer white bodice and capelet-inspired sleeves, the skirt was full and voluminous and in combination with its illusion Empire waistline, looking direct from the front, it didn't even look like she was expecting at all. Even from the side, one might be inclined to attribute the width of the skirt to the layers of tulle and fairy-tale-princess nature of the dress.

Rita could think of nothing better for the fairy-tale ending of her and Jag's story, which, it turned out, had been a love story after all.

As they celebrated their Western-style wedding, which was to be the first of many hosted events to make up for the rushed and administerial nature of their actual wedding, Rita reveled in the joy that she had gotten everything she had ever wanted.

She had a loving partner, a family on the way, and now, just six months after the exhibition, she had even begun to change the way the world drove.

Beginning with Hayat, she had been a part of overseeing the beginning of their transition to all electric transport, and she had messages from two American and two Japanese car companies to discuss her first-ever car design that could be mass-produced waiting for her to respond to after she and Jag enjoyed their first real honeymoon.

Like their celebratory events, he had assured her that their upcoming luxury yachting trip would be just the first of many romantic getaways they would share. Each had gone too long in their lives without the comfort and warmth of regular affection and celebration, and each was committed to making it up to the other.

They were a family, full of love and laughter, but also one equipped to handle disagreement and challenge. They had faced it all and come through the other side more dedicated to each other than they had begun, and it didn't get much better than that.

Or rather, it seemed it continually got better.

They had been lucky enough to find the right partners, the kinds of people who would poke and prod and encourage until evolution occurred.

Rita was only reminded of the truth of that as she smiled at her father before looping her arm through his.

That her father would be involved in any wedding of hers was a miracle in itself. That Jag had coordinated their reconciliation in time for the televised ceremony, the kind of sweet detail she would always love him for.

He was a master at planning, though perhaps still a bit high-handed about it all, as he hadn't told her what was going on through the process, simply shoved her into a room where her father already stood. In this instance, however, she did not mind. He made her brave and forced her to go after her heart's desires.

She could not lie and say it had been easy, but when they'd passed the reticence to speak and resentment and defensiveness, Rita, now practiced in the art of speaking up for herself when she needed to, was finally able to say the thing she had needed to say all those years ago but not known she had the right to.

"I'm so sorry for what I did, Papa," she started with. "I should have never lied to you. But what you did was wrong, too, and you owe me an apology. A parent shouldn't stand in the way of their children's dreams, happiness or future. It took me a while to learn it, but now that I am going to be a parent, it is even more clear. You didn't have to agree with me, but you were supposed to love me, no matter what I did. I deserve that."

And because everything she had said was true, and because words were insufficient to address everything that had passed between them, her father had merely nodded, tears streaming down his face, and opened his arms.

Smiling through her own tears, Rita had gone into them. And after they'd hugged, they stepped back from each other to look at how the years had changed them.

Her father had looked at her enormous belly and a thousand emotions flashed across his face. Settling on a soft smile, he said, "You got pretty fat."

And Rita had snorted and said, "Your hair turned gray."

With a chuckle, her father reached a hand to pat the salt and pepper of his hair. "A lot of time has passed. Too much. I'm so sorry, my sweet Amrita. I was a fool, but I have never stopped being proud of you. You did everything you promised to do, my girl."

And it had been enough to get to this point, her father walking her down the aisle in a beautiful dress to once again marry the man she loved, this time in the presence of her mother and father, her sister, and her uncles, and the family she was growing and would protect with her life.

It was a far cry from a judge and a jumpsuit.

Eleven weeks later

Rita went into labor in the wee hours of the morning, and like everything else she did, she raced through it fast and hard.

Their twins came into the world healthy and loud, their daughter first, followed by their son.

All of Hayat rejoiced in welcoming the new Princess and Prince, particularly eager to celebrate as a conclusion to their short and sedate mourning of the death of their old king. They went all out with parades and festivities to commemorate the birth, as well as their new, already much beloved, King and Queen.

They were especially excited about the Queen.

Their babies were like mirror images of them, their son taking after Rita, bearing her big round brown eyes and button nose, while their daughter's eyes were almond-shaped and amber, and her nose long and straight.

Their son they had named Martin Hatem Kabir Al Hayat, because Martin was as close to naming a child after a car as he would allow Rita to go, and their daughter, Benazir Summar Al Hayat because Jag had been moved when he'd learned that Rita's middle name, Benazir, was the same as his mother's first.

And three more years of joyous reigning and happy marriage after that, with two rambunctious royal pre-schoolers—a boy who loved to go fast and a girl with a mind for strategy—Rita told Jag she that was pregnant for the second time, this time completely without hesitation or fear, and they celebrated the news with their whole family.

* * * * *

ONE NIGHT WITH HER FORGOTTEN HUSBAND

ANNIE WEST

MILLS & BOON

This story is dedicated to
the Newcastle Romance Writers Group.

Here's to marvellous plots, words that flow
like warm honey and, above all, camaraderie.

CHAPTER ONE

A SHOUT DREW Angelo's attention. He stepped through the open French doors and saw Enzo, the gardener, leaning over the balustrade of the lowest garden terrace.

Enzo was staring down towards the sea. Then he spun around, saw Angelo and waved urgently.

'A body!'

Angelo frowned. Enzo's eyesight was cloudy and he was due to have cataract surgery soon. He must be mistaken. Yet he repeated it. 'There's a body on the beach.'

Angelo sprinted towards him. With every step he told himself it was simply a stray tourist, drawn to sun themself on the island's unique pale pink sand. Though, given the strengthening wind and ominous clouds spreading across the brilliant blue sky, they'd picked an odd time. The forecast was for a savage storm.

It must be a stranger who didn't know the cove was private and had swum ashore from a boat. Though every local boat owner respected Angelo Ricci's privacy. None would allow an outsider near his home.

Angelo slammed to a stop beside his gardener, staring down at the body. A woman, lying face down at one end of the beach.

His breath backed up in his throat, his brain cataloguing every detail.

Any thought that she might be sunbathing died. She lay mainly in the water, slender bare legs extended. The lap of waves made her oversized white T-shirt lift and ripple around her hips but it was the only sign of movement. She lay utterly, heart-stoppingly still. Nor was she lying totally on sand. Her head and one outflung arm rested on an outcrop of rocks above the water. It was clear, even from here, that her clutching hand was limp.

'Call the doctor!'

Angelo vaulted the balustrade to land in a crouch at the bottom of the first set of steps on the path down to the beach. He felt his bent knees absorb the shock. A second later he rose and pivoted, hurtling down the next set of steps that made the almost sheer rock face negotiable.

Mere minutes must have passed since he'd heard Enzo yell. Yet it felt like a lifetime.

Perhaps, for the woman below it *was* a lifetime. Each second could mean the difference between life and death.

Angelo felt each beat of his pulse as if in slow motion while his brain raced. He recognised the clarity of senses, the hyper-awareness of his adrenaline surge, from previous crises.

The last time had been while climbing in the Dolomites in the north of the country. When he and his climbing partner rescued a couple of beginners who'd got into trouble. One had broken a few bones in a fall and the other had frozen with fear. It had taken a lot of ingenuity to get the pair to safety.

Angelo's feet touched sand. He shunted the memory to the back of his mind as he powered towards the rocks.

She mightn't be dead. Surely there was a possibility…

Angelo dropped to his knees, careful not to touch her as he scanned both the woman and the empty beach. No footprints. No evidence anyone had been here, except her.

Even above the waterline the sodden T-shirt clung to her body and her hair was wet. So she hadn't been here long. It looked as if she'd walked or dragged herself partly clear of the sea before collapsing.

He reached out and gently circled her wrist with his fingers, searching for a pulse.

It was there, weak at first, but when he shifted his grip, stronger and even.

Relief rose like a warm tide. Angelo sat back on his heels and heaved in a slow breath. Alive and not obviously injured. From what he could see.

He surveyed her surroundings, the damp sand and dark rock. No sign of blood. He scanned her bare arms and legs, noting she had the smooth, unblemished skin of youth. There were a few freckles on her arms and, though lightly tanned, her pale colouring hinted she was likely a tourist rather than a local. Olive skin was more common here in the south of Italy.

Dare he move her? Turn her over?

He had no idea if she'd injured her back or head on the rocks that ran out into the sea from this end of the beach. Better to wait for a medical professional.

Angelo lifted his gaze to the cobalt sea, growing choppy as he watched. The mainland was close yet far enough to prevent people swimming across. There wasn't a boat in sight. But now he thought about it, he'd heard a speedboat earlier, in far too close to the rocks. But if she'd been on a boat, where was it now?

This was no time for speculation. He leaned over the woman and carefully lifted some strands of wet brown hair from her face.

She didn't move.

He reached again, drawing more tresses back behind her ear. The action uncovered the sweep of long eyelashes against the curve of her cheek.

Abruptly Angelo sat back, heart thrumming against his ribs. His breath was a snatch of air that made his lungs ache because he forgot to exhale.

He frowned. This was no time for flights of fantasy. He had an injured woman to deal with. He had to discover how badly injured.

Carefully he slipped his hand under the mass of wet hair and lifted it all off this side of her face.

He almost dropped it as he saw what lay beneath.

Shock jolted him. As if lightning had struck through him.

There was no blood. Yet what he saw horrified him.

His gaze traced the slant of her cheekbone, the line of her nose and delicately carved nostril, down to full lips that were too pale.

His hand shook.

Because he knew her.

It was impossible that she was here.

Yet there was no doubt. He'd know that profile anywhere.

He remembered leaning over her as the early morning sun flooded his bedroom. She'd stretched back into his aroused body, a feline smile of satisfaction curving those lips as she rubbed herself against him.

Angelo blinked, dispelling the memory.

Then he frowned. A smattering of freckles stood out against the unnatural pallor of her face. Those were new.

And her eyebrow looked different, still beautifully arched but more natural-looking than when he'd seen her last.

Slowly he released her hair so it fell behind her ear, leaving her face clear. He snatched his hand away. It tingled as if stung by unseen ants.

Of course she looks different. It's been five years.

Yet she didn't look older. If anything she looked younger than before.

Angelo snorted, feeling warmth begin to trickle back into his shock-numbed body. She'd spent a fortune, both in time and products, to maintain her looks. She'd claimed it was necessary because of her work, but he knew she'd been just as motivated by vanity. She'd see ageing as a personal affront.

Which didn't explain what she was doing here, of all places.

His eyes narrowed as he caught a smudge of colour on his hand. Blood?

Reluctantly he bent forward and there, if he wasn't mistaken, was a patch of darker colour in her wet hair.

He was just reaching out to investigate when her eyelashes

fluttered. Or did he imagine it? Angelo stared, alert to any movement. There it was again, the tiniest stirring.

A wrinkle appeared on her smooth brow and tiny vertical lines appeared above her nose. To his horror Angelo found himself thinking the frown looked almost cute on that clear, guileless face.

Guileless? His mouth twisted in a grimace of bitter derision.

That was one thing he couldn't accuse her of. This woman was an opportunist. Self-obsessed. Conniving.

She was an outright liar.

In fact, now he was here, on his knees beside her, he began to wonder about the convenient *accident* that had washed her up on his private beach. It was a little too unbelievable, surely?

Angelo Ricci was many things but gullible wasn't one of them. Once, definitely, and to his cost. But no longer. He'd learned distrust thoroughly and brutally.

If it were any other woman, he'd take her at face value. But not her. Was the blood in her hair actually some sort of dye?

Her frown deepened and tiny grooves appeared at the corner of her mouth. Her expression spoke of pain. Or the pretence of it.

Maybe she wasn't injured at all. Maybe she just feigned it and sensed his scepticism.

But why go to all this bother? She couldn't think he was willing to forget what had passed between them.

Her lashes moved again and she groaned. A soft, heartfelt sound that, despite his suspicion, wrenched at his conscience. Maybe she really was injured.

He watched her swallow, the movement jerky, then her tongue circled her lips.

Angelo moved to sit on the rocks on her other side so he was in full view when she opened her eyes.

Suddenly she did.

He still had a view of only half her face, the other half pressed to the rock, but there was no mistaking what he saw. Only one woman he knew had eyes like that. Eyes the colour of lavender or, she'd told him, the flowers of the jacaranda tree. A stunning colour between blue and purple.

His breath whistled out as his lungs cramped.

She didn't seem to see him straight away. It was only when he moved that her gaze tracked towards his face. Even then he wasn't sure she focused on him. There was no recognition in her features. No start of surprise or satisfaction.

'Hello, Alexa.' His voice was a gravel rumble, dragged out of him despite his will.

She blinked and then, after a moment's blank stare, closed her eyes.

Fear shot through him. Angelo didn't want her here. Wanted never to see her again. But the thought of her dying at his home, on his watch, was another matter.

'Alexa!'

Her frown turned into a scowl and she flinched.

Because she'd hoped for a warmer welcome? Or because she was really in pain? She might have a head injury. On the other hand she could be shamming. Either was possible.

'Alexa. Speak to me.'

Despite his doubts, concern filled him. Damn it, he didn't know whether to leave her as she was for fear of doing some damage or carry her up to the house.

Her lips moved. 'Not Alexa.' He had to lean in close, almost touching her, to hear the slow whisper. 'Ally.'

Angelo stared. She'd changed her name? But Ally would be a short form of Alexa.

Yet the woman he'd known hated being called anything but her full name. It was her brand as well as her personal name and she insisted on promoting it assiduously.

He heard a shout and looked up to the people picking their way down the cliff path. Medical help was on its way.

Relief stirred. The doctor would do what was necessary. Angelo would find out soon enough if her injury was real.

Her mouth was full of cotton wool. Cotton wool that tasted rancid. But the dry, sickening sensation that made her want to gag was nothing compared with the pain. It was so all-encompassing she couldn't pinpoint its source, though she had the mother of all headaches.

She lay there for a lifetime, knowing she was awake, not dreaming, but unable to summon the effort to open her eyes. Because she just knew that would make the hurt even worse.

The pain grew more defined. Her shoulders and arms ached. Her body and legs felt battered. Her hip was on fire. But it was her head… Even thinking about the pain hammering at her skull made it worse.

Dimly she became aware of noise. A rough, rushing sound. Or was that her pulse? Then, from nearby, the sound of someone moving.

Knowing she'd regret it, she opened her eyes. Instantly light jabbed at her in a blinding flash and she squeezed her eyes shut.

Someone spoke. A man with a warm, gentle voice, but she couldn't make out the words.

He spoke again and a firm hand took hers, testing her pulse.

She was hurt. Maybe she was in hospital. The voice spoke again and she frowned. She'd thought at first that she hadn't heard him properly because of the heavy pound of her pulse and her dull stuffed-with-cotton head. Now she realised there was something else. Something she couldn't quite grasp.

'*Bene, bene. Sei sveglia.*'

She frowned, then regretted it as even that movement sharpened the ache.

'I…' She swiped her mouth with a tongue that felt swollen and clumsy. 'Am I in hospital?' she whispered. Every syllable took effort.

'Not hospital,' a heavily accented voice replied. 'You're in Signor Ricci's home. He brought you up from the beach.'

Slowly she digested that. One word at a time.

She'd been on a beach. She was hurt. Someone had brought her to a house. Her breath exhaled in a fractured rush. 'Thank you.'

'Can you open your eyes?'

Her mouth twisted. Was she ready for more pain? But lying indefinitely in the dark was no real option.

She slitted her eyes open, hissing in a breath at the assault of light. But after a few seconds it got better, almost bearable.

She caught movement and her gaze focused on a thin man with a worn face and kind brown eyes.

'*Bene. Bene.*'

That was what he'd said before. It sounded familiar but as soon as she grasped at it the sense of familiarity faded.

'What…' She swallowed hard. 'What are you saying?'

For a second she caught concern on his face. But then it seemed she'd imagined it. He smiled and something inside her eased. 'Just that you're doing very well.'

A laugh escaped her dry throat. A chuckle more than a laugh and even that was cut short by a shaft of pain. 'I'd hate…' Her words trailed off, then his hand took hers again and she roused. 'Hate to see *poorly* if this is *very well.*'

'You're safe,' he reassured her and he sounded so certain she believed him. Or maybe she didn't have the energy not to. 'You'll be looked after. But first I need to examine you properly.'

The next time she woke the light wasn't so bright and the doctor wasn't there. She was alone in the dimly lit room and didn't know whether to be glad or worried. Her head ached but not so sharply. Nevertheless, she wasn't eager to move. She closed her eyes again, cataloguing how she felt.

Something hovered at the edge of her consciousness. Something disturbing. But that fuzzy feeling was a convenient reason to ignore it for now.

When she felt stronger she'd face whatever it was.

That rushing sound was still there, louder this time. After a while she recognised it as the wind tearing fast around the building. Occasionally it built to a buffeting surge and unease tugged at her. If the weather was this bad she needed to go outside and check on…

But the thought slid away half-formed.

A frown bunched her forehead. What was it she had to do? Why was it so urgent? Something that was her responsibility. Something important.

Whatever it was, it would have to wait. She couldn't pin down the details. Besides, she wasn't sure she had the energy to get up.

Experimentally she lifted one hand and discovered it had become a leaden weight.

At least it moves. At least it's not broken.

Instinctively she lifted her other hand, then twitched her feet, just enough to be sure they'd respond to her mental command. Relief rose.

The doctor had said there was no sign of spinal injury, she recollected now.

Instantly she felt better, remembering that worn face and his genial expression. He'd been gentle but professionally brisk, reassuring her that she'd feel better with sleep. A sigh escaped and she turned her head on the soft pillow.

This was incredibly comfortable for a hospital bed. Still with her eyes closed, she swiped her hand across the mattress. Then one foot. This was no single bed.

What was it he'd said? Something about a beach. Being carried up to a house. She must still be there. Maybe she'd better try getting up after all. She didn't want to be a burden. She'd need to make arrangements to get home.

Again that nagging feeling of something not right tugged at her. Something to do with going home? Anxiety niggled.

'You're awake, then.'

A different voice this time. A man's voice, deep and rich as homemade *dulce de leche*. She could almost taste the luscious caramel, sinfully addictive, on her tongue, just from those few words. She swallowed and found her mouth dry.

Slowly, wary of that horrible lancing pain, she slitted open her eyes.

A man stood beside the bed. A tall man with glossy dark hair. Her gaze tracked from strong thighs and trim hips in worn denim jeans, up a long torso that broadened as it went.

His pale polo shirt wasn't tight but she had no trouble making out the impressive musculature of his toned, powerful body.

For a second she wondered if this were a dream after all. This man was...spectacular.

It wasn't just his height and sexy body. Nor his strong-boned face that had passed *good-looking* and travelled on into *gorgeous but severe*. There was a magnetism about him that combined attraction and an air of aloofness.

Her heart gave a mighty thump.

He looked familiar.

Maybe she'd seen him on a billboard—that beautiful, stern dark face staring up at a mountain peak while he, in rugged climbing gear, sported the ultimate luxury watch on his wrist. She could imagine him selling something masculine and extravagantly expensive.

One black eyebrow rose, interrupting her dallying imagination.

'Yes,' she croaked and circled her dry mouth with her tongue. 'Awake again. Though I sort of hoped this...' she waggled her hand to encompass the bed '...was a dream.'

He stood, arms folded, watching her. He didn't even seem to blink. Finally he spoke. 'No dream, sadly.'

How had she thought his voice smooth and delicious? It was so brusque now she almost felt it graze her skin.

That steady gaze was unnerving too. Why did he stare? Her head hurt but she'd been assured she'd feel better soon. Surely she didn't look that bad.

'Are you a doctor as well?'

The man's nostrils flared and his mouth thinned and she had the distinct impression he was annoyed. But why?

Unease trickled down her spine. He didn't move towards her yet she felt abruptly vulnerable.

The instinct was so strong she didn't hesitate. Gritting her teeth, she rolled a little to her side, lifting one leaden hand and planting it on the mattress, then struggling to push herself up.

Pain screeched through her. Her body was clumsy and uncoordinated but she kept going, drawing herself higher with slow determination till she was half sitting against the bed head, trembling with the effort.

When she looked at him again his arms were no longer folded across his chest but hung by his sides, his fingers clenching. A muscle in his jaw flexed and she sensed he reined in emotion. But why? What had she done?

If she could get off this bed she would, but her legs felt useless and she didn't want to end up in a heap on the floor. All she could do was cross her own arms protectively and meet that dark stare head-on.

'Who are you?' she whispered.

A noise escaped his throat. Something between a snort and a huff of disbelief.

'Really? That's the best you can do?'

She shook her head, bewildered, then stopped, wincing, as pain darted through her head then bounced around her skull. Her eyes flickered shut as she breathed through the hurt, willing it to subside.

When she looked again he was a step closer to the bed, a frown lining his forehead.

'I asked who you are.'

Her words were strident, tinged with sudden fear. Did he hear that in her voice? Possibly. For, instead of moving closer, he shoved his hands in his pockets and leaned back.

'You know exactly who I am. And I've got no time for this game of yours.'

'Game? You think this is a *game*?' Her voice rose as she lifted one hand towards her throbbing head.

The man's attention moved from her face to her raised hand, then down, past her mouth to her shoulder. Something about his stare made her look down.

She wore a fine cotton shirt, buttoned at the front and with the sleeves rolled up around her elbows. The shirt wasn't hers. She knew that from the way it swamped her, lying askew and revealing the whole of one shoulder.

For a second fear stabbed. Where were her clothes? Why wasn't she wearing her own things?

She thrust the questions aside and yanked the cotton up over her bare skin, clutching it closed at the neck. Her hands were unsteady and she refused to try tackling the buttons under this man's hawklike scrutiny.

'I assure you Mr… Mr Whatever Your Name Is, that this is no game.'

'I agree. There's nothing remotely amusing about it. So let's cut the pretence. Tell me what you're doing here.'

'I was injured. On the beach.'

That was what the doctor said, but she struggled to visualise it.

Something darted through her brain and her breath caught. But again, when she tried to hang onto it, it vanished into foggy nothingness.

'How were you injured?' His voice had a remorseless quality she hated. 'And on this particular beach?'

'I don't…' She paused, trying to still the strange, quivery feeling inside. 'Which beach was it? Where was I found?'

Anxiety nibbled at her, growing stronger by the second. The question wasn't just where she'd been but where she was now. And much more. There was so much that, she suddenly realised, she didn't understand. The strangely vague quality of her thoughts took on a new, sinister cast.

He rattled off a name in a foreign language. It was totally unfamiliar.

No, not totally. '*Isola?* That means island, doesn't it?'

He raised his hands and clapped, his expression mocking. The applause was deliberately slow, making heat flood her cheeks. '*Brava*. A fine performance. But not convincing enough. I know you, remember?'

She wanted to protest that she wasn't trying to convince him. That she didn't care what he thought. But she had bigger concerns. Finally her hazy brain clicked into gear and she understood the implications of what before had been only vaguely unsettling.

It hurt to swallow, as if sandpaper lined her throat. But that was a minor inconvenience. It was nothing compared with the huge, scary truth suddenly filling her brain. The truth she'd been too dazed to realise earlier.

'You know me?'

He rolled his eyes. 'Spare me the playacting. Of course I do.'

She gripped the shirt closer with fingers that had turned clammy as she fought rising panic.

'Then you can tell me who I am. Because I don't remember anything.'

CHAPTER TWO

ANGELO STARED DOWN at the woman before him, disbelief vying with fury.

Experience told him she was up to no good. Yet, despite what logic said, he found himself noting how vulnerable she looked.

There was more colour in her face than there'd been down on the beach. Then she'd looked pale as a corpse. Yet even now she conveyed an impression of fragility.

Those extraordinary eyes were wide and shadowed and a smattering of freckles on her nose and cheeks gave her an unexpectedly wholesome, almost naïve look. As if the sophisticate he'd known had turned into an innocent farm girl.

Angelo suppressed a bitter laugh at the idea.

Her hair, dark honey now rather than the pale gilt she'd once favoured, was dishevelled and naturally sexy. The woman he recalled had done everything she could to appear sleek and well-groomed at all times.

Rosetta had given her one of his shirts to wear. He recognised it as one he'd earmarked for charity donation. The material was fine, but it was huge on Alexa and he kept getting tantalising glimpses of her body, her breasts jiggling when she moved and sending a line of fire straight to his belly.

That, above all, amazed him. As he remembered it, he'd been totally impervious to her feminine allure when he'd discovered the truth about her.

'You don't remember anything?' he drawled. 'How very convenient.'

It seemed ridiculous, especially after all this time, that she could come back here. She must be desperate to try conning him again.

One thing was for sure—she'd picked the wrong man. He wasn't as gullible as he'd been half a decade ago.

'Actually,' she snapped, 'it's very *in*convenient.'

Her chin rose and her eyes blazed angrily.

Her anger surprised him.

Alexa had always known on which side her bread was buttered. She'd been all sweetness and light around him, right until the end. He'd discovered later that others, like his housekeeper, Rosetta, had borne the brunt of Alexa's displeasure when she didn't immediately get what she wanted. But with Angelo she'd been all smiles and acquiescence.

He watched as suddenly her mouth wobbled.

Because she'd realised belatedly that annoyance would win no sympathy?

Yet, despite his cynicism, Angelo's protective instincts surged. He'd looked after his widowed mother and younger sister all his adult life. He was, it was generally agreed, a *decent* man, kind to animals, children and those less lucky than himself. The sight of someone in distress, especially a woman, tugged at his conscience.

But this woman was the exception. 'Don't try that on me. If you want chivalry, you can look elsewhere.'

'Chivalry?' Her voice cracked. 'How about common courtesy?' She breathed deep as if trying to master her emotions and he had to force himself not to notice the way her nipples pressed against the thin shirt. 'Why can't you tell me your name and where we are?'

Angelo sighed and shrugged. 'I have no time or inclination for these games, Alexa.'

'Alexa?' Two vertical lines ploughed down between her eyebrows. 'Alexa?' she repeated more softly, as if trying out the sound of it.

Arrested, he paused, taken in despite himself, by the sight of her bewilderment. A shudder raked her and she closed her eyes, swallowing hard.

Suddenly she didn't look defiant or scheming but…forlorn.

Something sliced through him. A momentary doubt. A flash of sympathy and concern. But only for a moment.

When he'd met Alexa she'd been a moderately successful model with aspirations to act. She'd proved herself adept at playing a role around him and it had taken a sudden revelation for him to see through her charade. Clearly her skills had improved, if she could elicit even a moment's sympathy from a man who knew her for what she really was.

He turned on his heel. 'I don't have time for this.'

'Wait!' Lavender blue eyes held his and despite himself something softened within him. There'd been an edge to her voice that sounded like fear and, as he stared back, he registered that her breathing had turned quick and shallow.

'Alexa who?'

Angelo frowned. Did she still persist with this charade? 'Alexa Barrett,' he said finally, wondering what she hoped to achieve, pretending not to know.

Her lips moved and she silently repeated the name, as if committing it to memory. 'And we're in Italy.'

It wasn't a question but a statement, yet her tone and knitted brow gave the impression she was perplexed.

'Southern Italy,' he murmured, leaning back and crossing his arms, curious, despite himself, to see what she'd do next. He couldn't figure what her plan was. His knowledge of Alexa told him she must have some scheme in mind to make her venture back here.

'The doctor.' Her gaze met his then skittered away. It was one of the few times he'd seen her discomfited and again it gave him pause. 'Will he come back soon?'

Angelo stared, trying to read her intentions in her features. But all he saw were hunched shoulders, the downward droop of her mouth and the fact that the hand grasping his shirt collar was white-knuckled.

He stifled automatic sympathy at the sight of a woman in distress.

'He'll come when he can. The weather's appalling and he had another emergency to see to. But he promised to return today.'

Angelo paused, his conscience grating. Whatever else was going on, Alexa *had* been unconscious when he'd reached her. That hadn't been a sham. The doctor had confirmed she'd had a knock to the head, advising that, for now, it was best she stay resting where she was.

Not what Angelo wanted!

But he couldn't throw an injured person out into the worst storm they'd seen in years. No matter how much he despised her.

'Is there something you need?'

That startled her. She actually jumped as if his words interrupted some deep reverie. Or as if she hadn't expected an offer of help.

Angelo's mouth firmed as guilt scored him. He didn't like this woman. Didn't trust her. But she'd been hurt and needed help.

'Water? Something to eat?' he persisted, watching her eyes widen and feeling annoyance rise. He wasn't an ogre. He was simply a man protecting his sanctuary.

She understood that. He wasn't the villain of the piece here.

'Thank you,' she said finally. 'Some water would be good.'

He nodded and strode to the bedside table, lifting the jug Rosetta had left and pouring some.

'Ah. Sorry. I didn't see it.' Alexa reached for the glass, carefully wrapping her fingers around the base of the glass as if intent on avoiding his touch.

Angelo's mouth curled. Who did she think she was trying to fool?

Then he swore under his breath as he released the glass into her hold and realised too late that she was trembling. Water spilled and he only just caught the glass, and her hand, in his.

She was so unsteady it was hard to believe she faked it.

What did you expect? She was unconscious a few hours ago.

Silently Angelo cursed. He could at least have held his temper in check till a more appropriate time.

'Here.' He raised the glass to her lips, his hand cupping hers.

She drank greedily. This close, he became aware that the trembling wasn't just in her hand. Her whole body shook. Did she have a fever? He put the back of his hand to her brow and heard her swift intake of breath. An instant later she moved her head away. As if she didn't want to touch him any more than he wanted to touch her.

'That's enough, thanks.'

Angelo transferred the glass to the bedside table and topped it up again from the jug.

When he turned back she was sitting up against the antique carved headboard. It didn't look comfortable.

'Are you going to lie down again?'

Her glance ranged from him to the door and back before she answered. 'No, I'll sit up, thanks.'

Now that flash of energy had seeped away, she didn't look well. Angelo hoped the doctor would be back soon. He was getting concerned about his unwanted guest.

'Right.' He reached over to a couple of pillows discarded onto a nearby chair. 'Sit forward. You'll be more comfortable with these.'

Alexa moved, not forward but to one side, her movements slow and stiff, but it was enough to make space for the pillows behind her. When she sat back her breathing was fast and her milky pallor worried him.

'Thank you.' It was a barely audible husky sound. Yet she didn't look at him to see if she'd garnered sympathy. She stared across the room towards the view of the sea as if she'd never seen it before.

The fine hairs on Angelo's nape prickled to attention. He straightened and stepped back from the bed.

She didn't even glance in his direction. Not that he minded.

Yet gut instinct stirred, telling him, as if he didn't know it, that something was wrong. Alexa had always been hyper-aware of him, alert to any little change of mood or counte-nance. She'd read him like a book, a fact that had chagrined him when he'd discovered how she'd abused his trust.

But now he'd swear she was barely aware of his presence.

'Why are you here, Alexa?'

Slowly she turned her head. Her features were curiously blank. 'That's just it. I don't know. I don't remember.'

She saw his head rear back and his mouth draw in a straight, flat line.

Why was he so set on rejecting the truth? Why wouldn't he believe her?

To her horror, her mouth crumpled and she swung back to face the huge window. Emotion bubbled in her chest, making it tight and heavy with distress, a good match for her dully throbbing head.

She'd been so numbed by shock and pain before, and over-whelmed by the effort of answering the doctor's questions, that things hadn't sunk in. It was only now that she realised how small her world was, consisting merely of what she could see, touch, taste, hear and smell. Everything else was hidden by the misty nothingness that blurred her brain.

Her memory was a blank space. So blank it terrified her. Every time she groped for some snippet of the past it slid away.

She blinked and stared at the view of white-capped waves and lowering dark clouds billowing and scudding across the sky. The seascape was stunning, terrible yet strangely beau-tiful through the lashing rain.

Like the man standing beside the bed, silently seething. His impatience was like static prickling her skin and charg-ing the air in the big, luxurious bedroom.

His stark disapproval matched the storm outside. As if he were a pagan weather god, living on a craggy hilltop, creat-ing terrible storms when his mood turned sour.

If he smiled, would the sun come out?

She couldn't imagine that happening. He looked too dour. Besides, she suspected he'd be too dangerously attractive if he smiled.

She blinked, her thoughts circling back to her predicament. How could she distract herself with such absurd ideas when she was in a crisis?

Because it's easier than dwelling on the mess you're in. No memory. In a place you're clearly not wanted. With a man who loathes you.

She swallowed. Why should he loathe her? Maybe she was dreaming. All this, from the storm thundering outside to her companion who looked like the hero of some gothic romance, could be a nightmare.

'What are you doing?'

She sighed and released the skin of her forearm that she'd pinched between her fingers. 'Just checking I wasn't dreaming this.' She turned and met his dark gaze, relieved to find the banked anger had been replaced by curiosity. 'You're *sure* my name is Alexa?'

He nodded. 'Absolutely.'

She bit her lip, letting herself sink back against the pillows he'd provided. Sitting up straight had taken too much energy when every muscle felt as if it had been strung tight for too long.

'It doesn't sound familiar.' Panic stirred. 'Surely it should if I've answered to the name for…' Her breath caught on a hiccup.

'What is it?'

He wasn't exuding sympathy but there was no one else to help her and she needed, urgently, to understand what was happening.

Grimly she told herself this must be a temporary thing, caused by her accident. Yet that didn't stop fear eddying deep inside. What if this lack of memory was permanent? Was it possible?

'I don't even know how old I am.'

For a second she didn't think he'd respond. His face was set in stern lines as if he battled the impulse to walk away.

Cravenly she hoped he'd stay. Despite his attitude, he knew her. He could explain who she was and why she was here.

'You admitted to twenty-three when I knew you, but that was five years ago.'

He looked at her from beneath lowered brows in a stare that was part accusation and part restlessness. Stoically she ignored his mood, silently rejoicing in the fact she was in her twenties, not the several decades older she felt at this moment with her aching body and muzzy head.

'Admitted? There was some doubt?'

Why would she lie about her age?

He shrugged, the movement dragging her gaze across his emphatic shoulders and down to expressive hands that gestured dismissively. 'I learned to take everything you said with a pinch of salt.'

Did he mean she exaggerated? Or that she outright lied?

She swallowed hard. The picture he conjured was anything but flattering.

What had happened to make him hate her?

Perhaps it was stupid to feel upset about something she didn't recall, but who wanted their first snippets of self-knowledge to be so negative?

Surely this wasn't right.

Surely she wasn't the way he painted her.

As if you'd know. You don't even know your own name!

She let her eyes slide closed, wishing the headache would go. She didn't have the energy for these unpalatable glimpses into the past. Maybe if she slept again...

'Alexa.'

Her eyes snapped open. Eyes the colour of espresso coffee stared down at her, intent as if they could read her very soul.

It scared her that this man, this disapproving man, knew her better than she knew herself. And that he didn't trust her.

'I don't feel like an Alexa,' she blurted. 'It sounds... foreign.'

Slowly he straightened, his gaze still holding hers. For the first time she noticed a flicker of something that wasn't hard and judgemental there.

'On the beach you called yourself Ally.'

'Ally?'

Her lips formed the name, her tongue lingering clumsily on the sound. Did that sound any more familiar?

The answer was *no*. Nothing seemed familiar. Not even the sight of her ringless fingers and lightly tanned arms that she must have seen every day of her twenty something years.

'Yes. Short for Alexa, presumably.'

Her mind whirled. How did she know what a panic attack was when she didn't know anything about herself? It was totally bizarre.

'Don't worry about it now.' To her amazement his voice dropped again to that low, lush note that made her think of rich caramel and comforting warmth. 'Just shut your eyes and relax. The doctor will be here soon and someone will sit with you till he comes.'

She wanted to protest. To assert herself.

But to what end?

The last ten minutes had left her exhausted and wrung out. Talking and trying to think had taken all her strength.

She just hoped when she woke she'd be better.

With luck her memory would have returned. She'd enjoy proving to this disturbing, disapproving man that her name wasn't Alexa or Ally and that she wasn't the liar he believed her. She was someone else entirely. Of course she was.

Clutching that thought close, she felt her eyelids grow heavy and then the world went black.

Angelo kicked his heels in the hallway while the doctor examined Alexa.

She'd slept solidly for hours, sliding out of consciousness so abruptly it had startled him. One minute she'd been a curious mix of fire and fragility and the next she'd been out for the count. So deeply asleep, so still, that he'd worried she wasn't merely sleeping.

But when he'd put his fingers on the silky skin of her wrist he'd felt her even pulse. Nevertheless, every half hour or so he'd risen from the armchair beside her bed, where he'd dealt with a slew of business messages, to check she was breathing.

Obviously she had some self-serving reason for coming to his home. He suspected her supposed memory loss was a crafty ploy for sympathy. Yet she really *was* injured and a blow to the head could be dangerous. The doctor had been infuriatingly non-specific after his first visit, promising an update on his return.

Rosetta had offered to sit with Alexa but Angelo had rejected the idea. He, personally, would keep an eye on her.

Finally the doctor emerged and Angelo led the way downstairs to his study.

'A drink?'

The doctor shook his head, sinking into a leather chair. 'Not with this storm still raging. I could be called out in the night. Now, about Ms Barrett...'

Angelo listened as the doctor talked at length about the woman ensconced in one of the guest suites. Listened with amazement.

'You mean it could be true? She could really have lost her memory?'

The other man frowned, his grave eyes piercing. 'You have some reason to suspect it's not true?'

Angelo paused. The doctor had only been on the island a few years, after Alexa's time here, and neither Angelo nor his staff had spoken about her since. As far as he knew there was no gossip about her on the island.

'I do. I knew her years ago. She wasn't trustworthy.'

'I see. But to fake amnesia...' He paused. 'It's possible. But that would be an extreme step.'

No more extreme than the lies Alexa had told before. The extreme lengths she'd gone to in order to get what she wanted.

'Amnesia isn't common but it's consistent with her injury.'

The doctor paused. 'You mentioned that Ms Barrett under-stands Italian.'

'She does.'

'Fascinating. She appears not to understand Italian now.' Did Angelo imagine an emphasis on the word *appears*? 'I must do some research and consult some colleagues.'

'Colleagues? Won't it be more efficient to move her to a mainland hospital?'

Then she'd be someone else's problem. Angelo suspected her convenient amnesia would probably dissipate then.

'No, no. That's not possible. Not with this weather. Did you hear about the chopper crash near Naples a few hours ago? Air ambulance is out and as for going by sea…'

The doctor looked towards the full-length windows. In the darkness beyond the wind screeched like the undead.

There'd be no sea crossing tonight or, if the forecast was correct, for a couple of days. This catastrophic storm, de-scending out of a clear spring day, was being described as one of the most destructive in living memory.

Which made him wonder again how Alexa had got to his private beach. No local would have brought her.

'She's best here, where she can rest quietly.' The doctor glanced around. 'It's good that you've got space to house her comfortably, and I'll come over regularly to check on her.'

'You want her to stay *here*?'

The other man's lips pursed. No doubt he thought An-gelo was being uncharitable, not wanting to house an injured woman. But the doctor knew nothing of the woman's charac-ter. The thought of keeping her under his roof indefinitely…

'It's not ideal. But we must do the best we can in the cir-cumstances.'

His stare hardened as if he expected Angelo to dispute that, but Angelo was a practical man. He understood that, for now there was no other option.

'Of course. She'll be well looked after.'

'I knew I could rely on you. Take heart, any memory loss is likely to be short-term. A few hours, maybe a few days.'

Unless she decided to spin it out, making the most of his charity.

But why? Angelo couldn't fathom what she hoped to gain.

The doctor reeled off a series of symptoms to look out for, in which case they should call him immediately. Then there were instructions about pain medication and the need for fluids.

Angelo listened carefully. Alexa Barrett would be well cared for. Hopefully she'd recuperate quickly and leave as soon as transport became available. Or sooner, if he could find alternative accommodation for her on the island.

Yet he had a deep-seated suspicion that it wouldn't be so easy to get rid of her.

Already she'd wormed her way back into his world, even his home.

The woman he'd vowed never to let near him again.

The woman who'd lied to him and betrayed him.

CHAPTER THREE

ALLY SAT IN an armchair near the window and stared at the boiling, dark sea.

After almost twenty-four hours she still had to make an effort to think of herself as Ally. But no other name had come to mind and it was better than Alexa, which just sounded wrong.

Or maybe it was the way her host said that name, as if repressing a sneer.

She shivered despite the warmth of the room and wished the rain would stop lashing the windows. Even to step out onto the balcony and draw a breath of salty sea air would be a relief.

All she'd seen was this bedroom and its adjoining bathroom. Partly because she didn't have the strength to go far with her weak knees and swimmy head, and partly because she hadn't been invited. She was here under sufferance.

Ally swallowed, forcing down the tangle of emotion that threatened to overwhelm her.

Everything will be all right. You just have to be patient.

She couldn't be claustrophobic. The suite was spacious and comfortable, with panoramic views of the sea.

Yet she was uneasy, and not just because of her missing memory. At a deep-seated level Ally knew she didn't belong here.

What sort of house possessed a massive guest suite like this? Everything was the height of luxury. From the huge cloud-soft bed to the beautiful original artwork. From the massive sunken bathtub, complete with gorgeously scented jars of bath salts and oils, to the expensive marble gleaming white with the faintest delicate tracery of pale green.

She knew barely anything about herself but she sensed such opulence, even though tasteful and attractive, was alien to her.

The grounds visible from here reinforced the fact that this was no ordinary house. Despite the storm damage the gardens set high on the clifftop looked superb and the place commanded a spectacular view. She tried to imagine it on a sunny day.

Ally knew southern Italy was famed for its wide blue skies, stunning coastal towns and clear water. How she knew it, she couldn't say. Just as she couldn't understand how she knew that the sun rose in the east and set in the west, or that it was sensible to wear a broad-brimmed hat in the middle of summer.

Yet she still couldn't remember anything useful like her name or where she was from.

He'd said she was Australian and, as she clearly wasn't Italian, perhaps he was right. It was one of the few personal details her close-lipped host had let slip and she'd pounced on it gratefully.

Not that she trusted everything Angelo Ricci said. Far from it. He was biased against her for some reason.

Simply getting his name from him had felt like pulling teeth, one laborious tug at a time. Teeth from a particularly ferocious-looking wolf.

The man unnerved her with his brooding silences and judgemental attitude. As if she'd *asked* to be washed up on his precious beach!

From here she could see a sliver of pale sand on what Rosetta had explained was the private beach where she'd been found unconscious. Rosetta the housekeeper who, like her employer, didn't seem happy to have her here. She'd been polite, and the food she brought was delicious, but there'd been no generous smiles or warm welcome.

Ally frowned. She'd thought Italians were renowned for their hospitality. Or was that wishful thinking?

Her thoughts circled back inevitably.

How had she got there? Why was she alone? Surely someone, somewhere, missed her? She tried to imagine people frantically searching for her. A family, boyfriend, husband even.

A sob rose in her throat and she stifled it. She couldn't afford to give in to despair.

Doubtfully she looked down at her fingers. There was no ring and no mark from a ring. Her nails were neat and short. Nothing there to hint at her identity.

She lifted her hand to her head, then dropped it. The headache was bearable now, just a low hum, but she didn't want to make it worse by probing.

'What are you doing?' The words, sharp and unexpected, lassoed her ribs, tightening her lungs so her breath caught.

Cautiously, not wanting to aggravate the pain again, she turned.

Angelo Ricci stood just inside the open doorway. She hadn't heard him enter and he stood with his hands jammed onto his hips as if confronting some malefactor.

Ally stared straight back, refusing to be cowed when she'd done nothing wrong. 'Looking at the view.'

Surely that was evident. Yet that frown made him look as if he'd caught her stealing the family silver. Was that what he thought? That she'd come to ransack his home?

Was he going to tell her next that she was a thief as well as a liar? Ally braced herself.

'You shouldn't be out of bed.' He stalked across the room and she marvelled at the way those long legs ate up the space so quickly.

Another reminder of his sheer physicality. She'd been aware of it from the first and, despite her wariness—okay, her dislike of the man who so obviously disliked her—she kept noticing.

Her chin hiked up to keep him in view as he stopped before her. Despite pride and logic, and all her determination, it wasn't just dislike she felt.

Something stirred deep within. A frisson of sensation that she had no name for and was glad she didn't. Because the feeling was *soft* when she needed to be hard and on her guard around him.

'The doctor said I needed rest and quiet. I've been resting all day.'

Those black eyebrows crammed close and she was reminded again of some angry god, about to hurl a thunderbolt because his temper had got out of hand.

What would Angelo Ricci be like in a temper? Her pulse quickened but with excitement, not fear.

Was she a secret thrill-seeker? Or a blatant adrenaline junkie? What else could explain the sudden impulse to goad him?

Ally tamped it down. See? She was a sensible woman.

'What if you'd fallen? What if you'd hit your head again?'

Surprised, she searched his grim features. Was that concern in his voice? She dismissed the idea. He was probably worried that if she hurt herself again it would look bad, as if he'd failed to care for her.

'But I didn't. I was perfectly fine.'

Well, not perfectly. She'd been wobbly and wondered if she'd make it to the bathroom and back, but her need had been urgent and there'd been no one around to ask for help.

Ally's brow puckered as another thought surfaced. 'Did I dream it or did you stay with me through the night?'

She had vague memories of a dark, broad-shouldered presence in the shadows beyond the dimmed bedside lamp. Of firm hands supporting her as she sipped thirstily at a glass of water.

Ally had assumed it was a dream but, seeing the slight smudges beneath his dark eyes, she wondered. If so, it was an unexpected kindness.

He shrugged. 'Someone needed to keep an eye on you. Rosetta took the day shift.'

So she had. Not that Rosetta had stayed, but she'd looked in so often Ally began to wonder if that explained her dour attitude. The housekeeper would have plenty to do without checking on her every twenty minutes.

'Thank you. That's very kind.'

His eyes widened and she had the impression he was surprised. Because he didn't think she had the manners to thank him for his efforts? Or because he didn't usually do anything to elicit gratitude?

She wished she understood him. But not as much as she wished she understood herself.

Ally didn't like this man because he was abrasive and unfriendly. Because he knew things about her she didn't and seemed determined to look down on her.

Yet something inside her sparked into life when he was near. She felt a surge of energy and curiosity then. Strangely, despite everything, she felt safe.

Maybe she had some faint memory of him carrying her from the beach. The doctor had mentioned that and, having seen the steep drop to the beach, it made her appreciate Angelo Ricci's physical power and determination.

'What are you thinking about?'

Ally realised she was staring into that chiselled face as if she'd never seen a man before.

Suddenly she laughed. As far as her brain was concerned, she *hadn't*. Angelo Ricci and the nice doctor were the only men she could remember seeing.

Was that why he drew her gaze like a magnet?

Had she imprinted on him, like an orphaned duckling attaching itself to the first living being it encountered? The idea was ridiculous.

Yet awareness skittered through her, tightening her skin and beading her nipples. Ally snatched in a stifled gasp.

This couldn't be...*attraction*, could it? That was the last thing she needed.

Her laughter caught in something like a sob and she wrenched her head round towards the stormy sea.

What would be worse, discovering she really was attracted to this sour man? Or that her reaction was nothing special and she was easily attracted to any man?

Ally blinked as the backs of her eyes prickled.

She felt totally lost. Like a tiny rowing boat adrift on those monstrous waves outside. There was nothing to cling to. Nothing certain except this room, this man, and the fact that she wasn't welcome.

'Alexa—'

'Ally!' She sniffed. 'Please. I prefer it.' Though it still didn't feel like her real name.

Would she ever know what that was?

Despite the doctor's assurances she worried she might never recover her memory.

'Ally.' From her peripheral vision she saw Angelo Ricci hunker down beside her. 'What's wrong?'

A laugh escaped her tight throat. It was jagged and bitter and revealed too much but, beneath the stoicism she'd aimed for, her emotions ran too close to the surface.

'What's wrong? Apart from the fact I have no memory, I don't know who I am or how I got here. I don't know *anything*.'

Hearing her rising panic she snapped her mouth shut and looked away, transfixed by a single ray of light that beamed down through the roiling clouds. It illuminated a tiny disc of dark water, turning it to pewter. Yet as she watched the tiny gap closed, the clouds bunching together, and everything turned dark again.

Would the clouds of confusion in her brain ever pull back enough for her to remember the past? Ally looked down to find her hands clenched in the long tails of the fine cotton shirt covering her thighs.

His shirt? Probably. The idea spilled heat into her cheeks and across her breasts. Suddenly she was hyper-conscious that she wore nothing beneath the oversized shirt she'd been using as a nightie. She smoothed it down her thighs then hitched the open collar high at her throat.

'The doctor is convinced you'll get your memory back. You just have to give it time.'

Angelo grabbed the other armchair near the window, turning it to face her rather than the balcony. An instant later he was blocking her view, sitting right in her line of sight.

'What if he's wrong? What if it never returns?'

He spread his hands in a gesture that spoke of patience and acceptance. Qualities that felt elusive right now.

'We cross that bridge when we come to it.'

'We?' She frowned. 'There's no *we*. Just me.'

His eyes held hers. Dark brown eyes that looked impenetrable and at the same time full of a knowledge she could barely guess at. She looked for sympathy. What she saw, or thought she saw, was wariness.

It made her push back in her chair.

He didn't *want* to sympathise, she realised. For some reason he was determined to keep her at arm's length.

'You'll be okay—'

'Don't let me keep you,' she said, maintaining an even tone despite the whirlpool of despair and fear threatening to suck her under. 'I've already taken up enough of your time.' She paused, searching for something else to hurry him on his way. 'You're right. Of course I'll be okay.'

Angelo looked her in the eye and tried to convince himself she was right. That she didn't need his help.

Because she had to be faking this so-convenient amnesia. He understood she'd had some sort of accident but she could only have come here as part of a deliberate scheme. To win his sympathy so he'd take her back?

Surely even Alexa couldn't believe that. Nothing on this earth would make him welcome her into his life. Logic told him she'd capitalised on circumstances to elicit his sympathy and let her stay. The storm had played into her hands. His island retreat was just that, a retreat. It wasn't the sort of place she'd visit on her way somewhere else. Which meant she'd sought him out.

Yet, seeing the anxiety in her shadowed eyes, the frown pleating her forehead and the nervous way she chewed the corner of her mouth, Angelo felt a tendril of doubt. He tried to recall her doing that in the past and failed. It was a new thing. Maybe a deliberate tactic.

He knew her acting skills of old, which was why he couldn't trust this woman. And yet…

Did he imagine that her face was slightly more rounded than he remembered? She *was* the same woman, wasn't she? Of course she was. Apart from her looks and voice, that eye colour was unique.

She looked away, fumbling to do up the top button of his shirt.

There it was again. Another reaction from her that didn't fit expectations. The Alexa he'd known had been proud of her body and loved to flaunt it. She'd thrived on male adulation, even when she was supposed to be in a committed relationship.

Was it possible she wasn't faking the amnesia?

It would take more than that to convince him.

'Alexa… Ally.' Angelo made his tone easy, gentle even. As if he had no suspicions about her motives. He'd treat her as what she ostensibly was, a chance met visitor. He'd give her sanctuary then send her on her way. 'You're safe here. The doctor expects you to begin regaining your memory soon. When that happens I'll help you get back to where you belong.'

Which, thankfully, was far from here.

Angelo ignored the traitorous little jab of heat to his belly as she stirred, her shapely legs sliding against each other as she tucked them further under the chair. Ostensibly the move was decorous, hiding some of her bare skin. In reality it reminded him of the fact she was clearly naked beneath his shirt. A fact he refused to dwell on.

'Thank you. I'm sure that will be a relief for you.'

'And for you,' he said easily. 'I can't imagine what it must be like, unable to remember anything.'

Her chin lifted in a movement that was suddenly completely familiar. Relief trickled through him. Occasionally,
despite logic, Angelo found himself wondering if he was
mistaken about his uninvited guest. But that movement was
pure Alexa. Once upon a time he'd found it endearing. Later
it had presaged obstinacy.

'It's unpleasant in the extreme.' Then, just as abruptly,
the fight left her and her shoulders slumped. 'You know my
name. Surely you can tell me more?'

'I have no idea what you were doing here. I hadn't seen you
for a very long time and I never expected to see you again.'

That was the way Angelo preferred it.

He watched her head rear back as she digested the finality
in his tone. Good. If she thought by staying here she might
worm her way onto his good side, the sooner she realised her
mistake the better.

'But you know more, don't you? Anything you can tell
me will help.'

She wrapped her arms around her middle, leaning towards
him as if hanging on anything he might contribute. As if she
didn't notice the way the gesture pulled his shirt across her
breasts, revealing tight nipples and surprisingly lush curves.

Angelo breathed out slowly and told himself he was too
canny to be taken in by the obvious ploy.

He'd play her game, for now. She was injured and there
was nowhere for her to go on this privately held island. No
hotels. Not even guesthouses. The locals, whether born and
bred here over generations, or rich incomers who'd bought
into the exclusive location as an escape from the rat race,
valued privacy.

'You're Australian.' She nodded, her bright eyes fixed on
his. 'When I met you you'd been in Europe for a while, modelling. Not top-of-the-range couture collections but sports-
wear, swimwear and lingerie.'

Something flickered across her face and her mouth turned
down a little. Maybe she wasn't pleased at being reminded
she hadn't hit the heights she'd aspired to.

'And my family? Where in Australia did I come from?'

Angelo shook his head. 'No idea. You never mentioned where you came from and said you had no close family.'

She'd been close-mouthed about both, airily saying she had no ties and no wish to live in the past. But she'd later mentioned her parents were dead and she was an only child.

In the early days he'd suspected some family tragedy, for he'd caught a flash of what looked like pain in her expression, so he hadn't pushed for details. After all, he knew how deep pain could run, losing his father too early.

'I see. What else? Where did I live?'

'You shared a flat in Rome but you gave it up. There was some disagreement with your flatmate.'

'Was she another model? Do you know her name? Maybe I can trace her.'

Angelo shook his head. Was Alexa really going to persist with this charade?

What if it's not a charade? What if she really has lost her memory?

The idea unsettled him. He didn't want to feel sympathy for this woman who'd barged through his life like a wrecking ball. Even now he was itching to get up and leave. It took all his control to maintain a polite façade. But he'd promised the doctor he'd look after her. Angelo would do whatever it took to get her physically mended so she could go and never come back.

'No idea. But your flatmate wasn't a woman. He was your lover.'

Her eyes widened and her mouth sagged and, if he didn't know better, he'd think he'd shocked her.

As if she couldn't imagine herself with a man. The irony pulled his lips into a grimace.

'My lover?'

'*Ex*-lover. You moved out. Took all your things.'

'I see.'

She nibbled her bottom lip again and Angelo felt his groin tighten. Did she know the action drew attention to the sweet shape of her mouth? It was one of the things he'd first noticed about her. That and the beckoning light in her stunning eyes.

And her body, lithe and seductive.

Despite himself, Angelo's attention dropped to her breasts, straining against his shirt. There was something disquieting about the fact it was *his* shirt she wore against her skin. The knowledge elicited an all too familiar tension in his belly. Sexual tension that had once led him to drop his guard, with calamitous consequences.

His gaze skimmed the indent of her waist, accentuated by her folded arms.

Alexa had changed since he'd seen her. She'd gained weight, her feminine curves more pronounced, though she was still slender.

Shocked at the direction of his thoughts, he snapped his gaze up, but she hadn't noticed his lapse. That, in itself, gave him pause. Once Alexa had been totally attuned to every nuance of his expression, voice and body. She'd studied him and learned to anticipate his desires.

Angelo sat straighter, resolution starching his spine.

Swiftly he catalogued the other changes in her.

She looked as young and fresh-faced as she had five years ago. But she did her hair differently, not sleek but loose and casual around her shoulders. It was a different shade too, dark honey instead of pale gilt, and there was a sprinkling of freckles across her face. He didn't remember those before.

She pushed a hand through her hair and he noticed her nails, short and unvarnished. So different to the long nails she'd once favoured, their colour changing to complement each new, expensive outfit.

She moved and suddenly Angelo found himself staring into wide eyes that were an impossible, entrancing shade of blue verging into purple. A shade he'd seen in no one but her.

His pulse thudded. She was a stunning woman despite her character flaws.

Which proved you couldn't judge on appearances.

'How do we know each other, Angelo?'

His attention caught on the way she said his name. Alexa had always prided herself on her perfect Italian accent. Now she said his name slightly differently. But then she was pretending she didn't speak Italian.

Or was that real, not pretence?

Either way it was far too confronting having her in his home. Deep-seated emotions bombarded him. Shame, regret and self-disgust at how he'd let her dupe him, and through him the people he loved.

He'd promised his dying father that he'd care for and protect his mother and sister, but he'd failed them and his *papà*. He'd broken that sacred trust when he'd allowed this woman to hurt them. His gut clenched as he fought nausea at how he'd let them all down.

'You need to rest.' His voice was rough. 'We'll continue this later when you're stronger.'

'No!' No weakness in her now. She was all determination. '*Tell* me. Did we know each other well?'

He folded his arms and looked her in the eye. He'd had enough.

'In some ways we knew each other as well as any two people can.' Her eyes rounded in a display of shock that made him want to smash through her ridiculous pretence.

'You were my mistress. Then you were my wife.'

CHAPTER FOUR

ALLY STARED AT the man before her, the man with cold eyes and a grimace on his lips, and felt her gorge rise. The fine hairs along her arms lifted and her nape tightened.

You were my mistress. Then you were my wife.

His tone was dismissive. As if she had no place in the world except in relation to Angelo Ricci.

Through her nausea, bitter amusement surfaced. That was still the case. With her memory gone, reliant on this man, she literally didn't have a life beyond the boundaries of his home.

A wave of terror crashed through her and she gritted her teeth, fighting down distress.

The inimical light in those dark eyes told her he'd been deliberately brutal. That was enough to make her harness what strength she possessed to stare him down.

Did something shift in his expression? Some flicker of emotion?

The very thought seemed inconceivable.

'Your *wife*?'

The word pulled a thread of heat down from her breasts to her belly and lower, to a feminine place that suddenly felt alive.

'Yes.'

'Are we still married?'

The abrupt sideways jerk of his head was eloquent enough, but he made it totally clear. 'Divorced.'

Every syllable dripped disdain.

For her? Or for the fact they'd divorced? Yet looking into those set features she couldn't believe he regretted ending their marriage. He looked anything but lover-like.

Her mouth thinned. 'Is that all you have to say?'

He shrugged. 'Isn't that enough?'

He was right. It was more than enough. Ally sank back in her chair, head spinning and heart thudding.

She had no memory of this man, despite the feeling, once or twice, that she'd seen his face before. Surely if they'd been intimate, she'd remember something?

Her cheeks burned at the thought of being his mistress. What did that entail? Sex on demand, pandering to his every whim? Fire swirled in her belly and she shifted on the padded seat.

Ally tried to imagine wearing glamorous gowns and jewellery, accompanying him to glittering parties. Tried and failed.

Or maybe—the thought made her insides churn—she'd been the sort of mistress to wear thigh-high leather boots and wield a whip.

Except one glance at that proud, stern face assured her that was unlikely. Angelo Ricci didn't look the sort of man to cede power to anyone.

Her head spun. The thought of being intimate with Angelo Ricci unnerved her. Her gaze drifted from the stark male beauty of that disapproving face to wide shoulders and a powerful torso that even now, despite his attitude, made her wish for things she shouldn't. Even his long-fingered hands looked capable and uncompromisingly masculine. As for those strong legs with their bunched thigh muscles straining the denim of his jeans…

Ally gulped as she felt a melting sensation between her legs. Something quivered into life deep inside.

She'd told herself she couldn't imagine herself with this dour man. Yet really she could imagine it too easily. Could almost feel the brush of warm denim and hard muscle beneath the pads of her fingers. Her hands tickled at the thought of touching the olive skin of his forearms with their smattering of dark hair.

As for touching him elsewhere, and being touched by him…

She looked up abruptly and met his eyes. That angry expression was gone, replaced by an expression that made her blood sizzle in her veins. Those dark eyes glittered, alive with something that might have been hunger. Something heated and primal.

Except the next instant it had gone, leaving her feeling… bereft.

His unreadable stare made it clear she'd imagined that momentary blast of longing. Which was all too believable given her malfunctioning mind.

Ally chewed her lip, fighting to get her brain working again. She told herself any fancied attraction to Angelo Ricci was a product of that knock to her head. It couldn't be real.

'You said I was your mistress.' She paused, hating the sourness on her tongue that the word invoked. She had to push herself to get the words out. 'Are you saying you were married before to someone else and I was…with you then?'

His head reared back and the look he gave her was full of disdain. 'Of course not. I'm an honourable man. I'd never break my vows and cheat on my wife.'

Ally's shoulders slumped in relief. The thought of being the other woman in some love triangle was abhorrent. 'So when you say *mistress*…?'

His nostrils flared, emphasising the finely chiselled shape of his nose. 'Maybe you prefer *kept woman*?'

No, she didn't. She hated it.

He implied she'd *sold* herself to him for money. What about her self-respect? Ally couldn't imagine doing anything so venal.

On the other hand, who was she to say what she would have done? She had no memory. Only an instinctive distress at the idea of being any man's paid sexual partner.

What did that mean? Was her mind playing tricks? Was

the sensation that this was all wrong, that she couldn't have done any of this, a subconscious effort at avoidance?

'I see.' Then on a burst of anger she blurted, 'Your word choice says a lot about you.'

He raised his eyebrows in query. 'You think?'

Ally nodded. 'It's deliberately demeaning. You could have said *girlfriend, partner* or *lover*. Instead you chose to be insulting.'

Maybe she'd been an English teacher, spending her days finding meaning in the written word. Or maybe she was simply a woman not used to being insulted and dismissed. Either way, she was grateful for the flash of anger that strengthened her sinews.

She arched her own eyebrows and met his stare, noticing the flex of his jaw and the quick flick of his pulse, as if her needling had struck home. Good.

'You're right.' He nodded stiffly, his discomfort obvious. 'I'd never describe any other lover as my mistress. I've let our history colour my word choice.'

Her skin tightened. She wasn't looking forward to hearing this, but she had to know. 'Go on.'

'We lived together in what we agreed would be a short affair. You preferred to live in luxury at my expense than work, which *did* make you different to my previous lovers. I paid your way and you were particularly pleased when I bought you gifts.'

His tone suggested those gifts were expensive. Ally's stomach dived. The more she discovered about her past, the more she wished it all a bad dream.

She brushed her hands up and down her arms, trying to stimulate blood flow to counteract the chill engulfing her. It was on the tip of her tongue to observe that maybe paying for a woman's companionship was the only way Angelo Ricci could get one to stay.

But he'd just laugh. Even when he looked down his nose at her, he was still a man who drew the eye.

Drew the eye! He was magnificent, dangerous and brooding. He'd attract women like moths to a flame. Until they discovered there was nothing soft or caring beneath that adamantine exterior.

Ally shuddered. 'Thank goodness that's over.'

Dark eyes narrowed on her as if he didn't believe she'd said that.

Let him think what he liked. She had more on her mind than whether Angelo Ricci was happy.

'Yet we married. Surely that means we were in love once?'

'Love?' His deep voice hit a jarring note that grated through her. 'Hardly. You married me for my money.'

It was like a slap to the face. She flinched, absorbing the shock. Yet another shock. When would they end?

His eyes glinted with pure dislike and, finally, Ally understood. That was why he didn't want her here. That was why he was so unfriendly and his housekeeper refused to smile. He thought her a gold-digger who'd tried to take advantage of him.

Ally was torn between disbelief, because that couldn't be who she was, and an absurd desire to say she was sorry. But apologising for something she didn't remember? That meant accepting his words at face value. Surely it took two to break a marriage, just as there were two sides to every story. She was hearing his version of events. What was hers?

She blinked and stared down at her hands, now clasped in her lap. Her head was throbbing again and the edges of her vision blurred. When she moved too fast she felt giddy. But she couldn't stop now. She had to know everything.

'If I was avaricious, why marry me?'

Her ex-husband shot to his feet.

Ex-husband. She still found it incredible.

He swung around to face the window and shoved his hands in the front pockets of his jeans. Ally's gaze caught on the tight curve of his backside in faded denim.

Suddenly the notion of them being together, being intimate, wasn't so difficult to believe. Her throat dried and she swallowed hard.

'It was a mistake. One I regretted almost immediately.'

She opened her mouth then closed it again.

What did it matter now? Did she really want to trawl through every last detail of something that had obviously ended acrimoniously?

She longed for something positive. To hear just one thing about herself that she could build on. To hear of one good quality she had. But she wouldn't get that here.

So far her skills were sex and spending money! If she'd kept this man, who exuded sexual chemistry, happy in bed, happy enough to promote her from mistress to wife, she must be very good at sex.

Ally grimaced and propped her head in her hands.

That *wasn't* what she was hoping for.

Was it totally naïve to think that somewhere in the world she had friends and family who liked her, missed her and worried why she wasn't in contact?

Was it weak to hope that someone cared about her? That she wasn't the black-hearted opportunist he painted?

A day later Angelo hunched against the buffeting wind, prowling the strip of beach that had narrowed with the high seas. The storm's fury had eased briefly and he needed fresh air. Being cooped up in the house with his ex-wife made him feel hemmed in. Even though he only saw her to check she was all right.

She was visibly improving, so hopefully she wouldn't be here long. But that still left the question of why she'd returned.

He kicked a pebble across the pale pink sand, listening to the slap of waves and the roar of the wind.

It was more than claustrophobia he suffered. His feelings were an uncomfortable mix of suspicion, fascination, doubt and guilt.

Suspicion because he knew her too well. He'd be crazy to believe her tale of accidentally washing up on his beach.

Fascination—his breath snagged—*that* was unexpected. Every time he was with her he was aware of her femininity, her feistiness and stoicism, completely at odds with the hatred he'd harboured for years. He admired her spirit and, more worryingly, the curl of her mouth when she smiled unexpectedly or the sound of her voice with its familiar accent that somehow wasn't quite the voice he recalled. As for his response to her flagrantly feminine and alluring body…no, better not to think of that.

Doubt. Now that was a surprise. Because, despite his well-grounded suspicion, he'd begun to wonder if, whatever her original scheme, she really had lost her memory.

She'd asked how he knew her and he'd told her. Then watched the colour flare in her cheeks before receding. Surely that wasn't an act. Her eyes had darkened, pupils too big against those vivid irises. He'd read stress in her restless hands and tense jaw and despite himself he'd felt pity. Perhaps this really was all new to her. He wouldn't bet money on it. Nothing would convince him to trust Alexa again, but maybe he'd been unnecessarily harsh. Certainly he had been if she truly suffered from amnesia.

Which led to guilt. Because he hadn't been gentle or conciliatory but driven by emotion. He'd made no allowance for the fact she was injured and that shamed him.

It wasn't enough to admit that he hated being reminded of their past. Of how easily she'd played him. Their fiasco of a marriage was as much his fault as hers. Because he should have known better.

He had a reputation for clear thinking. For cutting through complex situations. It had helped him turn the family's bank into an international powerhouse. It had helped him support his mother and sister, taking on the mantle of head of the family before his time. Yet still Alexa had deceived him spectacularly. And that had had awful consequences for those he loved.

Setting his jaw, Angelo clambered onto the rock platform at the end of the beach and looked out to sea. Even in this weather it was spectacular, his private slice of heaven.

He turned to go and paused, noticing something wedged

in a crevice. A flash of yellow and aqua. Curious, he climbed down and retrieved it.

It was a long paddle designed for use with a stand-up paddleboard. The logo of a hire store on the mainland was emblazoned on it, a place that rented jet skis and windsurfers to tourists. There was a chunk out of the blade and a crack up to the haft. Not surprising if it had been adrift during the storm.

Or involved in an accident.

The hairs on Angelo's nape stood on end as he wondered what accident might cause such damage.

He thought back to the afternoon before last. To the speedboat racing too close to shore. If someone had been swimming off the beach, or balancing on a paddleboard when it rounded the point…

Surely the boat would have stopped. Unless they hadn't realised there'd been an accident. If Alexa had been coming in to shore and lost her balance in the wake of the boat she could have knocked her head on a submerged rock.

Angelo's blood chilled. It was feasible. If true, she was lucky to be alive.

He spent another half-hour combing the rocks at either end of the beach for signs of a paddleboard, or other detritus. Finally the worsening weather forced him back up the cliff, paddle in hand.

Was that how Alexa had reached the island? She'd have to be proficient to do it and he'd never thought of her as athletic. On the other hand, she'd proved herself capable of anything in pursuit of her goals. Only someone reckless or utterly determined would make for the island with a storm bearing down.

Ten minutes later he was speaking to the owner of the marine rental shop. Yes, they were missing a paddleboard. They'd raised the alarm for a missing tourist but emergency services had been so busy on the coast there'd been no news yet.

No, they didn't have a name for the woman. The owner confirmed it *was* a young woman, his tone proof that she'd been attractive.

She'd rented a locker for her belongings while she was out on the water, but it had revealed nothing useful. They'd opened it to search for evidence of her identity when she hadn't returned. But, unlike every other tourist, she had no luggage or identification with her. There'd been a bag with water, a change of clothes, sun cream and some cash. No credit card, no passport. Not even a hotel room key. Nothing to show her name or where she was staying.

As if she didn't want to be identified.

The thought took hold as the other man expounded on how strange it was that she'd travelled so light. To Angelo, who knew the lengths Alexa would go to in order to get what she wanted, it confirmed his suspicions.

Amnesia or not, his ex was up to no good.

Angelo knocked on the door to her suite but got no answer. He waited and tried again.

'Alexa?' Silence. Yet she couldn't be asleep. Rosetta had spoken with her mere minutes earlier, sitting by the window. He knocked again, concern rising. Had something happened to her? Some medical complication? 'Alexa?'

Turning the handle, he stepped inside. The bedside lamp was on against the afternoon gloom but there was no sign of Alexa. His gaze swung towards the bathroom door as it opened.

A waft of fragrant air preceded her. His nostrils twitched as the scent of neroli reached him, rich and citrusy. Then she was in the doorway, wet hair combed back from her face, her feet bare and body covered past the knees in a white towelling bathrobe.

'You!' She faltered on the threshold, eyes rounding.

As if he didn't have a right to be in his own home. He ignored the fact he'd never normally walk into a guest's suite uninvited, especially a female guest's.

Angelo was about to say he'd worried something had happened to her but stopped himself. Better not to let her know of his concern. The woman he'd known would see that as weakness and twist it to her advantage.

'We need to talk.'

She smoothed back her hair in a gesture that might have signalled vulnerability if it weren't for those flashing eyes and the challenging upward hike of her chin.

'Unless you're in pain. If you need rest...'

See, he could be reasonable.

'I'm fine.'

She stepped into the room and Angelo silently agreed. She looked very fine indeed. Even wrapped in that bulky robe, Alexa was more alluring than he could recall her ever being in a minuscule bikini or lacy lingerie.

Was his mind playing tricks?

Maybe it was the wholesome look that appealed, a contrast to the subtle yet ever-present make-up she'd previously worn. Alexa had always looked polished, prepared for male adulation. At first he'd enjoyed the fact she made an effort to appear her best at all times. Till he realised how fixated she was on her appearance and that there was something lacking beneath her pretty façade. She ruthlessly wielded her looks and femininity like twin blades, determined to win what she wanted at all costs.

Now, with her face bare, she looked stunningly sexy and natural. Her eyelashes were spiked and her cheeks and throat flushed as if she'd been in a hot shower just moments ago. That idea was reinforced as he watched a single drip of water slide down her jaw.

Instantly Angelo had a vision of her naked in the shower. Of water cascading lovingly over the lush body he'd caught glimpses of the last couple of days through one or other of his shirts.

It was *that* intimacy, he decided, the fact she'd been naked but for clothes he'd once worn, that skewed his thinking down this unwanted path.

'Perhaps you'd like to sit.' He gestured to the armchairs near the window.

Instead of accepting his invitation she shook her head. Far from looking weak, she appeared energised. 'I'd rather you told me what you want then leave.'

Her voice was as sharp as a slap to the cheek.

Angelo's jaw clamped but he bit back a retort. It didn't matter if she accepted his olive branch. Still, her response rankled.

'I want to discuss how you got here.'

Her eyes narrowed, fire glinting there as surely as if ignited with a match. It intrigued Angelo. Alexa had always previously hidden her emotions.

'I told you I don't remember. What part of that don't you understand?'

His eyebrows shot up. It was unlike Alexa to show aggression. 'Actually, I have information to share with *you*.'

He folded his arms and watched her frown. She raised a hand and raked a hand back through her hair again. Did he imagine she suddenly looked fragile?

Maybe. Or maybe she was scared he'd discovered something she didn't want uncovered.

'I'm sorry. I shouldn't have snapped. I'm a bit…' She gestured vaguely. 'I'm not at my best.'

Angelo surveyed her for a moment then nodded. 'I understand.'

Strangely, he did. He didn't trust her but if she'd lost her memory totally…

'What have you got to tell me?'

Maybe he had news that would stir recollections.

'I think I know how you got here.'

Ally shoved her hands into the robe's pockets and tried to find her equilibrium. The way he looked at her told her to prepare for some new blow.

What could be worse than yesterday's revelations? She still couldn't get her head around them.

Then there was Angelo's patent dislike. It made her feel tainted and ashamed that anyone should dislike her so much.

At the same time she resented his brutal way of sharing their past. As if he'd enjoyed shocking her.

Ally straightened her spine. At least she'd regained her physical strength, despite some bruising and her scarily blank mind.

Yet she wasn't as confident as she tried to appear while she waited for him to continue. Cooped up in these rooms with no distraction from her thoughts was driving her crazy, leaving her emotions askew.

That had to explain her reaction when she'd seen Angelo in the doorway, looking from the bed to her. Something hot and needy had flared inside. There'd been a gleam in his eyes that spoke of awareness and for an instant she'd felt an answering flash of desire. She assumed it was desire. A dragging weight low in her body and a softening between her thighs.

How could she respond sexually to a man who despised her? Did she have no pride? No self-control?

Ally thought of the picture he'd painted of her and wondered if perhaps she didn't.

Suddenly she wished she'd taken the chair he'd offered. Her brain was whizzing and adrenaline shot around her body, making her poised for flight. Or fight.

And how it was she recognised that, when she didn't recognise her name, she had no idea.

'You came by sea. I've checked locally and there are no reports of a missing foreigner.'

'Go on.' There had to be more. It had always seemed obvious she'd come ashore at his beach.

'I found a paddle in the rocks at the end of the beach. The sort used with stand-up paddleboards.'

Dark eyes narrowed on her as if watching for some infinitesimal reaction. What did he expect? A flash of memory? Her lips tightened. If only…

'You think I paddled from the mainland?'

Her gaze shot to the glass doors onto the balcony where she'd caught a smudge of darkness earlier that might be the mainland. But the weather had closed in again and all she saw was thrashing rain and greyness. But his words jogged no memory. Ally breathed deep, trying to stifle disappointment.

'It's a fair distance but doable for someone fit enough.' His gaze flickered over her, as if assessing her physical fitness, and Ally's skin prickled. It wasn't a sexual look yet she felt hyper-sensitive to his scrutiny.

'Okay.' She made herself focus. 'If that's the case then I was staying on the mainland. If we search—'

'Already done.' His gaze turned laser sharp, making Ally wish she wore something more than the plush robe against her bare skin. 'I traced the guy who rented out a paddleboard for cash to a woman who meets your description. He'd already reported you missing to the authorities.'

Ally caught her breath, her hand going to her throat as anticipation swelled. This felt like progress at last. 'They've traced where I was staying?'

Surely, once she returned there and was reunited with her belongings, it would jog her memory.

Eagerly, she moved closer, only stopping when she caught a delicious hint of male scent, warm skin, citrus and cedarwood and realised what she'd done. She was a mere arm's length from the man who might be her host yet felt like her enemy.

Ally planted her feet on the antique carpet, refusing to back away. She wouldn't be cowed by him.

She breathed deep, telling herself she was intrigued to be able to identify the components of the scent, including a hint of pepper. This *wasn't* a response to him as an attractive man. It was her discovering more about herself.

Maybe she was a perfumer? Or worked in a department store, selling expensive colognes? Excitement stirred.

'Now that's the interesting thing, Alexa. There was no trace of a missing stranger staying locally. Your name on the rental book was an unreadable scrawl too, though it started with an A. They checked the locker where you left your belongings but there was nothing to identify you. Just a set of clothes and cash.'

'Ally. I told you I don't like being called Alexa.' Which was probably why he did it. 'What about a hotel key?'

Angelo shook his head. 'Nothing. It's as if you didn't want to be traceable. As if you carefully planned it that way because you were scheming something.'

She frowned, her mind working furiously. 'That's far-fetched, don't you think?'

He spread his hands, shrugging his shoulders. 'Nothing would surprise me.'

With you. He didn't say it but he didn't need to.

It was merely one more provocation on top of the others—his snarkiness as he'd described their previous relationship, his housekeeper's air of acting under sufferance, the lack of warmth from anyone except the doctor. On top of the terrible clawing fear that maybe she'd never regain her memory, it was too much.

Ally stepped forward right into his personal space, and poked him in the chest.

A surge of power filled her as she saw his eyes widen. It felt wonderful to take the initiative for a change.

'You're unbelievable! Do you know that? I'm the *victim* here but still you can't accept it.'

She pushed again into that hard chest, wishing she could shove him back, or make him feel some of the pain she'd experienced.

She wanted…she didn't know what she wanted precisely, but letting her emotions off the leash felt glorious.

'So what if I didn't leave a credit card in a locker? That's not a crime. And it's not proof of a conspiracy. Or are you so totally caught up in your own importance you think the world revolves around *you*? That the only reason I could possibly visit the area is because of you?'

She was panting, her breath coming in sharp tugs, but she didn't care. She looked into those liquid dark eyes and some devil urged her on. For the first time she felt alive and full of sparkling certainty instead of inhabiting a shadowy half-life.

'For all you know I was visiting a friend here.'

'No one has come forward to report their friend missing.'

Ally rolled her eyes. 'Maybe I rented a villa. Maybe I came here for sun, sea and relaxation. Maybe I didn't even think about the possibility *you'd* be here. Did you think of that?'

'Impossible.' Long fingers closed around hers, flattening them against his chest to stop her prodding.

Ally frowned, registering a heavy thud and realising it must be the beat of his heart.

'Why is it impossible?'

His mouth caught at the corner in a grimace and when he spoke it was in a whisper that scraped across her bones. 'Because of this.'

Then his head lowered and his mouth took hers.

CHAPTER FIVE

THERE WAS A moment when she could have pulled back or pushed him away. But she didn't.

Because she didn't want to.

The knowledge hit her as warm lips covered hers implacably yet with something curiously like gentleness. This was no hard mashing of teeth against lips.

This didn't feel predatory or like domination.

It felt…perfect, she realised as her eyes shut and her mouth opened and she leaned into him as if this was what she'd wanted all along.

Maybe it was.

The thought shivered through her.

Maybe the jittery uncertainty and the way she'd baited him were because she needed to discover what it felt like, being kissed by Angelo Ricci.

Held by him, for now his arms roped around her, hauling her close so she felt his solid heat all down her front. Every bit of him felt unforgiving, pure muscle and bone, and utterly spellbinding.

Or maybe that was because he worked magic on her.

Who'd have thought the thin-lipped mouth that had looked sardonic and disapproving could feel so wonderful?

Ally sighed and arched her neck as she leaned closer, cataloguing the rich taste of coffee and potent male. It was heady, addictive.

Did she subconsciously remember and crave physical contact with Angelo?

She should be horrified or at least embarrassed.

She wasn't. Instead she wallowed in sensation. The contrast of his hard maleness against her own body, which felt suddenly melting and soft. The taste of him as his tongue danced and slid against hers. The tang of his scent in her nostrils, the heavy pound of his throbbing heart beneath her now splayed hands. The easy, yet thorough way his mouth seduced hers.

Were kisses always like this?

Ally's head spun as she tried and failed to grasp at a comparison. She had none. To all intents and purposes this was her first kiss. She recalled none that had gone before, not even a hint of memory.

Surely she'd have remembered something so wonderful?

If kissing Angelo was like this, what would it be like to make love with him?

His hand caressed her cheek, cupping her jaw and angling her head for better access. Abruptly she lost her train of thought as she eddied into a whirlpool of bliss.

Her hands crept up his powerful chest and circled around his neck. His hair was short at the back, longer on top and silky to the touch.

Ally heard a sound, a gruff, low sound that dragged at her nipples and lower, at her pelvis. It took a moment to realise it was Angelo, the sound a rough growl from the back of his throat.

Delight shimmered through her and a new sense of purpose and power. For the first time since she'd woken on this island Ally felt strong, almost invincible. The sound of his desire did that to her. The proof of his hunger.

As if kissing Angelo, and discovering he shared the same need, made her feel whole. More than whole. Right.

It was the most extraordinary, unexpected feeling. And she couldn't get enough of it.

Ally murmured encouragement against his lips as she

threaded her fingers through his hair, shuffling still closer, discovering a ridge of potent hardness against her belly and—

Strong fingers settled on her upper arms and pushed her away. It took a moment to realise what was happening as she clung, limpet-like and lost in wonder.

Finally she blinked open heavy eyelids, her breathing ragged and her body feeling as if she'd run a mile. And wanted to run more.

Angelo's eyes were so dark she couldn't distinguish iris from pupil. He stared back intently, his hair rumpled and sexy, his lips parted and skin pulled tight over those amazing bones.

He looked like a fallen angel, dark, sensuous and utterly beguiling. Some hitherto dormant part of her brain came abruptly to life and she realised that was what his name meant. *Angel*. But definitely a fallen angel.

Ally sighed. If he weren't holding her from him she'd have lifted her hands to the back of his skull and pulled his head back to hers.

As it was, it took long, long moments of gasping breaths to come down from the sensual high where he'd taken her.

Tiny shudders ran under her skin, down her thighs and between them, across her nipples and up her backbone. Every part of her quivered with what she could only assume was unsated sexual hunger.

Her gaze dropped to his mouth, his lips darker than before and parted as he too dragged in great gulps of air.

That was a relief. At least she wasn't alone in feeling this way.

'Is it always like this?' Ally didn't have time to censor the words. She needed to understand.

'Sorry?' Sleek dark eyebrows scrunched as if he couldn't make sense of a simple question.

'Between us. Is it always like this?'

Emotions flickered across his taut features. So quickly she couldn't pin them down. Finally he shook his head. 'It was just a kiss.'

Just a kiss?

She felt as if he'd turned her inside out. Or, more accurately, as if together they'd soared close to the sun.

His gaze shifted from hers and Ally realised he was lying. Or at least avoiding a direct answer.

'What are you scared of, Angelo?'

That dragged his attention back to her. 'Scared? Me?'

He made a scoffing noise but it wasn't nearly as convincing as that deep-throated groan of pleasure that even now swirled in the back of her mind. It had been the most glorious sound.

'Yes, you. If it was only a kiss why avoid answering? It's a simple enough question.'

For a second, gazes locked, Ally felt the connection they'd shared mere moments ago. Even his hands on her arms softened, his thumbs stroking through the plush material of her robe as she canted towards him, feeling the thick fabric graze her bare skin.

Then, abruptly, Angelo let her go and stepped back. A long pace that put an acre of distance between them.

His eyelids lowered as if to conceal the expression glittering there as he surveyed her.

It did no good. She *felt* the intensity of that stare.

If the connection between them had always been so strong, it must have taken something incredible to sever their marriage.

Slowly he shook his head. 'I should never have kissed you. It was a mistake. Especially since you seem to have read too much into a simple kiss—'

'No! Don't lie.' Ally folded her arms over her chest and tried to ignore the scratch of fabric across her nipples. 'It wasn't a simple kiss. You said it yourself before you kissed me. You said I couldn't have come here by accident because of this…' she waved her arm between them 'this…thing between us.'

'You can put that down to the emotional baggage we share. Our relationship is definitely over. Though by turning up here it seems you have trouble accepting that.'

'It doesn't feel over.' She jutted her chin and dared him to deny it.

'Okay.' He lifted one shoulder as if trying to dislodge a little stiffness. 'I admit I was curious after all this time. But it's not an experiment I want to repeat.'

No, because you got burned. Because the fire between us is anything but gone, no matter what you say.

'The past is the past,' he insisted, and Ally wondered if he was trying to persuade her or himself. 'There's nothing here for you any more. I'm not interested in you. I don't want you any more.'

Liar.

His unblinking stare and belligerent stance were a masquerade to hide the fact he *had* wanted her just moments ago. She couldn't have imagined that.

Anyone seeing him from a distance would be convinced by his show of disdain. Not Ally. She'd felt the need welling inside him. Heard it, experienced it at a primal level that left no room for doubt. She knew they shared something powerful. A longing he fought with all his considerable determination. Even now she felt the golden shimmer of anticipation in the air between them.

'Maybe you're right,' she said finally. If she wanted answers she had to play his game. 'But the emotions run hot and heavy between us.' She watched his eyes flare but he said nothing. 'Help me understand what's going on so I don't... misinterpret things again. Tell me what happened.'

Angelo looked into eyes the colour of lilac in spring and felt something shift within him. A momentary weakening, he assured himself. It had been a long, long time since he'd fallen for this woman's lies. He wouldn't do it again. He'd learned from his mistake.

So what was that kiss if not weakness?

And why was the compulsion not just to kiss her, but possess her totally, stronger than anything he could recall?

Surely he'd never felt like this about her before?

Alexa had been available and eager to please. She hadn't loved him nor he her. He wasn't even sure he was capable of that, because he'd never yet felt about a woman the way his parents had felt for each other.

He'd witnessed their love and assumed, one day, he'd feel the same about someone, until he'd seen his mother almost destroyed by her adored husband's death. Since then he'd been wary of romance. He couldn't bear to risk the shattering pain of losing his other half.

Losing his father had been grief enough, compounded by the need to fulfil his promise to care for his mother and sister as well as the family bank. That had stretched him so thin for so long he'd been almost glad to put barriers between himself and the women he dated. He'd had no emotional energy to spare for anything more than short-term affairs firmly anchored in sex with no other expectations.

Yet he remembered his mother's romantic tale about locking eyes on his father and knowing instantly that he was *the one*.

The one!

If his ex-wife was the one, it was the one major disaster in his life.

The one mistake he'd never forget.

The one woman he'd never trust again.

Which made his actions totally bizarre. He'd kissed her out of frustration and found himself falling into... He had no word for it. Angelo refused to countenance ideas like *bliss* or *desire*. Not with her.

Though he knew he'd spend a sleepless night trying to explain why kissing her now had felt new and different and compelling. As if there was something more than convenient sex between them.

'You want to know about the divorce?' His voice sounded strained and he realised he spoke through a clenched jaw.

'It would help.'

Angelo doubted it, but if it meant she kept her distance...

'Why don't you take a seat?'

After all, she was still recuperating.

'I'm fine. I'd rather you just told me.'

'We met in Rome, at a party.'

She nodded, eyes bright, hands clasped together as if eager for more.

Because she had no memories of the past? Or because she hoped to open up communication between them and wheedle her way back into his world? He wished he knew. Every time he thought he did, she made him doubt.

'We went back to my place that night.'

Her eyes rounded and she blinked. If Angelo didn't know better he'd even believe she blushed, but it had to be a trick of the light. His ex wasn't shy about sex. Far from it.

'And then?'

He shrugged. 'You stayed. I had business in Rome. A few days later, when I came here for a summer holiday, you came too.'

It had seemed simple. He'd been working even harder than usual and had looked forward to a short break. Alexa had been fun at first and easy company.

'And I stayed? As simple as that?' Her brow furrowed as if wondering about commitments and work obligations. Five years ago none of that had mattered to her.

'Yes, you loved it here. The sea and relaxed lifestyle.'

She'd seemed genuinely happy. In retrospect Angelo was sure it hadn't been merely the chance to latch onto him as a meal ticket.

Alexa, no—she wanted to be Ally—frowned and looked towards the sea. 'I assume it's beautiful in good weather.'

'There's nowhere like it. Tourists come from the other side of the world to visit the Amalfi Coast and Capri.'

Fortunately fewer made it out to this smaller island, but the climate, architecture, scenery and food were the best in the world as far as Angelo was concerned.

His father's family had come from here generations ago and some of his most precious memories, of when his father was still alive, centred around summers holidaying in the region. Those halcyon days were the reason he'd bought this estate when he wanted a private escape.

'Okay, I loved it here.' Her gaze met his then danced away and he heard an unspoken question. Had she loved him, or he her?

His mouth firmed. The sooner he disabused her of that fantasy, the better.

'There was no great romance, if that's what you're thinking, Ally.' He paused, tasting her new name on his tongue. Strange how easily it came. 'We weren't in love.'

'Okay.' She looked doubtful but nodded. 'So it was a casual fling?'

'Something like that. I wasn't looking for a life partner.'

At twenty-nine he'd had more than enough to cope with at the helm of the family bank. His father had left a gaping hole and it had taken everything Angelo had to take his place and face down the doubters who thought the Ricci kid couldn't handle the job. That, and the need to prop up his grieving family, meant Angelo had had precious little time for a personal life.

Now those doubters were eating their words, and happily raking in profits as the bank outperformed most financial institutions, despite recent seismic shifts in the sector.

Ally wrinkled her nose in a way he'd noticed once or twice. The effect was…cute. Not in keeping with the sophisticated image she used to project.

Because her injury had affected her and she wasn't so good at maintaining that image? Or had she changed over the years? Curiosity stirred.

'Why did we marry if we weren't in love?'

She made it sound as if no one married for any other reason which, given their history, was laughable.

'Because you came to me with proof you were pregnant.'

It was like setting off a bomb. She goggled up at him, her face changing colour as she swayed on her feet.

Angelo almost reached out to steady her but she found her footing and straightened her shoulders. He watched her hand slide across her belly. Was that a conscious gesture, designed to convince him she couldn't remember?

This constant doubt messed with his head. He turned and paced away, swivelling round to find her not looking at him but into space. She looked bewildered. And bereft.

He marched back, hating the way her expression made him feel.

'No, you're not a mother and you didn't lose the child.' Belatedly he realised his words were too abrupt but instinct urged him to eliminate any doubt in her mind as soon as possible.

Slowly her head turned and her eyes sought his. 'It was a mistake, then? I wasn't pregnant?'

Angelo felt her confusion and shock and almost reached out to take her hands. She looked in need of support.

Hell! It was only a couple of days since she'd washed up on the beach. Guilt bit him. He wasn't managing this well.

'Come.'

He ushered her to the armchair and watched her subside abruptly, as if her knees gave way.

When she was settled he took the chair opposite.

'There was no baby.'

She opened her mouth to question him but Angelo raised his hand. Better if she just let him tell the story.

'You'd been here for six weeks. I'd had to return to the mainland to work after a couple of weeks but you stayed on. I commuted, staying here every weekend and working a couple of days a week from here. But in all that time you didn't leave.'

Her brows twitched as if she didn't understand the significance of that, but it was something Angelo had checked and double-checked, given what happened later. Nor had she had any visitors.

'Then one day you travelled to the mainland for an appointment. A medical appointment.'

He paused, taking in the way Ally leaned forward as if eager for more. Did she really not know?

'When I saw you that evening you were shocked but excited. Somehow, despite being on the pill, you'd got pregnant but you hadn't told me of your suspicions because you thought it couldn't happen. Then you showed me the foetal scan taken that day with your name on it, and a letter outlining your follow-up appointments with a gynaecologist.'

Angelo grimaced at the sour tang filling his mouth. 'Marriage wasn't on my radar but I love my family and I know my duty. I knew too that I'd love my child, no matter how it was conceived.'

A pang of regret pierced him. Would he ever know what it was to care for a child of his own? His lifestyle, reinforced by the lesson of distrust that he'd learned from this woman, made it less likely.

'We married out of *duty*?'

Her voice sounded small and wary and Angelo narrowed his eyes, trying to read her expression.

'What's wrong with that?' He frowned. 'I believed myself responsible for a new life coming into the world. I couldn't walk away from that.'

She surveyed him silently and Angelo had the feeling she was weighing him up. What did she see?

'Even if it meant marrying someone you didn't love?'

He hitched one shoulder. 'You think I should have chosen personal preference over fatherly responsibility?'

Ally sat back. 'Marriage isn't a necessity between parents these days. Or am I wrong?' Her brow twitched as if she grappled with the question. 'What you're talking about doesn't sound like a recipe for a happy marriage.'

Angelo snorted. 'You're right there.' But not for the reasons she implied. 'Yet, far from having doubts about marriage, you jumped at the idea.'

He should have seen that as a warning and taken his time. Instead he'd been young and firmly focused on his duty to his unborn child. He'd been inspired by his own father, determined to be the sort of father his own had been.

Though he and Alexa didn't love each other, he'd told himself they could work to create a nurturing family for their child. Having seen grief turn his mother into a shadow of herself, he'd even welcomed the fact that their marriage would be based on necessity rather than romantic attachment. He would love his child, that was enough.

He'd been conceited enough to believe he was in control of the situation, never doubting he was doing the right thing in offering marriage. Angelo shook off the thoughts. 'We married quickly and privately but it didn't last long. Within months I discovered it had been a lie. You weren't pregnant.'

'I *what*?'

He shrugged, the movement tugging at the rigid muscles of his shoulders and neck. 'There was no pregnancy. You'd faked it, and the so-called proof from the doctor.'

He, who'd thought himself awake to the ways of the world, had been sucked in by her lies. That had been a blow to his ego and more, he'd actually grieved the loss of a baby who'd never been real.

The news had shattered his self-belief. Already stressed by the challenge of proving himself professionally to a board and financial pundits waiting for him to fail, the realisation he'd been duped so completely, and about something so important, had made him question his judgement more than anything else could have.

Ally gaped at him, mouth working, and he realised he'd had enough. He had to end this quickly.

'Your plan was to fake a miscarriage but you were found out. Rosetta suspected things weren't what they seemed. When I confronted you and you realised you couldn't get away with lying you admitted it. For a while you tried to pretend you'd lied because you were in love and desperate to be with me. But you weren't convincing.' He paused, watching his words sink in. 'You wanted me for the money. The lifestyle. The husband who'd support you in style so you never had to work again.'

'Maybe I *was* in love.' She scowled at him. 'Maybe you misjudged me and it was all a terrible mistake.'

Bitterness filled him. Angelo had experienced love with his family and knew what he'd shared with her was too shallow to deserve the name.

He looked into Ally's apparently earnest eyes and felt himself wishing things could have been different. That *they'd* been different. Not because she could ever be the sort of woman he could love, but because for so long he'd felt empty inside.

Maybe it was time to make changes in his life, forget casual affairs and search for something more satisfying. Because after all these years he finally admitted he wanted something more.

The truth that he'd avoided for years was that he'd run scared of meaningful relationships with a woman.

Angelo remembered his grief when his father had died and he'd witnessed grief almost destroy his mother. He'd shunned anything that might bring him such pain, like a relationship that might make him vulnerable because he cared too much. He'd stuck to shallow sexual relationships because it seemed safer.

The irony was that policy had led to his affair with Alexa. In a twist of fate, by holding himself back from the possibility of a real relationship, he'd fallen into the trap set by a woman who saw only his bank balance. She'd targeted him because he could give her a life of luxury and because of that the people he loved had suffered.

Because of *his* error of judgement.

'It wasn't a mistake.' His voice was gruff. 'It was a calculated lie.'

She frowned. 'Maybe I was trying to get your attention the only way I could. If I loved—'

'Enough!' He refused to let her bandy that word about. 'Don't try to rewrite history. You didn't love me. You admitted it when I challenged you. In fact you seemed pleased at the way you'd fooled me.'

He'd been left feeling that, far from experiencing unrequited love, Alexa's feelings towards him and men in general were much more negative.

Now he watched her stunning eyes grow wide. If this was an act, she was impressive.

'So we divorced. You've never set foot in one of my homes since the day I discovered the truth about you, and that's how I prefer it. We've had no contact since.'

CHAPTER SIX

ALLY STARED IN the bathroom mirror, trying to read something, anything, into the image she saw there.

But, like mirrors the world over, it gave no clue to her character. She saw an ordinary woman with hair that in today's bright sunlight looked dark blonde instead of light brown. Her mouth was pinched and there were shadows under her eyes but those spoke of tiredness and stress, not personality.

The only noteworthy thing about her was the colour of her eyes. The vivid blue-purple colour of jacaranda blossom.

Yet even that unusual shade didn't spark any insights.

You've never set foot in one of my homes since the day I discovered the truth about you, and that's how I prefer it.

Ally forced down bile at the memory of Angelo's words yesterday. They were engraved in her brain, especially after a night when she'd tossed and turned, fruitlessly trying to switch off her thoughts long enough to get some rest.

Just her luck that a brain that couldn't remember anything earlier than a few days ago should have perfect recall, not just of his words but Angelo's tone and expression as he'd said them.

As if he tasted something disgusting on his tongue.

As if he never wanted to be reminded of their shared past.

Ally couldn't blame him. She was disgusted too.

Her skin crawled when she thought of faking a pregnancy to get a man to marry her. Her mind kept shying away from what Angelo had said, that she'd done it for purely mercenary reasons. But even if that weren't the case, even if she'd acted out of love and the need to be with him, that didn't excuse her actions.

How could she have done that?

How could she have thought it a reasonable thing to do yet be so horrified by it now? Did that mean she'd changed? Or was her dismay due to the fact she'd been found out?

Surely not. Ally just couldn't imagine doing anything so devious or venal. But perhaps her mind was playing tricks and one day soon she'd get her memory back and discover he wasn't the only man she'd tried to dupe.

She wrapped her arms around herself, shivering.

No wonder Angelo didn't want her here.

Now the attitude of his housekeeper, Rosetta, made sense. She'd been here through their relationship. She'd had doubts about the pregnancy and knew Ally had lied. It was a miracle the woman continued to check on her and bring her delicious food. Given her severe demeanour, Ally guessed she was firmly on the side of her employer and saw Ally as trouble.

An hour ago, when Ally had taken her breakfast tray downstairs, she'd seen Rosetta's stare turn piercing with suspicion. As if she thought Ally aimed to wheedle her way into her good graces.

It had taken all Ally's courage to go downstairs. Physically she felt stronger so the stairs weren't a problem, but facing anyone after what Angelo had revealed took more courage than she thought she had.

But Gran had always said that sooner or later you had to face the consequences of your actions and it was better to do it sooner.

Ally was turning towards the bedroom when her brain clicked into action.

She planted a palm on the bathroom counter and leaned in hard, her breath a sharp gasp.

Gran? She had a gran?

Slowly, not daring to hope, she pondered the word. Not Nanna or Grandma but Gran. A definite person.

Yet when she tried to delve deeper and put a face to the name she hit that infuriating blank wall. The misty nothingness that fuzzed her thoughts when she tried too hard to remember.

Frustration rose. She sensed that for the first time she was close to a genuine memory. Yet pushing only stressed her and left her feeling useless and scarily empty.

Looking down at her fingers splayed on the marble counter she told herself it was a positive step. It was something from her past.

She had a grandmother and, by the sound of it, one who was sensible and cared about her. That was a positive, right?

It beat being told she was a scheming liar hands down.

Excitement stirred. It was the first sign she'd had that her memories might be accessible. True, she couldn't recollect a specific event, but knowing she had a gran and remembering her words had to count for something.

Relief shuddered through her. For days she'd feared the doctor was wrong and she might have to face the rest of her life with no memory of her past.

Her eyes squeezed shut as she thought of those fragments of her past she knew about. The bits Angelo had told her. Instantly her stress levels hiked up as tension filled her.

Was it weak, not to want to face this? The constant disapproval? The knowledge she wasn't wanted?

Surely she'd recover more quickly somewhere else. Ally turned to look out at the spectacular view of terraced gardens, cobalt sea and azure sky. The weather had finally cleared. Maybe it was time to find somewhere else to recover.

Angelo tried to focus on emails but his thoughts kept straying.

To last night's kiss. To the yearning that had opened up inside him for more than just the taste of her.

It was utterly, irrefutably wrong to lust after his ex-wife. It should be out of the question. Yet Angelo couldn't lie to himself. He'd been on the brink of taking things too far.

With a woman he couldn't trust.

A woman he'd told himself he hated.

Yet she'd got underneath his skin in ways that defied logic and his determination to keep her at a distance.

Everything about that kiss had felt fresh and wonderful. There'd been no taint of past lies. Instead it had felt like a new beginning. What enticement had she woven around him?

He'd had yet another discussion with the doctor, who was adamant that his ex-wife's memory loss was the result of head trauma. Adamant too that she needed rest and calm.

That, combined with the guilt that clawed Angelo's belly whenever he thought of last night's revelations, left him ill at ease.

He could have handled it better. Yet whenever he dealt with Ally he found himself running on emotion, not logic. Beneath every contact were memories of her bare-faced lies and selfish greed.

She'd hurt not only Angelo but his family. *That* had been unforgivable.

He'd promised his papà he'd look after the family, yet it was *he* who'd introduced Alexa and her poison into their lives. Because of him *they'd* suffered. Angelo had failed them, breaking his deathbed promise to the man he'd admired above all others. That knowledge carved a gash through his soul.

His mamma had been thrilled at the prospect of a *bambino*. She'd come alive for the first time since Angelo's father died, finally focusing on the future not the past.

His heart had lightened and he'd found himself for the first time thinking about a family of his own.

Then when the truth emerged he'd had to watch his beloved mamma withdraw into herself all over again.

And his sister grow wary to the point of paranoia. Giulia was a lovely person with her own unique beauty, yet she feared falling into the same trap as Angelo. She rarely dated, suspecting men were only attracted by her fortune, and he feared she was in danger of becoming a recluse. His once bright, gregarious sister!

That was Angelo's fault. If he hadn't fallen for Alexa's lies, acting impetuously with a youth's confidence in his own judgement, they wouldn't have suffered.

Yet that hadn't prevented his response to Ally. Despite the negative memories and suspicion, there was an insistent tug that kept drawing him to her. Physical attraction, yes, but something more too.

He was torn between wanting to protect her and make her smile and wishing she'd leave and never return.

Angelo raked his hand through his hair, swearing under his breath, and looked up to see he wasn't alone. Ally stood in the doorway, her hand raised as if to knock.

Like last night she wore that voluminous towelling robe and like last night he had no trouble imagining her naked body beneath it.

Angelo snagged a rough breath and surged to his feet.

The sooner she had new clothes so he wasn't constantly seeing her half-dressed, the better. He glanced at his watch. With the fine weather, Rosetta had left for the mainland and its shops early. Any time now—

'I won't keep you long. I'm sure you're busy.'

Ally's voice was crisp. He wished he felt half so business-like around her. Instead he felt too much. It was a new and disturbing sensation.

'Come in.'

He gestured for her to take a seat before his desk.

'I prefer to stand.'

Jaw set, hands clasped before her and shining hair loose around her shoulders, she looked like a teenager called before the headmaster. Until he looked into her eyes and read determination.

'What can I do for—'

'I'd like to leave.'

'Leave?'

Angelo scowled. It was the last thing he'd expected. Surely

her reason for being in the area was to get back into his home? Even if she had amnesia it was the only logical explanation.

'Yes, please.' Her gaze flickered and he realised she wasn't as sure of herself as she tried to project. 'Now the weather's improved I can get to the mainland, can't I?'

Surprise shot through him. 'You have somewhere in mind?'

Was she finally going to admit to her scheme?

She shook her head, her mouth thinning. 'No. But I thought, in the circumstances...' She waved her hand vaguely around his study. 'You don't want me here and I can understand, given what you told me.' Her voice wobbled a little and she swallowed. 'I'd like to think I had a reason for what I did. That my motives weren't as simple as you believe. But I just don't *know*. All I know is I hate what you've told me and it makes me uncomfortable being here.'

Heat drilled from Angelo's gullet to his belly.

Shame. A searing streak of fire that made him shift his weight. He had every right not to trust her and everything he'd told her was true, but that didn't alter the fact she was injured and needed care. Where was his decency? So much for living up to his *papà*'s example.

The doctor's words rang in his head.

Care, rest and quiet. That's what she needs. No stress.

Yet she was asking to leave because she felt uncomfortable here.

So she should, after the way she'd behaved.

Yet Angelo had to rise above that. He knew his duty to a guest, much less an injured one. Besides, if he wanted to learn the reason for her presence, he needed to keep an eye on her.

'I'm sorry you're uncomfortable. But I don't think you realise the damage done by that storm,' he said eventually. 'Many coastal towns were hit. Hospitals are full and emergency services are stretched. If anyone on the mainland has room to spare they're hosting neighbours whose homes have been wrecked.'

'I see.' She swung her head to look out at the garden, her

nose wrinkling in that trademark move he'd come to realise meant she was thinking hard.

'Look, Ally.' It got easier all the time to use her new name. Maybe because memories of Alexa were so poisonous. The name Ally didn't have the same negative connotations. 'You're welcome to stay here.'

'Welcome?' Her eyebrows disappeared under her fringe.

'Yes.' He held her eyes, ignoring the throb of energy that passed between them and focusing on what had to be done. 'There's plenty of room here and, whatever our past, you're *safe*. And it would be better if the same doctor could monitor you, don't you think?'

He paused to let that sink in. 'I admit I reacted badly when you arrived.' With sound reason. 'But the past is the past. Maybe you've done me a favour. It's done me good to confront that finally.'

He still couldn't relax around her but he realised, with a flash of insight, hoarding hatred all these years wasn't healthy. He'd thought of how his mother and sister had been scarred by his marriage breakup. He had been too, becoming suspicious and judgemental. Maybe it was time to cultivate the more generous side of his nature.

'You're injured and need help. I can provide that. Then when you're better you can move on.'

She stared as if she'd never seen him before and Angelo silently acknowledged that it was a significant turnaround, from enemy to ally. But he had an obligation to care for her till she was well enough to return to her normal life. Lashing out over her past actions did no one any good. She needed quiet to recuperate, not his jibes.

'And what—' she paused '—if I don't get my memory back?'

Her chin tilted high and she stood taller, as if shoring up her defences against such a possibility. Angelo glimpsed fear in her eyes and felt the hard kernel of bitterness inside him melt a little. She was trying to be strong though she clearly feared the worst.

Angelo moved from behind the desk and walked towards her, stopping at arm's length. 'According to the doctor that's extremely unlikely. He thinks that the best prescription for regaining your memory is rest and a lack of stress, both of which you can get here.' He breathed deep. 'I promise to be a better host and—'

'There's no need. I understand why you don't like having me around.'

That wasn't quite true. Mainly he'd prefer she'd never come. Yet part of him was fascinated and wanted to discover what it was about her that drew him so relentlessly.

'I haven't behaved well,' he admitted, 'and that pains me.' He was a proud man but he'd been raised to be decent, not a bully. 'Let me make it up to you. How about a truce? I'll try to set the past aside and you try not to worry about the future and we'll see how we go.'

Suspicion glinted in her narrowed eyes. 'Why would you do that?'

'Because I don't like the man I become when I dwell on the past.'

The words surprised him. He'd only just acknowledged that their shared past had changed him. And realised he wanted to move in a more positive direction. He hadn't meant to blurt it out. But it seemed to have been the right thing to say because she nodded and her high shoulders sank a fraction.

'I don't like the woman I was in the past either.'

Angelo scoured her features, wondering how much he could trust her words. Were they designed to lure him into trusting her?

It would drive him insane if he second-guessed her every move. He had to stop that. What could she do to him anyway? Forewarned was forearmed so there was no possibility she'd dupe him again.

'Then how about we focus on the present?'

Still she hesitated. 'And if my memory doesn't return?'

'We'll take the doctor's advice. In a week or so, if there's no change, no doubt he'll organise more tests.'

Angelo watched Ally consider that. Strange that, when she finally nodded assent, he felt relief.

'You've got a deal.' She stepped forward, extending her hand, something Angelo didn't remember from the past. She'd preferred kisses on the cheek.

'Deal.' His hand met hers and he was surprised by her firm, businesslike handshake.

Ally shook his hand, feeling for a change as if she weren't totally powerless. 'Excellent. I'll do my best not to get under your feet.'

The words were calm but clipped and she felt proud of herself, given the way her emotions had wobbled all over the place.

She slipped her hand from his. Maybe her job made her a confident speaker, or at least able to appear confident. Was she a teacher? Lawyer? Journalist? Certainly she'd felt at home shaking hands, even if the tingle along her palm and fingers proved this man still had the power to rouse her.

But there'd be no more kisses. No more getting carried away. No matter how much she craved the mindless physical pleasure of it. Craved this man.

It was as if she had a long-standing addiction to him that even time, disgrace, shame and willpower couldn't conquer.

Ice trickled down her backbone as she remembered what he'd told her. That she'd trapped him for his money. It must be true. His housekeeper would back him up on that, yet Ally couldn't get her head around the idea.

Far better to do what he suggested and concentrate on the present.

'One thing before we move on.'

Angelo's deep voice burred through her, making her wonder what it would be like if he didn't want to move on. If instead he wanted to devote his attention to a woman, not because he distrusted her but because he desired her.

Ally's pulse raced, that flicker of heat stirring again, despite her attempts to stop it.

'Yes?'

The single syllable was husky as her throat constricted. She hated that she was drawn to him sexually. It felt like a betrayal by her body yet she didn't know how to stop it.

'I'm sorry for distressing you when I told you about the past. I could have found a better way to tell you.'

Ally stared up into unfathomable dark eyes. No, not quite unfathomable. In the past she'd read anger and distaste there. Then passion. Now she saw regret.

It made him look human. Appealing. Too attractive.

That was all she needed...

'Reliving our past brought a lot of long-buried feelings to the surface. It won't happen again.'

'Thank you, Angelo.' The apology felt significant. An acknowledgement that she wasn't the only one who'd behaved badly.

Carefully she surveyed him and once more glimpsed a different man. One who wasn't hard or brooding.

What had he been like when they'd first met? Surely not so dour. Had he been charming? Seductive?

Had she fallen in love with him five years ago?

She blinked as the suspicion took hold. Could that really be why she'd behaved so appallingly?

It might explain why she was attracted to him now, when everything she knew about their past made her cringe with shame. Was it some subconscious recollection of her deeper feelings for him?

Ally's breath seized. She only remembered to breathe when she caught movement in her peripheral vision and noticed Rosetta in the doorway. The housekeeper's expression was blank but her eyes burned. With suspicion?

Hurriedly Ally stepped away from Angelo as the other woman said something in Italian.

'Excellent,' Angelo said. 'Bring them in.'

Her face set, Rosetta moved closer and Ally realised the woman understood English. Communication between them had been limited, the other woman choosing not to speak, and Ally had assumed it was because of a language barrier.

Heat flushed her cheeks as she realised Rosetta had simply preferred not to talk to her. Because of what had happened before. The skin across Ally's shoulders and nape crept tighter as if skeletal fingers pinched her there.

Had she really been so appalling?

She let out a shuddering breath. The answer to that was clear.

The woman held out two big shopping bags to her.

'Rosetta went to the mainland to get you some clothes.'

'You did?'

She needed clothes, badly. All she had was a T-shirt and bikini. And the use of this robe and some shirts for sleeping that must be Angelo's. She'd recovered enough to find that disturbing. Though they smelled of sunshine and fresh soap rather than potent male, she couldn't help being aware of whose they were as the cotton brushed her skin.

'Thank you so much, Rosetta. That was good of you. I appreciate it.'

She guessed the other woman had a busy schedule given the pristine state of the mansion and the exquisite food she prepared.

'You're welcome.' Ally caught her surprise, quickly masked. 'You needed something decent and my clothes wouldn't fit you.'

At the word *decent* Ally felt her blush intensify, conscious of the robe that gaped a little as she bent to accept the bags. Rosetta barely came up to her shoulder. No wonder Ally had been given Angelo's shirts in lieu of pyjamas instead of borrowing something from her.

'Aren't you going to look at them, to see if they fit?' Angelo asked. 'Rosetta took your swimsuit as a size guide but still…'

'Of course.'

Yet she felt self-conscious as she put the bags on a chair

and plunged her hand into one. She withdrew it to discover she'd grabbed a handful of black lace, a see-through bra and G-string, not the T-shirt and shorts she'd expected.

Hurriedly she shoved them back down, feeling the tips of her ears burn. She was *not* holding those up against herself.

Interesting, though, that Rosetta had chosen that underwear. What had Ally expected? Cotton? Something plain and practical? If so, what did that tell her?

Putting the idea aside, she delved into the second bag and withdrew a strappy sundress in a delicate floral print of pinks and lavender blue.

'Oh!' She held the fabric against her. 'How pretty. Thank you, Rosetta.' The material was a soft cotton that draped beautifully. 'I love it.'

She looked across to find two sets of eyes fixed on her, both looking startled.

What had she said? Ignoring the puzzle, Ally smiled at the housekeeper. 'I'm sure it will be a good fit and if it needs adjustment maybe I could borrow a needle and thread?'

Rosetta nodded slowly. 'Of course.'

Still the other woman looked at her strangely. Ally told herself to ignore it, delving further into the bag to discover more clothes, this time in solid colours, cut stylishly. They looked trendy and well-made but maybe a bit dressy for around the house.

'Thank you,' she said again, looking from Rosetta to Angelo. 'Can you give me the receipt please, so I know how much I owe you?'

Ally heard a choking noise that could have been shock or disparagement, then the housekeeper said something in Italian and, at a nod from Angelo, left the room.

'What did I say? Is something wrong?' The housekeeper already disapproved of her and Ally didn't want to get her further offside.

'Nothing's wrong.'

Yet his tone and quizzical look said otherwise.

Ally put the clothes down. 'Please, Angelo. We called a truce, didn't we? I'd rather you told me what the problem is.' Surely nothing he said would be as upsetting as the facts he'd already shared.

He spread his hands in a gesture that struck her as intrinsically Italian. 'No problem. Just something interesting.'

'Go on.'

He tilted his head to one side as if taking stock of some curiosity. 'First, you looked uncomfortable with the lingerie Rosetta chose. But in the past you had no qualms about wandering around the house in just that.'

Ally blinked, trying and failing to picture herself letting anyone else see her in those tiny wisps of nothing.

'Second, the one item you gushed about didn't have a designer label.'

Ally folded her arms. 'Let me guess. In the past I only wore expensive clothes?'

Angelo shrugged. 'They were your preference and I know for a fact you never wear florals. Your taste in clothes is more…dramatic.'

Ally's forehead twitched as she looked again at the clothes. Of the lot, the one that appealed most was the sundress. It seemed her tastes had changed in half a decade.

'Anything else? No, let me guess.' She swallowed, hating what she knew was coming. 'That I intend to pay you for the clothes.'

Slowly he nodded. 'That and the fact you mentioned altering it to fit. Your strengths didn't lie in dressmaking.'

Heat swirled deep inside as Ally thought of what she *had* been good at. Lying and sex, as far as she could tell. She lifted her chin. 'That was years ago. Obviously I've changed.'

For a second Angelo said nothing. Then he inclined his head and it felt like a win, as if the truce they'd called were real. 'Clearly you have.'

He gestured to something else Rosetta had brought. A

small backpack embroidered with daisies. 'There's this too. The belongings you left in the locker on the mainland.'

Instantly Ally forgot about clothes and personality changes and reached for the pack. It was light, too light, if it held all her worldly possessions.

She clutched it close, trying and failing to be optimistic that this might jog her memory.

'Ally?' Was that concern on Angelo's face? It felt like it when he steered her to a deeply padded chair and guided her into it. 'It will be all right. I promise.'

His words, soft and deep, wrapped around her chest, easing the tight breath caught in her lungs. Making her realise she was, quite suddenly, terrified.

'Do you want me to open it?' The unexpected tenderness in his tone almost undid her. She could stand up for herself against aggression or disapproval. But against kindness...

'No. Thanks. It's fine.'

With trembling fingers she opened the fastening and upended the contents. Faded jeans. Sneakers, a blue T-shirt that said *Roma*, which she knew to mean Rome, a nude bra and knickers. A comb, lip balm, water bottle, sun cream and euros. She didn't know the currency so couldn't tell if it was a lot or a little.

Nothing to divulge her identity. No name tag or address. Worse, nothing familiar. Her hands strayed over the collection again and again, willing herself to remember, but nothing came. Just that yawning blank.

She shivered, the lip balm rolling off her lap.

'There's nothing,' she gasped. 'Nothing I can recall.'

Suddenly Angelo was there, squatting before her, holding her unsteady hands in his big, firm ones.

'It's early days. You need time. Ally, do you hear me?' His hands squeezed hers and she looked up to find his dark eyes glowing with concern.

A weight shifted inside her and she breathed again.

'Of course.' She wasn't sure she believed it but if she said it often enough… 'Soon I'll remember everything. Then I can go home.'

Ally's breath caught. *Home*. It sounded wonderful.

She just prayed she *would* remember where that was. And that she'd survive living with Angelo Ricci until then.

CHAPTER SEVEN

ALLY SMILED AS Enzo laughed. It was the happiest sound she'd heard in the four days she'd been here.

Her smile became a grin as she jammed the hat down, turning her head to give him a profile view as if she modelled haute couture instead of a tatty straw sunhat.

It was kind of him to produce the hat for the sun beat down brightly. The sky and sea were a brilliant blue and even the storm-battered garden was vivid with colour.

'The hat may be worn but it'll do the job. Thank you, Enzo. *Grazie.*'

It was one of her two bits of Italian, the other being *per favore*, which meant please.

He nodded and said something she didn't understand. It didn't matter. She'd puttered happily beside him in the garden for half an hour and gestures had been sufficient.

Ally kept catching her breath at the nooks and stunning vistas in this garden perched high above the sea. It was like something from a travel brochure or a sophisticated magazine. Stunningly beautiful.

Yet it wasn't familiar. Surely, as Angelo's ex-wife, she should feel *déjà vu*?

In Angelo's arms she'd experienced, if not *déjà vu*, then at least a sense of rightness, as if, finally, everything had fallen into place. Yet since then, nothing.

Shouldn't she remember the elegant wisteria loggia, where she'd found Enzo raking up leaves stripped by the storm? Or the rose arbour, sleepy with the hum of bees? Or the secluded pond with its exquisite marble statue of a boy fishing?

Each garden within a garden made her pause as pleasure washed through her.

That, she suspected, was why Enzo let her tag along. He saw how she admired the place. To her delight she even knew the names of some of the plants.

Did that mean she had a garden of her own somewhere? The idea tantalised but led nowhere. Her past was still a blank. Frustratingly, scarily so.

Putting on the gloves he'd provided, Ally gathered up bougainvillea cuttings and put them in the wheelbarrow. The hot pink cascade of battered flowers was so bright it almost hurt the eye and she paused, mesmerised.

Everything here seemed saturated with brightness and warmth, from the vibrant red geraniums to the blazing white of the garden balustrades against the opalescent sea beyond. It was so different to what she was used to. So—

'Ally? What are you doing?'

She blinked and shivered, vainly trying to grasp the thought that had entered her brain so easily and now disintegrated like a tantalising wisp of smoke.

Not what she was used to. Different to...what?

'Ally?' That deep voice was closer and the thought was gone. Completely disappeared.

She drew a shuddery breath and tried not to mind. Surely it would return. But dismay and frustration feathered her spine. Would she *ever* remember?

Warmth encompassed her bare elbow and she turned, gaze locking with eyes the colour of her morning espresso, rich, dark and addictive.

She blinked, scurrying to revise that thought. Not addictive. She wouldn't let it be so.

Even if she found herself thinking about Angelo too often. Even if her dreams featured a dark, enigmatic man who seduced her again and again, leaving her breathless and unsettled, wishing she weren't alone in her vast bed.

Wishing he'd take her in his arms and kiss her again.

No, no, no! She refused to go there.

'Hello, Angelo.'

Her voice was a husky croak that she feared betrayed her libidinous thoughts.

Because Angelo Ricci was extraordinarily handsome and he'd actually been pleasant these last couple of days. He'd been gentle and supportive when he'd presented the daypack with her meagre belongings and her hopes had taken a nosedive because they didn't spark recognition.

He'd been kind as well, giving her free run of the English language books in his library and organising new clothes for her. Not just any clothes. They were beautifully made and expensive. Rosetta had obviously been told to buy the best.

But Ally refused to find him addictive. Or attractive. Others might, but her taste ran to...

Her breath snagged. She had no idea what her taste in men was like.

Like Angelo Ricci, insisted the voice in her head.

Once she'd found pleasure with this man. Earthy sexual pleasure. For all his air of buttoned-down control, there was a raw masculinity about him, an air of sensuality, that beckoned to some breathless, needy part of her.

Ally stifled the thought.

'I thought you were going to read by the pool.'

He frowned down at her. Not with anger like before but with something that made her pulse trip faster because it made her feel cared for. How crazy was that? Was she so desperate for affection?

'I'm helping Enzo.' She ignored the catch to her voice, just as she ignored the way Angelo's hand on her elbow sent warmth spilling through her.

'You're supposed to be resting.'

There it was again. That note of concern appealed too

much. She pulled free, not liking the way her nerve-endings sparked and crackled at the contact as if from an electric shock.

'I've been resting for days, Angelo. I got bored sitting by the pool. Besides, this is restful. I'm just strolling, passing tools to Enzo and putting a few prunings in the wheelbarrow. It's lovely to be in the garden.'

She didn't add that she'd also been drawn by the company. Rosetta had still to crack a smile in Ally's presence, though she wasn't quite so frowningly remote. And Angelo, despite his changed attitude, wasn't a comfortable presence. The undercurrent of awareness or doubt or whatever it was between them was palpable.

Ally fought it by peppering him with questions at mealtimes. About Italy, his home, the island—anything impersonal. Because when things became personal between them everything got out of control.

Her blood effervesced whenever his hand brushed hers or she discovered him watching her, eyes glinting with something she couldn't identify.

Once or twice she'd imagined it was approval she saw there, even attraction. After all, he'd kissed her passionately. But then his expression would change and she knew she was fooling herself. Angelo had admitted to curiosity about kissing her. But now he'd moved on.

'You have to be careful not to overdo it.' He turned and spoke to Enzo in Italian.

Ally watched, frustrated. She'd felt at home pottering among the plants, like it was something she was used to doing. That, of itself, made her want to stick at it, in case it sparked a memory. It gave her hope, made her feel she was doing something useful.

It also kept her mind off her fraught relationship with her host.

'No, please.' Ally interrupted. 'Don't say I can't help.' She heard the desperation in her voice and stopped. After a breath she continued. 'Enzo's been very kind and I enjoy his company. I'm not doing any damage, I promise.'

Angelo stared down at her, wishing the brim of that disreputable hat didn't shadow her face.

Had he imagined that taut, woebegone look? The edge of panic in her tone?

That made him wonder if she should be in hospital after all. It would be easy to get her there now. But the doctor thought it best Ally stay quietly here. Which made her Angelo's responsibility.

'I'm sure the garden is in no danger from you.'

He smiled reassuringly, conscious as always of the disparity in their sizes. For despite her feistiness he'd been shocked to read something like fear in her eyes a couple of days ago. That look had stopped him in his tracks, making him abruptly aware that he loomed over her.

He'd felt shame course through him, an emotion he wasn't accustomed to, since he'd spent his life trying to be as honourable and honest as his father.

The woman he'd married had never looked at him with fear. She'd understood that, no matter how she provoked him, he was protective of women. He'd never resort to violence.

These past days had convinced Angelo that her amnesia was real. Either that or she'd become the best actress he'd ever met.

As a result, his suspicions had taken a back seat. It was pointless reminding himself she'd used and betrayed him. That woman was a far cry from the one before him.

He liked this new Ally who asked so many questions about his homeland and its customs. Who seemed intrigued by everything and eager to discover more.

The Alexa he'd known had been more interested in his income than local traditions. Was it time that had changed her or simply memory loss?

And why that panic in her voice now? What was so wonderful about traipsing after Enzo? In the past she'd never seemed to notice anyone else when Angelo was around, especially staff.

'You can help Enzo later. It's time for his lunch break.'

'Oh, of course,' she said immediately, taking off her hat and gloves and putting them on the laden wheelbarrow. 'I hadn't realised the time. I didn't mean to keep him from his break.'

She approached Enzo, thanking him in halting Italian and winning an approving grin.

Angelo watched, intrigued. Enzo was Rosetta's husband and knew the circumstances of Angelo's failed marriage. Yet the older man's response was warm.

She always was good at wrapping people around her little finger.

Angelo stifled the doubting voice as they walked towards the house. Ally wasn't bluffing about the amnesia. She'd been an accomplished liar in the past but over this she was telling the truth. Whatever her reason for returning, and knowing her she had a reason, he pitied her predicament. Shame stabbed him, as he remembered the harsh way he'd treated her. He'd tried to make that up to her, offering the care an injured guest deserved, and she seemed to be improving, physically at least.

Yet he was intrigued about the bond between her and his gardener.

Everything about her fascinated him. She seemed at the same time so familiar and yet so changed.

'You and Enzo get on well, considering he doesn't speak English.'

She shrugged. 'I suppose we have gardens in common. There's nothing quite like being out amongst growing things, is there?'

Angelo met a sideways glance from guileless eyes and felt as if he'd walked into a wall.

It was the sort of comment he expected from his mother, who loved tending her roses and herbs. Not his ex.

Had she undergone a personality transplant?

His wife had been lively, sociable and good at getting on

with people. But always, he'd learned, for a purpose. Never had she expressed an interest in anything as domesticated as gardening. As for sewing or altering clothes, Angelo wouldn't have believed it except he'd heard it with his own ears.

This new Ally was a puzzle.

One he intended to solve.

More and more she disconcerted him. Even something as simple as walking beside her felt different. He was aware of the feminine contours of her body. Lusher and more pronounced than in the past. Maybe she wasn't dieting so strictly these days? Had she given up modelling?

Nor did she seem as tall. That had unnerved him till he realised it had to be because she wore flat shoes or went barefoot, whereas in the past she'd worn heels, even lazing around the poolside.

Small things but unsettling.

For the first time in years, five years to be precise, Angelo felt he wasn't in complete control of the situation. It wasn't a sensation he liked.

'So, you enjoy gardening,' he said as they took their seats on the terrace looking over the sea.

A wide awning gave shade and, like yesterday, Ally took her time admiring the view and the urns perched on the balustrade that overflowed with bright flowers.

'Apparently. I found it relaxing this morning. Besides, how could you not enjoy it with surroundings like these?'

Angelo always found it restful here, but seeing her admiration made him view it with new eyes.

Maybe he should listen to his family, who urged him to take more time off to enjoy the luxuries he'd worked so hard for, like this estate on an exclusive, sought after island. Perhaps there were changes he needed to make in his life.

'Is this your permanent home?'

'Sadly no. I spend more time in Rome and elsewhere.'

Ally frowned. 'But you spend a lot of time here, surely?'

She might have read his mind. Angelo shrugged, stifling discomfort. Because she was right, the place was special but he rarely allowed himself the downtime to enjoy it as he should. 'Not as much as I'd like.'

Her head tilted to one side. 'Why?' Then her eyes rounded. 'It's not because of me, is it? Because coming here reminds you of what happened—?'

'No!' She looked so aghast he had to cut her off. 'Nothing like that. It's still a retreat for me, the place I come to get away.'

Strange that, though this was where he'd been with Alexa, it wasn't here that the painful past usually haunted him. It was when he was with his mother and sister, seeing the damage his fiasco of a marriage had inflicted on them.

The fact that the villa didn't usually evoke memories of Alexa showed how little she'd meant to him as a person. They'd never connected emotionally and there'd been no depth to their relationship. Just physical attraction then a sense of duty when she'd announced her pregnancy.

In fact, Angelo realised abruptly, he cared far more for her now than he had when they'd been lovers. He surveyed her sun-kissed features and rumpled hair and felt none of the anger he'd harboured so long.

'So why not visit more often?' When he didn't immediately respond she said, 'Not that it's any of my business.'

'It's a fair enough question.' He stared into those bright eyes and wondered why he didn't mind talking about it with her.

Because she was like a stranger? They said it was easier to talk about personal things with people who didn't know you.

He shrugged. 'Ever since I took over from my father I've devoted myself to business. I rarely take time off.'

When he did his time was punctuated with video conferences, calls and emails. Even his weekends here were interrupted by work.

'Ever since?' A tiny frown creased Ally's brow. 'Was there a problem when you took over?'

'It wasn't easy to begin with. My father died suddenly and—'

'I'm sorry. That must have been tough.'

Sympathy glowed in her eyes and to Angelo's amazement he felt his throat tighten. It was a long time since his *papà*'s death, yet he still missed him. Nor was he used to sympathy. He was the one who'd held everything together for his family. The one they looked to for support.

'Thank you. He was a special man.' He paused. 'I've worked hard to live up to his standards and, yes, there were lots of people who doubted I could fill his shoes. I was seen as inexperienced. But I've proved them wrong. The bank is an even bigger, more successful enterprise now.'

'I'm sure he'd be proud of you.'

Again she surprised him. Her empathy and insight were unexpected. Five years *had* changed her.

'I hope so.' Some thought ego had prompted him to try to outdo his father. Instead he'd worked to live up to his father's memory and provide for his mother and sister.

Later, after his divorce, his drive had been fuelled by the need to harness negative emotions and direct his energy somewhere positive. The failed marriage had dented his ego and confidence in his judgement, inflicting a burden of shame at not protecting his family, at letting his father down.

He'd been determined not to fall for any woman's wiles and had reinforced his policy of confining himself to brief hook-ups that were sexually satisfying and didn't interfere with his well-ordered world.

Strange that having his ex here made him wonder what a permanent relationship would be like. To make this place a home rather than a part-time retreat.

To be here with his wife and children.

He hadn't thought in those terms because thinking about starting a family was like probing an unhealed wound. Instinctively he'd retreated from the idea of making himself vulnerable to love, having seen loss devastate his mother. Then the debacle with Alexa had shut down a part of him. Was he a lesser man for that?

'But if the business is so successful, surely you can delegate and take more time off?'

Angelo focused on the woman across the table from him. 'You sound like my mother. She tells me to relax more and my sister...' He paused, realising that oddly he didn't mind mentioning them to Ally.

'Your sister?' she prompted.

'She calls me a workaholic.'

Ally released a gentle huff of laughter that whispered across his skin before curling deep inside, where he felt a nugget of glowing heat. 'I like the sound of your sister. Clearly she's a very brave woman.'

The glint in her eyes was teasing and Angelo's mouth crimped up at the corners. Giulia was the only other person who teased him. Strange that he enjoyed it now with Ally.

Maybe his family was right. Maybe it was time to reconsider what he wanted from life. Angelo had no plans to follow his father into an early grave. The divorce had changed him, made him bitter. Perhaps it was time to focus more on the positives.

'If I owned this place I wouldn't want to move.' Ally waved a hand towards the view. 'Just look at that hot pink pelargonium trailing over the white of the balustrade with the deep blue sea beyond. It's stunning.'

Angelo sat back, watching Ally's enthralled expression and listening to her unvarnished enthusiasm.

When she'd been here before she'd loved the place but had been too sophisticated to gush about it. Now he found her appreciation engaging.

His thoughts were interrupted by Rosetta, arriving with bread and antipasti.

Ally enthused about the garden as they served themselves from the delectable spread. She seemed to know what she was talking about. She mentioned plants by name and was particularly interested in the garden's design and its different sections, or rooms as she called them.

'The rose arbour in particular...'

She trailed off as if lost in admiration at the memory.

Angelo nodded and reached for a bottle of sparkling water, topping up their glasses.

His mother was fond of that sheltered corner of the garden, with its rich scent and abundance of blooms. It struck him that she'd enjoy sharing this meal with Ally, discussing plants and design.

It was only as he put the bottle down that he realised Ally was sitting bolt upright and her expression was stunned. He leaned closer, concern rising, particularly at the way she held a piece of bread in the air as if frozen in the act of taking a bite.

'Ally?' His nape prickled. 'What is it?'

She didn't even blink.

'Ally!'

Still she seemed absorbed in something she could see beyond him. He swung round and noted a yacht in the distance but nothing else. Nothing to stun her into silence.

He shoved his chair back, worry rising, when she spoke.

'Gran,' she whispered, with such yearning in her voice that it stopped Angelo mid-movement.

He scoured her face for signs of pain or distress. All he found was a curious blankness that contrasted with a furrowed brow that spoke of concentration.

Then, abruptly, she sat back, blinking, her suspended hand dropping to the table, her eyes overbright.

Angelo didn't stop to think. In a second he was around the table, crouching beside her chair. He covered her hand with his. Was it imagination or was her flesh chilled?

'Talk to me, Ally.'

Finally she swung her head around and he expelled a breath that felt like relief as her gaze caught his and he read recognition there. It had only lasted seconds but he'd felt unnerved by those moments when she'd been unresponsive, as if far away in her head.

Had she overdone it, helping Enzo? Had she somehow worsened the damage to her brain? Guilt stirred. He should have kept a better eye on her. Made her to rest.

'I remembered,' she whispered, so low that he had to lean close to hear. The scent of sweet neroli-scented soap and warm female flesh tickled his nostrils, distracting him for a second.

'You remembered? That's excellent.'

They'd been waiting for a sign that her memory would return. Angelo hadn't let himself think about what would happen if it never did. About the complications that would ensue if he had to play the host until they discovered enough for her to take up her life again.

Yet, instead of looking delighted, her face was drawn and her eyelashes spiked with tears.

He squeezed her hand. 'What did you remember, Ally? Your life? How you came here?'

She lifted her other hand to her face, wiping the back of it across her eyes the way a child would brush tears from her face.

'Not that much. But it made me feel…' Her mouth wobbled and for a horrible moment it looked as if she'd cry.

Angelo had never seen this woman cry in all the time he'd known her. Even faced with recriminations when her lies were exposed, she'd been defiant rather than broken, certain rather than upset. The sight of her blinking back tears tugged at something deep inside him.

Angelo moved closer and wrapped his arms around her. Ally's head subsided against his shoulder, her hands clinging to his shirt as she sniffed.

'Sorry. I'm sorry,' she whispered.

She buried her face against his throat and he felt dampness on his skin. Despite all his caution Angelo also felt an upsurge of sympathy and protectiveness as he tightened his embrace. Whatever had happened, it had totally thrown her.

He held her firmly, feeling the tremors racking her body, the shaking breaths that heated his skin, the smudge of tears.

It felt different from any past embrace. He knew this woman and yet in this moment she felt unfamiliar.

No, that wasn't it. His body cradled hers easily, as if the

weight of her slim frame against him was the most natural thing. It was her distress that was unusual. His ex-wife had never displayed fear or sadness, just an unwavering certainty that she had a right to whatever she wanted.

'Sorry, Angelo,' she said again. 'I don't know what came over me.'

She pulled back and, to his surprise, he was reluctant to release her.

Angelo tore his thoughts from that and focused on Ally. 'What happened? Did you remember something bad?'

She shook her head, sniffing, and smoothed her hair back from her face in a gesture he remembered from the old days.

Strange how the sight of her doing that, while wearing the pretty floral dress and blinking back tears, messed with his head. As if the unwelcome past melded with the present.

'No, nothing bad. That's what I don't understand. I should be happy to remember something, shouldn't I? And it was a nice memory.'

She blinked tear-glazed eyes and Angelo thought he'd never seen anything so sad yet so beautiful.

'Tell me about it.' He took her hand again, rubbing his thumb rhythmically over the back of it, ignoring the thud of his heart against his ribs.

For a second longer her eyes locked on his, as if frantic for reassurance. Then she looked away and Angelo felt it as an abrupt release of tension.

'It was the scent of the bread.' She lifted her other hand and he realised she still held a piece of focaccia.

'Rosetta is renowned for her baking.' Though in the past his ex hadn't indulged, too busy watching her intake of carbohydrates to eat even the best home-made bread.

'Not the bread. The rosemary sprinkled on top. That's what made me remember.'

She swallowed and it was easy to see she still battled strong emotion.

'Go on.'

She flashed him a lopsided smile that hit him hard. It

wasn't practised or sultry but it was real, something Angelo found incredibly enticing.

He found *her* incredibly enticing. Not because she aroused protective instincts but because of her enthusiasm, her air of honesty, her lively interest in so many things.

Angelo waited for the cynical inner voice to crush that idea but for once it was silent. He didn't know whether to be relieved or concerned.

'I smelled the rosemary and it hit me. I remembered being on the veranda of a house, looking out over a garden. I was standing, pouring a rosemary hair rinse over a woman with white hair. My gran.' Her voice wobbled on the last word. 'I knew who she was even though I was behind her and couldn't see her face. We were talking about how well the rinse had turned out. One of my best yet.'

Angelo met Ally's bright eyes and read turbulent emotion there. Another new experience. In the past she'd revealed only what she wanted him to see. Now he sensed she wasn't even thinking about what she revealed. She was simply dealing with what her disordered mind had thrown up.

He frowned. 'Surely that's good? A positive memory about a person and a place? That's a start.'

She nodded, her lips crimping at the corners as if holding back emotion. 'You're right. Of course you're right.'

'But it's not that simple?'

She looked at him with something like gratitude and Angelo felt a chip of the reinforced concrete he'd constructed around his heart crack and fall away.

Ally's voice dipped low. 'No, it's not. The memory itself is nice, comforting even. And the way we spoke, I know we're very close.' She shot him a glance then looked away. 'After what you told me I'd begun to wonder if there was anyone, anywhere who cared when I didn't come home.'

Another lump of reinforcing sheered away, leaving Angelo feeling scraped raw. He had nothing to be guilty about, he told himself. He'd merely told her the truth about their relationship.

But he'd enjoyed it too much, hadn't he? The chance to inflict hurt on the woman who'd hurt him years before.

Angelo wasn't proud of himself in that moment.

'Now you know there is.' He squeezed her hand and was relieved when she returned his grip.

'Yes.' Yet still she didn't look happy. 'The problem is that the memory made me incredibly sad. Which makes me scared of what I'll discover when I finally remember everything.' Her hand clutched his. 'I'm not sure I'm ready to face that.'

CHAPTER EIGHT

'THIS IS AMAZING.' Ally stopped on the last step of the cliff path and took off her sandals, taking in the deserted cove with the deep blue sea sparkling beyond. Stepping onto the unusual pearly pink sand, she wriggled her toes. 'It's as soft as icing sugar too.'

Angelo turned and looked over his shoulder, eyebrows lifted at her delighted reaction. The twist of his body accentuated the breadth of his shoulders and the narrowness of his hips.

Instantly she forgot all about the secluded, perfect beach, her gaze feasting instead on him.

He was breathtakingly masculine. In black swim-shorts and a thin T-shirt he looked toned and taut. Ally had to drag her attention away from those heavy thigh muscles and powerful arms.

'I like it. The private beach was one of the things that attracted me to the villa.'

'It must be great, having the place to yourself.'

On a public beach Angelo would probably be mobbed by admirers.

Ally swallowed hard, telling herself she was too aware of him as a man. It had grown worse in the last couple of days, since Angelo had dropped his antagonism and wariness.

Yesterday when she'd had her mini meltdown at the lunch table he'd been kind and understanding. He'd drawn her close and let her snuffle out her tears without making her feel in the least foolish that she didn't even know what she was crying about.

But that sadness had been piercingly raw. It had hit out of nowhere, stealing her breath and her strength and turning the bright day gloomy with despair.

She'd tried to tell herself her brain wasn't working properly. That she was imagining things. Yet the awful suspicion lingered. That when she *did* remember everything she'd wish she'd remained in ignorance. Because something awful had happened.

Since then she'd spent as much time as possible with Angelo. Being with him took her thoughts off the unknown, scary past.

Yeah, because you're busy lusting after him.

Nonsense. She was just *appreciating* him. Any woman would.

But did other women toss and turn all night, alternately wishing he were with her and dreaming that he was?

Heat scored her cheeks and Ally watched his gaze sharpen. Sometimes it felt as if Angelo read her thoughts, or at least her body's response to him.

Maybe he could. They'd been lovers.

Ally wrinkled her nose, concentrating on not shifting her weight as that edgy, needy feeling started up again at the apex of her thighs. She mightn't have any memory but she was pretty certain it was her body's way of telling her she wanted sex. With Angelo Ricci.

Which was *not* going to happen.

'So, are you going to show me where I washed up and where you found the paddle?' Her voice sounded strident with forced cheer. But better than hoarse with arousal.

'You're sure you feel like clambering over rocks? There's nothing to see now.'

Angelo had been solicitous to the point of smothering since that scene at lunch yesterday. He'd insisted she lie down until the doctor came and pronounced she was doing well. Even this morning, when Ally said she was going to the beach, he'd tried to persuade her not to.

He seemed to think she was physically fragile, whereas it was only her mind that wasn't working. Her body seemed fine.

Too fine, considering how it responded to those delicious pheromones he exuded, and his sheer physical presence.

'Absolutely. I'd rather be outdoors. I'm not used to being cooped up. It doesn't feel right, lounging about.' She saw his sharp look and hurriedly added, 'Though I'm enjoying the books you've lent me.'

He didn't say anything, just surveyed her as if she were a puzzle to be solved. Then abruptly he nodded. 'This way.'

He led her to an outcrop of rock at one end of the beach. 'You were lying here with your head and arm on the rock and most of your body in the water.'

Ally's body iced at the image he conjured. She could almost see herself, unconscious, head just above water. She'd been lucky not to drown or be more severely injured.

'It's okay, Ally.' His low voice wrapped around her reassuringly, as did his warm fingers, covering hers where she rubbed her hands up her arms. His touch stopped the movement, drawing her eyes to his.

She read sympathy in that dark chocolate gaze. Yet it wasn't sympathy she wanted. It was desire.

She wanted Angelo to want her again, even if fleetingly. Being constantly on tenterhooks, close to him but keeping her distance, was too much to ask.

Abruptly she stepped clear of his touch and looked out across the water. She could make out buildings on the mainland, clustered around the sea and climbing the steep slopes.

'You really think I came from there?' It was too far to swim, but maybe on a paddleboard...

'It seems so. I sent that photo you let me take of you to the hire company owner. He's sure you're the woman who rented the missing board.'

Her heart thudded. A real lead then, not just supposition.

Now they just had to work out where she'd come from. 'Did he say how much he's out of pocket for the loss?'

She turned to find Angelo staring at her. 'Don't worry. It's covered by insurance.'

Ally expelled a breath. One small thing less to worry about. She had plenty of big things to worry about. 'Where did you find the paddle?'

He led her further over the rocks to a place where they ran like a ragged spine out into the sea. 'There, wedged under that outcrop.'

Of course there was nothing to see now. It was days since the storm. Even so, Ally had to clamp down on disappointment.

Had she really hoped that coming here would help her remember?

'I'm sorry, Ally. The whole island is on alert for any flotsam that might have come ashore in the storm, in case there's some sort of clue. But so far there's nothing.'

Her head jerked up. 'Thank you. That's very kind.' It shouldn't surprise her, after all he'd done for her. Of course he had a vested interest in helping her retrieve her memory so she could leave. 'I suppose the paddleboard is halfway to Sicily by now.'

Understanding warmed his gaze. 'Come on. Since there's nothing more to see, let's have that swim.'

He reached out a hand and she took it, some of the tension in her upper body easing at the contact.

Ally knew the gesture was just because Angelo didn't want her tripping on the uneven rocks and further damaging herself. But any human contact was welcome.

She'd felt so alone, isolated in a claustrophobic world where she didn't belong.

Surely that was why she'd become fixated on Angelo. It was simpler to focus on her hormonal reaction to a supremely sexy man than face the grim reality of her amnesia.

Any diversion was welcome. So as soon as they were on

the sand she stripped off the lightweight trousers and top she wore over her bikini and headed for the water.

From the corner of her eye she saw Angelo yank off his T-shirt and toss it on the sand with the beach towels. The sun caressed the taut, muscled lines of his frame, burnishing his olive skin so that he seemed to glow.

It reinforced that fantasy she'd had before, of him as a fallen angel, beautiful, mesmerising and untouchable.

Ally's fingers tickled as she imagined touching his firm chest, tracing a line down to his navel, then following the dark thread of hair that disappeared beneath his shorts.

Her breath hissed between her teeth and she ran into the water, barely noticing its cool caress against ankles, knees and thighs before she shallow-dived beneath the surface.

Angelo watched her rub her hair dry with a beach towel.

But it wasn't her hair he was watching. It was the effect of that vigorous movement on her body. Ally's breasts, deliciously full in that bikini top, jiggled enticingly and her taut rear shimmied when she turned.

She was even more alluring than he remembered, still slim but with fuller curves.

Yet it was her expression that dug down past his defences. Not because of sultry glances or pouting lips. Instead Ally wore a wide, open grin and the sight of it made something within him sit up and beg.

She looked radiant, her skin flushed with exertion, her eyes bright with pleasure and her hair a tangle of old gold, glinting in the sun as she dropped the towel.

'Wasn't it glorious? The water is so clear.'

'You definitely have an affinity with the sea.'

'Maybe that's why I loved it here before. You said I never left the estate.'

Slowly Angelo nodded. It was true. Yet his memories of the past were of her lounging in the shade by the pool and occasionally taking a quick dip to cool off. He didn't recall her swimming laps of the cove. Ally had only stopped when he'd reminded her of the need to take it easy or risk possible repercussions and the doctor's wrath.

People change. Obviously she's taken up new habits since she left you.

Yet it surprised him. In Angelo's mind she was fixed in time and character, unchanging from the way she'd been five years ago.

Had their destructive relationship been a catalyst for change in her too? For the first time he wondered what had made her the grasping woman she'd been when they'd met. He'd never taken time to think about that.

Because their relationship had been shallow, grounded in sex and then the fiction of her pregnancy. He hadn't probed deeper.

Now Angelo discovered he had more in common with his ex-wife than he'd had at the time of their marriage.

A love of the sea and of books for relaxation. A penchant for straight talking.

Last night, needing something to divert him from the intimacy of her company, he'd found an old classic film to watch, something he hadn't done in ages. To his surprise Ally had not only enjoyed it but commented on it knowledgably, revealing a knowledge of vintage films that led to an animated discussion.

Angelo had enjoyed the evening more than any he could remember in a long time.

Now he enjoyed watching his ex-wife dress.

He told himself to look away and he did turn to shake out his towel. But from the corner of his eye he caught the wriggle of her hips as she pulled on loose trousers. For some reason they looked particularly sexy with the shadow of her bikini bottom clearly visible through the white fabric. As for the floaty green top, it settled around her, sheer and spangled and disturbingly tempting, giving tantalising glimpses of her body underneath.

'Ready?' he asked.

Another bright smile and it struck him that she was right. She seemed happier out of doors.

'Sounds good. I thought I'd help Enzo after lunch. The storm played havoc with the garden. There's still a lot of raking and pruning to do and tying things up.'

Angelo nodded, trying to get used to this new woman who'd rather work in the garden than sip cocktails on a lounger. He gestured for her to precede him up the steps so he could help her if she suddenly flagged. Though, given the way she seemed to spark with energy today, that was unlikely.

He realised his error when he found himself mesmerised by the seductive sway of her hips and the sight of her trousers clinging to her damp bikini, giving him a perfect view of her shapely derriere.

His body tightened and he forced himself to stop and look away, turning his thoughts to business calls he needed to make. Work would be a welcome diversion from this woman. There was an issue in New York to sort and—

Voices snagged his attention and he looked up to see Ally had stopped ahead on the bend where the track zigzagged back across the cliff. At that corner the path reached the side boundary of his property.

Loping up the stairs Angelo found Ally smiling at his neighbour, who was leaning towards her through a gap in the thick planting. She seemed rapt in what he was saying.

'Here he is now,' she said as Angelo stopped behind her. 'You can ask him yourself.'

But Oliver Branston, Angelo's new American neighbour, didn't instantly look at Angelo. Instead his gaze rested on Ally as if he too found her mesmerising.

Angelo bristled, the skin drawing tight between his shoulder blades. 'Hi.' He pasted on a smile. 'Is there something I can help with?'

Branston had only bought the property a month ago and had so far kept to himself.

'I'm having a housewarming party.' He raised a hand as if fending off objections. 'Don't worry, it's not a noisy Hollywood blow-out with strobe lights and circling helicopters. I'm just inviting some neighbours over for a barbecue. To get to know you all and maybe allay fears people might have about me being here.'

Angelo smiled, liking the guy's self-awareness. Some of the locals had worried about having their cherished peace and privacy disturbed by a man as well-known for his partying as his impressive film-making.

'Thanks. I'll look forward to it.'

It would be a good opportunity to take the man's measure.

'Excellent. The day after tomorrow, wander over any time in the evening.' Branston nodded and shifted his attention to Ally. 'You too, Miss Ally. I expect to see you there.'

With a wave he was gone, leaving Angelo to ponder the way he'd looked at Ally with obvious approval. Maybe he looked at every woman that way. If Rosetta were to be believed, the man had been romantically linked with dozens of the world's top actresses.

It didn't matter. Ally would be resting at the villa, not going to a party.

The thought settled the edginess that had stirred in Angelo's gut when he'd discovered Ally smiling up at a Hollywood heart-throb. Oliver Branston might be a director, not an actor, but with his golden good looks and movie mogul power he drew women like bees to nectar.

Angelo and Ally walked together the rest of the way, chatting about their swim and the view, and that too settled his ruffled senses.

In the old days she'd have been beside herself with excitement after meeting Branston, given her dream of moving from modelling to acting. But Ally showed no excitement over meeting their famous neighbour.

More and more Angelo found himself liking this new version of the woman he'd known.

'There you are, Ally. A gorgeous drink for a gorgeous woman.'

Ally looked from Oliver's dancing blue eyes to the extraordinary drink he held out to her. It was outrageously decorated with four sorts of fruit, a paper umbrella and a fizzing sparkler.

A laugh bubbled in her throat at his over-the-top comment. 'You're wasted in the movies. You should be a full-time barman.'

It was the second mocktail he'd made her tonight. The doctor hadn't specifically banned alcohol but Ally didn't want anything to hinder her brain's recovery.

Yet for some reason she'd felt shy, requesting a soft drink when all around were glamorous people quaffing fine wine and cocktails.

Maybe she felt on edge because Angelo hadn't wanted her to attend the party. First he'd warned that she needed rest, though she felt fine. Then he'd insisted the doctor wouldn't approve. Thankfully the doctor had agreed that the stimulation of company might be good for her.

Ally had been growing quietly desperate with the need for something to take her mind off Angelo. Since their truce, it grew harder to rein in her attraction. A night spent with other people was a heaven-sent opportunity.

Oliver grinned. 'It's good to know I've got another career option if my next film flops.'

'As if! I looked you up. Even if it did, you'd still have backers. You've made so many great movies.'

'You had to look me up?' His eyebrows rose. 'I knew you weren't a groupie out to get a part in one of my films, but I'd sort of hoped my name was familiar.'

Ally hesitated. Her medical condition wasn't something she'd mentioned. She didn't want to seem more of an outsider than she already felt, surrounded by all these wealthy, privileged people. Some had been friendly but they'd preferred talking to people they already knew than making small talk with a stranger.

'The fact is, Oliver, I have a slight problem. My memory...'

As she briefly told him of her accident he moved closer, concern and interest on his face.

'For real? Sorry. Of course it's for real. You wouldn't joke about anything like that.' He peered down at her, exuding a sympathy that warmed her. 'You're one gutsy woman. Coming here, acting as if everything's normal when it must be as scary as hell.'

She blinked, her eyes suddenly too hot. 'Thank you. The doctor says I'm doing well but it doesn't feel that way.'

'Aw, Ally, I'm sorry. I didn't mean to upset you.' He wrapped his arm around her shoulders and squeezed reassuringly before stepping back.

'You didn't. I mean, it is upsetting when I think about it but you didn't upset me.' She drew a slow breath. 'It's good to talk about it with someone else.'

As she spoke she felt a familiar prickling up the back of her neck and turned to discover Angelo on the far side of the wide pool deck, staring at her from under frowning brows. Again.

He'd spent most of the evening at her side, but he was popular among the guests and more than once he'd got caught up by people wanting to talk with him. Ally had been happy to wander on her own for a little and enjoy the stunning setting.

Now he didn't look supportive or understanding. He looked like a thundercloud about to burst.

'Your lover looks ready to strangle me.'

'Angelo's not my lover and he's probably angry with me, not you. Though why he's upset I don't know.'

It hurt and annoyed her. She'd thought all that was in the past.

'That's easy. He's jealous of you being with me.'

Ally stared at the American, his outrageous words jangling in her brain. When she turned back it was to see Angelo moving purposefully towards them, until an older woman with rubies at her throat and ears stopped him, her expression worried.

'Jealous?' Ally shook her head and turned back to Oliver. 'No way. There's nothing between us.'

'Obviously he wants there to be something between you.'

Oliver's mouth curled into a seductive smile. 'But if you're not lovers that means there's a chance for me.'

Again he made her giggle with his over-the-top chivalry. 'You really play up the louche playboy routine, don't you?'

For a second she saw surprise in Oliver's blue eyes. Then he shrugged. 'Habit. And you *are* intriguing and beautiful.'

Suspicion stirred. 'You want something, don't you? What is it, Oliver?'

By the time Angelo extricated himself politely from his mother's friend, Ally and Oliver Branston were nowhere to be seen.

He prowled inside to the reception rooms but there was no sign of the pair. The agitation in his gut worsened.

He'd *known* he shouldn't have brought Ally here. He'd told himself it was because she still needed to recuperate. But since he'd seen her and Branston, giggling like a couple of teenagers over the cocktail he'd made her, Angelo realised it was more than that.

He didn't like the expression in Branston's eyes when he looked at Ally.

Angelo hadn't enjoyed the way *any* of the men looked at her tonight.

What had possessed Rosetta to buy that skin-tight dress in electric blue that drew every eye?

Heat circled his throat and he lifted a hand to loosen his collar, only to discover the top of his shirt was open.

'Angelo. I'm glad to see you. I wanted your opinion—'

'Sorry,' he interrupted before an acquaintance could detain him. 'I have to find my companion—'

'The lovely blonde? I don't blame you. Last time I looked, Branston was monopolising her, leading her into the garden.'

'Thanks,' Angelo shot over his shoulder, already halfway to the French doors. 'I'll catch you later.'

His pulse beat a quick tattoo that matched his short, sharp breaths. He plunged across the terrace and into the rambling garden.

Ally loved gardens. Maybe Branston was just showing her his plants.

Yeah. And what else is he showing her?

Angelo needed to protect her.

He swallowed a growl of fury and strode down the path, noting how secluded and private the garden seemed after the chatter of guests mere metres away.

If Branston laid a finger on Ally...

The thought died as he rounded a corner and found the pair strolling together in a small courtyard. Their heads were together as if whispering secrets. As he watched, Ally stopped and Branston moved closer and took her arm.

Fury at Branston exploded in Angelo's belly.

The denotation sent shockwaves through his body, making his heart pound. What would he have found if he'd waited another twenty minutes to follow them?

He waited, breath severed, for her reaction. But, instead of pulling back, Ally leaned into the other man and Branston's arms went around her, his head dipping towards hers.

This time it wasn't an explosion radiating out from Angelo's belly. It was a piercing stab of pain shearing from his throat, through his chest and right down to his feet, soldered to the ground.

Ally didn't need saving. She *wanted* Branston's touch.

The revelation hit like a smack to the face.

Angelo felt his lungs collapse as the air inside rushed out on an exhalation of realisation and hurt.

How could he not have suspected?

How could he not have *known*?

Suddenly everything became clear.

Amazing that he hadn't worked it out earlier.

From the first he'd understood his ex-wife would only come to the island because she expected to get something from it.

In his hubris, Angelo had assumed she was angling for a reconciliation. Then, over the last week, she'd convinced him that her amnesia was real and she was, at the moment at least, guileless and needing support.

How she'd played him.

Again.

Pain shot through his jaw and around his skull as he ground his teeth. To be gulled by a predatory woman once was a monumental blow. To be gulled twice…

It wasn't Angelo she wanted. He'd just been a convenient tool in her latest scheme.

She'd come to the island because Branston had bought the estate adjoining Angelo's. If there was one thing she'd always wanted as much as money it was the chance to become an actress.

Her performance this week really had been superb. She'd convinced Angelo, who of all men should have known better, that she was wounded and fragile. All the while she'd been waiting for a chance to connect with the top Hollywood director who had a reputation for taking unknowns and turning them into stars.

Angelo remembered her on the cliff path two days ago, eyes wide as she'd simpered up at Branston. She must have been waiting for an opportunity to meet him.

No wonder she'd been adamant about attending the party. Now her decision to wear a dress that left little to the imagination made sense.

Except Angelo refused to be a pawn in her plans. He strode across to the pair, gravel crunching underfoot. Even then Ally didn't look up. She was too busy sinking against Branston as if she knew she only had seconds to make an impact.

'Branston, you—'

'Good thing you're here,' the other man said. 'Ally's not feeling well. I think she needs to go home.'

She does indeed, all the way to Australia. The sooner the better.

'Angelo.' Her voice had a husky throb that caught something in his chest. Except now he knew the emotion he heard was fake. Like that wide-eyed look of fragility.

For a moment he was tempted to walk away, leave her to make her play for Branston and be done with it. But he refused to make it so easy for her.

Instead he moved close, wrapped her arm through his and led her away. Branston came all the way to the front gate, obviously concerned. She'd certainly made an impact in an incredibly short time.

The realisation fuelled Angelo's fury. But he wasn't into public scenes. In silence he led her into his villa. Even then she didn't stop her act. How far would she take this pretence?

He led her upstairs, noting her earlier faltering steps had become firm and she leaned on him less.

Finally, at her suite, she opened the door and went inside, turning to face him.

Before she could speak he followed her, making her step back. 'That was quite a performance. It's almost a shame your scheme won't work.'

'Performance? I don't understand.'

Angelo crossed his arms, staring down into her bewildered face.

He hated that, even now, he was attracted to this lying woman. Supporting her back to the villa, he'd been bombarded with her scent, sweet and enticing, and he still felt the effect of her body against his.

He was aroused with an unholy combination of physical desire and fury.

Fury, not even because she wanted to use Branston to boost her career. But because she'd pressed herself against him, when it should have been *Angelo* she seduced.

Because, despite everything, Angelo still wanted her.

'Then what *do* you understand, Ally? This?'

With one long step he closed the space between them and wrapped his fingers around her wrist.

CHAPTER NINE

ALLY STARED UP into eyes so dark they looked like the midnight sky on a moonless night. No light, no softness.

Yet it wasn't softness she craved.

Her body fizzed with adrenaline from being so close to Angelo. Even this harsh Angelo who looked more like the dark angel who'd sat in judgement on her in the early days, instead of the kind, nurturing man she'd come to know.

She was torn between shock and delight. Because finally her secret craving for closeness had come true. So instead of pulling free she simply tipped her chin higher and held her ground.

'There is no scheme, Angelo. Oliver and I were talking and suddenly I felt woozy.'

It had hit out of nowhere, that sudden weakness as her legs wobbled and her brain clouded. She'd brushed against a low shrub, releasing a heady wave of scent. The next thing she knew she was faint, her pulse racing and her head turning woolly as fragments, not of memory but of emotions, bombarded her. She'd felt so much and so abruptly, it had cut her off at the knees.

'Talking? It didn't look like you were talking from where I stood.'

'You were spying on us?'

Ally frowned, trying to make sense of his *volte face*. The man who'd been so solicitous, worrying that the party might be too taxing, was nowhere to be seen. Angelo's severe expression looked as if it was cast from unforgiving metal.

'I was concerned for you. But I needn't have bothered. Stupid of me not to have realised earlier that you only came here to get close to *him*. You want him to make you a star, don't you?' Angelo's face dipped towards hers, his mouth curling in contempt. 'Were you going to sleep with him to get a role? Or was the plan to leave him dangling?'

Ally moved to smack his face, but he held her easily.

She sucked in a frantic breath, needing an outlet for her anger.

'It was *nothing* like that. In case you missed it, I'm too busy trying to remember who I am to worry about planning future career moves!'

Her chest rose and fell as outrage filled her. She tugged her hand and he released her.

Strange. She'd hated the sense that Angelo held her where he wanted her. Yet now she didn't know what to do with her hands. Almost as if she missed his touch!

'Oliver is simply a *nice man*.' Something she'd actually begun to believe Angelo might be. 'He saw I wasn't really comfortable and kept me company. Plus he was interested from a professional perspective in my amnesia, said it would make a great story premise.'

For once Ally hadn't minded talking about her predicament, especially as Oliver's interest made it seem, for a short time, more like an intellectual puzzle than a frightening disaster.

She'd been grateful for his company. Earlier she'd been fine with Angelo beside her, but when he got caught up in conversation she'd felt out of her depth among all those sophisticated people. Even wearing the only dress she had that seemed suitable for a party, she'd felt self-conscious and it was only partly due to the amount of bare skin her dress revealed.

'We both know your weakness for *nice men*, don't we, Alexa? How you like to use them to get what you want.'

On a surge of energy Ally stepped away, crossing her

arms and scowling up at him. She hated being called Alexa
and he knew it.

'If you mean yourself, Angelo Ricci, then you're wrong.
You're not at all nice.'

'Excellent.' His smile was a baring of teeth. 'Then I don't
have to feel guilty about this.'

He was in her space again, his body flush with hers, his
arm looped around her back as his gleaming gaze captured
hers.

Ally heard a whoosh of breath as her breasts rose on a
sharp intake against his hard chest. Or was that the sound of
a conflagration igniting inside her?

Heat engulfed her, flames licking higher as she absorbed
the sensation of his powerful thigh muscles against hers and
his torso pressing close.

She should be intimidated by his size and strength, by
the fact that they stood flush against each other, with nowhere to hide.

Instead Ally revelled in it. In every glorious centimetre of
arrogant masculinity crammed up against her.

The truth hit her in an instant of stunning acknowledgement.

This was what she'd craved for the past week.

This and more.

She wasn't intimidated by him. Not a bit of it. She was
challenged and she wasn't in the mood to back down. Or
deny herself. She'd felt herself growing stronger by the day,
but along with her recovery had come an ever-increasing
need. For Angelo.

Ally grabbed the lapels of his jacket, tugging hard. As if
that could shift him!

Yet remarkably he did move, his face lowering, centimetre by achingly slow centimetre, until his warm breath feathered her lips.

'There's no point trying to seduce me,' he rumbled. 'I
know you and I'm awake to your schemes.'

Ally laughed. The sound was harsh as he reminded her of

her unenviable situation. That almost everything she knew about herself came from Angelo Ricci.

But he didn't know everything. He had it wrong when he thought her attracted to Oliver Branston. It was *this* man, this darkling fallen angel who attracted her.

She was tired of feeling weak and unsure. Of letting others dictate what she should do and taking responsibility for her.

Out of nowhere, or more probably out of a week of fear, despair, fragile hope and bitter disappointment, rose a confidence born of the knowledge this man protested too much.

'You're immune to me? Is that it?'

Ally lifted one hand to the back of his neck and urged his head down.

There was no resistance, though his eyes glittered brighter.

His mouth met hers and there was a moment of stillness. Ally felt an invisible shockwave shudder through her. An amazing instant of recognition and anticipation.

A second later there was a surge of movement and she found herself pushed up against something solid. A wall? The door? She didn't care. All she cared about was that it anchored her against Angelo's tall frame as a tumult of sensations bombarded her.

His tongue slid deep, his mouth turning a kiss into an act of possession. His hands roving her taut frame, creating shudders of delight wherever he touched.

Ally rolled her head back to give him better access to her mouth, at the same time taking the offensive, kissing him with all the pent-up passion that had brewed for a week.

A week with the man who'd once been her husband.

Had they kissed like this when they'd been married? If so she wondered how she'd had the strength to walk away. It felt as if they'd been made for each other. As if they were yoked together by something so elemental it simply couldn't be denied.

Large hands clamped her hips, lifting her up so she teetered on her toes and she welcomed it, grabbing him for support. He moved in, one thigh thrust between hers so she couldn't fall.

Ally swallowed a soft, whimpering sound at the pressure of that solid thigh right there where she ached for him. She felt his hand on her bare leg, shoving her hemline higher, lifting the dress up so all that separated them was the light wool of his trouser leg and a scrap of red lace.

Angelo moved his leg, or maybe he lifted her against him. Either way, she felt the friction of lace and hard masculine muscle against that damp place between her thighs.

Lightning forked through the darkness behind her closed eyes. She juddered and would have gasped except Angelo swallowed the sound. He took her mouth with an insistent eroticism that turned their kiss into something new. Something that undid any last restraints her overloaded brain might have harboured.

Strong hands urged her up and she followed eagerly, pressing herself against his thigh, questing for more. If only she could get higher, to the source of all that wonderful masculine heat.

She dropped one hand from his shoulder, zeroing in on that rigid shaft of arousal.

Instantly Angelo stopped her. She thought he'd tug her grasping fingers away. But as she rose against him again, a low keening sound emerging from her throat, he froze, holding her hand against all that potent promise.

It was too much and nowhere near enough. Ally's thoughts fogged, especially when he insinuated his other hand behind her, dragging her higher and closer. Until suddenly her hips were bucking in uncontrolled movements and fire burst in her veins.

Ally shuddered with it, hot and cold. Shattering in a bright explosion of colour and sensation such as she'd never known.

She screamed, but the only sound was a muffled echo as Angelo took her ecstatic cry into himself as he kissed her.

That kiss felt...tender. Intimate.

That undid something within her, leaving her wide open and wondering.

For a suspended moment Ally was on the world's pinnacle, shimmering with delight. Then she fell, collapsing into nothingness.

It might have been a mere second later or long minutes, but when she came back to the real world she was in Angelo's arms and she'd never felt so good. Her face was pressed against his soft jacket and unyielding chest. His scent, tangy and enticing, surrounded her and she felt the strong pulse of his heart beneath her ear.

It felt strange, cradled in a man's arms. So strange she wondered if she'd ever experienced it before. Every nerve-ending tingled with delight at the feel of Angelo's powerful arms holding her close.

Dimly she remembered she should be furious with him for his accusations. But Ally had no interest in anger, not given the indescribable, blistering joy she'd experienced. There'd be time later to talk sensibly. For now she wanted more of what she'd just had. She felt floaty with delight as if she'd never before experienced sexual pleasure.

'What's so funny?'

Intriguing how Angelo's voice rumbled out from beneath her ear.

She shook her head, not wanting to get caught up explaining that this felt like an utterly new experience and it had blown her mind.

He studied her face, his eyes shining with something that made her already softened muscles turn to mush.

Angelo turned with her in his arms then lowered her to the bed, following her down. Ally's brain atrophied as his long, athletic body covered hers. He nudged her knees apart and sank between them, his erection pressed intimately at the juncture of her legs and up her belly.

Were all men so big when aroused? Her heart fluttered as if in trepidation, yet at the same time her fingers gripped his backside, eagerly drawing him towards her as her pelvis tilted up.

Angelo murmured something low and heartfelt in Italian, then, before she could stop him, lifted himself away, supporting himself on hands and knees.

Their breaths mingled as their gazes locked. With his body blocking the lamplight, Ally couldn't read his expression, but she sensed his taut control and read his heavy breathing.

'You want me,' she whispered, not sure if it was a challenge or an invitation.

'I shouldn't.'

'Nor should I want you after the way you insult me.'

Did he stiffen? 'But you do.'

Angelo's voice dropped to a deep scrape of sound that made her skin prickle all over and her nipples pucker. It was all she could do not to drag him down on top of her so she could rub herself against him.

How could she want him now when she'd just climaxed so hard she might have blacked out for a second? Was that normal?

'Don't you, Ally?'

Was it childish to clamp her lips shut rather than admit the words? After all, he hadn't admitted it either.

Then one large hand drifted down to her breast, so soft at first she couldn't believe it, until he cupped her harder, his thumb brushing her nipple through her dress, and her whole body jolted.

'Or are you too scared to say it out loud?'

Ally refused to let him feel superior. She lifted her hand, stroking the straining fabric that covered his thigh, then covered his erection with her palm.

Angelo's hissed breath was magic, as was the sudden shudder of his body.

'And you want *me*, Angelo. This is mutual. Stop pretending you're not interested.'

Above her he shook his head, his expression bordering on

incredulous. 'Not interested? You've been driving me out of my mind ever since you washed up on my beach.'

At last. Honesty. Honesty and desire.

Ally felt something take off inside her, as if a flock of birds had risen from a tree and soared into the bright sky.

'Good.' Her voice was husky, only just audible. 'Because you've been doing the same to me.'

There was such freedom in admitting it. Not holding herself in any longer.

For a moment longer they remained unmoving, yet it felt as if everything shifted, the world turning over like a giant kaleidoscope and locking into a new, unfamiliar pattern.

'Hold that thought.'

Angelo crawled backwards, down the bed. He shouldered his way out of his jacket and reached for her feet, slipping off first one sandal then the other.

It was a simple thing. It shouldn't be erotic at all, but Angelo took the time to massage her instep and Ally had to bite back a moan of delight as her eyes closed and she gave herself up to sensual pleasure. This man knew his way around a woman's erogenous zones. She could barely believe she'd climaxed against him while they were still fully clothed and now she was blissing out from the touch of his hands on her feet.

Finally he skimmed those clever hands up her bare legs, so slowly that her breath came in tortured gasps as she waited for him to reach the edge of her short dress. Soon he was pushing it higher, and she shifted her hips so he could free the material.

Callused hands caught the narrow lace at her hips and rolled it down, lower and lower, finally drawing her panties off her feet.

Yet he didn't return to lie over her. Ally finally opened her eyes to see him drop and settle with his shoulders between her thighs.

The sight was…arresting. Incredibly erotic, especially when he sensed her regard and lifted his head to meet her stare. Something passed between them, hot and hectic, and

Ally felt her heartbeat pound against her ribs and lower, between her legs.

Angelo's mouth curved up in a smile that melded desire with greed. As if he wanted to taste her there. The idea made her quiver in arousal.

'Angelo—'

'It's okay. I'll take care of you.' He was already lowering his head when Ally leaned up, putting out her hand to stop him.

'No! I don't want that.'

Glittering eyes met hers and she read surprise in his pared-back features.

Exciting as it was, seeing him there, Ally wanted something else. Next time she exploded in ecstasy she wanted to be *with Angelo*, not alone.

She needed him desperately.

'I want *you*.'

Ridiculous to feel heat scorch her throat and cheeks. They must have had sex lots of times and, from what Angelo hinted, she wasn't shy. But Ally felt shy now, lying with her legs sprawled wide and Angelo there between them. Shy as she hadn't felt when she'd climaxed against him.

'Please, Angelo.'

Ally had no doubt that Angelo would make it good for her. He was experienced and obviously knew how to please her. Yet she could only go with her instinct. She wanted them, together. To lose herself in his arms.

A sigh of relief eased from her lungs as he reared back and, holding her eyes, hauled off his shirt.

Ally's gaze flickered to his straight shoulders and down the leanly sculpted chest she'd so admired when they'd swum together. He really was stunning. How would it feel when they came together, naked?

'Take your dress off, Ally. Or do you want me to do it?'

For answer she scrambled to sit up and reached for the zip at her back. Her tongue was stuck to the roof of her

mouth. She doubted she could speak anyway, not when
Angelo was unbuckling his belt and reaching for his zip,
every movement slow and methodical, in contrast to the
movements of her damp, fumbling fingers.

In the end she had to sit up and pull the fastening around
to her side so she could see where she'd caught fabric in
the teeth of the zip. Finally she dragged the zip down and
shoved the dress low, wriggling to get out of it.

That was when she remembered she was braless, as her
breasts swung free and she heard an intake of breath.

A deep voice murmured, 'Don't stop there.'

Angelo felt the air back up in his lungs as he surveyed her,
dishevelled, rosy-cheeked and heart-stoppingly alluring.
For a second she looked as if she contemplated pulling the
dress back up to cover herself. But as her eyes met his, Ally's expression morphed into one of excitement.

He felt the heavy drag of her stare as it dropped from
his face, down his body to his sheathed penis. His erection pulsed in response to that hungry stare and he almost
chuckled at her look of surprise.

A tiny part of his brain puzzled over Ally's reactions.
The way she'd stopped him going down on her was new.
The shock he read now on her face. Was it possible he'd
been wrong? Maybe she really did have amnesia.

Maybe he was mistaken about her and Oliver. Had he
allowed his bias against her, not to mention plain, old-fashioned jealousy, colour his perceptions?

Angelo didn't have enough brainpower to puzzle it out
now. His mind was fixed on Ally shimmying out of that
slinky blue dress, her breasts bobbing enticingly.

His breath sheared off as she dragged the material lower.
The contrast between plump, rose-tipped breasts and her
narrow waist dried his mouth. Then the gentle curve out
to her hips...

The years had changed her, filled out her curves a little more, but he liked that. The thatch of dark blonde hair

between her thighs had surprised him. She'd always been bare there, ready for her bikini modelling. But he liked the natural look. Even the unfamiliar way she blushed appealed, enhancing the feeling that this was special and new.

Angelo swallowed hard. It was only as the dress fell to the floor that he found his voice again. 'You're even more beautiful than I remember.'

Stunning eyes the colour of a dusk sky met his. Electricity zapped across his skin and arrowed to his heavy groin. She swallowed, like him teetering on the brink.

He kept his eyes locked on hers as he prowled up the bed. He was already so aroused he didn't trust himself to survey her lovely body again.

Angelo paused above her, swallowing air that tasted of Ally, sweet and hot. He shuddered, too aware that any incidental touch might send him over the edge.

'Ready?'

She nodded, her eyes huge and brilliant, and he felt himself sinking into them like a man without a life raft.

He wasn't sure if he was reassuring her or himself as he cupped her cheek and watched her gaze soften. All he knew was that this was different. He'd thought he'd known this woman so well, but now, despite the past, this moment felt unique. He couldn't remember ever being so close to losing control so quickly.

Angelo shook his head, pushing the thought away as he focused on the mechanics of bringing them both the utmost pleasure without spilling himself prematurely. It was a problem he hadn't had since his teens but he was so aroused this was going to be tough. Wonderful but tough.

'Relax,' he murmured, bending to brush his mouth across hers. As he did she sighed and reached up to clasp the back of his neck with both hands as if claiming him for herself.

The idea appealed, as did the husky little murmurs she made as he kissed the corners of her mouth.

Ally tugged at his neck, trying to bring him closer, and he obliged, covering her delicious body with his own.

For a second they were both absolutely still, absorbing each new sensation. Angelo felt a shudder begin in his groin, race through his buttocks and all the way up his spine to make his nape tingle and tighten.

'You feel so good,' he growled against her mouth.

'So do you.' She shifted beneath him and he sank deeper between her thighs, heat meeting heat.

Suddenly Angelo couldn't wait any longer, despite his best intentions to take his time.

Kneeing her thighs wider, he stroked her breast and felt her quiver. He kissed her there, feeling her move needily beneath his mouth as he slid his hand between her legs. Gently he explored, finding that tiny nub, smiling against her breast as she tensed beneath him.

He explored further, deeper, and she responded with a rise of her hips that spoke of an urgency that matched his.

No more foreplay. Not when they were both so needy.

Lifting his head so he could watch Ally's expression, he hooked one of her slender legs over his hip and positioned himself. Her eyes weren't wide now. They were slitted and slumbrous, pure invitation.

Angelo smiled as he tilted his hips and pushed.

It was all he could have hoped for and more. Ally's expression, the soft embrace of her body, that searing, close heat enfolding him. He felt like some conquering hero about to claim the world's greatest prize.

Angelo gave himself up to beckoning bliss and thrust, hard and smooth, into paradise. Only to freeze, a split second too late, as he felt a barrier that was there one moment then gone the next.

Ally stiffened, her lovely, limber body turning rigid.

Stunned, he looked down into wide eyes and a mouth drawn back in pain. He saw her pulse pound frantically, felt her fingernails dig into his shoulders as a great tremor passed through her.

Some part of his brain was still working, trying to tell him something. But it couldn't be.

Yet, as Ally's eyes welled with unshed tears and she gulped in a shuddery gasp of hurt, he realised it was true.

Ally was a virgin!

CHAPTER TEN

THROUGH A HAZE of shock, Ally saw Angelo frown and felt him pull back.

'Stop! Don't move!'

She clutched at his shoulders and tried to hold him to her.

The pain was starting to ease. She drew an unsteady breath, grateful for Angelo's stillness as her body adjusted to this strange new sensation.

Ally's brow crinkled. How could it feel that way when they'd done this before, and when she'd wanted it so badly? Even if she hadn't been sexually active for a while, surely it wouldn't feel like this.

The answer was obvious but too perplexing to take in now. For, as she relaxed a little under his weight, the uncomfortable tightness changed to anticipation.

Ally would make sense of it later. For now what she wanted, *needed*, was the pleasure that had beckoned so brightly.

She drew a deep breath that didn't seem to fill her cramped lungs. 'You can move now.'

To her consternation, Angelo withdrew totally, leaving her bereft.

'Not like that,' she gasped.

'What do you want, Ally?'

He spoke through gritted teeth, the tendons in his neck standing proud and his features stark, as if his skin had shrunk. He looked like she'd felt a second ago, hurting and holding it in.

'I want you, Angelo. Please don't stop.'

He was shaking his head before she finished. 'We can't. You're not—'

'None of that matters. I want you, Angelo.' She swallowed the last of her pride as she reached for him. 'I *need* you. Don't leave me like this.'

Troubled dark eyes held hers for the longest time. Until finally, with a guttural whisper of something she couldn't catch, he knelt over her again.

Wide shoulders blocked off the room as the heat of his body blanketed her, but she kept her eyes on his, willing him on. His touch was light, each movement careful, so that when he took her again it was in slow motion, allowing her to absorb and revel in each incredible sensation. On and on it went, till Angelo and she lay together as one.

This time it felt amazing.

'No pain?' His voice was gruff.

'None at all.' She frowned, trying to find the words. 'It feels strange but not bad.'

Angelo grimaced, his laugh tight, and she realised he was probably used to more wholehearted compliments.

'I'm sorry, I didn't mean—'

'Don't be sorry. You're being truthful. That's what matters.'

Ally saw that he meant it. Despite the grim look on his face and the aura of ruthlessly shackled energy that she supposed came from holding back. For her.

It was a reminder that he'd already given her one release but he'd had none. As simple as that, she discovered that she wanted to give him pleasure as much as she wanted it for herself.

Ally smiled up into that serious face, smoothed her hands over his shoulders and tugged him closer.

'Make love to me, Angelo. Please.'

What came next was a revelation. That a man so large and powerful could be so tender and careful shouldn't surprise her, yet again and again Ally found herself stunned by his consideration. And his capacity for discovering erogenous zones she hadn't known existed.

His every movement was slow and deliberate, calculated to delight.

It wasn't just what Angelo *did* either. The very act of holding him close thrilled her. So did the occasionally harsh sound of his breathing and his sighs of approval as she discovered some of the places where he was sensitive.

Inhaling his scent, rich with citrus, pepper and cedar, excited her. As did the taste of his skin. Ally couldn't get enough of him, kissing, licking, even nipping gently with her teeth, to be rewarded with the sight and feel of this big, powerful man shuddering with pleasure.

When he moved inside her it seemed as if the world shifted too, so profound and amazing were the sensations Angelo evoked.

Until suddenly she was clinging to him, panting for breath, feeling the rise of something inside that was both inevitable and all-consuming.

'Come for me, *cara*.'

Angelo's words caressed her cheek before he gently bit down on her earlobe, and suddenly she was arching her back, matching his rhythm with a desperation that wiped everything from her mind.

'Angelo!'

Her voice was a broken cry as she convulsed around him.

A second later, as if he'd been waiting for her, his movements altered. The slow, easy glide becoming a charged drive into pleasure.

They clung, bodies striving, as the world burst apart and enveloped her in bliss. She'd experienced sexual release a short time ago but this was more intense, more profound, and far more than she'd expected.

When Ally came back to herself she was wrapped in Angelo's arms, his head in the curve of her neck, his breath humid on her flesh and his chest heaving. She loved the feel of him slumped there and wrapped her arms around him.

Her heart was pounding and so was his. She felt it hammering behind his ribs.

A moment later he muttered something in a low, voiceless rumble and lifted himself off her.

Ally couldn't stop a muffled protest at the idea of him moving away. At least he only rolled onto his back beside her, his body touching hers all the way down her side.

She drew a shaky breath and tried to comprehend what had just happened. It had been stunning, not just physically but emotionally. Instinctively she shied from examining her feelings too closely because she feared what they might reveal.

She was groping for something to say when Angelo levered himself up from the bed and strode into the en suite bathroom without a word.

Ally frowned. But what had she expected? Kind words?

It had been sex, pure and simple. They'd goaded each other into it, angry as well as sexually aroused. It would be a mistake to read anything more into what had happened.

Yet she recalled Angelo's expression as he'd joined with her the second time. The patience and care he'd shown. More than that, she'd felt real tenderness, almost reverence.

Could it be that, despite the circumstances, they had found something special? It *felt* as if they'd shared something that transcended simple carnal lust.

But what did she know? She'd been a virgin.

The knowledge was like an earthquake, undermining the few certainties she'd managed to cobble together. If she'd been a virgin then surely that meant she wasn't the woman Angelo believed her.

Where did that leave her?

Who was she?

Suddenly fear stirred. Fear of being adrift again. Of that grey world of nothingness that had engulfed her when she'd first woken to no memory.

Angelo planted his palms on the marble benchtop and stared at himself in the mirror. He looked the same as usual but he felt completely different. As if the world had tilted on its side and everything he knew or thought he knew had shattered.

His body still pulsed from orgasm and his brain was foggy from the remnants of explosive ecstasy, but his belly roiled with a sickening mix of guilt, shock and awe. It felt selfish to dwell on how wonderful their sexual encounter had been when the implications were so mighty, turning everything upside down.

How badly had he hurt her? His gut clenched as he recalled her stunned gaze, eyes wide and pleading.

How had he got everything totally wrong?

He squeezed his eyes shut, trying to identify a moment when he might have withdrawn and walked away from tonight's tempestuous events. But there wasn't one. Making love to Ally had been inevitable from the moment they'd marched into her room, sparking fire off each other.

No, earlier than that. From the moment he'd seen her with Oliver and rage had boiled in his blood along with jealousy. It had already been too late then.

As it had been even earlier in the evening. From the moment she'd sashayed into the living room in that slinky blue dress and something inside his brain had shorted. He'd tried and failed to keep her away from the party because he'd known the alternative, spending the night at home, trying to ignore how much he wanted her, was inconceivable.

Angelo tried to comfort himself with the knowledge that what had happened had been mutual. She'd wanted him as much as he'd wanted her.

Want. Such a weak word for that tremendous surge of desire, possessiveness and sheer desperation.

He hung his head. It didn't matter how fated it had seemed. Or that they'd both been desperate for it.

He'd just deflowered a virgin.

An innocent.

Not his ex-wife. Not a woman who understood that, however compelling their drive for intimacy, this wasn't about love but about raw, unvarnished lust.

Ally wasn't the woman he'd believed her. Yet she'd had to withstand his withering scorn. He shrank at the memory of how he'd treated her since her arrival, taking his anger out on her.

This wasn't Alexa but a woman he didn't know. A woman who didn't know him.

He might not have seduced her into sex. It had been entirely mutual. Yet that didn't stop his guilt. It tormented him, curdling his stomach. He should have been caring for her, not giving in to lust.

His mother and sister told him he was over-protective, shouldering too much responsibility and trying to safeguard them from every hurt. Maybe they were right. But tonight, again, he'd failed spectacularly as a protector.

Angelo raked a hand through his hair and straightened, sucking in a deep breath.

It was time to see how Ally was.

He paused in the doorway to the bedroom, heart slamming into his ribs as he saw her lying, curled on her side, looking spent and fragile.

How badly had he hurt her? The question made him feel queasy, but he had to know.

He crossed the room and gingerly sank onto the bed beside her. She didn't look up, though she must have felt the mattress sink.

She was shivering and he reached out to drag a cover over her nakedness, then paused, noticing the small but tell-tale smudge of colour on the bed behind her.

Angelo's heart shrank.

He should have followed his instincts there and then and got right away from her. But when she'd looked at him with those big eyes, wide and pleading, he hadn't been able to turn away.

Because you didn't really want to leave.

Because being with Ally felt essential to him.

'Ally? Talk to me.'

He heard a muffled sniff and brushed her hair back from

her face. Relief filled him when he saw she wasn't crying, but that didn't ameliorate his guilt.

'Are you hurting? What can I do?'

Finally she turned her head to look at him. 'No. I'm okay.'

'You don't look it.'

He was used to lovers who sighed and snuggled and talked about next time. By contrast Ally looked strained and pale, but who could blame her?

A gurgle of laughter surprised him and her mouth tilted up into a tiny smile. 'Thanks for the compliment. Just what a woman wants to hear.'

'You're shivering. Of course I'm concerned.' His mouth firmed. 'I hurt you. I can't tell you how sorry I am. If I'd known—'

'You didn't know. Neither of us did.'

Angelo shook his head. 'I should have realised. I can't believe I didn't work it out before.'

Yet, as he said it, he marvelled at how much this woman looked like his ex-wife. The bone structure, the shape of her mouth and nose, even her gestures. And those memorable eyes. How rare was that colour? He'd never seen the like anywhere else.

They could have been twins. Except Alexa had said she was an only child. That was one of the reasons he'd been so sure of Ally's identity.

Sure, but wrong.

'I must be very like her.'

Ally might have read his mind. Her expression as unreadable, yet Angelo heard a wealth of emotion behind her words. Silently he nodded. What could he say?

Angelo stroked Ally's hair off her face, filled with tenderness and regret for the hurt he'd caused. But not for the actual deed. He still couldn't regret that.

'Did I hurt you very much? How are you now?'

He'd never been with a virgin.

She shrugged. 'It only hurt a little.' Her gaze avoided his, making him wonder. 'I'm okay now.'

Angelo wished he could believe her. 'If I'd known I would have been more careful.' What was he thinking? 'If I'd known I would never have touched you.'

At least he *hoped* he'd have been strong enough to keep his distance. But he'd never before been so devoured by passion. It made him uneasy, doubting his willpower. No other woman had ever threatened his control in this way.

'Don't!'

In a flurry of movement, Ally pushed his hand away and scrabbled further up the bed, reaching for the bed covering in a bid to conceal herself.

Angelo rose enough for her to pull the cover up then sat again, eyeing her warily. He shouldn't be surprised at her impulse for modesty, yet it felt like she was shutting him out.

Who could blame her?

'Ally, I'm sorry.'

'Stop saying that!' Her mouth tightened. 'There's nothing to be sorry about.'

She paused to draw a deep breath and Angelo forced himself not to follow the rise of her breasts beneath their thin cover.

'There's no harm done. It was just sex. Millions of people do it all the time. You used protection so there won't be consequences.' Yet Ally's voice was clipped and her shrug looked anything but insouciant. Angelo read tension in the movement. 'And if it wasn't as good for you as it usually is...' another lift of tight shoulders '... I'm sure you'll get over it.'

Angelo frowned at her. 'Not as good as usual?'

He reeled. Her dismissive *just sex* comment had thrown him, and now she implied what they'd shared was substandard.

Ally turned away, but Angelo was so close it was hard to avoid looking at him. Plus he was naked, sitting there unfazed by his lack of clothes, while her stupid pulse pattered faster and her insides turned to mush all over again.

Given his magnificent body it wasn't surprising that he was comfortable naked. More comfortable than she was. He'd probably had plenty of lovers too, considering his charisma and good looks. And given his obvious expertise in pleasing a woman.

Ally shivered and tried to rein her wayward thoughts back in, away from the memory of him using his mouth, hands and toned, virile body to bring her to ecstasy.

'Ally, I—'

'No. Please.' She lifted her palm. 'Don't apologise again.'

She didn't think she could cope with him saying sorry any more, reinforcing how much he regretted their spur-of-the-moment coupling.

She'd already had time to work out that Angelo had been driven by fury at what he'd believed to be his ex-wife's scheming and now he thoroughly regretted what had been, for her, an amazing experience. He'd shot out of bed without a word.

'I wasn't going to apologise.'

Was that impatience in his voice? She met his eyes then looked away again, horrified by the fluttering feeling in her chest. Just the sight of him undid her.

'Good. I think—'

'I was going to say that what we just shared was anything but disappointing. It was fantastic.'

As if tugged by an invisible string, her head turned towards him. Did he mean it? She wanted to think so, but she couldn't tell if his words were just to reassure her. He met her stare easily, but what did that prove?

'I'm glad you think so,' she said carefully.

'Of course I do.' He leaned closer, his expression earnest. 'It was…spectacular.'

It sure was. For her, at least.

But she couldn't shake the idea that Angelo tried too hard to reassure her. He'd climaxed but, on a scale of one to ten, could intercourse with an inexperienced virgin compete with hot sex with someone who matched him for sensual experience?

Someone like his ex-wife.

The woman he'd thought he was bedding.

The woman, Ally realised, with a sick feeling in her middle, he still desired, despite what had passed between them.

That was why his emotions had been roused tonight, fuelled by his unwilling attraction for the woman who'd betrayed him. The woman he still wanted. He'd been jealous, imagining her with Oliver.

That explained his sudden and complete withdrawal when he'd discovered she wasn't Alexa. He'd only kept going because Ally had pleaded with him. Fierce heat swamped her at the thought. Pity sex, they called it.

'So, we've sorted that out. It was very nice and now it's over.'

One large hand reached out and captured hers, planting it, palm down, on his bare thigh. Ally felt the furnace heat of his body, the twitch of powerful muscle and the tickle of dark hair under her hand. It sent some signal to her brain which immediately stirred her crazy hormones back into action.

As if, having had her once, Angelo might be interested in more!

Ally kept her gaze down, not wanting him to read her thoughts. Until she realised her attention had strayed to his groin. She swallowed. No wonder there'd been pain. Angelo wasn't a little man in any respect.

'Far more than *very nice*, Ally.' His deep voice slid across her body's pleasure points, making her skin tighten and her nipples peak.

Horrified, she looked up and met his dark stare. This couldn't go on. She had to pull herself together.

She nodded, as if everything was clear and easy. 'And now it's finished. Time to move on.'

Ally watched his black eyebrows climb, as if in surprise.

But there was no going back. She had to begin as she meant to go on. Not as a victim, or an object of sympathy.

'So, Angelo, the million-dollar question is, if I'm not your ex-wife, Alexa Barrett, who am I?'

CHAPTER ELEVEN

'I WISH I KNEW.'

Angelo hated seeing the pain and confusion in her beautiful shadowed eyes. Just as he hated that perfunctory tilt of her chin and her cool tone as she spoke dismissively about sex being over.

Of course it's over. She's out of bounds. She should have been out of bounds from the first.

Yet he felt dazed by the most memorable lovemaking of his life. He told himself that was an exaggeration but didn't believe it.

Clearly it hadn't been the same for Ally.

It had been no tender seduction. In the beginning it had been too hot and fast for an innocent. When he'd learned the truth, he'd belatedly done everything he could to make up for the initial pain. He'd thought he'd succeeded. But maybe, despite her orgasm, the whole event had been too traumatic.

If he'd known, he'd have taken more care.

If he'd known, he'd have found a way to resist her!

'We'll find out who you are.' He leaned close, aiming to reassure. 'Trust me. I have the resources to help. We'll discover your identity, you'll see.'

For the longest moment her lavender gaze locked on his and he'd have given half his fortune to know what she thought.

Was it possible that, despite the shock of what had just happened, she too felt the connection he did? Even now he felt it, more strongly than anything he'd experienced with Alexa.

Finally she nodded. 'I hope so. It's rather tough, not knowing who you are.'

Angelo's heart went out to her. There she sat, clutching the bedclothes and, if he wasn't mistaken, trying not to shiver, but downplaying her shock. She was so gallant. She gave him a lesson in true courage.

'On the upside,' he offered, trying to match her light tone, 'at least you're not my ex-wife.'

Was it selfish to be glad she wasn't the woman he'd learned to despise?

Ally laughed aloud, the sound pulling his lips into an answering smile. 'You're right. Every time you spoke about her it was to reveal something awful. I was on tenterhooks all the time, wondering what dreadful thing you were going to tell me next.' She snuggled lower into the bed. 'It's a relief to know that wasn't my life.'

Again, Angelo admired her attitude. Ally was strong, forthright and refreshing.

She needed help and he needed to begin thinking with his mind not his libido. Even if some greedy part of him wanted her to reach out to him for reassurance now everything they thought they'd known about her was disproven.

Angelo stilled at the realisation of his selfishness. No, it was far better that she was confident, even though he sensed some of what she projected was a façade.

'You said you felt suddenly woozy at the party.' It wasn't a word he was familiar with but from the context he guessed she meant unwell. 'But you were okay by the time we got back here.' He paused, thinking of how much more than simply *okay* she'd been. 'Is there anything else I need to know? Should I call the doctor?'

She shook her head, her rumpled hair sliding around her bare skin like a curtain of dark honey.

'No, it's nothing like that. I think it was a memory, or part of one.'

Yet, instead of being excited, Ally's expression grew tense. That wasn't a good sign.

'Do you want to tell me about it?'

'There's nothing much to tell. It was confused and more about feelings than a recollection of an actual event.'

'And it made you feel sick?'

Angelo's belly hollowed. Was her past so bad it affected her like that? The doctor had mentioned the possibility she'd suffered some recent trauma and that was part of the reason her brain refused to remember, as a defence against something it didn't want to face.

Ally gnawed at the corner of her mouth. She looked vulnerable, her veneer of confidence slipping. Angelo wanted to pull her to him and assure her everything would be all right, but he held back. He had no right to touch her without an invitation, no matter how much he wanted to.

'It made me feel...' She shook her head. 'Upset. But I don't know why.'

Angelo heard the fear in her voice. He could barely imagine how it would feel to have no knowledge of yourself or your past. 'Don't read too much into that. It's a big thing, regaining your memory. It's bound to knock you off-balance.'

He just hoped the doctor was wrong and she wouldn't have to face past trauma on top of all she'd already been through.

'You're right.' She scrunched up her nose in that cute way she had, then sent him a swift sideways glance. 'Despite what just happened—' she gestured to the bed '—I suppose there's no way I *could* be her?'

'Absolutely not.'

Ally mightn't know much about how sex felt but there'd been no mistaking her virginity. He almost told her about the bloodstained bedding but wondered if it might embarrass her.

'Which means I really do look like Alexa.' She shook her head. 'It seems too fantastic to be real.'

'I know what you mean.' That was why he'd been so convinced of her identity, despite the couple of differences he'd put down to time or an imperfect memory. 'But the likeness is uncanny.'

An idea occurred and Angelo shot to his feet. It only took

a minute to grab his phone from his discarded trousers. He sat down again beside Ally and started searching. 'I'll show you.'

'You kept her photo?'

Ally's voice held a note he couldn't interpret.

'No.' He'd eradicated every trace of Alexa from his life. He didn't want reminders of his worst ever mistake. 'But I can find one. There.'

After a short media search he held out his phone.

Ally took it gingerly and he heard her indrawn breath.

'She's stunning!'

Angelo leaned over to look again at the photo, snapped by a press photographer as he and Alexa entered a red-carpet event in Rome. She wore a shiny sheath dress of deep purple that hung from one shoulder. It hugged her body and the long slit up the side of the skirt revealed most of one slim leg.

'She looks exactly like you.'

'I don't look like that!'

Something in Ally's voice made him look up from the phone. 'Your hair is a few shades darker and done differently.'

Ally shook her head. 'The features are very similar but she's glamorous and so incredibly poised.'

Angelo stared. 'Did you look in the mirror tonight? You're every bit as stunning. More so because it's all natural, not contrived for effect.'

His voice hit a rocky note as he remembered Ally appearing at the head of the stairs looking utterly gorgeous. She'd stolen his breath and set desire pounding through him so hard he'd tried every excuse to make her stay here in the villa.

And didn't that work out well?

That thought gave him the strength to look away when Ally stared at him wonderingly. Needing distraction, he took the phone and searched for another photo.

'Do you have wedding photos?'

Angelo flinched. 'No.' Hearing how brusque his voice was, he searched for something to soften the denial. 'It was a private wedding, with only my mother and sister as witnesses. With a baby supposedly on the way there seemed no

reason to wait and Alexa said she preferred a simple ceremony.' Because she'd wanted to hook him as quickly as possible. 'Here's another.'

He passed the phone back and couldn't help noticing the
brush of Ally's fingers on his.

He made himself focus on the photo. This one was of
Alexa alone, modelling the sort of swimsuit designed never
to get wet.

'You're right.' He couldn't tell if Ally sounded deflated or
just tired. 'We're very similar, though I think we're a couple
of dress sizes different.'

Angelo bit back the urge to say he much preferred her feminine curves to Alexa's thinner body. But he'd made enough
mistakes for one night.

'And look at this.' Ally expanded the photo. 'Here.' She
leaned, in peering over the phone and expanding the photo.

'What is it?' He saw nothing but an expanse of lean hip.

'There's no scar.'

Angelo frowned. 'Alexa never had a scar there.'

'Exactly.'

Ally thrust the phone at him and pulled aside the bedding
to reveal her upper thigh and the curve of her hip. Angelo's
mouth dried as he recalled the satiny texture of her skin and
the sweet woman and spice scent of her body. Desire thundered through him and his hand tightened around the phone.

As he watched she tilted her body and there, on her hip,
was a thin silvery scar he hadn't noticed earlier.

Because his mind had been on other things.

'More proof that you're not her.' As if any were needed.
'It doesn't look new.'

'No, I've had it for as long as I remember. Gran said I fell
off a swing...' Ally's voice petered out and before his eyes
her face paled, the sprinkling of freckles suddenly standing
out across her nose.

Ally's hand went to her throat in an unmistakably defensive gesture.

'Are you okay?'

'I...' She shook her head, frowning. 'I remember, *almost* remember, her voice. My gran's voice.' She blinked and raised drowned eyes. 'I should be excited but it all feels wrong somehow.'

She swallowed hard, as if forcing down a lump in her throat. Angelo clenched his hands, knowing better than to reach for her.

'What can I do, Ally? How can I help?'

For several seconds she didn't answer. Finally she spoke, her voice strained. 'Would you mind just holding me? I feel cold inside and I know it's stupid because nothing's really changed, but I feel so alone.'

'Of course.'

Angelo felt as if a piece of his heart had broken away, listening to her hesitant request. After all she'd been through it was no wonder she needed comfort. He leaned over and put his phone on the bedside table.

But instead of leaning into his embrace Ally slid down under the covers. That was when he realised her teeth were chattering. Not from the temperature in the room but from shock.

He grabbed his discarded boxers, because there was no way he'd dare share a bed with her naked. Then he pulled back the bedclothes and slipped in beside her.

Instantly Ally turned onto her side and he gathered her close, her head on his shoulder, her hair tickling his chest and her bare, beautiful body flush against him.

Angelo wrapped his arms around her in a loose embrace. 'Rest now. Everything will look better in the morning. I promise.'

She nodded and he caught her sweet woman scent. It was pure temptation. But this time Angelo conquered his urge for more. Because Ally's needs came first.

Ally woke to delicious warmth. She lay on her side with her knees bent and Angelo behind her, his arm heavy across her waist, heat radiating from him.

She breathed deep, luxuriating in the feel of them lying together.

'You're awake.'

His deep voice wrapped around her like his embrace. She felt the sound rumble through his body into hers and bit her lip as familiar, needy excitement stirred.

Just like that.

She'd gone to sleep grateful for simple human contact but in an instant she was aroused by this man. A coil of heat circled low in her body and her breasts felt fuller at the thought of what they'd done together and might do again.

Ally tried to tell herself it was because he was her only lover.

Yet surely it wasn't so simple. She'd wanted Angelo from the first. Even when they were at daggers drawn there'd been a sizzling undercurrent of awareness, urging her to challenge him if she couldn't understand him.

That sexual awareness hadn't changed, even if her pride insisted she should distance herself. Because he'd bedded her thinking she was someone else. Common sense told her any attraction he felt for her was because she looked like the woman who still, obviously, evoked incredibly strong responses in him.

Ally gulped down a hot tangle of emotions and dragged in a breath that felt like shards of glass in her tight chest. Forcing her eyelids up, she was amazed to see bright daylight outside.

'You stayed all night?' She half turned, looking over her shoulder and meeting his enigmatic dark stare.

'You needed me.' The simple statement made her greedy heart tumble. 'I didn't like to leave in case I woke you.'

Unlike his hot body, Angelo's voice was cool and detached. A reminder that he was here for her, not himself.

As she thought it he lifted his arm off her waist and rolled away. Ally stifled the cry of dismay that rose to her lips.

'Thank you, Angelo.' She pulled the bedding tight around herself and turned to him, but he was already getting up from the bed. 'That was kind of you.'

That halted him in his tracks. 'Kind?' He paused, a wry expression on his face. 'It was the least I could do after...'

He shook his head and her mood tumbled. It couldn't be clearer that he felt uncomfortable about having sex with her. That he didn't want a repeat.

Ally wrapped her fragile defences around herself and pasted on a smile that hopefully looked more real than it felt. 'Of course. But, again, thank you.'

This time his gaze held hers and a frisson of connection crackled through her. Was she the only one to feel it?

'Rest now. I'll have Rosetta bring you breakfast.'

Under veiling eyelashes she watched him pull on his clothes, his movements quick, almost urgent. Because he had business elsewhere or because he didn't want to be around her any longer? Maybe he feared she'd read too much into the sex they'd shared. Still, she couldn't stop the question. 'And what are you going to do?'

'Start the search for your identity. With luck, and my resources, it won't take too long to find out who you are and where you came from.'

'Wonderful.' She pinned on a smile that felt too tight across her cheeks. 'Thank you.'

It would be a relief finally to know who she was, so she could resume her real life. Yet why did she feel desolate at the prospect of leaving the villa? No, not the villa. Leaving Angelo Ricci.

Realisation sheared through her like a dropping blade.

Angelo said he despised Alexa but hatred was close to love. He still felt incredibly strongly about his ex-wife and that was what Ally had tapped into.

But had she done more? Had she done something silly, like fall for a man who saw her only as a pale imitation of the woman he'd once cared for?

Suddenly Ally was terrified that was exactly what she'd done.

CHAPTER TWELVE

ALLY HAD SPENT a week with the man she'd believed to be her ex-husband. Now, three days into her second week with Angelo Ricci, everything had changed.

Angelo was the perfect host, ensuring she was comfortable while he pursued his quest to uncover her identity.

He was considerate and supportive. Yet Ally longed for more. A spark of the emotion they'd shared. Of the passion that still twisted, like a slow-burning flame, deep within her. Even a flicker of anger would do if she couldn't have his desire. Anything to indicate he felt *something* for her.

She told herself she shouldn't crave his touch. But that made no difference. No matter how hard she tried she couldn't forget that magical interlude when he'd shown her a whole new world. With him she'd come alive in ways she hadn't thought possible. As if sex were more than a physical experience.

But Angelo didn't share her feelings. He was friendly and considerate but that was all.

No more burning glances. No more sizzling passion.

Because you're not the woman he really wanted. He thought you were Alexa.

Ally shivered. The speed with which Angelo had left her bed that morning had confirmed it. He'd spent the night with her out of pity and guilt. Ally had read that in his eyes, and in the shadows that darkened his features when he thought she wasn't watching. He felt sorry for her and blamed himself for what had happened between them.

As if she hadn't been a more than willing participant!

Ally tried to tell herself she'd been carried away by anger that night. But she'd wanted Angelo from the first. She'd been attracted even when he was furious and dismissive, and when he'd been nice…he'd undone her utterly.

She pulled her borrowed gardening gloves higher up her hands and frowned at the arching rose bush before her. Instead of blush pink blooms she saw dark eyes and a haunted, handsome face in her mind's eye.

Angelo was doing everything he could to track down her name and her past. He must be paying a fortune for the investigators but he was determined to get answers for her.

Because he wants you gone as soon as possible.

She drew herself up, searching for the strength she needed. Was it any surprise she felt as if she was living a half-life? Maybe her anguished feelings weren't just because of Angelo. It made sense she was unsettled from not knowing who she was.

Surely it was impossible to fall for a man she'd known a bare week.

If she kept telling herself that…

'Ally?'

Adrenaline shot through her at the sound of his voice. She spun around and felt that familiar dazzle of excitement as their eyes met. How could a man grow more scrumptious by the day?

'Hi Angelo.' Did she sound breathless? Her pulse was pounding so fast she couldn't tell.

'Enzo's trusted you alone with the roses?' He nodded to the secateurs in her gloved hands. 'He must really respect your gardening skills. He watches my mother like a hawk when she wants to get involved here.'

Ally shrugged. Angelo made too much out of something simple. Was he trying too hard to sound casual? But, taking in his relaxed features, she dismissed the notion. *She* was the one pining for things she couldn't have.

'I'm just deadheading. Nothing major.'

'Even so, it's no small thing, winning his trust, believe me.'

Angelo paused and her pulse thudded. 'Do you have news? Have you found out anything?'

She had recurring nightmares about never recovering her past, living the rest of her life in this strange limbo. It would be fantastic finally to get a lead on who she was. Yet at the same time she felt butterflies inside at the idea of leaving and never seeing Angelo again.

'I'm afraid not.' He frowned. 'But we *are* making progress. Eventually I'll have good news for you.'

He smiled reassuringly and Ally felt that familiar warmth inside her chest. She knew that, as well as trying to trace her movements in Italy, Angelo had hired people to locate Alexa, figuring there must be a familial link between her and Ally. Surely soon there would be a breakthrough.

'I came to see if you felt like an outing. It's a glorious day and I thought an excursion might be welcome. You've been here nine days and the only place you've been is next door.'

Ally fought to keep her voice calm, while inside she felt like dancing a jig. An outing with Angelo, just for fun and not because he thought it was his duty. 'What did you have in mind?'

His cheeks creased as he smiled down at her, as if reading her pleasure. 'Capri. It's calm enough to see the Blue Grotto. Then we could eat at a restaurant I know with the best views in southern Italy.'

'I'd love it!'

'More salad?'

Angelo held out the bowl so Ally could help herself. He liked her enthusiasm for good food, sampling each dish slowly, identifying the flavours, before tucking in wholeheartedly.

They had a secluded spot on the restaurant terrace and inevitably his attention was riveted to this fascinating woman rather than the glorious view.

'My mother would like you,' he said, surprising himself.

Ally stopped with a piece of fish poised on her fork. 'She would? How so?'

'She's a fine cook, she'd like the way you appreciate what you eat.'

Angelo watched Ally pop the morsel into her mouth and chew. He tried not to stare at those full pink lips and reached for his wine, gulping down a mouthful and ignoring the tightening of his jeans. In that pretty sundress and wearing a wide-brimmed sunhat purchased at a shop by the port, Ally looked fresh and alluring.

It had been two days since they'd made love and there hadn't been an hour of that time when he hadn't imagined or dreamed about doing it again.

Angelo reached again for his glass then put it down. He needed to keep a clear head around her.

He guessed Ally didn't realise how seductive she looked or how enticing her smiles. Unlike Alexa, her warmth was real and natural. She'd dazzled the young boatman who took them into the Blue Grotto so much that Angelo had wondered if the guy would follow them ashore and become a nuisance.

'I'd never dream of wasting food, especially when it tastes like this. I know how much effort goes into cooking a great meal. Even something simple, like a good, old-fashioned apple pie, takes time and know-how to get the pastry just right.'

Angelo caught the significance of Ally's words though it appeared she didn't. She was a cook as well as a gardener?

'Besides, it would be criminal not to make the most of this place.' Her gesture encompassed the terrace, perched high with a view over the town below and the sea that changed colour as the sun moved. 'Thank you for bringing me here, Angelo. It's brilliant!'

No, it was her smile that was brilliant. And her enthusiasm. She'd been enthralled by everything, her questions about the sights they visited revealing a questioning mind and a readiness to be pleased.

'It's absolutely my pleasure, Ally. I'm enjoying myself too.'

How long since he'd made the effort to play tourist with someone? Or enjoyed it so much?

He truly had become a workaholic as his sister claimed. He attended black tie events for charity or business but couldn't recall his last meal out simply for pleasure. Maybe too he'd grown selfish since Alexa, rarely exerting himself for anyone except his family.

'There's something I need to tell you, Ally.' She looked up questioningly. 'I apologised for my behaviour when I thought you were Alexa but you deserve an explanation.'

Sharing intimate details of his life didn't come naturally but he couldn't ignore the urge to explain to Ally. Not to excuse his actions but because she deserved to understand.

'Go on.'

Looking into her bright gaze, this didn't feel nearly the chore it had seemed before. There was no judgement there, only encouragement. She was a remarkable woman.

'I never explained why Alexa's betrayal cut so deep.'

'You're a powerful, successful man, used to making major corporate decisions. Finding you'd been tricked would undermine your confidence in your judgement.'

Angelo's eyes widened. 'I'm so transparent?'

She shrugged. Was that a flicker of amusement? 'Hardly. At first I found you almost impossible to read.'

'And now?'

His heart thundered as he met that stunning lilac gaze. For the first time he found himself drawn by the idea of someone, *this woman*, having his measure, understanding him. In the past he'd cultivated an air of impenetrability, a valuable tool as he grappled with corporate challenges.

But life wasn't all about work. Increasingly he'd begun to think about finding more satisfaction in his private life. To actually *have* a private life, rather than casual flings and too-brief breaks from work.

Colour caressed Ally's cheekbones. 'Now I see the caring, decent man behind the powerbroker.'

Did she? It felt as if he'd done too little for her.

'Alexa *did* hurt my pride and made me question my judgement. But her real sin was hurting my family.' He twisted the stem of his wineglass. 'Our family was close and when my father died we were devastated. My mother in particular. She fell apart.' He paused, remembering how her breakdown had made him vow never to be so vulnerable, even as he'd understood her pain. 'I tried to fill the gap, taking care of her and my younger sister. I'd have done it anyway, but it was the last thing I promised my father.'

'That's a big responsibility.'

'So was stepping into his shoes as CEO. All the pundits said I was too young. They waited for me to fail. But I refused to let my father down. It was a rocky road but I eventually proved myself.'

He'd worked ridiculous hours, barely taking breaks.

'But still I worried about my mother. She'd lost her joy in life. It was only when Alexa declared she was pregnant that I saw the old spark in Mamma's eyes.'

'Ah.'

Angelo nodded. Ally had guessed what came next. 'My mother and sister were thrilled at me settling down and at the prospect of a baby. It began to feel like the old days, until the truth came out. That crushed my mother, not just that there was no baby but that the woman I'd married was so awful. I had to watch her slide back into depression.' He paused, his gut cramping. 'My sister was damaged by it too. Ever since then she's avoided relationships, worrying the only reason a man would pursue her is for her money. It's destroyed her confidence and ability to trust.'

'Oh, Angelo, I'm so sorry.'

'They're doing better now.' His mamma was, at least. 'But I blame myself for the hurt I brought them.'

'It wasn't your fault!'

'I was the one who brought Alexa into our lives and let

them believe in our marriage. They thought our family was healing with a new generation. That's why I reacted so badly to you. Why I refused to give you the benefit of the doubt. Seeing you dredged up all that pain and reminded me of how I'd failed them.'

Warm fingers closed on his hand. 'I'm sure they'd disagree.' Angelo met her eyes and was surprised to see her look stern. 'You take too much on yourself.'

He shook his head. 'I promised to protect them.'

'You care about them very much, don't you?'

'Of course. More than anything. They're family.'

Something flared in her eyes then disappeared. 'It was Alexa who lied, not you. What about the damage she did to you?'

Angelo withdrew his hand. Not because he disliked Ally's touch but because it made him feel too much. Made him want too much.

'I just wanted you to understand. You deserved an explanation.'

Ally regarded him silently and for the first time in for ever it felt as if someone saw past his persona of power and competence to the fault lines deep within.

'Thank you. I do feel better, understanding a little.' She paused. 'Tell me about them. You said your mother is a good cook. What's her speciality?'

Gratitude filled him at Ally's understanding and acceptance. At her change of subject, as if she knew how hard it was to speak of this.

'Seafood.' He forced himself to smile, though he felt wound too tight. 'Her family is from Venice so that's a speciality. But my sister developed a seafood allergy, so Mamma has branched out a lot. Her beef *ragù* has to be tasted to be believed, and her desserts…!'

Ally chuckled, the sound like liquid sunshine, bright as she leaned close, her face alight. Angelo felt his rigid muscles relax.

'You have a sweet tooth? What's her speciality? Tiramisu? Zabaglione?'

He was about to say she knew a lot about Italian cuisine but stopped himself. If Ally became self-conscious about the information she revealed it might stop.

'She makes those, but her lemon cake is my favourite.'

'Really? I have the best recipe for a citron tart. It has a luscious lemon filling, topped with slices of lemon sprinkled with icing sugar that you caramelise under a flame. My gran taught me to make it. It's her favourite.'

Ally's words stopped with an abrupt snap of teeth. Slowly she lowered her knife and fork to the table. Her gaze sought his, a hazy lavender stare that now looked lost.

'I did it again, didn't I?' She gulped a shaky breath. 'I can remember tiny things. I can even, almost, picture the kitchen where I learned to cook, but nothing else. Not even her face. Just her silver hair and the warmth of her voice.'

Ally sounded so forlorn, her eyes huge with emotion, that Angelo didn't think twice, just took her hand in both of his. This generous woman needed support.

'It's a good sign that you're starting to remember snippets.'

'But why *little* things? Why not my name or address? Or who my family is?'

Her voice rose to a wobbly note that pierced him. She'd been so brave and positive. It was too easy to forget how frightening her memory loss must be because of her determined good humour. Yet knowing what she'd endured because of him cut a sweeping gash through his belly.

'It's little things now but soon it'll be bigger things. Just be patient and it will all work out.'

Angelo had no idea if that were true but he willed it to be so.

He couldn't recall wishing for anything so hard. Not since his father had died, leaving Angelo alternately wishing for more time with his beloved *papà*, and to be the man he had to be for his family's sake.

'You'll see, Ally. Stay positive and it'll all eventually come back to you.'

'But what if it's something awful? Something I'd rather not face?'

He squeezed her hand, wishing he could take her in his arms and hold her, comfort her with an embrace. His arms ached with the effort of holding back. 'Whatever happened, you won't be alone, Ally. I'll be with you. I promise. You'll be safe.'

Angelo leaned in, close enough to inhale her delicate scent. Close enough to kiss those trembling lips.

But he didn't, despite the almost overwhelming urge to do so. Because it wasn't simple reassurance he longed to give her.

He wanted to kiss Ally for *himself.* To satisfy his own greedy longing for her.

One night with her was nowhere near enough. He wanted so much more. But he had no right. She needed his support, not his lust, no matter how fantastic they'd been together. He had an obligation to care for her.

Maybe, one day, when she'd regained her memory of the past... But he couldn't allow himself to fantasise about that now.

'Thank you, Angelo. It makes a huge difference to know I'm not totally alone.' Ally's eyes shone and her mouth pulled up in a crooked smile that tugged at his heartstrings. 'You're very kind.'

Angelo almost snorted in self-disgust. Kind? Kind would have been giving her the benefit of the doubt earlier.

'Now you're exaggerating. I was an ogre in those early days. But keep saying it, Ally. I like hearing it.'

Far too much.

As expected, his words drew a genuine smile. Angelo liked her ready sense of humour. 'Well, you're a lot easier to handle now than you were a week ago.'

'That's something, at least.' Angelo tried and almost succeeded in not thinking about Ally handling him in the way he wanted, naked flesh to naked flesh. Maybe that was what made him blurt out, 'I have an idea. Something that might trigger your memory.'

As soon as he said it, and saw excitement brighten her features, he wondered if he'd been wise to mention it. Because there was a risk involved, a risk to Ally, and she'd already been through enough. That was why he hadn't spoken of it sooner. But it was too late.

'Tell me!' Her hand turned in his as she gripped his fingers. What did you have in mind?'

'You were walking in Oliver's garden when you started to remember something so strongly that you felt ill. Maybe there was something there that triggered your memory. Something about the place maybe?'

Her brow furrowed in concentration. 'Maybe there *was* something…' She paused. 'Some smell. Maybe from a plant? Or am I imagining that?'

Angelo nodded. 'Perhaps, if nothing else comes to mind in the next few days, we could visit Oliver and retrace your steps. See if anything happens.' He wasn't sure it was the best idea, given how it had affected her last time, but Ally was getting upset and he hated to see her distraught.

'Why didn't I think of that? It's brilliant.' She smiled up at him and it felt like a burst of sunlight exploding inside. 'Thank you, Angelo!'

It was late when they returned to the villa. The violet dusk had fallen, settling like a dark blanket on the island. Ally revelled in the warm evening air. It felt like a caress on her bare arms as they entered Angelo's home, the scents from the garden creating a heady perfume.

Angelo's original plan for a couple of hours on Capri had turned into a full day excursion to see the sights, ending with them sharing dinner at a restaurant which had been both spectacular and charming.

Ally had loved every minute. Seeing new things. Mingling with other people. The beauty of the island. But especially the ease between her and Angelo. The barrier between them had dropped and she didn't feel so obviously that he held back from her. Though it was clear he wasn't about to sweep her into his arms like she wanted.

But they'd spent the day as friends, which Ally treasured. It wasn't as good as being lovers, yet Angelo made her feel special.

'Thanks for a wonderful day, Angelo. I had the best time.' Her pulse quickened as she met his dark eyes. Would she ever get over him? The answer had to be *yes*. She had to find out who she was, the sooner the better. 'Do you think Oliver is home?'

Angelo's frown told her he wasn't eager to go there, which was odd, as it had been his idea.

'It's easy enough to find out.' He took his phone from his pocket just as it rang. His expression as he glanced at the screen told her the incoming call was important. 'I'll answer this first. It won't take long.'

Ally nodded and headed for the stairs. She might as well put away the sunhat Angelo had bought her.

But once in her room she couldn't settle. Her thoughts kept turning to Angelo.

He'd opened himself to her in a way she'd never expected. Understanding his self-blame over the impact of Alexa's behaviour and how it had coloured his attitude when she'd washed up on his beach made her feel better. She was drawn by his protectiveness to his family, despite believing he laid too heavy a burden on himself.

He was a complex, thoughtful, surprising man.

His apology and his promise to be there for her if she needed him had broken through the brittle casing of fear around her heart. That made her feel stronger and ready to face her past, even if at the same time she realised how vulnerable she was to him.

With Angelo at her side she felt she could face almost anything. But soon they'd have to go their separate ways.

Regret was a sour tang, filling her mouth. Yet at the same time impatience grew. He wasn't interested in her. She wasn't one of the chosen few who truly mattered to him. His tender expression when he'd spoken of his family had made her almost jealous of them! How selfish was that?

The longer she stayed here, the harder it would be to hide her feelings. She was living in his home, seeing him every day. Even the clothes she wore had been bought by him. Was it any wonder she felt tied to him?

As Ally paced the lamplight caught the sparkle of purple and blue on her feet. The gorgeous strappy sandals that Angelo had bought her on Capri. They were pretty and jewelled and Ally knew instinctively they were the sort of expensive treat she would never have bought for herself.

She loved them.

She swallowed hard, her throat aching as an upswell of emotion caught her.

It wasn't just the sandals she loved. It was Angelo.

Ally had tried not to think about it but hiding from such a blatant truth didn't work.

Nor did telling herself it was impossible to feel so much after such a short time.

Falling for a man who was emotionally attached to his ex-wife was asking for trouble. It could go nowhere. Because, despite the damage she'd caused, Alexa was still important, still at the centre of his thoughts. He'd made love to Ally, believing she was Alexa.

She *had* to get back her memory and leave. Go somewhere where she could try to get over him.

Ally hurried from the room, her skin prickling with urgency as if ants crawled over her.

When she got downstairs she heard the murmur of Angelo's voice from the study. He'd only been on the phone a few minutes but she couldn't wait. Besides, she didn't want to face him now. She'd rather do this on her own.

Soon after, Oliver's housekeeper led her onto his terrace and turned on the outdoor lights. Signor Branston was tied up on a video call but of course she could wait in the garden until he was free.

Ally resisted the impulse to break into a run as the house-keeper left. Instead she took her time, trying to breathe slowly as she approached the enclosed garden where she'd walked with Oliver.

She paused at the entrance, her palm on the column of a jasmine-covered pergola. The scent filled the evening air but it wasn't the perfume that had sparked her memory.

Fighting anticipation and nerves, she stepped onto the path and approached the sundial at the centre of the space.

Still nothing. Maybe Angelo was wrong. Maybe it was the conversation with Oliver that had brought back her past. Perhaps…

Ally slammed to a halt as a heavy waft of perfume engulfed her. Her nostrils twitched and something feathered the back of her neck, the dance of phantom fingers across tightening skin. Slowly she inhaled, drawing the pungent aroma deep into her lungs. It was familiar.

Looking down, she saw blue-grey foliage and purple spears of flowers.

Lavender.

On the word came a jumbled rush of memory. Sights. Voices. Faces. Laughter. The warmth of home.

Relief filled Ally and she smiled, the fear she'd held in so tight finally lifting.

There was Uncle Ben on a tractor, his tatty hat shading his face. Long rows of lavender, dark purple and pungent in the midday sun. White blossoms in the orchard, birds singing in the branches. Cobwebs glistening with jewels of dew in the dawn light. The comforting cluck of chickens as they pecked their way through the garden. The smell of wood smoke curling from the old chimney on a winter's morning and the cuddly warmth of a hand-knitted jumper protecting her from the cold as she stepped onto frost-stiffened grass.

Wonderful as they were, the bombardment of recollections rocked her and Ally made for a stone bench. Her fingers closed tight around it as she sank, anchoring herself as she grew lightheaded.

She closed her eyes, hearing rain drumming on the iron roof of the old farmhouse. The chirrup of frogs in the dam. Belle's eager bark, telling her to hurry. The sound of humming, an old lullaby she'd known all her life.

Abruptly the relief and lightness vanished.

Joy was eclipsed in a devastating rush of desolation that froze everything inside her.

Ally heard herself gasp. A sliver of ice pierced her chest as fragmented recollections shifted and pieced together.

Then the tears started to slide down her face.

CHAPTER THIRTEEN

Angelo found her in a secluded part of the garden. Near where he'd seen her with Oliver.

She sat with her back to him but even in the muted light he knew something was wrong. Her shoulders were hunched and her head hung low. Fear punched the air from his lungs.

He hurried forward, silently cursing. His sister had had a small crisis days ago so he'd felt compelled to take her call. It had been good to hear her bright and confident, having dealt with her problem, but he regretted those ten minutes on the phone.

Today with Ally had been special. He'd revelled in her delight and the sparkle in her eyes when she looked at him. He'd basked in her approval at his idea to jog her memory but he should have kept quiet, respecting his sixth sense that it could be devastating for her.

'Ally.'

He sank down beside her, registering the tight pull of her lips and the rigid set of her jaw. Something dropped from her chin and he realised she was weeping.

His chest turned over. It reminded him of the roiling pain he'd felt when his father died.

Seeing Ally lost to grief undid him. He felt helpless though he wanted so much to make things better.

He covered one cold, trembling hand with his.

'I'm here, *cara*. You're not alone.'

Angelo moved closer, wrapping his arm around her, feeling her shudder as she drew in each breath. She felt fragile. Her feistiness and determination had been swamped by something. Bad news, he guessed.

He should have been here with her, not left her to face this alone. He should have guessed she'd be impatient to know, deciding not to wait for him.

'Whatever it is, Ally, we'll face it together.'

She took a shuddering breath and lifted her head. The sight of her pale features, drawn with pain, made him ache.

Angelo lifted her hand and pressed his mouth to it. It was a heartfelt kiss, not of physical passion but of something stronger and deeper. He wanted to give her his strength and help her through this crisis.

Her lips curved in a sad parody of a smile that cracked his heart. 'I'm okay, Angelo, just coming to terms with the past.' She paused. 'The good news is I'm not dying of some terrible illness. I'll be fine. I just need time to adjust.'

Angelo didn't release her. 'What can I do? Do you need to be somewhere? Do you want me to make arrangements?'

Ally shook her head. 'There's nothing. Thank you.'

Angelo said nothing, wanting to give her time and space. Whatever had caused this grief, it was her choice whether to share it with him. He wouldn't intrude.

Ally was grateful for Angelo's presence. It calmed her, made her realise she could face this. When he'd kissed her hand it had felt as if he shared something vital with her. Something that made this marginally easier.

How different he was from the man she'd first met.

She could imagine herself building a future with this Angelo, a man who could be gentle as well as strong. But it wasn't possible. Whatever he felt for her was mixed up with his attraction to his ex.

Ally sat straighter and wiped the tears from her face with her free hand. Angelo didn't move his arm from around her shoulders. For that she was grateful. It felt better to be held.

Still he didn't question her. She looked into his eyes, black in this light, and her heart swelled with tenderness. He could be understanding as well as demanding.

'My name's Alison Dennehy, but I've always been called Ally.' Her whispered words to Angelo on the beach that first day had been right. 'I come from Tasmania, the island state at the south of Australia.'

Angelo nodded his encouragement but didn't press for more. He was letting her take her time and the realisation made something shift hard inside her.

'It was the lavender.' She pointed to the clump growing near the sundial. 'I brushed it and the smell brought it all back.' She smiled and felt her facial muscles pull high on one side. Maybe it was more of a grimace. 'I grew up on a lavender farm and apple orchard.'

'No wonder the perfume sparked memories.'

Ally nodded. 'It's a potent scent and they say there's nothing like smell to evoke the past.'

That was something which had particularly interested her in her work with essences.

So much was coming back. There were blanks still but she had enough sense of herself and her past to understand what had happened. She rubbed her hand up her bare arm as a glacial shiver prickled her skin.

'Your family is still on the farm?'

'Yes,' she said quickly, feeling pain stab. 'My uncle lives in the old farmhouse now with his wife and children.' Ally swallowed hard. 'I lived there from the age of four. After my parents died in a car crash my gran raised me.' Angelo squeezed her hand and she was grateful for his understanding. 'The pair of us lived together there for years.'

'Just the two of you?'

His voice told her he'd guessed what was coming. She inclined her head. 'Just Gran and me. Uncle Ben worked on the farm but lived in town.'

'And you liked it there.'

It wasn't a question. Ally wondered what Angelo heard in her voice.

'I adored it. No wonder I like helping Enzo in the garden.' She forced a laugh. 'It's where I'm most at home. Growing things, keeping bees, making things from what we grew, like herbal essences, soaps and scents.' She met Angelo's gaze. 'I'm good at it too. I'd developed a range of lavender and honey products.'

She'd planned to make that her future.

'I'm sure you are. You seem a natural.'

Ally looked at their linked hands, knowing she should withdraw from him but not having the strength.

'I'm not a city girl like Alexa.'

She felt him start. 'So you *are* related?'

'We're cousins. Our mothers were identical twins. That's why we look similar, but she's a few years older.'

And in experience even older. Poor Alexa. Despite what Angelo had revealed, Ally knew there were reasons for her cousin's behaviour, if not excuses, starting with an abusive stepfather who'd skewed her ideas about relationships.

'You've seen her recently?'

'Not for years. She visited Gran and stayed for a while. That's how I knew about this place. She spoke about the island with such affection, said it was the most beautiful, peaceful place in the world. I always thought that if I had the chance I'd visit.'

She paused, remembering why she now had time for travel. 'I think she must have visited soon after your divorce. She was troubled and Gran has always been good at listening to problems in a way that helps you work out what to do about them.'

Ally swallowed that hot ache in her throat. 'Alexa was at some sort of crossroads.' She flashed him a look. Her impression was that Alexa didn't like the woman she'd become. 'She's living interstate now, working for an organisation that supports victims of sexual violence.'

Angelo's eyebrows lifted in surprise. 'She sounds like a different woman to the one I knew.'

'Perhaps she is.'

Ally waited for him to pump her for more information

about the woman who'd figured so large in his life. The woman he still desired.

His next words surprised her, for they weren't about Alexa.

'You remember something else, don't you, Ally?' His voice was coaxing and gentle tears prickled the back of her eyes again. 'Your grandmother?'

She inclined her head. Of course it was Gran. Every memory she'd had until now had been linked to her.

'She died.' Ally's voice was harsh, the words sticking to her tongue so she had to force them out. Her chest ached as she drew air into tight lungs. 'She was driving the tractor while I was out. They say she had a heart attack at the wheel and died instantly, probably before the tractor overturned on an embankment.'

'Ah, *tesoro*.' Angelo gathered her close and somehow she was sitting on his lap, her head tucked beneath his chin. The warmth of his big frame and the steady beat of his heart against her ear were reassuring in a world suddenly fluid with broken images and shocking hurt.

Another painful breath, another painful memory. 'I came home and found her and Belle lying there.'

Her words ran out. The memory was too vivid.

'Belle?' Angelo's voice was sharp.

'Our old border collie. We'd had her since I was young. She was devoted to me and Gran.' Ally bit her bottom lip, willing it not to wobble, though the anguish had reached an unbearable level.

'A double tragedy, then. When Rocco, my childhood dog, died it almost broke my heart.'

Ally nodded, suppressing a snuffle. She could picture Angelo with a dog. He had a kind heart, she'd discovered. She could imagine him loyal and loving.

'It seems silly, but losing them both together made it more devastating.'

Especially as she'd been confronted with the sight of them both— She sucked in a sharp breath and forced her thoughts elsewhere.

Ally barely had any memories of her parents. It was Gran who'd looked after her when she was sick, listened to her dreams, encouraging her and laughing with her. As for Belle, Ally remembered her as a puppy, her raspy tongue licking, and as an older dog, slowed by arthritis but still faithful and loving. Still insisting on riding the tractor though she needed help to get up.

'It's not silly at all. It makes perfect sense.' He paused. 'No wonder you took a holiday to get away for a while.'

'It's not quite like that.'

Ally straightened in his embrace and immediately his arm slid away, releasing her and giving her the chance to move away if she wished. She didn't wish. She wanted to stay in Angelo's arms for ever, but it was enough to remind her it was time to look after herself, not turn to him for comfort.

She forced herself to rise, swaying a little before finding her balance. She sensed him stand behind her, felt his body heat.

'What is it, Ally? There's more, isn't there?'

It was as if he read her emotions, despite her determination to control them.

Ally gave a strained shrug. 'I had to leave the farm. Gran and Uncle Ben were joint owners and when Gran died…' She took a deep breath, staring across the beautifully manicured garden. 'Uncle Ben lost money on a separate business deal, an investment gone wrong. He's badly in debt and his family lost their home. They needed somewhere to live.'

Angelo's voice was hard. 'So they moved onto the farm and forced you out while you were grieving?'

'They didn't *force* me. It made sense to move out.'

Besides, it wouldn't be the same living there without Gran.

'Don't you have a share in the property? Especially if you were helping to run the farm?'

Angelo stepped in front of her, his face sombre, and she saw the businessman in his expression, looking for leverage on her behalf.

Warmth trickled through her cold body at his earnest look.

He really was concerned about her. She reckoned he'd be an indomitable ally should she need one.

But the sad truth was that the sooner she got away from his orbit the better for her peace of mind. He tied her in knots and made her long for what could never be.

'I inherited a minority share of the farm. But Uncle Ben can't afford to buy me out at the moment and I'm not pressing him for the money.' She forced a smile to stiff lips. 'As for sharing a small farmhouse with my aunt, uncle and four rambunctious boys under ten, that's not an option.'

Angelo didn't smile back. His brows contracted in a scowl.

'Look, Uncle Ben isn't trying to cheat me. He'll buy me out when things turn around. Meanwhile Gran left me a bit of cash. That's what I used to travel here. I'm on my way to the south of France, to visit the lavender fields and the perfumeries. But I wanted to see this place that Alexa raved about. That's why I flew to Rome first.'

Angelo nodded. 'A holiday. An excellent idea after all that's happened.'

Ally spread her hands. 'Originally it was going to be more than a holiday.' That was in the days before Gran's death when she'd dreamed of a fact-finding trip. 'I've always been interested in scent-making. I'd planned to use the lavender farm as a springboard into that.'

She stopped. Without the farm, she needed to find a new dream. Uncle Ben had plans for the place that didn't include perfume-making or bee-keeping. When she returned to Australia she'd have to find a new job and a new home. A different dream.

'But, yes, it's a short vacation. A once-in-a-lifetime opportunity to see something of the world.'

Because she'd had to get away and it was easier to head for the place she'd always wanted to visit than devise a new itinerary.

Ally didn't have formal qualifications. When she did find work it would probably be poorly paid. She doubted she'd have another chance for overseas travel.

She looked from the garden to the tall man watching her, the man she cared for too much, and told herself it was a good thing she was moving on.

Angelo was protective but that was all. His first thought, on learning she remembered her past, was to ask where she wanted to be and if he could help her get there.

He didn't want her as she did him. He merely felt sorry for her and obliged to help her. Even the sexual attraction between them had been short-lived, a mistake on his part because he'd believed her to be someone else.

Ally felt her heart crumple as the last of her dreams shrivelled. She angled her chin up and turned away. 'Shall we go? I'd rather not see Oliver tonight.'

Angelo poured a glass of red wine with numb fingers. His muscles were taut, his movements uncoordinated, because witnessing Ally in distress had undone him.

He knew about grief, but he still had his beloved mother and sister. Who did Ally have?

'Here. It will warm you up.'

She looked up from the settee where she'd collapsed on their return. For a moment he thought she'd refuse, as she'd refused all alcohol before. Instead she reached for the glass, carefully grasping it so that their hands didn't brush, before taking a cautious sip.

Regret pierced him. A yearning for her touch. The profound need to *connect*. She was hurting and he wanted to hold her, comfort her.

It would comfort him too, having her in his arms. Because he'd missed her there, though they'd only had one night together.

He swung away and poured himself a glass of wine, despising his neediness. This wasn't about him but what was best for Ally.

It seemed that, despite her readiness to sink into his embrace half an hour ago, she didn't want solace from him now. Would that change if he gave her time and space?

An unseen weight pressed between his shoulder blades.

'What can I do, Ally? What would help?'

If he could be useful he'd feel better. He was accustomed to taking charge and making things happen.

Shadowed eyes met his. They looked dazed and his fingers curled tighter around the stem of his glass.

'You offered to arrange transport.'

Angelo's heart shrank. 'Of course. When you've had time to sort yourself out—'

She shook her head, her honey-coloured hair sliding around her neck. 'There's no point in delaying.'

Her gaze shifted to the ruby wine in her glass.

Because she couldn't bear to look at him? He stiffened.

Angelo had imagined today that they'd reached a new level of understanding, friendship even. But tonight's revelations made it starkly clear how poorly he'd treated her, a woman grieving the loss of a loved one and, if he read the situation right, her dreams too.

'I'd like you to stay. Take your time and recover completely. I'll look after you—'

'No!' Her strident syllable gashed his windpipe, stopping his words. 'I don't need you to look after me! I'm not your responsibility. What I *need* is to leave.'

Angelo heard the hard, cold truth in her voice. The distress. He shouldn't be surprised that she wanted to escape from here, from him, as soon as she could.

It was a mistake, letting her go. He felt it in every atom of his body. But he remembered his sister telling him he was overprotective, remembered Ally concurring, saying he'd gone too far in shouldering responsibility for Alexa's actions. Protective instinct and selfish need battled against the desperation he read in Ally's face. Her need for freedom, away from him.

'If that's what you want…' It nearly killed him to say it.

'It's time I got on with my real life.'

A life that didn't include him. It was a hammer blow.

Once he'd wished this woman elsewhere. Now he didn't

want her to go. Not only because he felt protective but because he wanted...more.

That was a first. He was an expert at ending relationships with women but had no experience maintaining them. He hadn't had the guts to seek a meaningful long-term relationship because he'd feared that caring led to too much pain.

Yet suddenly that was exactly what he wanted, to be with Ally long-term.

Everything about her called to him. Not just her looks, but her stubborn strength, her determination to make the best of her difficult situation. Her stoicism as she'd weathered one blow after another. Her charm, humour and the friendly way she had with everyone, from the movie mogul next door to the gardener and various strangers.

She was thoughtful yet engaging. She was sexy in a way that made every atom in his body sit up and beg for another taste of her body.

She was exactly what he'd never realised he wanted.

He, who'd never permitted himself to imagine feeling so much for any woman.

The knowledge didn't strike like a blow. Instead it infused his blood, spreading through every vein, artery and capillary until it was a glow warming his body from the inside. Angelo had never experienced anything like it.

But it was *not* what Ally needed to hear tonight. She had enough to deal with.

After what had passed between them he *had* to give her freedom to make this choice without interference. He owed her that much.

Reluctantly he spoke. 'I'll make some calls—'

'Thank you. I'll leave tomorrow.' Angelo's pulse skipped. So soon? 'I need transport to Naples. I stayed at a *pensione* there and left my luggage in storage while I came down to the coast for the day.'

Ally waited for him to nod and agree but the words wouldn't come.

A primitive part of him wanted to do whatever it took to keep her here.

Angelo exhaled slowly. He could never do that. Ally's independence was crucial, especially after she'd been cooped up here so long, hemmed in by memory loss.

'I'll call the doctor. He'd better check you over first. When he gives the all-clear, I'll organise transport.'

Angelo paused, mind racing, searching for an excuse to delay because, no matter how much she wanted to leave, it didn't *feel* right. Yet how could he impose his will on her? The way she'd flinched from him, stridently rejecting his suggestion she stay, was too revealing.

'Give me your contact details, in case you run into trouble.' A new thought struck. 'Or if there are consequences from the other night. Condoms can fail.'

The idea of a child evoked powerful emotion but it wasn't the trapped feeling he'd experienced when Alexa had told him she was pregnant.

Ally's face jerked up, such dismay on her features that his nebulous imaginings disintegrated along with his pride.

That look said everything. Ally might resemble her cousin physically but the thought of being tied to him, even with his fortune and social standing, clearly held no allure.

His conscience told him he'd got his just deserts. She'd made her preference clear. Her first thought was to get away from him as soon as possible.

He wanted to rage and protest. To stop her leaving.

But Angelo Ricci was a civilised man who respected a woman's wishes. He swallowed his wine in one gulp, put down his glass and wished Ally goodnight, amazed he could still speak given the almighty ache opening up inside him.

Then he strode from the room before he did something utterly selfish, like ask her to stay, for *his* sake.

CHAPTER FOURTEEN

ALLY HUNG UP her damp towel in the tiny hotel bathroom and wrapped a cotton robe around herself.

Tonight was her last night in Provence. She'd spent a week exploring the countryside, the quaint stone-built villages, seeing the fields of lavender and other flowers and visiting a perfume factory.

It had been exciting, memorable and poignant. Because it made her think of her beloved gran and the plans Ally had had for the future.

When she returned to Australia her life would change. She'd have to look for work in the city. Uncle Ben couldn't afford to employ her. He planned to run the farm alone with his wife till their finances were better. Ally didn't want to live nearby, hankering for what she couldn't have.

She shook her head and grabbed a comb, pulling it through her hair. It was the story of her life right now, clearing out of places because she couldn't bear to be close to what she couldn't have.

Angelo.

The name feathered into her brain like a waft of beckoning lavender-scented breeze from the surrounding fields.

She'd left him nine days ago and the yearning hadn't subsided. Would it ever? She'd so wanted to stay with him, until he spoke of looking after her, as if she were yet another responsibility he'd taken on. A duty. Not because he couldn't bear to be without her.

'You have to give it time,' she told herself.

No more thinking of Angelo, who'd left her in Naples with such a severe, brooding expression that she guessed some problem had arisen at his bank. She'd cut short their goodbyes, not trusting her emotions, giving him a quick handshake and running into the *pensione* where she'd stored her luggage before he could say anything.

Of course, that hadn't been the end of it. He'd been on her mind every hour since.

She'd imagined she saw his gleaming dark sports car as she'd made her way through the thronged Naples streets. Her spirits had soared at the railway station when she thought she saw him, head and shoulders above the crowd, as if he'd come for her. But, whoever the man was, he'd kept his distance. There'd been no one and nothing to stop her getting on the northbound train.

She looked in the mirror and grimaced at her shadowed eyes and pinched mouth. She'd better get out her make-up.

Tonight was her last night. Tomorrow she'd leave for Australia. She was determined to put on a pretty dress and treat herself to a nice meal and a glass of wine at that cosy restaurant across the square. She'd pretend she was just another tourist enjoying a night out.

Instead of a woman with a broken heart.

Her teeth sank into her bottom lip but Ally refused to cry. She'd be strong because she had no other choice.

A rap on the door made her swing around, frowning. She didn't know anyone here except the staff and they'd have no reason to come to her room at this time.

She unlatched the door, opened it and sucked in a hissed breath. Her pulse thundered in her ears.

'Angelo?'

In the dim light of the hall he was little more than a silhouette, yet totally unmistakable. Proud head, broad shoulders and that utterly masculine frame in a dark suit tailored to his superb body.

Ally's mouth dried and she swallowed convulsively, trying to make sense of him, here, when her brain told her she must be dreaming.

Was she hallucinating? Was this some delayed reaction to her head injury? Maybe she'd begun seeing things.

'Ally.'

Her skin tightened all over and something swooped low in her belly at the sound of her name on his tongue. It wasn't his rich, melting caramel voice. It was rough-edged and a little husky as if he hadn't spoken much lately. Yet that single word undid her. It made her think of midnight loving and raw desire. Of warmth, passion and the love welling up inside that she couldn't suppress.

Ally's eyes widened and her knees weakened with the force of that emotion. She tightened her grip on the door to keep upright.

He couldn't be here.

'Can I come in?'

He stepped forward and she knew something was wrong. His straight shoulders were unbowed but lines grooved deep around his flattened mouth and the chiselled features that usually looked proud and beautiful seemed too angular.

Instantly Ally stepped back, admitting him.

Yet when she'd closed the door behind him and sagged back against it, Angelo didn't speak, just stood, taking in the small room.

Her skin prickled from the crackling energy he radiated. It was as if her body came alive in his presence and that terrified her. How could she pretend to be immune?

'Angelo?' She found her voice. 'What are you doing here?'

It must be something important for him to come so far. He must have spent a lot of money to track her down.

He swung around, his brooding gaze locking on hers. Ally felt it in the band of heat that tightened around her chest, impairing her breathing. And the leap of her foolish heart.

'I'm not pregnant,' she blurted, not sure where the words came from, or even if they were true, since it was too early to know.

Yet that was the only reason he could be here, to check if there were *consequences* from their one night together.

Was it so important to Angelo to cross off that possibility? To ensure there was nothing left to bind them together? Her mouth turned down on the thought.

'You're not?'

He frowned and Ally told herself her imagination made him sound disappointed.

She hiked her chin up. 'That's why you followed me, isn't it?'

Or could it be something altogether different? Maybe he wanted Alexa's contact details. Maybe he'd finally realised it wasn't hate he felt for her sophisticated cousin but love. That was why he'd been attracted to Ally and why he'd taken her to bed.

She took a deep, shuddery breath and saw his attention drop down her body.

Looking down, she saw her thin robe gaping open from neck to hem, revealing a swathe of pale skin. Fumbling, heat searing her cheeks, Ally covered herself, twisting the belt into a tighter knot.

Angelo's gaze rose, slowly, and she felt it like the brush of his hand, warm, deliberate and arousing, from her belly to her breasts and up her throat. While at the apex of her thighs her pulse thrummed a heavy, needy beat.

She couldn't take this any more. 'I—'

'That's not why I came.' If Angelo's voice had sounded husky before, it was frayed now, a gravelly rasp of sound that abraded every nerve-ending and set her hormones jangling.

'I'll send you Alexa's phone number when I'm in Australia. I don't have it with me.'

Angelo looked blank. 'Alexa's phone number? Why would I want that?'

Ally gathered the lapels of her robe close, wrapping her other arm around her middle. 'I thought…'

His eyebrows rose. 'You thought I want to talk to her?'

He sounded horrified, or was that her imagination playing games?

Ally lifted one shoulder. 'I know you feel strongly about her.'

'Dead right. I never want to see her again.'

'I don't believe you.' She met his stare and refused to be cowed by the frown gathering on his forehead. 'There's something about her you can't get out of your system. Look at the way you were attracted to me. You even had sex with me because you thought I was her.'

'Made love.'

'Sorry?'

'It might have started out as sex, but in the end we made love together.'

Ally's brow scrunched in a frown. 'I don't understand what—'

'Believe me, *tesoro*, there's a difference.' He took a step closer, his dark gaze pinioning hers. 'Sex is a purely physical act but making love…' He lifted his shoulders, spreading his palms wide. 'It's about much more than a physical act and it matters a whole lot more.'

Angelo swallowed and it struck Ally out of nowhere that he looked uncomfortable. More than uncomfortable. On edge. She wanted to read special significance into that but didn't dare let herself. Despite what he seemed to imply.

'You're splitting hairs, Angelo. Just tell me why you're here.'

While she still had the strength to pretend his presence didn't affect her. By her calculations that would be all of three minutes.

His mouth quirked up at one side as if in reluctant amusement. 'Trust you to cut straight to the chase, *amore mio*.' Then his amusement faded and his expression grew serious again. 'I came here because of *you*. I can't let you go. I didn't try to stop you leaving because I knew you needed time and space to deal with everything you've been through. But there are things I have to say, things you need to hear.'

Ally stared up into his strained, handsome face and wondered if she dared trust her ears. This was too like one of those fantasies that she hadn't been able to stop imagining, no matter how hard she tried.

Pride rose to her aid. 'I'm not a substitute for Alexa. And I'm not some obligation or responsibility. I might have washed ashore on your beach but I don't need your protection or your guilt.'

Angelo's head snapped back as if slapped.

'You think I feel…obliged to look out for you?'

'You said it yourself. You have an overdeveloped protective streak. But I'm not a member of your family, Angelo.' Hurt resonated deep inside. 'I'm not some duty to be taken care of.'

Dark eyes held hers and a quiver of longing engulfed her.

'I do want to look after you, Ally, but I fully understand you're strong and independent and you don't *need* me to protect you.' His voice dipped strangely. 'As for being a substitute for Alexa, never! It's true that in the beginning I believed you were her but that's not why I'm attracted to you and definitely *not* why I made love to you.'

Stunned, she gaped at him, watching him rub a hand around the back of his neck as if, like her, his muscles bunched too tight.

'Your resemblance to Alexa kept me at a distance initially. It's the *differences* between you that attract me. Your personality, your mind, your attitude and generosity. That's why I care for you. That's why I want to be with you.'

'You *care* for me?'

Ally's death grip on her collar tightened till her fingers ached.

'I do.' Angelo lifted his arms in a wide shrug. 'I practised what I'd say to you all the way here but I've forgotten all my prepared words.'

She blinked. He was dangerously persuasive as it was.

At the look in his eyes, lush heat spread through her taut body in rolling waves. It was a look Ally had never seen before. Like wonder and desperation and something far more profound, all rolled together.

Her heartbeat quickened as he stepped closer.

'What Alexa and I shared was shallow and brief. It would have ended a lot sooner except business was frantic and I spent a lot of time away from her. I was about to end things when she announced she was pregnant.'

He breathed deep and went on. 'It was *you* I made love to that night, Ally, not some memory of your cousin as you seem to think. For the record, I find you infinitely more desirable than I ever found Alexa. And while you might have been the virgin that night, I can tell you it was a first for me too. It was the first time I *made love* to a woman with my mind, body *and* heart.'

He paused and she heard his harsh breathing, as if from supreme exertion. Or strong feelings.

A perfect match for the raw emotion welling up inside her.

'I've never connected with any other woman like that, ever.'

Dumbfounded, Ally watched his hand cover his heart and her heart melted in response.

'Laugh if you like, but it's true.' His deep voice grated across sensitive flesh, leaving her trembling with shock and excitement. 'I've held back from emotional relationships because I feared they would make me weak. I saw my mother's pain when my father died, saw the way it almost killed her, and was terrified of the same thing happening to me. *That's* the real reason I've only wanted short affairs before now, not, as I told myself, because I was too busy with work.' He paused, his gaze holding hers. 'Yet with you I tumbled into love in just a week and that's not going to change.'

Ally licked her lips, wondering if she could find her voice. There must be more she needed to ask because surely this was too much to believe. Her heart was hammering and it felt as if a whole flock of swallows swooped and dived in her abdomen.

All that emerged, in a mere scratch of sound, was, 'It's not going to change?'

He shook his head, that rich espresso gaze pinioning hers in a way that rooted her to the spot.

'Never. I might be new to love, Ally, but I'm sure. This isn't a passing fancy. This is the real thing. And it's not about duty. It's about what's in my heart.'

He paused and, dazed, she watched his chest rise high on a deep breath. 'The question is whether you feel anything for me. Whether, given time, you might come to care for me too. I know this is sudden and you're still adjusting to having your memory back. I know you've been through a lot and I have no right to push—'

Ally tumbled forward, hands to his chest, face upturned and body flush against his so that all his heat began seeping into her, melting the frost that had turned her bones brittle.

On tiptoe she lifted her face, curled one hand around the back of his neck and pulled his mouth down on hers.

She saw wide, stunned eyes, felt his jolt of surprise. Then there was nothing but the taste of Angelo, luscious on her tongue, the lemony cedar masculine scent of him in her nostrils, his tall frame against her, powerful thighs shifting wider as he drew her in hard and yet harder, until it felt as if they were one. Almost.

Ravenously she kissed him, one hand anchored in the luxuriant hair at the back of his skull, the other slipping beneath his jacket to splay across his shirt and the warm contours of his chest. She swiped his pectoral muscle and felt him shudder as her thumbnail brushed his nipple.

'Ally.'

Even muffled the sound of him saying her name made her heart fly. She smiled against his mouth. Her world had turned on its head in mere moments.

Firm hands planted on her hips, holding her, as Angelo stepped back, breaking their kiss.

'Don't go!' She was beyond caring that she sounded needy. She was beyond anything but the craving for this remarkable, unexpected man.

'I'm not going anywhere.' His glittering eyes had a hungry glaze that made her insides squirm with delight. 'But I don't want to rush you.'

'Rush me?' He had to be kidding. She'd done nothing but yearn for him from the day she'd left. 'I'm crazy for you, Angelo. I've been so lost without you. Not because I wasn't capable of managing on my own, but because I left part of myself with you and never thought I'd get it back.'

That possessive look in his eyes softened into something that made everything inside her go still.

'*Amore mio*.'

There it was again, that delicious *dulce de leche* voice that flowed like hot caramel through her veins and melted her bones.

'Please, Angelo. Show me.'

Those powerful hands didn't hold her back now as she moved in close, nor when she nudged him against the bed.

Instead his mouth curved knowingly as he wrapped his arms around her and fell back onto the mattress. He rolled and a moment later she was pressed into the bed with him sprawled above her.

There was nowhere else on earth she'd rather be. 'I feel like all my Christmases have come at once.'

Angelo's smile was tender though his body was rigid with arousal. 'I know the feeling. I can't believe I'm so lucky. We've known each other such a short time and it was mired in misunderstanding. I thought I'd have to fight even to have you hear me out.'

'I'm listening.' Her fingers reached for his top button, delight and excitement fizzing like champagne bubbles in her blood. 'But you're wearing too much.'

'There's a remedy for that,' Angelo murmured as he shrugged out of his jacket and ripped his shirt open.

Ally sighed and palmed her hands across his hard chest, enjoying the contrast of silky skin and crisp chest hair.

'Shall I tell you now all the reasons we should stay together?'

His sultry voice was hot temptation whispering in her ear, making her shiver.

'Soon.'

The sight and feel of him distracted her. Her hands dipped to his belt and Angelo's breath caught on a hiss.

Minutes later, after a flurry of movement, they were naked, breathing hard and fast, looking into each other's eyes as their bodies settled against each other.

Her restless hands swept his flanks and up over his broad back. Would she ever get used to the sheer magnificence of this man? 'You feel so good.'

Angelo lowered his head, rubbing his nose against hers, then peppering her eyelids, ears and jaw with tiny kisses. 'That's my line, beautiful Alison.'

She sighed, the breath stalling in her lungs when he swept one hand to the apex of her thighs and into the slippery heat there. Instantly she lifted her hips, pressing into his touch.

'*Amore mio.* I love how you want me too. I love everything about you.'

His voice was spiky with emotion, making Ally reach up to cup his face in her hands, tenderness filling her. Angelo's eyes shone so brightly, she felt she could fall into those rich depths and stay there for ever.

She shivered as a rising tide of desire, gratitude and love flooded her. The best, most remarkable part was seeing those same emotions in Angelo's face. She felt them in every reverent touch, every careful breath.

Slowly they joined, gazes locked, and Ally felt as if together they entered into one of life's most profound mysteries. As they moved together their tender touches grew more needy, movements quicker and their breathing turned to gasps as rapture exploded, flinging them into bliss.

Yet through it all, the carnal joy and the ecstasy, was a poignant sense of coming home to where she belonged.

A lifetime later they lay, spent and dreamy, in each other's arms.

'I love you, Angelo,' she said when she finally found her voice. Yet she saw his brow knot. 'You don't believe me?'

He raised her hand to his mouth and brushed a kiss to

her knuckles. 'I do. But you've just got your memory back. You're in the process of adjusting to your past and who you are. You need time to be sure.'

'I *am* sure, Angelo. You're not the only one who's never felt this way before.'

Still he looked too serious. She reached up and rubbed her finger over the crease that formed above his nose.

'You're not convinced.' She sighed and stretched, surprised to discover awareness build again as she shifted against his naked body. He felt so amazing. 'Maybe,' she murmured, 'you feel the need to remind me again why being with you is a good idea.'

Ally let her hand slide from his face, down his throat to his chest and lower. Angelo's hand caught hers as she traced an intriguing muscle near his hip.

'Remind you?' he growled and tiny sparks of fire ignited all along her backbone at that sound of pure masculine promise.

'Well, I *have* had memory troubles.' She pouted up at him, trying to stop the grin that threatened to break out. 'You don't want to take any chances on me forgetting, do you?'

'Absolutely not.' His expression turned from tender to voracious in the blink of an eye. A moment later his lips closed around her nipple, making her gasp and arch up against him.

Ally gazed at the man who'd won her heart and soul. 'I think you're onto something there,' she whispered unsteadily.

The wicked gleam in his eyes undid her even more than his erotic caress. 'You're right. I need to know you're sure about us together. I'll have to remind you regularly, over a long time.'

Ally threaded her fingers through his dark hair and grinned at the man she loved. 'That sounds like an excellent plan.'

EPILOGUE

ALLY STOOD ON the wide terrace as the sky began to darken to purple and indigo, feeling the end-of-day warmth seep up through her soles from the sun-warmed flagstones.

She breathed deep, inhaling the rich scent of lavender from the rolling fields beyond the lavish gardens. It mingled with the heady perfume of roses, jasmine and a hundred other flowers blooming in the garden.

It was her favourite time of day, the view over fields and valleys to distant hills lit with the last glowing daylight. Angelo's wedding gift had been this beautiful antique villa on the mainland with an adjacent lavender farm. His thoughtfulness and generosity had almost undone her, for in the process he'd changed his life to accommodate her dreams.

Now, after two years, the house had been renovated to suit them, her business was taking shape and they still managed weekends away at their special island retreat. Angelo telecommuted a lot more and when he went to the city for a few days Ally usually went with him.

She couldn't believe how lucky she was. Not just to be here, but to have Angelo in her life.

She shivered suddenly, thinking of the unlikely circumstance that had brought them together. It would have been so easy for her to visit Italy and never meet him.

'You're cold?' A deep voice sounded behind her and strong arms slid around her, holding her close.

Ally grinned as Angelo's lovely heat enveloped her.

'Not any longer.'

She leaned back in her husband's hold as his hand settled lightly on her purple-blue silk dress, covering the tiny swell of her abdomen.

Ever since she'd shared her news he hadn't been able to stop touching her there, as if still not quite able to take in the fact that they were going to have a child.

She turned in her husband's arms. He looked a million dollars in his tailored dark jacket and his crisp shirt undone at the throat. Ally loved that V of olive-gold skin there, so tempting. But nowhere near as tempting as the soft light in his gleaming eyes.

'What is it, *amore mio*?'

She shrugged. 'I've just been counting my blessings. Thinking how incredibly lucky I was to wash up on your particular beach on that particular day when you were there.'

'Luck?' Ebony eyebrows arched as he shook his head. 'Not luck. It was fate. We were destined for each other. Don't you understand that yet?'

'Oh, really?' She suppressed a delighted smile. 'Yet you refused to marry me for a full year after we met.'

Not that she was annoyed. She'd understood and been touched by Angelo's need to be sure he wasn't rushing her. He'd insisted on giving her time to get her bearings and be absolutely sure that she loved him. He'd even accompanied her back to Australia for a long visit to see family and friends and sort out her affairs.

Angelo's hands moved, roving across the thin silk of her new dress in a way that made her body spark with arousal and her breath hitch. 'Ah, but didn't you enjoy being courted?'

'Is that what you call it? It felt like pure seduction to me.'

His mouth widened into a slow smile she could only describe as wolfish, and a trickle of heat beaded down her spine and dipped low in her abdomen. 'Whatever works, *tesoro*, to keep you happy.'

'*You* make me happy, Angelo. Always you.'

She read the profound emotion in his eyes and felt her

heart swell. 'And I never knew I could be so happy, *amore mio*. Because of *you*.'

He leaned down, his lips about to brush hers when a door slammed and a babble of voices echoed through the house. Someone called their names and Angelo paused, whispering words under his breath that Ally, with her improving Italian, knew weren't for public consumption.

'Whose idea was it to have a party tonight?' he growled.

Ally laughed. 'Yours, darling. You said I should invite all our friends and your family to celebrate my birthday. And unless I'm mistaken Giulia and your mother have arrived with some of your cousins. Or maybe that's Oliver's deep voice I hear in the distance.'

'Branston?' Angelo's pulled her in closer. 'The man always flirts with you outrageously. I think he sometimes forgets you're a married woman. I have to watch him like a hawk.'

But Ally read the glint of humour in her husband's eyes. 'And I think you just like an excuse to keep me close.'

He grinned disarmingly and her heart gave a little flutter of pure delight. 'You know me so well, *tesoro*.'

Angelo ignored the approaching voices and swept her back over his arm, settling his mouth over hers in a passionate yet tender kiss that made her silently agree that their meeting really had been destined. Because there was no other explanation for such perfect joy.

* * * * *

COMING SOON!

We really hope you enjoyed reading this book.
If you're looking for more romance, be sure to
head to the shops when new books are
available on

Thursday 26th May

To see which titles are coming soon, please visit

millsandboon.co.uk/nextmonth

MILLS & BOON®

Coming next month

THE SECRET SHE KEPT IN BOLLYWOOD
Tara Pammi

It was nothing but sheer madness.

Her brothers were behind a closed door not a few hundred feet away. Her daughter…one she couldn't claim, one she couldn't hold and touch and love openly, not in this lifetime, was also behind that same door. The very thought threatened to bring Anya to her knees again.

And she was dragging a stranger—a man who'd shown her only kindness—along with her into all this crazy. This reckless woman wasn't her.

But if she didn't do this, if she didn't take what he offered, if she didn't grasp this thing between them and hold on to it, it felt like she'd stay on her knees, raging at a fate she couldn't change, forever… And Anya refused to be that woman anymore.

It was as if she was walking through one of those fantastical daydreams she still had sometimes when her anxiety became too much. The one where she just spun herself into an alternate world because in actual reality she was nothing but a coward.

Now, those realities were merging, and the possibility that she could be more than her grief and guilt and loss was the only thing that kept her standing upright. It took her a minute to find an empty suite, to turn the knob and then lock it behind them.

Silence and almost total darkness cloaked them. A sliver of light from the bathroom showed that it was another expansive suite, and they were standing in the entryway. Anya pressed herself against the door with the man facing her. The commanding bridge of his nose that seemed to slash through his face with perfect symmetry, the square jaw and the broad shoulders…the faint outline of his strong, masculine features guided her. But those eyes…wide and penetrating, full of an aching pain and naked desire that could span the width of an ocean…she couldn't see those properly anymore. Without meeting those eyes, she could pretend this was a simple case of lust.

Simon, she said in her mind, tasting his name there first…so tall and broad that even standing at five-ten, she felt so utterly encompassed by him.

Simon with the kind eyes and the tight mouth and a fleck of gray at his temples. And a banked desire he'd been determined to not let drive him.

But despite that obvious struggle, he was here with her. Ready to give her whatever she wanted from him.

What did she want? How far was she going to take this temporary madness?

Continue reading
THE SECRET SHE KEPT IN BOLLYWOOD
Tara Pammi

Available next month
www.millsandboon.co.uk

LET'S TALK
Romance

For exclusive extracts, competitions
and special offers, find us online:

f facebook.com/millsandboon

🐦 @MillsandBoon

📷 @MillsandBoonUK

Get in touch on 01413 063232

For all the latest titles coming soon, visit
millsandboon.co.uk/nextmonth

JOIN US ON SOCIAL MEDIA!

Stay up to date with our latest releases, author
news and gossip, special offers and discounts, and
all the behind-the-scenes action
from Mills & Boon...

 millsandboon

 millsandboonuk

 millsandboon

might just be true love...

MILLS & BOON
Desire

Indulge in secrets and scandal, intense drama
and plenty of sizzling hot action with powerful
and passionate heroes who have it all: wealth,
status, good looks…everything but the right
woman.

MILLS & BOON

HEROES

At Your Service

Experience all the excitement of a
gripping thriller, with an intense romance
at its heart. Resourceful, true-to-life
women and strong, fearless men face
danger and desire - a killer combination!

MILLS & BOON
MEDICAL
Pulse-Racing Passion

Set your pulse racing with dedicated,
delectable doctors in the high-pressure
world of medicine, where emotions run
high and passion, comfort and love are the
best medicine.

ht Medical stories published every month, find them all at:

millsandboon.co.uk